PRAISE FOR DOON

"*Doon*, by Carey Corp and Lorie Langdon, is a YA retelling of *Brigadoon* that is fresh and enchanting."

— *USA Today's* Happy Ever After blog

"*Oz* meets *Once Upon a Time*."

— City Book Review

"… An imaginative reboot of the classic *Brigadoon*."

— *School Library Journal*

"Musical-theater fans will rejoice … Give this romance to fans who can't get enough of 'Will they? Won't they?' plot twists."

— *Booklist*

"The perfect mix of mystery, magic, and romance; be prepared to get lost in another world!"

— Maria V. Snyder, author of the *New York Times* Bestselling Poison Study series

Other books in the Doon series:

Shades of Doon

Carey Corp and Lorie Langdon

BLINK

BLINK

Shades of Doon
Copyright © 2016 by Carey Corp and Lorie Moeggenberg

This title is also available as a Blink ebook.
Visit www.zondervan.com/ebooks.

Requests for information should be addressed to:
Blink, 3900 *Sparks Drive SE, Grand Rapids, Michigan 49546*

This edition: ISBN 978-0-310-74241-8 (softcover)

Thank you to the Alan Jay Lerner Estate and the Frederick Loewe Foundation for
use of the *Brigadoon* premise.

Cover design: *Magnus Creative*
Interior design: *Greg Johnson/Textbook Perfect*

Printed in the United States of America

16 17 18 19 20 21 22 23 /DCI/ 18 17 16 15 14 13 12 11 10 9 8 7 6 5 4 3 2 1

Dedication

For the weak who choose bravery,
the broken who find their strength,
and the oppressed who rise up and fight:
Never bow down to your fear.

CHAPTER 1

Veronica

Cheating death tends to make you live with your whole heart—to take risks and enjoy each moment, no matter how gritty. I reminded myself of this as all of Doon stood in hushed anticipation of a potential bloodbath. One involving the boy I loved.

A resounding boom split the silence, and a line of drummers emerged from the arched opening at the east end of the arena.

Their leader in full highland regalia, including a headdress over a foot tall, marched into the stadium while brandishing a bronze staff. The drum beats quickened, echoing in time with my heart as they ushered in flag bearers waving standards from every Doon citizen's nation of origin.

Italy, Africa, China, America, India, Australia ... the flags kept coming, their kaleidoscope of colors snapping in the breeze. Everyone in the stadium rose to their feet, and the realization washed over me that this was my kingdom—the beautifully diverse land I was so very privileged to lead.

Sensing my flood of emotion, my best friend, Kenna, wrapped her arm around my shoulders, and we leaned our heads together as the procession filed into rows, and then continued to march in place. The grand marshal twirled his staff and threw it high into the air. The second he caught it, the drums cut off.

Several dozen bagpipers, dressed in traditional kilts, high socks, and matching black tams, streamed in from both sides of the stadium. Their music wove its spell around me, and when the drums joined in, the effect was breathtaking. This dramatic ceremony ushered in the final day of the festival celebrating both our freedom from the evil limbus that had almost destroyed us all and my seemingly miraculous recovery.

The final notes of the song faded away, and the grand marshal gestured for everyone to be seated. I smoothed the fabric of my full-length skirt and adjusted the MacCrae tartan draped across my bodice. Fiona, my ever-wise advisor and friend, had suggested a traditional Doonian dress of celery and forest green stripes. She'd also insisted on fixing my hair herself, plaiting the length into a side braid adorned with silk butterflies and matching ribbons.

The stadium began to shake as two massive war horses, manes and tails flying out behind them, galloped onto the field. Warmth rose in my cheeks at the exhilarating sight of my prince astride his chestnut stallion, Crusoe.

"What are they doing?" Kenna asked, both of us sitting a little straighter as the MacCrae brothers hurtled full speed in our direction.

I glanced down at my schedule of events, but didn't see anything between the closing ceremonies and the big fight. "I have no clue."

The brothers, bare chested and wearing identical kilts in

blue and green MacCrae tartan, pulled their mounts to a stop directly in front of the royal box. Duncan, riding his ebony mare, Mabel, quirked a lopsided grin as Jamie dismounted and jogged up the stairs to where we sat in the stands.

Jamie stopped on the stoop in front of us, his gorgeous face a study of contrasts — eyes glinting with mischief while his lips and jaw were set in solemn lines. He bowed with an exaggerated flourish of his hand, drawing giggles from my self-appointed ladies-in-waiting — Gabby Rosetti and her gaggle of girlfriends.

Playing along, I lifted my chin and hiked up my brows, adopting the most royal expression I could manage. But the moment Jamie's dark gaze met mine, my pretense melted into a wide smile. His stare grew warm as he stated his request in a deep, resounding voice. "I fight this day in your honor, my lady queen. And would humbly request a token to take into battle."

The Doonians clapped and hooted their encouragement. I bit my lip. *A token?* Was I supposed to give him a kiss, or something more tangible? I tried to remember what I'd seen in movies.

Kenna tugged on the tip of my braid and instructed, "Give him something he can wear, Highney."

I shot my smart-apple friend a glare at the nickname she'd taken to using recently — a combination of *Highness* and *behind*. To keep me humble, she claimed. I rolled my eyes at her as I stood and pulled an emerald ribbon from my hair. Getting into the spirit of the moment, I cleared my throat and proclaimed, "Prince James Thomas Kellan MacCrae, my bravest knight, I bestow my favor upon thee!"

There were whoops and applause as Jamie took a knee and bowed his head over his flexed right arm. I would never get used to the boy who'd been groomed from birth to be king, kneeling to *me*. Hastily, I tugged him to his feet.

With the entire kingdom watching, I brushed my fingers over his sun-warmed skin and wrapped the ribbon around his bulging bicep, just below his tattoo. Even placing it at the indention of his muscles, the ends of the cloth barely met. As I pulled the knot tight, Jamie leaned down and murmured against my ear, "Thank you, my heart."

A shiver ricocheted up my spine, and when he caught my gaze with that wicked spark in his eye, I knew he'd felt my reaction.

I adjusted the band of fabric and whispered, "Try not to get yourself killed. I may require your services later." Jamie grew still and I arched a brow at him, curling up one side of my mouth. "As a chaperone for the festival, of course."

A low chuckle escaped his chest and our eyes met in silent understanding before he turned and jumped off the bleachers. Once on the field, he swung up onto Crusoe's back, took the reins, and wheeled the horse around in one graceful, seamless motion. Then he glanced back over his shoulder to make sure I was watching. *Show off.*

As Duncan guided Mabel away from the stands, Kenna shot to her feet and shouted his name. Just as he turned back, she chucked a dark ball in his direction. Duncan reached up and caught it. Then, to the delight of the crowd, Kenna yelled, "Go get 'em, ogre!"

He gave a salute and then galloped after his brother. Together, they rode to the center of the arena, where the pipers had cleared off and a group of boys were constructing a fighting ring made of ropes and weighted poles.

I glanced at my BFF just as she slipped her pale foot back into her shoe.

"Did you just give Duncan your sock?" I squeaked.

"Yep." She nodded and then turned to me with an impish grin. "I just hope he ties it somewhere far away from his nose."

With a hoot of laughter, I grabbed her hand and pulled her against me. "I love you."

She wrinkled her nose and shrugged. "I know."

Back on the field, Duncan was wisely attaching Kenna's sock to the weapon holster at his waist while Jamie loosened up by rolling his neck from side to side. The brothers' competitors had arrived — Fergus and his only slightly less mountainous cousin, Ewan Lockhart. Fergus tied the length of his strawberry-blond hair back from his face and blew someone in the audience a kiss. I leaned forward and saw Fiona catch it and hold it to her chest, giving her husband a broad wink. They had to be the cutest married couple I'd ever known.

"Esteemed ladies and gents of Doon!" the announcer boomed.

We took our seats and Kenna tilted her head to the side. "The acoustics in here are great. That guy isn't even shouting."

But I was barely listening. I smoothed the hair around my crown, tugged on the sleeves of my blouse, and worked to paste a calm expression on my face. I hated this part.

The announcer continued. "Today, an ancient feud that dates back hundreds of years before the Covenant will be played out before our eyes! The esteemed clan Lockhart versus the noble clan MacCrae!"

The crowd roared, the reverberation of their joined voices and stamping feet signaling the beginning of the fight. Duncan and Fergus exited the ring. Apparently this was a tag team match, and Jamie was up first.

Ewan Lockhart crouched in one corner. With his thick build, shaggy dark hair, and beard, he resembled a Sasquatch ready to pounce. In the diagonal corner, Jamie drew his weapon and bounced on the balls of his feet, my pulse jumping with him. The Doonians had been chattering about this match for weeks, making friendly wagers and trash talking — it was the highlight of the games. Too bad I wasn't going to get to enjoy it.

"Vee, open your eyes," Kenna hissed. "This fight is happening whether you watch it or not."

She had a point. I squinted open one eye and gripped the arms of my chair so hard I broke a fingernail.

The referee gave a signal and the competitors leapt forward. Jamie swung his sword in a forceful arc, the blade angled toward Ewan's head. I leaned forward, both eyes wide as Ewan blocked the blow with a deafening clang. Their swords clashed and they forced each other across the ring and back, neither one of them gaining an advantage, until Ewan's ham-sized fist connected with Jamie's jaw. I cringed as he stumbled back several steps. With a shake of his head, he recovered and charged.

"Don't worry, Vee," Kenna whispered. "It's not real. They're just putting on a good show."

I wasn't so sure about that. I'd seen Jamie and Duncan training in the Brother Cave. They were out for blood. Not to kill or maim, of course, but first blood was a big deal — bragging rights for weeks after. And this was a tournament in front of the entirety of Doon.

Jamie landed a kidney punch just below Ewan's chain mail vest as Duncan and Fergus yelled advice from the sidelines. With a snarl, Ewan lunged, his blade coming within millimeters of my boyfriend's exposed throat. Jamie dodged, but it was way too close for comfort.

Oh yeah, they were taking this seriously. I shot to my feet, but as I yelled, "Stop!" the spectators surged up around me, their screams and applause drowning me out.

Kenna made her way to her feet a moment later. "He knows what he's doing. Have a little faith."

As if to prove her point, Jamie landed a blow to Ewan's back with the flat of his sword, making the giant stagger forward. Kenna clapped in response and shouted, "Whoohoo! Go Surfer Dude!"

I choked on a laugh. *Surfer Dude* was the name she'd given Jamie when we first arrived in Doon, and it in no way described my intense, fiercely protective leader of a prince — other than his longish tawny hair, of course.

A spastic movement down in the front row caught my eye. Lachlan MacPhee, the cute boy who'd first shown me Jamie's playful side with a mock sword-fight in the marketplace, mimicked his royal idol's every move. He rotated his arms in a wide arc, as Jamie's sword smashed against Ewan's with a clang. The other pre-teens surrounding Lachlan shouted and pumped their fists like zealous fans at a professional wrestling event.

Their rapt excitement reminded me that this was supposed to be fun. But as Ewan swung wide and Jamie ducked, avoiding the blade at the last possible second, my attention riveted back on the match. Jamie rose and whirled behind the bigger guy, hooking his arm around Ewan's neck. With a snarl, Ewan flipped Jamie over his head. Jamie landed in the dirt, but didn't even pause. Muscles flexing, he sprang to his feet with powerful grace and the two were back at it, sparring in a complex sequence that had them dancing all over the ring.

"Oh, they're good," Kenna commented, not taking her eyes from the action.

Ewan charged, and one side of Jamie's mouth curled as he climbed the ropes and then jumped and spun, delivering a roundhouse kick to his giant opponent's chest. Ewan teetered back and then fell face-first into the dirt. Jamie, who'd landed on his feet, pumped a fist in the air and the crowd exploded in cheers. My neck and shoulders slumped, the tension breaking free. Ken was right; I needed to trust Jamie. Clearly, he could hold his own.

When Ewan staggered to his feet but couldn't maintain his balance, Duncan and Fergus tagged in. The size discrepancy between Duncan and Fergus was roughly the same as Jamie and his opponent, but the bigger guys moved with less agility and more force. As Duncan and Fergus clashed swords, Kenna stilled beside me. I smirked and opened my mouth to tease her, but bit back the comment when Fergus disarmed Duncan, his sword clanking across the ring.

A hush descended on the audience and my vision went blurry. I rubbed my temples and took a few cleansing breaths before I opened my eyes and — saw a car on the far side of the arena. Not a horse-drawn wagon or a carriage. A freaking modern-day car.

Shimmering like a mirage, the dull red Toyota chugged along and cruised behind the ring. My veins turned to ice as my eyes followed the vehicle until it vanished from view.

Someone to my left gasped, and I twisted to see my assistant, Emily, clapping. Back in the ring, Duncan had regained his sword. My eyes locked on Jamie as he gripped the ropes, shouting at his brother. But it was like I watched him through a window screen. I blinked, desperate to recalibrate my vision, but the walls of the stadium, the people, even the bleachers began to fade around me. The noise of the crowd became muffled, sounding farther and farther away. The floor tilted beneath me. This could not be happening again.

Was Doon disappearing, or was I?

CHAPTER 2

Mackenna

oly Schwartz! I watched the red car disappear down an asphalt lane that had materialized in the center of the coliseum. The ground, which had been flat dirt moments ago, was now covered in gently sloping grass littered with billboards. Duncan, Jamie, and the rest of the Doonians shimmered like ghostly mirages while I grappled with my bearings.

Queasy and coated in a fine sheen of sweat, I dug my nails into the palms of my hands — an old trick for stage fright. The sharp sensation pulled my focus inward and away from the cirque du bizarre happening in the arena. Around me I heard the crowd cheer, but it was muted, as if someone had turned the sound down low.

I took a deep breath as I closed my eyes, and when I opened them again — the road was still there. A blue minicar appeared, following in the red car's path. At the opposite end of the stadium, a flatbed truck barreled toward the tiny car at high speed.

This had to be some sort of sun-induced delusion. Heat stroke or something. Squinting skyward, I discounted the explanation almost immediately. The early morning sun had not yet crested the stadium bleachers. And the temperatures were fall-like, not scorching.

My surroundings were eerily quiet, and although I could still see the Doonians, my head ached when I tried to focus on them. Beside me, I heard Vee's unmistakable yogic breathing. I glanced in her direction and then followed her wide-eyed stare to the impending collision of the truck and the car.

Without so much as a honk of its horn, the truck smashed into the much smaller vehicle. The sickening crunch of twisting metal filled my ears, along with a strange buzzing noise. The sound surged and became thunderous cheers as Doon snapped back into place. The car accident was gone, leaving me with a discomforting sense of vertigo as I noted Duncan and Jamie standing over their disarmed opponents. They'd won the match.

Fighting the urge to barf, I clapped for Team MacCrae, whom I'd dubbed *Surfer Dude* and the *Amazing Ogre* in honor of Vee's and my first time in Doon. So much had happened since then. My Indiana bestie had defeated the evil witch and, in doing so, became queen of the legendary Scottish kingdom. I'd faced my fears in order to destroy the zombie fungus and gotten a second chance at happily ever after with the boy of my dreams. It was the stuff of fairy tales ... and yet, Cinderella's epilogue had never included delusions of a head-on collision between two horseless carriages.

I glanced at Vee, who was wildly applauding her Charming. She had that manic aspect of someone committed to avoiding their present reality. When she caught my eye, her facade cracked. Her face turned a sickly shade of yellowish-green that mirrored how I felt on the inside.

Jamie, Duncan, Fergus, and Ewan exited at the opposite end of the arena. Guessing that we would not see them again until they'd cleaned up, I placed my hand under Vee's elbow and lifted her to her feet as I stood. "The queen and I need to use the royal restroom."

Vee's brow furrowed. "No, I don't."

"Well, I do." I tugged at her sleeve. "Are you sure you don't need to tinkle?"

Tinkle was the code word we'd used in junior high when we wanted to chat privately in the girl's room. Vee's eyes widened slightly as she nodded. "Actually, I do need to go."

As she stepped toward the back of the royal box, Emily Roosevelt and Gabriela Rosetti, who'd recently joined the royal entourage as Vee's ladies-in-waiting, moved to follow. Vee stopped them with a wave of her hand. "Thanks, but I think Kenna and I can do this alone."

In tandem, we climbed down the stairs and walked a short distance away from the festivities to a short brick structure. There were several such bathrooms ringing the arena, but only one had a private guard and required a crown to enter. This particular building had two doors, one for the king and another for the queen.

The guard stepped aside and we entered a private sitting room. Divans and oversized ottomans in plush cream fabrics dotted the area. Interspersed tables provided a variety of fruit, sweets, and drinks — all decidedly unappetizing after what I'd just witnessed.

Vee headed straight to a set of sinks at the back of the room, where she turned on the taps and splashed water over her face. One of my first and most favorite discoveries about the kingdom of Doon had been its running water — a pleasant surprise given the medieval kingdom's lack of other modern conveniences like electricity, refrigeration, and microwaves. *Yay for modern plumbing!*

My bestie took her time patting her face dry before speaking. "What's up, Ken?"

She looked so composed that I instantly doubted what I thought I knew. "Uh," I stammered, unsure how to begin. "That was a surprising turn of events out there."

Her brow pinched. "You mean with Jamie and Duncan? 'Cause they were the favorite to win, regardless of Fiona's trash talk."

Though Vee and I shared a brain more often than not, this didn't seem to be one of those times. Rather than fish for confirmation that my hunch about her was correct, I blurted out, "Cars. I saw cars. Actually—two cars and a truck, and they collided with a crunch and I'm pretty sure I'm Coco Puffs."

The corner of Vee's lip twitched, and then her careful composure cracked with a gigantic sigh. "Oh, thank heavens."

"That I'm cuckoo?"

She shook her head as she sank onto a plushy divan. "That you saw it too. I thought it was just me — that I was getting sick again or something."

I sat in the chair opposite her and searched her vibrant blue eyes. "So we're both crazy?"

"No. It means what we saw was real."

Her words were hardly reassuring. "So how come the villagers didn't freak out?"

"Kenna, you really have to stop referring to the other citizens as 'the villagers.' You're one of them now. They're not about to come after you with pitchforks."

No matter how many times Vee said that, I still felt like an outsider. Duncan said to give it time, so I was trying not to obsess about being the new kid on the block. But I was mentally digressing. Returning to the topic of tales from the weird side, I said pointedly, "No one else seemed to see the collision except us."

"I'm not sure why." Vee bit at her lip, signifying she was

deep in thought. "None of the other Destined seemed to see it either. Just us ... Maybe it has something to do with our gifts, or our connection to the Rings of Aontacht or the modern world. Or maybe — "

"Or maybe it was PTDS. A post-traumatic Doon stress."

She responded just as I hoped, with a half-hearted chuckle. I'd heard somewhere that a sense of humor meant you hadn't gone completely off your rocker. "I think you mean post-traumatic stress disorder. It's an interesting theory though. We should probably do some research, see what we can find about visions appearing to those called to Doon."

"Okay — let's not do any of that." Vee started to protest, but I rushed on. "Wait. Just hear me out. There's no reason to believe that we'll have more hallucinations. For all we know, it was an isolated thing, like the adrenaline rush bus drivers get when they need to lift a car off a baby. So please don't make a big deal about this."

"But — "

"No buts." The sound of bagpipes drifted in from the coliseum, signaling we were almost out of time. If we didn't hurry back, people would come looking for us. "Let's pretend that nothing happened and enjoy the absence of conflict for once. We've got princes who adore us and a *ka-lay-lee* to go to."

"A *céilidh*." She pronounced it *kay-lee*, like a girl's name. "I'm really looking forward to it."

Fiona had described it as a gathering with traditional folk music and dancing. Apparently the weekly dinner-dances held in the Great Hall of Castle MacCrae were also céilidhs, but the one tonight in the village marketplace, marking the end of the highland games, would be the mother of all gatherings. In addition to dancing, there would be folk art and storytelling — the closest Doon had to a thriving arts scene.

Rummaging through my bag, I pulled out a tube of mango-granate lip gloss and handed it to Vee. "Doesn't a Kaylee party sound better than research?"

Vee contemplated the gloss like it was a horse full of Trojan soldiers before taking it out of my hand. "Besides," I prompted, "what do you think is going to happen if you tell Jamie about this? Do you really want to go on lockdown again?"

Even though Doc Benoir had declared Vee recovered from whatever had caused her to collapse the day that I'd decided to stay in Doon, the cause was still a mystery. And without a reasonable medical explanation, Jamie tended to hover over her like a male version of Mama Rose searching for the slightest hint of a relapse.

"Fine," Vee capitulated, "we can chalk whatever happened out there up to PTSD — for now. But if anything like that happens again — to *either* one of us — we're going to tell our friends immediately and then do everything we can to get to the bottom of it. Deal?"

She held out her hand and we shook on it. "Deal."

After the drama of the Eldritch Limbus, we were entitled to time off for good behavior. In the last couple months we'd rescued Doon not once but twice from evil, and it was high time to enjoy the benefits of saving the world. Her Royal Highney and I had waited long enough for our happily ever afters.

CHAPTER 3

Veronica

A cool breeze from the open window flowed over the nape of my neck, chilling the sweat beading on my skin. I scrawled my name across the bottom of the page and then dripped hot wax in the corner and impressed the royal seal beside my signature. Adding the sheet to the growing pile of accepted petitions, I rubbed the now dulled points of the crown on my luckenbooth pendant. The ornament had belonged to a long-ago queen of Doon, a young girl named Lynnette who had died trying to save her kingdom from a band of witches.

Normally, the pendant brought me comfort and a sense of connection, but today it wasn't doing its job. I tucked the long chain back into my blouse. After stealing the necklace from the forbidden ground of the witch's cottage — the home of the very witches who had killed Lynnette while attempting to take her throne — I hadn't shown it to anyone. Even if Kenna and I had journeyed to find the one book that could help us break the curse trying to destroy Doon, when I'd stepped foot on that cursed ground, I'd committed an act of treason.

Suddenly so cold that my teeth chattered, I pulled a shawl around my shoulders. Memories of what I'd seen that morning in the arena burned against my closed lids. My eyes popped open and I grabbed the next petition. The paper shook in my hands. I set it down on the desk and wrapped my arms around my waist. Even if I could pretend to believe what Kenna and I had seen was benign, or some shared delusion, deep down I knew there was more to it. All I wanted was to be settled, to enjoy my new lease on life. To have a happy, peaceful reign with my amazing co-ruler by my side and to have something I hadn't had since I was eleven years old — security.

How wonderful would it be if the trivial disputes and appeals on these pages were the most dramatic thing in my life? If I could do the work I'd come to love, leading and shaping a kingdom, and then end each day snuggled up on the sofa with my incredible boyfriend and a good book, or having dinner at Rossetti's Tavern with friends … I sighed, the picture in my mind one of pure bliss, and perhaps a pipe dream.

I shivered hard and pulled the soft wool of the shawl tighter around my shoulders, as I skimmed the document before me; a request to use an empty storefront in the village, the one down by the loch. A name jumped off the page — Analisa Morimoto. Ana was one of the Destined who'd crossed the bridge during the most recent Centennial. An orphan who'd survived the streets of London as a petty thief and document forger. She'd fast become a friend and ally.

She wanted to start a kickboxing gym for women. An image of the women of Doon shedding their skirts for "short trousers" and sleeveless shirts, kicking and punching their way out of the conventions of the past, made me chuckle. Doon was about to experience a revolution.

I signed Analisa's petition with a flourish, hoping she'd

welcome my help to flesh out her ideas. I'd be her first customer. The stamp sank into the dollop of wax, and I extracted it with a satisfying pop. I was moving on to the next paper before me when a knock sounded on my office door. Before I could answer, my prince charming strode into the room.

"Are ye ready?" He quirked a roguish leer as his eyes swept over my face, reminding me he was at least one quarter villain. "You certainly look ready. Good enough to eat, in fact."

And right on cue, my heart did a pirouette inside my chest.

He crossed the room and leaned down, placing his heated lips against mine in a kiss that chased every last chill from my skin. But the moment his mouth departed, the cold shook through me and my headache returned with a vengeance. Jamie perched on the corner of my desk facing me, his eagle-sharp gaze searching mine. I couldn't reveal that I was feeling less than perfect or he'd rush me to the clinic faster than you could say "carrageen moss." I swallowed a wave of nausea at the thought of the seaweed-like herb tonic that Doc Benior had forced me to drink by the bucket load during my recovery.

Jamie's warm fingers brushed my cheek as he tucked a lock of hair behind my ear. "Are ye feelin' all right?"

When I awoke after my collapse, the first thing I saw was Jamie, Kenna, and Fiona red-eyed and whispering as if someone had died. Apparently that person had been me. But after sleeping for forty-eight hours straight, I'd felt fabulous, and Doc Benoir had given me a clean bill of health. Jamie, on the other hand, had been wrecked. My usually stoic boyfriend hovered over me asking every thirty minutes if I felt all right or if I needed to rest, the fear in his eyes heartbreaking.

"I'm fine. Are you all right?" I stared at the purplish bruise shading the skin beneath his light stubble.

He gripped his jaw and moved it from side to side with a

wince. "No' bad. Better than wee Ewan, I'd wager." He smirked. "Now, about that dance …"

I picked up a stack of papers and tapped them against the desk to align the edges. "I just have a lot of paperwork to catch up on. Why don't you head to the festival and I'll meet you down there later this evening?"

The thought of putting on my queenly smile and kissing babies as if nothing was wrong, as if I hadn't just witnessed the modern world converging on my enchanted kingdom, sent a sharp pulse of pain through my temple. Hopefully, a cup of tea and a nap would kick this headache, but the other issue was not so easily solved. I opened my mouth to blurt the story to Jamie, but stopped. The tension lines that normally rested between his brows were gone, the planes of his face relaxed and mobile — for the first time since I'd met him he looked like an eighteen-year-old boy. I couldn't steal that joy from him simply because Kenna and I had shared some abstract vision.

"Vee." Jamie set a wide palm on the pile of my unfinished work. "I can help you with this in the morn'. The people want to see their queen. To celebrate with her. As do I."

I nodded, pushed back my chair, and stood. "Okay, let me go change. But the paperwork will have to wait until after lunch tomorrow. I'm spending the morning with Kenna." I kissed him quickly on the cheek. "Give me fifteen minutes."

"Aye. I'll meet ye in the courtyard." He slid off the desk and sauntered out the door, calling over his shoulder, "Dinna be late!"

After a ponderous journey up the one hundred and twenty-seven steps to my tower suite, I was beginning to rethink my decision. My body didn't seem to want to cooperate, every move laborious as if I were trudging through the southern bogs of Doon. Breathing hard, I finally reached the landing, pulled myself up the last few steps with the handrail, and almost bumped into Eòran's broad form.

"Yer Majesty!" My personal guard's bushy brows lowered until they almost touched his equally shaggy mustache. "Is anything amiss? Should I get the doc?"

I paused at the top of the stairs and rubbed the back of my head, which was now throbbing in time with my temples. On the tip of my tongue was an order to send word to Jamie, telling him I wouldn't make the festival after all, but I knew that would only send my already on-edge boyfriend into panic mode. So I lowered my hand and forced the grimace off my face.

"I'm fine. Just ran up the stairs too quickly." I breezed past him, but heard his uneven footfalls pursuing me around the curve of the hallway. The poor man hadn't fully recovered from his battle with Sean MacNally and his band of insurgents, who had been convinced Kenna and I were committing treason instead of working to save Doon from a curse. The slight pause and scrape of his steps twisted my gut. He'd been so tenacious in trying to protect me that MacNally had broken his femur to stop him. Though Jamie had doubled the guards at the base of my tower, Eòran refused to stay off the job a moment longer, even if it meant serving before he was fully healed.

"May I at least ring for a bit of tea, Yer Majesty?"

Warm tea and a cozy blanket sounded like heaven. I let out a sigh as I pushed open the massive wood and iron door to my suite, longing to curl up in the pillowed window seat of my sunroom turret. But instead I replied, "No, thank you, but you can accompany me down to the carriage in a few moments and then take the rest of the day off."

Before I finished speaking, the guard shook his head, his eyes widening.

"I won't take no for an answer, Eòran. I'll be perfectly safe with Jamie, and I won't have you standing up here all alone while all of Doon is celebrating."

He'd stopped shaking his head, but his jaw was set in a stubborn line.

"Surely you have someone you'd like to hang out with rather than me?"

The man's impossibly broad shoulders slumped as he cast his eyes to the ground. "There's no one ... my queen."

The man had to be at least forty years old. How could he have no one?

"Well, that settles it then. You'll attend the festival as my guard."

He lifted his gaze, his eyes alight with purpose.

"And my friend." I shut the door in his bewildered face before he could argue, and strode to my bedroom. Traditional Doonian dress was lovely, but I was ready for something more "me." I shucked the heavy skirt, and then lifted the blouse and sash over my head in one movement. Noticing my pendant had come off with it, I tucked the necklace into a box in the back of my wardrobe, where I stored it each night. As much as I enjoyed wearing the pendant, there would be nowhere to conceal it in the new maxi dress I planned to wear.

I lifted the dress from the hanger and laid it out on the bed, admiring my creation. I'd designed it during my forced bed rest, and the finished product had been delivered last night. It had turned out even better than I'd imagined. Slipping the scarlet cotton sheath over my head, I let the soft fabric fall into place just above my knees. But that was just the first part of the dress. I stepped to the full-length mirror to tie the overskirt around my waist, a sheer fabric embroidered with a swirl of fall colors that fell to my ankles. Short kid-leather boots and a matching shrug completed the outfit. The effect was stylish, yet feminine, and definitely pushed the boundaries of Doon propriety.

Feeling a sudden burst of energy, I removed Jamie's mother's circlet from my head, unbraided my hair, and finger combed the waves around my shoulders. I jogged to the dresser and found the new tiara Emily had commissioned for me — one I'd been saving for a special occasion. The gold filigree design was more ornate than what I usually wore, yet still lightweight, and ended in a peak of blood-red rubies that matched my outfit to perfection. As I secured the royal circlet into my hair, I realized my headache was gone.

Grabbing a small clutch, I left my room with Eòran following closely behind. In the castle courtyard, framed by the glow of late-afternoon sun, Jamie waited for me by the open carriage. He'd changed into leather trousers and a forest green tunic, the thin material hugging his chest and broad shoulders. And he'd retied my ribbon around his bicep.

His most recent gift to me sat by his booted feet — a Scottish deerhound puppy. The moment the dog saw me, his shaggy tail wagged so hard that his entire back end shook, his blue-gray fur quivering in anticipation. The breeder had named the dog *Blaz* — German for "unwavering protector." I'd decided the name fit, since he was also the fastest thing I'd ever seen on four legs.

The pup strained toward me, and Jamie made a sharp noise as he nudged the dog's neck with two fingers. Blaz lowered to his haunches with a whine. Jamie'd made it his mission to train him as a proper guard dog. But I didn't give a care about that. I had more than enough guards. I'd fallen head over heels in love.

With a baiting grin, I stopped several yards away, lowered to the dog's eye level, and made a kissing sound. Before Jamie could react, Blaz shot forward, almost knocking me over when his over-sized paws landed on my shoulders, his warm tongue coating my face. I laughed and pushed him away. "Hey, buddy." I scratched his silky ears and then stood, the dog glued to my side as I walked to join Jamie at the carriage.

"That just isna right." Jamie shook his head, shooting Blaz a look of betrayal.

"You wanted him to be devoted to me, right?"

"Aye, but not blindly so." Then Jamie's eyes shifted to me, darkening as they swept over my face. "Though I canna say as I blame him. He's besotted with you, just like every bloke in this kingdom."

I leaned against the strong heat of his chest and rose on my toes to press a kiss to his delectable mouth. "Well, then take me on a proper date," I whispered.

Jamie's strong arms encircled my waist and pulled me closer, igniting tiny sparks all over my skin. A cross between a cough and fake sneeze stopped us just before our lips met again. I'd completely forgotten about Eòran.

As Jamie and I separated, my loyal guard limped into view. "Excuse me, my queen, but I believe the céilidh is about ta begin. And ye wouldna want to miss the openin' dance."

"Yes, of course." For some reason, my cheeks flamed as if I'd been caught doing something naughty by a parent. "Then let's be off."

"Och! I almost forgot." Jamie snapped his fingers and then jogged around to the other side of the carriage. "Wait right there! And close your eyes."

I shook my head in wonder before squeezing my eyes closed. A whoosh of air informed me that Jamie had returned, but his normal masculine scent was masked by a beautiful aroma. Sweet, fresh, and green. I drew in the unmistakable fragrances of lavender and honeysuckle. And for a brief moment, I was a little girl chasing hummingbirds in our backyard in Indiana while my dad cooked hamburgers on the grill. *"Come on, Vee-Vee! It's time to eat."*

I opened my eyes to a riotous mix of color. The blooms were beautiful, but the memory hit me like a snowball to the chest. I hadn't thought about my dad's nickname for me in a long time. Hadn't allowed myself to remember how good things had been *before* — before drugs had stolen him from us.

My eyes flooded with tears as Jamie said, "I picked them myself in that meadow down by the loch … Why are ye cryin'?"

As his face became a stark mixture of hurt and panic, I swiped the moisture from my cheeks and pushed my dark thoughts away. "It's just that no one's ever given me flowers before." It was true. And I had to fight the rise of emotion for an entirely different reason.

Jamie's crouched brows rose, and a slight pink washed over his smooth, shaven cheeks. "Oh, well … I … just thought ye might like them since — "

"I love them, you crazy boy!" I took the bouquet and threw my arms around him. "Now let's go get some dinner. I'm starving!"

After instructing a page to put my flowers in water, we all piled into the carriage and the driver took off at a quick trot. Blaz claimed the seat beside me, leaving Jamie to share the opposite bench with my guard. From the pinched look on Jamie's face, and the fact that he'd arranged to have a driver other than himself, I figured this wasn't the romantic beginning to our date that he'd envisioned.

The crisp afternoon breeze ruffled my hair and skittered through the russet and scarlet leaves of the oaks framing the road. As we neared the end of fall, Doon only became more beautiful.

Soon, we rounded a bend and turned onto the packed streets of the village. The Doonians called out greetings as we passed by. I smiled wide and waved like I was in the Scottish version of the Macy's Thanksgiving Day parade. Lively music floated through the air. The vibrant colors of a maypole twirled in the distance. Hot spiced cider and fresh hand pies from a nearby vendor's cart filled the air with the mouthwatering scents of autumn. And just like my first carriage ride into the market, I couldn't wait to escape the confines of the vehicle and experience the sights, sounds, and tastes of everything around me.

Jamie shot me a knowing look before instructing the driver to pull over and park on a side street. We rolled to a stop and Jamie jumped down. I stood, ready to follow behind him.

"Wait. Let me assist you this time," Jamie said with a wink before he reached up and encircled my waist, lifting me down as if I weighed next to nothing.

"What? You don't want me to tackle you to the ground?" I batted my eyelashes at him innocently.

A naughty grin tilted his lips. "Tackle me all ye like, love. 'Tis never a hardship to break a pretty wench's fall."

I pulled away from him and swatted his inanely hard bicep. "I'm a wench, am I?"

Jamie's laugh was rich and deep as he put an arm around me and led me away from the carriage. "Aye, but a bonny one. You look exceptionally lovely today. I especially like this new crown." He leaned over to inspect the tiara more closely. "These stones practically glow against your dark hair."

"You don't mind that I'm not wearing your mother's crown?" I lifted my head and met his melting dark eyes.

"Nay. I think she'd greatly approve." He gave my waist a squeeze. "And no' just of the crown."

I swallowed the sudden baseball in my throat as Blaz shot

past me into the crowd, Eòran close on his heels. The people parted for us as we approached, dipping into bows and offering well wishes.

A thrill of pure happiness rushed from my heart to my toes, making me want to dance. Kenna's assessment had been dead-on. For once, all was right in our world. And I wasn't about to let a few headaches or PTSD hallucinations stop me from savoring every single perfect moment.

CHAPTER 4

Mackenna

In my experience, the best — and worst — things often happened while dancing. With each whirl, the present became clearer while the world beyond, with its future worries, dissolved into a dizzying blur. But eventually, when the music stopped, a terrible reality would come crashing in to shatter the illusion.

In the past, dancing with Duncan had always been bittersweet. But this time was different, because when the music stopped the only thing we'd be facing was our happiness. Tomorrow we would still be together with our arms around each other, and we'd never have to come down to earth again.

That comforting thought urged me to snuggle even closer to the boy who held me. My nose burrowed into the hollow of Duncan's collarbone as I inhaled his summery scent of saddles and soap. His Adam's apple brushed against my temple as he swallowed. Embracing the moment, I tipped my face up and kissed his throat.

He smiled down at me, his dark eyes twinkling with surprise. "What was that for?"

Blue and green paper lanterns, strung between posts so that they crisscrossed the open air pavilion, swayed gently over our heads. With my heart near bursting and my head about to pop, I replied, "For being you. And for not giving up on me."

"I couldna if I tried."

I settled my face against his neck, only to notice the odd scrap of black cloth peeking out of his breast pocket where his handkerchief should have been. "What in the world are you wearing — is that my sock?"

"Nay." With mock solemnity, he said, "It is a priceless token given to me by my most esteemed and beautiful lady. Her footwear is more precious to me than rubies or gold."

I missed a step, laughing as I swatted his bicep. "Dork."

"If my lady commands it, a *dork* I shall be."

Duncan was in rare form tonight. I had missed his sunshiny demeanor. Needing a moment to catch my breath, I asked, "What if your lady commands a cold beverage?"

He captured my hand and bent down to kiss it. "As you wish."

As Duncan disappeared into the crowd, Fiona waved at me. Next to her giant-sized husband, she looked like a doll, although she definitely wore the pants in that relationship. Fergus was a big old softie, but lethal with a blade — that, plus a petite yet formidable wife, made for an interesting combination. Adjacent to them I spied Analisa and the oldest Rosetti boy, whom I was really trying to think of as Giancarlo and not just local arm candy. Now that Duncan and I were together, Ana had made her relationship with the hot half-Italian, half-Scotsman official. Ana, who was half-Japanese and a forger by trade, was exotic in her own right; together she and Giancarlo were a walking, breathing *Teen Vogue* cover.

Ana offered me a wink, to which I nodded in reply —

probably the friendliest we would ever get. I wasn't sure I'd ever entirely get over feeling jealous about her close friendship with my boyfriend. However, she'd proven her trustworthiness by helping us out of more than one tight spot. When Vee and I had been taken by an angry mob, Ana had secretly followed. While we faced the limbus, she'd infiltrated the opposition and untied the princes, who then overpowered their captors. By the time Vee and I had returned from the limbus covered in ash, Jamie and Duncan were in control — all thanks to Ana.

Duncan approached with two mugs as Vee and Jamie spun past. Their dancing on the whole seemed far more ambitious than that of the rest of the villagers. They shimmied and high-stepped like something straight out of *Dancing with the Medieval Stars*. When the music swelled, Jamie plunged Veronica into a low dip and then held the pose as the tune ebbed into silence.

The Doonians applauded their queen and her royal hottie as Jamie skillfully raised my bestie back to standing. For the first time since Vee's collapse, Jamie seemed to let his guard down. But I harbored no illusions that the slightest case of indigestion on her part wouldn't cause Jamie to relapse into Prince Overprotective mode.

Truth be told, I couldn't blame him. I still had nightmares about Vee crumpling to the ground, impossibly pale and as still as death. I thought my best friend was dying. Could I really blame the boy who loved her more than life for doting on her in the extreme? They were lucky to have one another — we were all lucky.

I took a sip of cold, berry-infused water as the commotion died down and the elderly Reverend Guthrie took the stage. From the services I attended at the Ault Kirk, I knew him as an engaging and charismatic speaker. He cleared his throat and paused dramatically, waiting until all eyes were riveted to him before speaking in a strong, rolling brogue. "Many of our citizens have been learnin' the art of storytelling from Calum Haldane, our verra own *seanachaidh*."

Duncan's mouth brushed my ear, and the reverend's words faded away as he whispered, "Seanachaidh" — which he pronounced *shan-ah-kee* — "means 'storyteller.' Calum's family have been official storytellers in Doon for generations."

I nodded, caught between Duncan's intoxicating nearness and Reverend Guthrie, who pointed in my direction. "Calum's latest story, 'The Piper and the Boots,' should be o' particular enjoyment ta our newest addition, Mackenna Reid."

The crowd's focus shifted to me as I pasted on a polite smile. After a moment, Reverend Guthrie recaptured the audience, saying, "Now I give to ye, Calum Haldane."

Everyone clapped as a stocky, middle-aged man took the stage and began to speak in animated tones. As he recited, I couldn't help but feel like an alien observing a far-off civilization. My muses were modern, like the Stephens — Sondheim, Schwartz — not seanachaidh, with their old Scottish wives' tales. The drama of this world wasn't mine. As if she were reading my mind, Vee glanced over her shoulder, catching my attention before I could look away. Her concern caused my eyes to sting. My vision swam and I refocused just beyond the little stage in the hope it would seem like I was watching the show. In my peripheral vision, I sensed more than saw as she turned back to the performance.

Although Vee's assimilation into Doon did have challenges, the conviction of her heart had never wavered. As I stared at the seanachaidh, I envied her certainty. Would I ever feel like this place was home? Could I really have a career here? What if I just ended up a baby-making housewife ... producing little princes and princesses while my husband helped lead the kingdom? A tear slipped down my cheek as I grappled to discover my songs for this new world.

Duncan's warm hand found mine in the darkness and gently squeezed my cold fingers. His warm breath tickled the hairs on my neck as he whispered, "Come with me."

I started to question him, but he silenced me with a "shhh" and a gentle tug on my hand. Fingers intertwined, we slipped out of the performance and away from the festival. Cool air chilled my wet cheek as we walked in silence. When we reached the edge of the farmers' market, I expected us to head toward the village, but Duncan gently led me in the opposite direction, down the deserted lane that led to farm country.

"Where are we going?"

He shrugged elegantly. "Ye will see."

Despite my melancholy mood, he piqued my curiosity. A low, full moon lit up the countryside so that I could clearly see the fence posts and dark clusters of sleeping sheep in the fields. In the distance, the trees gently swayed. The breeze reached me, carrying the familiar scents of heather and dung, and something sharper, like rosemary.

After a few minutes, we came to a crossroads, and Duncan nudged me toward the grassy field. At the far edge of the paddock, I could just make out the larger shapes of cattle. In confirmation, a cow lowed.

I'd recently confessed to Duncan the dream I'd had when we'd crashed in the icky barn during our journey back into Doon. I'd dreamt about Duncan kissing me and then I woke up to a moony-eyed cow giving me some unwelcome tongue action. Duncan thought it was outright hilarious and Vee had taken to referencing my kiss with Elsie the Amorous Cow as my "experimental" phase.

I stopped at the edge of the lane where gravel road met grassy slope. "Wait. We're not going to visit Elsie, are we?"

Duncan turned and stepped into my space so that his body fit against mine. "Why? Do ye fancy her kisses more than mine?"

"Difficult to say." I pretended to consider his question. "She's very fond of me."

"So you're needing proof of my fondness, is that it?" He captured my face between his large, callused hands and examined me at an intense, yet leisurely pace. His eyes — the color of molten chocolate — studied my brows, my nose, my cheeks, and finally my mouth. After a breathless eternity, his gaze lifted to mine, his lips slightly apart as he closed the space between us.

Kissing Duncan was like falling down a rabbit hole, the known world dropping away as I discovered a new, fantastical reality. It was equally as satisfying as being on stage ... but less practical than drama as a vocation.

Deepening our kiss, Duncan repositioned one hand on my waist while the other twisted into my hair. I wrapped my arms around his chest, my fingers digging into his muscular back as I urged him closer. My body came alive on a cellular level, feeling everything: his breath tickling my cheek, tiny goose bumps on my arms from the breeze, the searing heat of his body pressing into me, our frenzied hearts beating in duet as his soul intertwined with mine.

Trembling, he pulled back enough to search my face. "Proof enough for ye?"

"Maybe just a wee bit more." I flung myself at him, and we resumed kissing until we were both senseless.

When we finally parted, the world seemed sharper. Every molecule in my being zinged with awareness as Duncan slipped his fingers through mine and stepped into the grass.

Despite his gentle tug, I refused to budge. "Where are we going, really?"

He favored me with a crooked smile that was both cocky and mischievous. "Just a ways into the field."

"But I'll get my boots dirty." Before I'd even returned to Doon, Vee had commissioned a half dozen pairs of boots in my size in a variety of colors. They were a surprise for when I decided to stay. The soft moss-green suede ankle boots matched perfectly with my hi-lo dress — the latest design in Vee's Royal Rock Star collection.

"They'll clean," Duncan said with a chuckle.

He gently tugged my hand again while I stared at my feet in dismay. "They're new."

"Oh, for heaven's sake, woman." Without another word, he scooped me up and threw me over his shoulder like a sack of turnips. In spite of my half-hearted protests, he remained silent. When it became clear that resistance was futile, I calmed down and enjoyed the view — which was spectacular.

When Duncan reached the center of the field, he carefully set me down on a thick patch of grass. Feigning irritation, I smoothed my skirt before meeting his expectant gaze. "Now what?"

"I own this field." His accompanying gesture swept his arms outward in a wide arc. "It's not part of the MacCrae holdings. I purchased it outright last week."

So he was the proud owner of an empty field? Big whoop. He must've read the confusion on my face because he turned to the side, picked up a shovel, and presented it to me like a Tony Award. "Here. Take a scoop of the earth."

"You brought me all this way — in the middle of the night — to be a farmer? Or are you planning to kill me? Am I about to dig my own grave?"

Rather than take the bait, he placed a butterfly kiss on the tip of my nose. His long dark lashes fluttered hypnotically as he asked, "Mackenna Reid, do ye trust me?"

"Yes."

"Then dig." He reached for my hand and wrapped it around the handle. "One shovel-full of earth will serve."

Admittedly, I was intrigued. I scooped up a divot of dirt and deposited it next to the hole. When I met Duncan's bright grin, he said, "Ye've just broken ground on Doon's new Broadway Theater."

Astonishment clogged my throat as the tears I'd been struggling to keep at bay flowed like a faucet stuck in the on position. This was the site of my theater — the one Duncan would construct with his own hands. The kind, loving gesture elicited a whole new level of weeping.

I felt Duncan's arms wrap around me as he asked, "Why are ye cryin'?"

"'Cause — you're building me — a theater," I moaned between sobs. I'd never been a dainty crier. In fact, if you looked "ugly cry" up in the dictionary, you'd see a picture of my red, blotchy face.

He pulled back. His fingers grazed my chin, coaxing my face up until I looked at him. "I told ye that I'd build one for you. Here." He handed me my sock.

"I know," I gasped. "It's — " I blew my nose, a honking and singularly unattractive sound, into his priceless token. "It's just so nice."

His index finger brushed my jaw as he peered into the depths of my being. "I love you."

"I love you, more."

He shook his head. "Doubtful."

Before this turned into an all-out "Anything You Can Do

(I Can Do Better)" – style throw down, I conceded to my hand-some benefactor. No matter how much I struggled to find my place, Duncan would never stop reminding me that he believed I belonged in his world.

"Okay. You love me more. And I am so lucky to have you."

Urging Vee to forget the freaky modern-day delusion had been the right thing to do. This was finally our time. And together we would create a life in which all our dreams could come true.

CHAPTER 5

Veronica

The céilidh was like a Disney movie come to life. My handsome prince lifted me into the air and we spun in a circle, my skirt fluttering in an arc behind me. I held on tight to his broad shoulders, the fiddle and bodhrán driving us faster and faster, while paper lanterns whirled into a kaleidoscope of fairy lights above our heads.

A quick strike of the drums signaled the end of our umpteenth reel and I fell against Jamie's chest with a laugh. I'd wanted to dance and I'd certainly gotten my wish, but I was relieved when the musicians announced they were taking a break. A refreshing breeze brushed my flushed face as we made our way off the dance floor and back to our table. The warmth had leached from the autumn air as soon as the sun disappeared behind the horizon, and people gathered around cheerfully crackling fires in large brass basins, roasting sausages or warming their hands.

Jamie headed off to get us drinks while I plopped in a seat at our empty table and fanned my steamy face with a napkin. I

43

scanned the area for Kenna and Duncan before remembering they'd disappeared sometime during the storytelling. Kenna was still adjusting to the slower-paced life in Doon, and, not unlike many of the Destined, trying to find her place. As much as I enjoyed hearing the old folktales and legends, I imagined our storytelling was not the type of performance she felt she could sink her teeth into. Personally, I couldn't wait until she realized the missing theater scene was a blank canvas waiting for her genius. Not only would it give her a purpose, but with no television or computers in Doon, we were sorely lacking in the entertainment department.

Propping my aching feet on an empty chair, I picked at the glittery nail polish stuck to my fingernails like superglue. Mani/pedi time had been fun until Kenna declared she'd forgotten to bring remover with her to Doon. As I peeled off a strip of Caribbean-blue sparkles, I recognized that, not unlike the stubborn adhesive, my best friend would let go of her misconceptions and self-doubts in her own time. But making her feel welcome was something I *could* help with, which is why I'd blocked off my entire morning the following day for some pure, unadulterated girl time.

The table jerked and slid three inches as Blaz pulled against his rope to get to me. He whined and then gave a short yelp to inform me of his displeasure.

I went around and knelt in front of him. "Oh, buddy, what happened? Did we leave you all alone?" He'd wound his leash around the legs of the table, so I unclipped it from his collar.

At the first click of freedom, he slathered my face with dog saliva and then curled the edges of his mouth, his tongue lolling out of his head. Who knew a dog could actually smile? But I had no doubt that was exactly what he was doing. I led him around the table, and when I sat, he tried to crawl onto my lap.

"Blaz, down!" At the sound of Jamie's deep voice, the dog stilled immediately and flopped at my feet with a whimper. "Where's Eòran?" Jamie handed me a cup of chilled cider.

Where *had* my guard gotten to? He'd said he had no one he wished to spend time with at the festival. "He probably just went to get some food."

"Speaking of, can I get you anything, love?"

"Maybe a — " A sharp bark cut off my words, and Blaz — true to his name — took off like a racehorse out of the gate. Jamie and I jumped to our feet and watched in horror as he bumped into Adam, a scientist from Ireland, who balanced three overflowing mugs of ale. The dog whooshed past him and Adam spun on his heel, liquid sloshing all over his shoes.

Then Blaz ducked under a table and sent the cobbler's wife to her feet with a squeak, before darting into a stand of trees after a bushy-tailed cat.

"Blasted mutt! Some guard dog he's turned out to be," Jamie grumbled as he ran after my rapidly disappearing puppy.

I sat down again, laughing out loud at the Tom-and-Jerry-spectacle and the good-natured ribbing from those seated nearby.

"Might want ta trade that pup in for a *real* dog, yer Majesty."

"That wee beastie needs a good wallop."

"The Laird'll take care o' tha'!" the cobbler shouted, inciting sniggers all around.

I certainly hoped Jamie wouldn't hit my sweet Blaz. I sat up straighter and craned my neck, but could no longer see either of them.

The music began again as I settled into my seat and took a sip of the cool, spiced cider. Several couples began a slow waltz-like dance, Fergus and Fiona among them. Fergus, sporting a dark purple bruise under his left eye, whirled his diminutive wife around the floor — his meaty hands held her as if she were an exquisite china doll. Gabby Rosetti danced in the burly arms of the blacksmith's son. And her petite older sister, Sofia, breezed by with her father, Mario.

Something about the precious way Mario looked at his daughter hit me like a punch to the sternum. My vision darkened and another couple took their place...

"Dad, you're supposed to lead." I squeezed his arm under the soft jersey of his sweatshirt and looked up into his laughing eyes. The same aqua-blue as mine.

"How can I when my daughter is a ballerina?" He took my hand and spun me out.

I did a quick pirouette, extending my leg out and back again as he held my hand above my head.

"Bravo!" He twirled me back in with a chuckle. "See, I could never compete with such grace."

"You don't have to compete, silly daddy. It's just a pretend dance..."

Six months. That had been six months before he disappeared. Had his eyes been unnaturally bright or was I superimposing what I knew now over the memory? Had he already been thinking about leaving me? Was I such a heavy burden to bear?

My attention snapped back to the present and I noticed Sofia and Mario swaying on the edge of the dance floor, tears tracking down Sofia's face. I didn't mean to eavesdrop, but I couldn't help hearing her strained words.

"Why won't the dreams stop, Papà? I canna wait to go to bed each night, but each morning when I awake I grieve for him." She clutched a fist to her chest. "It's like a physical ache I carry with me every moment of every day."

"I do not know, *la mia bella*. But I do believe *i sogni*, the dreams, mean there is still hope. *Spereremo*."

Sofia shook her dark curls. "*Non è possibile*. The bridge is closed until the next Centennial and both the Rings of Aontacht are in Doon. I've missed my chance at a true Calling, haven't I?"

"I have to believe the Protector will find a way. Just look at the extraordinary circumstances that united Jamie and Duncan with their soul mates." He tucked a stray ebony curl behind her ear, his dark eyes liquid. "Never give up hope. *Mai!*"

"*Mi dispiace, Papà*. It hurts too much to hope. I have to move forward with my life." She stared down at her feet. "Somehow."

Mario tipped up his daughter's chin and brushed the tears from her cheeks. "You'll always be *il mio tesoro*."

My treasure.

Unable to listen to another word, I shot to my feet and began to make my way through the crowd. There were too many people, the laughter around me too loud. I didn't know where I was going but I had to get away. My people could not see me break down. Not here, not like this.

I'd reached the last row of tables when a deep, honeyed voice filled my ears. The crowd let out a cheer, and I stopped. I didn't recognize the words of the song, but the familiar rich tone, edged with that enticing hint of a rasp, resonated deep in my soul. *Jamie.*

Someone grabbed my hand, and I turned to meet Gideon's skeletal face. I started and jerked my fingers from his. It was still a struggle to trust the ex-captain of the guard, who'd caused Kenna and I so much trouble when we'd arrived in Doon. But the man's genuine, almost apologetic expression kept me rooted to the spot. The witch, Addie, had controlled his every move via a curse. This was the *true* Gideon. "Yer Majesty, pardon my intrusion." He bent in a short bow. "But the Laird sings for you."

"How do you know?"

"'Tis an ancient Gaelic ballad w' a verra special meaning." His eyebrows arched into his scarred forehead.

I pivoted to see Jamie on the stage facing me, standing tall and strong, his gaze confident yet beseeching. As he sang, the wind tousled the waves of his hair across his forehead. He shoved a tawny lock out of his eyes and then extended his hand in my direction. Giggles drew my attention to the foot of the stage, where a cluster of girls had gathered like groupies at a boy-band concert, their adoring eyes glued to my boyfriend as they looped arms and rocked in time with the music. I couldn't say that I blamed them; Jamie's charisma was off the charts, but why was he singing for me? Why now?

"Ged nach eil sinn fhathast pòsd'..."

The words flowed through me like the first time I'd tasted ale — warm and smooth, leaving me lightheaded. "What is he saying?" I whispered.

"Ye should go find out, eh?" Gideon's voice rose at the end in barely contained excitement.

The man clearly knew something he wasn't telling me. Jamie's eyes never left my face as I walked toward him feeling like I was smack dab in the middle of an episode of *Glee.* But I was no Rachel Berry. I couldn't sing. Not a note. Kenna had tried to improve my voice, but we finally determined music moved my feet, not my tongue.

When I reached the last row of spectators, I saw my puppy sitting obediently at Jamie's feet, as lulled by his voice as the group of sighing girls around the stage.

I stopped at the edge of the crowd, and Gabby, along with Emily and Analisa, parted the sea of people so I could get closer. If there was a sound associated with swooning, I heard it all around me as Jamie crouched to my level, his broad smile bringing out both dimples in his cheeks. I took his extended hand, and he pulled me up beside him. Gazing into my eyes, he sang the last note of the song, and I melted into a puddle of spineless girl-goo.

He took both my hands in his broad palms, and suddenly my heart catapulted into my throat. This was no pointless romantic serenade. Nothing Jamie did was pointless. The intense lines of his body and the emotion pouring from his eyes said this was a declaration. I swallowed, hard. *Was he about to propose?* I loved this boy more than I thought possible, but marriage? I was barely eighteen.

My vision narrowed in panic. I couldn't say no in front of our kingdom.

Jamie's throat bobbed in a rare show of nerves before he spoke. "Verranica Welling, I feel like I've been dreamin' of you since before I could talk ..."

Oh no. I was dead in the water. My chest tightened as I gazed into his heartbreakingly handsome face — a face I wanted to wake up with and go to sleep to every night for the rest of my life.

The people sent up a cheer, along with someone who sounded suspiciously like Fergus shouting, "Get on with it, laddie!"

Jamie's eyes sparkled, but a muscle twitched in his jaw, and I realized he was taking a huge risk by putting his feelings out there for everyone to see, especially without knowing if I would accept or reject him.

He cleared his throat before continuing. "Vee, you're the only one I'll ever love ... Would ye become ..."

He swallowed again, and I thought my chest might burst.

" ... my handfasted mate?"

"Your what?" The words surged out of me with no finesse whatsoever, provoking a roar of laughter from our audience.

Jamie's eyes darted to the crowd and then back to my face before he leaned in and whispered, "'Tis a Celtic ceremony tha' signifies our engagement."

"Would we have to do it right now?"

"Nay, my heart. At a date of your choosing."

"Then, sure."

He leaned back and arched his brows in challenge. He wanted me to pronounce it. So flooded with love at that moment, I'd cartwheel through the crowd in my underwear if it would make him happy. I turned to the people of Doon. Keeping one of his hands locked in mine, I proclaimed, "My answer is yes!"

Blaz jumped up and gave a sharp bark of agreement as the Doonians showed their support with clapping and cheers. I scanned the faces and saw tears in the eyes of a few dear friends, including my bestie, who grinned from ear to ear and gave a fist pump. Beside her, Duncan cupped his hands around his mouth and yelled, "Kiss her, you dolt!"

And in a perfect *Little Mermaid* moment, the people began to chant, "Kiss her! Kiss her!"

Jamie spun me around, took my face in both his hands, and kissed me until the entire world faded away.

The next morning, I was floating on air. The sun shone warm on our shoulders as Kenna and I strolled down the cobblestone path, peeking in shop windows and brainstorming ways to decorate her suite. We'd decided on an eclectic mix of jewel tones with accents of traditional plaid. We'd even had a painting of the Brig o' Doon commissioned by Bahati MacPhee, Lachlan's mom and a gifted artist who'd been Called to Doon from Africa. I'd been having so much fun, I hadn't thought about the work waiting for me back at the castle in twenty minutes. Amazing what a little shopping could do for the soul.

As we passed the market square, I was astounded to see the only signs of the previous night's merriments were a few lanterns swaying in the trees. It'd been well past two in the morning when the festival had wound down, and the streets had been absolutely trashed.

"Where did everything go?" Kenna asked, mimicking my thoughts.

"I don't know, but I know where I can find out."

Following the mouthwatering scents of fried dough and coffee, I led Kenna and Blaz across the street to Alsberg Bakery. After handing Blaz's leash to Eòran, and piling our packages into his arms, we pushed open the door and were greeted by the tinkling of a bell and a waft of sugary heaven. The selection was insane, but we eventually decided on coffee and apple fritters the size of my head.

As we waited for our order, I asked Mr. Alsberg, "How did the square get cleaned up so quickly? Do we have a Doon janitorial staff I don't know about?"

"Or house elves," Kenna muttered under her breath. I swallowed a laugh as the baker handed us two paper-wrapped pastries.

"The Creu," he answered, as if I knew what he was talking about.

"I'm sorry?"

The German shook his head with a smile and pronounced the word more carefully. "The *Crew*."

Adding cream to my coffee, I stopped mid-pour. "The crew of what?"

Mr. Alsberg gestured us to a free table and then sat and explained that "the Crew" was a group of older children whose job it was to awake at first light and tidy up after all events. He listed Lachlan and several other names I recognized as being part of the team.

When I asked how they managed to get a bunch of pre-teens to do such an unglamorous job, I was told it is considered a privilege to serve the Kingdom in this capacity. And with a wink, the baker added, "It does not hurt that Prince Yahmie leads the Creu."

Quickly sorting through his accented words, I set down my coffee with a plunk. "Wait. Did you say Jamie heads up the Crew?"

Mr. Alsberg nodded. "Yes."

Amazing! Jamie had seen me to my door, and with our extended goodnight kiss would've gotten to bed sometime after three. Yet he'd still risen at the crack of dawn to lead the cleanup.

Two hours and three shops later, my jaw still dragged on the ground. The more I learned about my future king, the more astonished I was by his many layers. I knew, like me, he was an early riser, but I'd assumed he spent all his mornings training in the Brother Cave. Apparently, not all of them.

"So, are we going to talk about the heffalump following us around or should I shoot it in the head?" Kenna asked as we made our way to the textile shop. "I'm assuming that dreamy expression on your face has something to do with a certain hysteria-inducing prince?"

When I didn't answer right away, she clasped her hands next to her cheek and squealed, "Oh, Prince Jamie! He's sooo gorgeous!! Doesn't he have the best voice eveeerrr?!?"

Blaz jerked on his leash and howled in response to the grating whine in Kenna's voice. Agreeing with his assessment, I gave her a well-deserved smack on the arm. "Stop already!"

"Well, you did pretty much get engaged last night and you haven't even mentioned it."

We turned a corner and I glanced behind us to make sure Eòran hadn't returned from taking our bags to the carriage. The man had been hovering like my second shadow all morning. I tugged Kenna into a narrow backstreet and turned to her with an unguarded grin — the kind that was so uncontrollable it almost hurt my face.

Her eyes flew wide as she pulled me into a bear hug. "I'm so happy for you guys! When can I help you design your dress? I'm thinking princess style, of course, with — " She squeezed me until I wiggled away to avoid a cracked spine.

"Whoa there, girly. We aren't engaged yet. It's like a ... I don't know." I shrugged. "A pre-engagement."

Her ecstatic joy melted into confusion. "Like a promise ring? Lame. Then why was everyone so excited?"

"Well ..." I looped my arm through hers and led her down the darkened alley, Blaz walking ahead of us. "The Handfasting is a public ceremony where multicolored cords are braided and wrapped around the couple's joined hands, symbolizing the integration of their lives with each other and the Protector." I'd been unable to sleep the previous night until I'd read up on the Handfasting.

"Doesn't that whole Completing thing mean you're engaged?"

"Umm ..." I wrinkled my nose. All the formalities in Doon could get confusing, even for me. "No, I think that was more about the throne. Doon requires a king and queen to balance one another's strengths. This is more of a personal thing. Anyway, once we go through the ceremony, we become officially engaged for a year and a day. Handfasting is like a trial period to see if the couple really wants to tie the knot — which incidentally is where the expression originated."

Kenna rolled her eyes at my random trivia.

But I ignored her. "Some couples even live together during the trial."

"Will you and Jamie live together?" She raised her fingers in air quotes and wiggled her auburn brows suggestively.

"We kind of already do —"

"What?" she squeaked. "When did this happen?"

"*I meant,* we live in the same castle, weirdo." We reached the end of the shadowed lane and stepped into a slant of sunlight bisecting the flagstones. "I've never even been to his roo —"

My vision blacked out and something yanked me forward, like a rope intertwined with my intestines. Pain bloomed from my core. For a nanosecond, I was floating, in a zero-gravity spacewalk. In complete silence.

Then a pressurized pop.

Nausea burned in my throat as the invisible tether twisting my gut fell away. Sensation returned by degrees. I blinked, and my senses snapped into focus.

A body pressed tight against my side. Kenna and I stood on a sidewalk. A concrete sidewalk. The sun sank behind the trees, where moments before it had been late morning. With a tiny electric buzz, streetlights flickered on all around us. Raw chills skittered across my shoulders and raced down to my fingertips.

A car whizzed past, and I stumbled back, digging my nails into Kenna's arm to keep my balance. I squeezed my eyes closed, willing the illusion away. *This isn't real. This isn't real.*

"Can I assist you ladies with anythin'?" My eyes popped open to find a man wearing the black polyester uniform and checker-brimmed hat of the Scottish police. The officer glanced at my crown and then back to my face. If this was a mirage like before, how could he see us too?

"Miss?"

Because this was real.

"No, no, no." I paused and swallowed my panic. "I ... mean ..."

"No ... thank you, sir. We're fine." Kenna finished for me, her voice as shaky as I felt.

His dark brows crouched over his eyes as they darted between us, then he shook his head and walked away. I glanced around at the whitewashed buildings and tree-lined street. The sign for Poet's Corner Coffee House swung gently in the breeze just ahead. I stumbled to the sewer and emptied the contents of my stomach.

This was no hallucination. We were in present-day Alloway, Scotland. On the other side of the Brig o' Doon.

CHAPTER 6

Mackenna

You know that feeling you get when there's an abrupt scene change in a movie? The main character drives down the road, and an instant later is sipping a latte in a café. Or they lock eyes on a stranger in a club and the next second they're in an apartment making out? Without a transition, it takes a moment — sometimes several — for your brain to fill in the gaps.

This was a zillion times worse — because it was real.

Vee straightened after vomiting into the street. I grabbed her arm and steered her down the sidewalk, away from the mess and the suspicious copper who kept giving us the stink eye. When we were out of earshot, I whispered, "What just happened?"

She stopped. Her pale face accentuated the confusion in her eyes as she stared listlessly at the sidewalk. "I don't know."

"But we're in Alloway."

Her head jerked up to face me as she snapped, "I can see that."

Although misplaced, I understood her angry reaction and held up my hands, palms out to remind her that I wasn't the enemy. "So what happened?"

"Let me think for a minute." She sank onto a nearby bench.

"Okay." I knew better than to push her when she needed time to process, so I paced up the sidewalk. The evening sun sat low on the horizon. In this part of Scotland, anything near seventy was considered a heat wave, and the temperature was indeed brisk. As soon as I had the thought, it was impossible not to feel the cold. Soon my teeth began to chatter.

Ahead I could see the sign of the Poet's Corner Coffee House — one of my favorite places in Alloway. While Vee was thinking, I would get a strawberry scone to settle her stomach and some cinnamon cocoas for us both. I took a couple of steps before realizing that I didn't have any money. In Doon we charged everything to the castle — the perks of royalty — but here we were just two broke teenagers. At least our maxi dresses fit in with current fashions.

I turned back toward the bench, watching as a group of girls emerged from a pub at the other end of the block. They pointed at Vee, commenting to one another in whispery giggles. Although her dress was stylish, her tiara seemed a bit much. And without a jacket to ward off the chill, she shivered conspicuously like some homeless fashionista. The whole scene was so surreal.

Acting on impulse, I walked over to my bestie and pinched her arm.

"Ow!" Vee leapt to her feet. "What was that for?"

Dang. "I was hoping it was a dream," I explained apologetically.

She shook her head. "Nope. This nightmare is real." She slumped back down to the bench.

At the far end of the block, I spied the copper keeping tabs on us. Casually, I leaned over the bench. "We should go to Dunbrae Cottage."

"Why?"

I shrugged. "To regroup, get supplies, get off the streets and away from the fuzz. Figure out how we're going to get back."

That's when it hit me. Every time we'd crossed in or out of Doon other than the Centennial, we'd had the aid of my aunt Gracie's rings. They were special, magical in a supernatural kind of way. Without the rings, we were stuck.

My insides turned to ice as I contemplated never seeing Duncan again. The princes would eventually come looking for us. But time moved slower there; how long until they noticed we were missing? We could be in our thirties before they showed up. I could be middle-aged by the time I was reunited with my eighteen-year-old boyfriend. I was already older than him — thanks to my chasing dreams in Chicago stunt — but now I could end up a cougar creeper. Did Duncan even like older women?

"Get a grip, Kenna!" Vee shook me back and forth so hard my head rattled. Somehow I had wound up on the bench beside her. As I sputtered, she stopped shaking me and leaned in. "You were babbling. Something about Chicago and cougars and creepers."

Oh my! I didn't realize I'd been internalizing out loud. Rather than explain, I asked, "How are we going to get back to Doon?"

"With these." Fishing around in her tiny clutch, Vee pulled out a satin drawstring pouch. Inside were the Rings of Aontacht. "I know you wanted to pretend that the vision in the arena never happened, but I felt it was better to take precautions."

Bless her over-reactive heart. As she placed the gold and ruby ring on her finger, I slipped the silver and emerald one on mine. The cool metal instantly soothed me. Thanks to Vee's brilliant mind, we would not be stranded in the modern world.

Feeling tons better, I sprung up from the bench. "Should we head to the bridge?"

Vee made a sucking-on-a-lemon face before answering. "I think you had a good idea about going to the cottage. It's right by the bridge, and the princes probably won't figure out we're missing for a while. Plus, they'll search the village and the castle before thinking about the bridge, which means that we'll have to make our way back on our own. We should get flashlights and water. And anything else that seems logical."

"Ding Dongs."

Vee frowned at me, so I clarified, knowing they were her go-to stress snack. "I've been dying for some good old junk food. There should be a box in the pantry—and those things don't have an expiration date."

"Kenna, we need to be practical."

"I am being practical." I started to list things off, using my fingers to count. "Flashlights, water, Ding Dongs, Little Debbies, fashion magazines, more nail polish, polish remover, and some hair product."

Enticed by my litany of modern conveniences, she groaned. "I would trade my throne for some decent conditioner."

We walked past the Poet's Corner, both of us hesitating slightly at the thought of tasty treats we couldn't afford. At the end of the block, we followed the jog in the road that would take us to the roundabout at the southern edge of the tiny town. From there, it was a couple more blocks to the cottage.

Clutching one another for warmth and stability, we hunched forward as we walked into the bracing wind. Except for the hike, and the wind, and being sucked out of Doon, this wasn't such a bad thing. We didn't know why we'd ended up back in the modern world, but we had a way to get home and we could stock up on supplies.

When I said as much to Vee, she shook her head. "You can't treat this like a field trip, Ken. Something isn't right."

As if I hadn't figured that out on my own. The million-dollar question was, why was this happening? Fiona had said on more than one occasion that Doon had need of us. Though now that the witch's limbus curse had been thwarted, maybe we weren't needed anymore. "What if Doon's done with us?"

"Done?" Vee halted midway through the roundabout to face me.

"Yeah. Like we've accomplished what we were supposed to — defeating the witch and all — and now the Protector's sending us back to our own world."

"No." The wind turned her hair into mini whips that lashed at her cheeks. Impatiently, she wound her hand through the mess and gathered it into a smoothed knot at the base of her neck. "None of the Destined have ever been cast out. We were called to Doon and we chose to stay. We're a part of the Covenant now. Doon is our home."

But what if it didn't feel like home? Could the Protector sense that I was having trouble adjusting? Or maybe I'd been deemed unworthy. Maybe this was about me — Doon trying to kick me out.

"Kenna, look at me."

I focused on my best friend's grim face, knowing she'd picked up on my thoughts on account of us sharing a brain and all. "You belong in Doon, whether you feel like you do or not. And entertaining these doubts just wastes energy that could be spent on what's really going on."

She was right. At least in the part about wasting effort on questions with no clear answers. "Okay. So what *is* happening?"

"That, my friend, is what we need to find out." We resumed

our journey to Dunbrae Cottage. "Something tells me we're going to need a little help from the brightest minds in Doon."

Scooby Gang time.

It gave me an immediate sense of relief that greater minds than mine would be helping figure this out. Each one of our friends brought something special to the think tank. Fiona could discern the supernatural and knew a wealth of folklore and historical information. Fergus was tactical. Jamie, who was nearly as crazy smart as Vee, had a gift for understanding complex problems. Duncan, the perfect counterbalance to his brother, tended not to overcomplicate things and instead saw issues in their simplicity. Adam, a newer member to our group, whom we'd met during the limbus fight, had a brilliant, scientific mind. Emily thought of details the rest of us didn't, and Analisa — although she wasn't a friend and probably never would be — was crafty in a dodgy, breaking-the-law sort of way. Reluctantly, I had to admit that Ana's particular skill set had come in handy on more than one occasion.

By unspoken agreement we picked up our pace as Dunbrae Cottage came into view. My aunt Gracie's cottage, with its overgrown English garden, looked like something from a Shakespearian faerie story. We crossed under the arched trellis at the foot of the walk and made our way to the front door. I reached for the rock that doubled as a hidey hole for the key and thought about the last time I'd been here with Duncan. So much had changed since then — we were finally together and he was building me my very own theater.

I hurriedly unlocked the door and replaced the key. By the time I had the rock back in place, Vee was already in the foyer. She sat on the steps leading to the second level, with her face in her hands.

"Are you okay?" I flipped on the lights as I closed and locked the door after us.

"Yep." Other than a head jiggle, she didn't move. "Just dizzy is all."

Dizziness had been the first symptom when she collapsed and nearly died. I rushed over and knelt beside her. "Are you having another episode?"

Her muffled voice replied, "I don't think so … Jus' need a minute."

I gently touched her temple. It was burning up.

"Vee, look at me." I helped her lift her head. Her cheeks were flushed, her eyes glassy and unfocused. After a moment her lids slid shut. "Are you sure you're not having another episode?"

"Mmm-hmm." Her head bobbed again. "Must be the flu or something. I think I jus' need to lie down for a moment."

She lurched to her feet and I reached out to steady her. With my hand on her back, I followed her up the narrow steps, guiding her to the bedroom overlooking the River Doon. She stumbled toward the bed and flopped face-first onto the comforter. "Don' let me sleep too long. 'Kay?"

"Okay …"

I watched her burrow into the blanket, and within seconds she was out. Was she really just under the weather or was this another episode that would bring her to death's door? I still vividly recalled the way she had collapsed in the courtyard. That incident had filled Vee, and those who loved her, with terror. This time there was no fear, no gasping for breath, or clutching at her heart. As her bestie, I needed to take her at her word that she was simply under the weather. As if she were reading my mind even in her sleep, Vee gave me a soft snore of confirmation.

Leaning over her, I unfastened the delicate tiara from her hair. As I removed the final hair pin, I noticed a chain across the back of her neck. The halter-style top of her dress had concealed it. Slowly, I unfastened the clasp and removed the necklace so it wouldn't strangle her in her sleep. Attached to the chain was a gorgeous silver pendant, a jewel-encrusted heart topped by a crown — a Scottish luckenbooth — identical to one I'd seen in a painting in the library of the Castle MacCrae. As I set the necklace on the desk next to the tiara, I wondered if Vee wore a replica of Queen Lynnette's or if it was the real enchilada. More importantly, why had I never seen it before?

With another dainty snore, Vee turned to her side. I wasn't sure how long she would sleep, but I decided to be packed and ready to head home when she woke up. With a little luck, she'd rally after a catnap and we would be back in Doon before anyone realized we were gone.

CHAPTER 7

Veronica

The dregs of sleep fell away in slow layers, revealing the ache pulsing in my temples. I kept my eyes closed against the sun heating my face. So much to do, so little time. Petitions, a meeting with my advisors ... What else? Oh yes, I'd agreed to meet with Analisa about her new gym. Then, golden-brown eyes and Jamie's dangerously handsome face appeared behind my closed lids. Definitely no time for a headache.

I sat up and threw the covers off in one quick motion. And blinked at the cool blue walls, cherry furniture, and eyelet curtains framing a view of trees, the glint of a river, and ... the distant arch of the Brig o' Doon. Memories rushed back in and a scream curdled in my throat. "Keennaaa!"

Kenna appeared almost instantly, hair sticking straight up on one side, her eyes extra wide. "Vee, you're awake."

"Why did you let me sleep all night?" I hissed as I plucked my sweater off the end of the bed and shoved my arms into it, before realizing I'd put it on upside down.

"I tried to wake you up. You're the one who practically passed out. Here …" Kenna peeled my sweater off, turned it right side up, and held it out for me. "So, you're feeling better today?"

Finding my half-boots, I plopped into a chair and yanked them on. "I'm fine. But we have to go."

Kenna yawned and smoothed down her tidal wave of crimson hair. "What's the rush, Cinderella? It's not like you're going to turn into a pumpkin. You said it yourself, hardly any time will have passed in Doon."

"At this point it will have been several hours. And what if …" I let my words trail off, not wanting to dump my worst fears all over her blissful oblivion. Standing, I wiggled my ankle until the rest of my foot slid into the boot. "And Cinderella doesn't turn into a pumpkin. Her carriage does."

That earned me a patented Mackenna Reid eye roll as she scooped up my crown and silver luckenbooth pendant and handed them to me. "Okay, we'll leave soon. Where did you get that necklace? It's really cool."

I grabbed my old travel bag, shoved the necklace and tiara inside, and looped the strap across my chest. Taking Kenna's arm, I lead her into the other bedroom. "I found it in the witch's cottage. I recognized it from Queen Lynnette's portrait and couldn't stand the thought of leaving it there to rot. Now, will you *please* get dressed?"

"Of course, Highney." She gave me a mock bow before tugging her night shirt over her head, her next words muffled by fabric. "Heaven forbid Prince Freak-Out discovers you aren't where he left you for five minutes."

Pausing halfway to the bathroom, I spun around. "Did you just call Jamie *Prince Freak-Out*?" She was trying to diffuse my anxiety with humor. Just like when we were munchkins in our fifth-grade play and I refused to go on stage until she made some joke about the Lollipop Guild being the future juvenile delinquents of Oz. I'd giggled all the way through "Ding-Dong! The Witch Is Dead." But right now — with the sum-total of my life at stake — her teasing was having the opposite effect.

I marched back into the room and got in her face as she tugged her skirt over her hips. "Jamie is *not* a freak-out! He's a teenage boy who has carried the weight of an entire kingdom on his shoulders since he was old enough to understand it was his duty. And yes, he's protective of me, but it's only because without each other neither one of us would be able to survive."

My voice broke and I pivoted away, swiping at my stupid tears. Why did I always cry when I was angry? A shudder scraped through me, and I pressed a fist to my mouth. We had to get back to Doon. I couldn't allow myself to imagine the alternative.

"Hey." Kenna rested her hand lightly on my shoulder. "I'm sorry, all right? I didn't mean to upset you. I'm scared too."

With a shaky breath, I turned around and threw my arms around my best friend, squeezing her tight. "I know. I'm sorry too. I'll be fine, as soon as we're home."

Kenna pulled back, her eyes shimmering silver. "Then what are we waiting for?"

🏵️ 🏵️ 🏵️

Kenna locked the front door behind us, and my gaze caught on the lion-head knocker — the MacCrae family's royal symbol. It touched me that Gracie and Cameron had maintained their allegiance to the kingdom even in Alloway. It had been their Calling to leave Doon and protect its secrets from the outside.

"Where should we hide this?" Kenna held up the key as her eyes searched the front garden. "I don't want to forget where it is again."

The last time she'd forgotten, Fergus had been two steps

away from smashing the door down in order to find out if the witch was holding Jamie captive inside. Which she was.

I didn't know how, but I feared Addie was responsible for us getting booted out of Doon. With renewed urgency, I scanned the overgrown greenery. My eyes landed on an ivy-covered trellis, propped in front of the chimney. "How about over here?" I pushed aside the curtain of vines, squatted down and loosed a stone toward the base. Kenna handed me the key and I set it inside the hole, then shoved the stone back into place, hoping I'd never have need of the key again.

Standing, I dusted off my hands and then dug in my satchel. I handed Kenna the emerald Ring of Aontacht, and then slipped its ruby twin on my finger. "Now, let's get out of here."

We rounded the house and set off on the path to the river at a jog. "Did you get all the supplies we talked about?"

"Yep, even nail polish remover," Kenna announced in triumph, hefting a bulging pillowcase over her shoulder like Santa Claus.

"But did you get the flashlights and extra batteries?" By my estimation, it would be late afternoon, but the walk back to the village from the bridge was a long one.

"Yesss. Duh." Kenna called from several lengths behind me. "And a couple boxes of blueberry Pop-Tarts."

I trotted back and grabbed her hand, pulling her beside me. "We're almost there."

The rush of water and the tang of fresh mineral-rich air greeted us as we rounded the bend. But when we reached the end of the path, we both stopped short. The stones of the Brig o' Doon glittered in the late morning sun, the entrance shaded by leafy green trees. It was straight out of a painting — except for the people. Three couples and a family of six crowded the bridge, pointing and taking pictures.

A curse slipped from my lips as I shoved a hand into my hair. I should've anticipated this. It was summer here, prime tourist season.

I must have voiced my last thought aloud because Kenna led me to a nearby bench and asked, "And what could you have done about it if you had? Put up crime scene tape to block the entrances?"

"Not a bad idea, actually." I perched on the edge of the seat, contemplating where I might acquire a believable blockade.

"Well, I don't think you're going to find some just lying around. So you might as well relax and wait it out."

After twenty minutes passed and the steady stream of tourists continued, I sat back and crossed my legs in resignation. I was tempted to drag Kenna onto the bridge and unite our rings to see if they would light up at all. But I wasn't sure how fast they would transport us back into Doon, and I didn't want to give anyone a heart attack when the two American girls disappeared into thin air.

But what if the rings didn't work? What if the force that had pushed us out of Doon blocked us from getting back in? We had both rings, so there was no way for anyone to come after us. I hadn't wanted to tell Kenna, but the truth was that if the rings didn't work, we'd be cut off from Doon until the next Centennial . . . and we wouldn't be middle-aged, we'd be dead.

My breath constricted until I was panting like I'd sprinted a half marathon.

"Vee, sweetie, look at me." I worked to calm my expression before I turned to face her. "I can see the wheels spinning in your head. Talk."

I smoothed my hair into a ponytail and then twisted the length into a knot, reluctant to voice my deepest fear. Words held power, and I refused to give the evil at work here an ounce more fuel.

Kenna's wide gray eyes searched my face. "They're probably missing us by now, huh?"

"Maybe." I turned back to watch the Brig o' Doon before reasoning out my answer. "If we were forced out of Doon at …" A young family exited the far side of the bridge, leaving one older couple strolling across hand in hand. Preparing to bolt, I tensed and touched Kenna's shoulder. But as the couple reached the far side, another group approached. This time it was a bunch of college-aged students, posing for goofy pics and taking selfies.

With a groan, I slumped back and focused on Kenna's earlier question. "So, if we were forced out of Doon when it was late morning there, it's been almost twenty-four hours here in Alloway. Functioning on the theory that Doon's time moves at approximately one-fourth the speed of the outside world — "

"Just get to it already, Einstein. I don't need a math lesson. Will Duncan be freaking out, or not?"

Arching a brow at her choice of words, I explained, "I'd estimate five to six hours have passed in Doon. So, yeah, I'm sure they know we're missing by now."

I sank lower on the bench and twisted the ring on my finger, examining the engravings on the band — Celtic symbols for substitution, protection, and unity. These rings had proven over and over that they conducted the will of the Protector of Doon. They'd seen us through every spell and curse thrown at us. They were incorruptible. We just had to have faith.

The students made their way off the bridge, leaving a young couple chasing a small toddler. Ignoring all the doubts fighting for my attention, I said a quick prayer, grabbed Kenna's hand, and stood. "Come on."

"What about the people?" she asked, but let me drag her forward across the grass.

"We can't worry about that."

Once we reached the edge of the stones, I let go of her hand in case the rings activated, and we exchanged a knowing glance. Strolling forward side by side, Kenna began to chatter about the bridge and the play that had made it famous. Just two tourists visiting a celebrated landmark for the first time. We reached the arch and paused directly across from the small family, who leaned over the edge with their backs to us. We were so close to home, I could smell the earthy crispness of autumn and a fresh batch of Alsberg Bakery's pumpkin spice scones.

Could we chance it while they weren't looking? How long would it take for us to disappear? I glanced at both entrances. There were no other people around. My heart began to pound, and I reached for Kenna's hand just as she stepped toward the young family.

"Excuse me." She'd pasted on a polite expression, but I could see her fingers trembling. "Would you like me to take your picture?"

The mother turned around. "Sure, that'd be wonderful," she replied in a chipper Aussie accent.

The woman handed Kenna the camera she had slung over her shoulder. Hurrying them along was a brilliant idea. They posed, and Kenna snapped several shots. After thanking us, the father hoisted the little girl in his arms and they made their way down the other side of the arch.

Unable to wait another second, I held out my hand. "Ready to fly over the rainbow?"

"You know it." Kenna reached out, muttering, "Duncan, here I come."

The second our fingers linked, the power of our rings connected, shooting red and green sparks that fused into a brilliant white glow. I glanced to the end of the bridge and met the wide gaze of the tiny girl looking over her father's shoulder. I smiled and waved as the light enveloped us, so bright I was forced to close my eyes. Maybe after today, that little girl would always believe in miracles, even if she didn't remember why.

When I blinked, spots floated through my vision. I let go of Kenna's hand and raced forward. Gleaming white castle turrets soared above a sea of apple- and pumpkin-colored leaves. The unmistakable slate, white-capped mountains of Doon rose in the distance. My chest expanded and I pushed out the air I'd been holding in my lungs.

Home.

Kenna squealed as she tackled me in a bear hug. We danced around in a circle and then rushed off the bridge arm in arm. We ran — or jogged, in Kenna's case — through the burnt-out woods of the Brig o' Doon path, still barren since our recent encounter with the Eldritch Limbus, all the way back to the main road.

Kenna bent over to catch her breath, while I repositioned the bag slanted across my chest.

"You know Analisa's opening a kick-boxing gym in town. We could join together."

I blinked innocently as she gave me the stink eye. Such was every conversation we had regarding her physical conditioning.

"You might get to punch Analisa ..." I tempted as we began to walk.

"Now that I could get behind."

"Do you really hate her so much?"

Kenna paused before answering. "Hate is a strong word. Let's just say I distrust her."

"Speaking of trust ... I hate to do this, but when we find the guys, let's not blurt out the whole story of what happened at once." Kenna bit her lip, so I said it for her. "Yes, okay? If I don't ease Jamie into it, he'll put me on complete lockdown."

I wasn't complaining. Jamie MacCrae loved me with a commitment and intensity that I'd craved my entire life. His protective instincts where I was concerned just required a bit of finessing.

"Is there a safe room in the castle?" She threw me a cautious expression. "I'm not criticizing Jamie, I just want to be able to find you after he locks you up."

I laughed, but didn't state the obvious — that if any safety measures were taken, she'd be with me. "Actually, the castle keep is a panic room of sorts. Before Doon was separated from our world, it was where the Laird and his family would hole up during a siege. You know that old, dark dining hall off the throne room?" Kenna nodded, her cheeks flaming up. "I see Duncan's already introduced you to that part of the castle."

She shrugged and lengthened her stride.

"So this is how I can get you to speed up." I jogged to reach her side. "When *did* you two investigate the keep?"

She walked faster. I laughed and caught up to her again.

As the sun began its slow descent toward the mountains, I shivered in my thin sweater, and my feet began to drag as my adrenaline faded into exhaustion. Surely a cart or horse would come by soon and we could hitch a ride the rest of the way to the village. I hated the thought that Jamie and the others might be worried about us.

Kenna rubbed her arms and turned to me. "Can we take a brea—"

But her words were drowned out by approaching horses. Moving fast. I grabbed Kenna's arm and pulled her off to the side as two riders rounded the bend at a gallop. Broad shouldered and regal, one light headed and the other dark. I instantly recognized the MacCrae brothers and threw my arms in the air to wave them down. Jamie turned in our direction, his tawny hair pushed off the strong bones of his face, a familiar, fierce determination in every line of his body.

"Our knights in shining armor have arrived," Kenna cried as she hopped up and down beside me.

They might not have been wearing armor, but as my prince pulled his mighty steed to a stop, its massive hooves clawing the air before he swung his leg over the horse's back and leapt to the ground in one fluid motion, I almost swooned. I was in his arms in an instant. Tempted to melt into his warmth, I forced myself to pull back and paste on a serene smile.

Jamie's hands framed my face, a furrow appearing over his left brow as his dark eyes searched mine. His thumbs swept over my cheeks in a gentle caress. "Are ye all right?"

I took his hands in mine. "I'm fine." I glanced over to where Duncan held Kenna close. "*We're* fine."

Duncan ran a hand over the back of Kenna's hair. "Where've ye been, woman?"

Kenna shrugged, glancing pointedly in my direction.

"Yes, where have ye been?" Jamie squeezed my fingers. "Eòran said you disappeared from the village hours ago."

I disconnected our hands, stepped back from him, and forced a casual tone. "Somehow we ended up in Alloway. I'm not sure — "

"You what?" Jamie roared.

"Modern-day Alloway?" Duncan demanded.

I lifted my palms. "Settle down! We weren't hurt. I had the rings with me, and we crossed back over the bridge. No problem."

Jamie scrubbed a hand over his mouth, a million questions battling in his turbulent gaze.

"Jamie." I grasped the hard muscle of his bicep. "I'll explain everything, but can we not do it in the middle of the road? I'm starving. We haven't eaten in twenty-four hours."

His eyes flew wide. "By the Saints, lass! Ye've been gone for an entire day of modern time? What took ye so blasted long to get back?"

So much for giving it to them in small doses. I sighed at my own stupidity. Kenna shook her head and then gave me the "watch and learn" look.

"Duncan." She leaned into his chest and gave a little shiver. "I'm cold and tired. I promise we'll explain everything over a nice cup of tea back at the castle."

Duncan and Jamie exchanged a nod and then helped us up onto their mounts. Jamie swung up behind me and told me to lean back and relax. His way of saying he'd hold off his questions — for now.

He wheeled Crusoe in a circle with one hand on the reins, his other arm tucked around my waist, holding me close. The horse gave a snort and then trotted forward with a rhythmic sway. Snuggled into Jamie's warmth, my head resting on his shoulder, his delicious stormy scent filling me with every breath, I tried unsuccessfully to keep my mind from going to the dark side. What if it happened again? What if next time I couldn't get back? And I was separated from everything and everyone I loved, forever?

CHAPTER 8

Mackenna

Duncan's massive chest pressed against my back as he leaned down to whisper in my ear, "Let's keep going..."

Mabel bristled in her stride and tossed her black mane, causing me to focus more on the beast beneath me than the hot boy behind me. Duncan straightened and tightened the reins to bring his steed into instant submission. He murmured to her in a soothing voice that sounded infuriatingly similar to the one he occasionally used on me, and she obeyed.

The horse loved him. Me, she tolerated only when absolutely necessary.

Now that I had no concerns of Analisa poaching my boyfriend, Mabel had become my new nemesis. Whenever Duncan wasn't looking, she yanked my hair with her teeth, slapped me across the face with her tail, or nudged me into the filthy hay in the corner of her stall. One time I swear she bit my butt, but when I said as much to Duncan he'd defended her saying she didn't have a jealous bone in her body. On that we could agree. Mabel didn't have *a* jealous bone, she had *two hundred and five* of them — a fact I'd looked up in the castle library just to be sure.

" … could bypass the castle and be to the hunting lodge by nightfall." It took me a minute to realize that Duncan's two thoughts were connected and he that he was suggesting we not go straight back.

Around the bend in the lane stood the village of Doon, and rising into the distance beyond, our destination, the Castle MacCrae. *Home* … I tested the word out. It felt foreign, like when Mario Rosetti lapsed into his native Italian. I couldn't remember the last time a place had felt like home. Not my studio in Chicago, or the house in Arkansas that my dad had uprooted me to at the start of senior year. Maybe before that, in my old house in Bainbridge, Indiana … but even then, only when Vee was there with me.

It was the same way with Dunbrae Cottage. My aunt Gracie's death had left a void, as if the magical spark had ebbed away, leaving cold wood and plaster behind. Home wasn't a place, it was the people I loved — my royal best friend, the amazing boy at my back, and friends who were more like family than actual blood relatives. Because of them, I belonged here and, in time, I hoped I would feel the truth of it.

At the bend, the road forked leading to the village on the right and the start of the high road into the mountains to the left. As we approached, Duncan slowed Mabel to a walk. "Hmmm? Which shall it be?" The intimacy of his voice, pitched low and close to my ear, sent shivers rippling across my neck.

Why would he want to go to the hunting lodge if our best chance of figuring out what had happened to Vee and I was joining the brain trust back at the castle? I leaned back against him and slightly off to the side so I could look up at his face and ask. He prefaced his answer with a pained smile. "To pretend —

even if just for a little while — that nothing could ever separate us again."

He looked out toward the village with a frown. "Because I'm half mad with the need to lock you away in a tower where ye'll be safe." His dark, imploring eyes fastened on mine, starting a butterfly chorus line in my stomach. Although I never fancied myself as a cloistered princess, I could indulge in a little cosplay for my prince's sake. "Humor me and say we'll go — if not at present then soon."

"Okay. Soon." I promised, before straining upward to plant a kiss on his jawline. He responded by tipping his face down to capture my mouth with his. The kiss wasn't sweet. It was rough and desperate, like we were both trying to hold on to the other person to keep the moment from slipping through our grasp. Which happened anyway as the horse beneath us reared up.

Duncan immediately broke off the kiss and pulled at her reins. Ears pinned flat, she bared her teeth and tossed her head in annoyance. "Mabel!" Duncan admonished. "What's gotten into ye?"

Her tail swished back and forth as she snorted, stamping her feet. Her owner looked at me with chagrin. "Mayhap, she's a wee bit jealous o' you."

"Ya think?" I couldn't help but roll my eyes. In her defense, she did have him first. But she was going to have to deal with the fact that he was mine too. And I wasn't going anywhere — at least, not if I could help it.

With a sigh, Duncan reluctantly steered Mabel toward the village of Doon. "I guess I'll just have to content myself with sleeping at your doorstep."

Just like at the cottage in Alloway, when he'd slept in the hallway in front of my room ... I'd nearly forgotten about that.

At the time I'd assumed that he'd been trying to keep me on lockdown because he was following orders. "Why did you do that? Sleep in the hall in front of my door at Aunt Gracie's?"

"I desired to be as close to you as possible." He chuckled softly. "That was a wretched night."

"Because the floor was so uncomfortable?"

"Nay. Because you weren't nearly close enough. Plus, it was the first time ye'd been out of my sight since our reunion. The separation was so unbearable, I couldna sleep."

"I was out of your sight when you took a shower at my apartment." That had been unbearably torturous for me, but I wasn't about to admit to it.

"That was wretched too. There wasn't enough cold water on the planet to numb me to your presence." He guided Mabel around the outskirts of the village, clearly in no hurry to catch up to his brother and Vee. "I knew from the moment I laid eyes on you in Chicago that I never wished to be parted again. I couldna bear it."

Exactly how I had felt. Whenever he left my sight I'd been plagued with irrational fear that I was dreaming and would wake up at any moment to find myself alone in my studio apartment. If Duncan was my home, I was his heart. Without the other, we would cease to function. That was the point of the Calling, I supposed. A gift from the Protector, revealing the person who was not only our other half but the one who would challenge us in the best ways possible to grow into the people we were destined to be.

Not consciously thinking about my words, I blurted out, "What do you think about Vee and Jamie getting handfasted?"

Geez! I sounded like a desperate girlfriend in *Bye Bye Birdie.* *Did you hear about Hugo and Kim? They got pinned, the lucky ducks. I sure wish it would happen to me.*

"Aye," Duncan said evenly so that his tone betrayed nothing. "I think it suits them."

"Not that I'm jealous — 'cause I'm not." I immediately started backpedaling so Duncan wouldn't think that I was fishing for a commitment. "I'm just making conversation, since it's a fairly recent development." *Shut up, Kenna.*

Duncan brought his horse to a stop. The front gates of Castle MacCrae loomed just ahead. Carefully dismounting, he stood looking up at me, his soul bared in the depths of his chocolate-brown eyes. Taking my free hand, he placed it flush over his heart. "Mackenna, I am committed to ye in every way a lad can be committed to a lass. Ye need never doubt that."

"I don't."

He blinked up at me, love radiating from his eyes. "What is it, then?"

I shrugged. "I guess I'm just afraid. There are so many things that could separate us. What if I get sucked back to the modern world? Or something happens to you?"

"Shhh." His hands circled my waist, and he helped me to dismount. As soon as I was on solid ground, he gently captured my chin and tipped my face up toward his. "I dinna believe we've come all this way just to be at the end of our story. I trust that we've many wonderful chapters ahead."

This time when his lips met mine, the kiss was soft, as if I was fragile — no, not fragile, *precious*. He slowly pulled back, his fingers cupping my jaw as he pressed his forehead against mine, and his eyelids fluttered shut. I closed my eyes as well, hoping we could prolong the moment forever. Which lasted all of about five seconds before Mabel butted me in the side and nudged us apart with her freakishly hard head.

Like a jealous house pet, the mare positioned her body

between us. As my boyfriend took her reins, she gleefully flicked my cheek with her whip-like tail.

Snicker all you like, Horseface. This is only round one.

If it came to a livestock showdown, I was fairly certain Elsie and the whole bovine community would have my back. We'd go all *West Side Story* on Mabel before she had a hope of rallying her equine posse.

Horses and cows as Sharks and Jets made me remember this great gender-bending production of the Bernstein musical I'd seen at the Windy City Players. The star-crossed lovers, Antonia and Mario, instead of Tony and Maria, were *meh*, but the girl who'd played Riffy had blown me away.

Duncan firmly forced Mabel to the outside so that he could walk between his two girls. "What are ye thinkin' about?"

"Chicago. I wish circumstances had been different. I would've loved to show you around."

"Do ye wish you were back in the modern world?" His words were light, but there was a wariness in his eyes.

"No," I replied without hesitation. "But there are things from my old life that I would've loved to share with you."

Duncan wrapped his arm around my shoulder, pulling me closer. "Ye still can. Tell me about them — and I will cherish every detail."

I had no doubt that he would … but no amount of words would be the same as him experiencing my world first-hand.

Flanked by the princes and Eòran, Vee and I wound our way through the castle to the appointed meeting spot. When I stepped into the council chamber, eight sets of familiar eyes greeted me. Our little Scooby Gang had grown. Although I had some reservations about more people joining our group, I had the feeling we were going to need all the help we could get.

As well as Fergus and Fiona, Doon's happy newlyweds, four of the Destined had joined our inner circle. Typically the Destined were called to Doon for love, a soul mate waiting for them on the other side of the Brig o' Doon. But during the last Centennial a few months ago, an unprecedented number of individuals had been Called from the modern world because the kingdom had need of their skills — something that, if you really pondered it, felt both troubling and reassuring.

Of the four newcomers in the council room, only Emily had been Called to Doon for love, and unfortunately her soul mate had been the first victim of the zombie fungus. Analisa had been called for her unique-yet-questionable criminal talents. Adam had an extensive background in environmental science, which had proved invaluable in figuring out the nature of the limbus. Oliver Ambrose, seated next to him, was the other scientist — a mechanical engineer, to be exact. And although I didn't understand what he did, he was crazy smart. Vee referred to him as the Tony Stark of the Destined, but even with his unruly dark hair and manscaped goatee, I failed to see any resemblance to Robert Downey, Jr.

The final additions to the gang were the oldest Rosetti boy, Giancarlo, who according to Duncan was fearless with a sharp strategic mind, and his little sister, Gabriella.

As soon as Vee cleared the doorway, Gabby rushed her. "We're so glad you're back, Your Highness — I mean, Vee — Veronica." The force of the hug sent Vee stumbling backward into Jamie, who clasped her arms to keep her from toppling over.

Mortified, Gabby simultaneously let go and hopped back. She had attached herself as Vee's lady-in-waiting and doted on her queen with something akin to hero worship. She always reminded me of a puppy, due to her gangly body and unchecked enthusiasm. Gabby tucked a wayward lock of blonde hair behind her ear and smiled sheepishly. "Sorry, Veronica — I mean, Your Highness. Please pardon my behavior."

My best friend chuckled self-consciously. "Vee's fine. And there's nothing to apologize for." Placing a hand on Gabby's back, Vee diplomatically guided her to the table. "Why don't you take a seat so we can get started?"

Eòran stood dutifully by the closed door as Vee settled herself at the head with Jamie to her left and me to her right. Duncan sat on my other side. I could smell his fragrance of summer sunshine and fresh leather as his fingers twined with mine under the table. It felt soothing to have him so close.

An empty chair remained between Gabby and Fiona. Vee nodded to it, but before she could get her question out, the door opened. The oldest Rosetti sister, Sofia, burst into the room. Hair disheveled, cheeks flushed, she stared at our little gang with bright, feverish eyes. "Sorry! I wasn't going to come, but then …" She looked helplessly around the room until her eyes found Fiona, who gave her an encouraging nod. "I thought I might be of use."

Glancing between Sofia and Fiona, I sensed some unspoken agreement. Fiona continued to smile, saying, "I asked Sofie to come. Thirteen is an unlucky number for a council and I have a feeling that she has much to contribute." Fiona tapped her temple, indicating her gift — her sense of the supernatural world. In my experience, if Fiona had a feeling, it would undoubtedly come to pass.

Vee indicated the empty chair. "Of course. You are most welcome, Sofie."

As Sofia took her seat, I noted the change in her eyes, a

nearly manic determination to engage in her surroundings. A definite shift from the lackluster girl I'd seen at the céilidh.

As soon as Sofia settled, all eyes turned toward our end of the table. Vee cleared her throat nervously, her eyes darting briefly to Jamie for reassurance before facing the group. "How much does everyone know about what happened?"

"Jus' that you and Mackenna went missing," Fergus replied.

"Aye," echoed Eòran from the far side of the room near the door. "And ye weren't nary ta be found."

"Yes, we — that is, well, we're not exactly sure ..." Vee began and then trailed off cryptically. "I mean, we know *what* happened, but it's just ..."

"Oh, for the love of Lerner and Loewe, out with it already. We got sucked out of Doon," I explained.

The table erupted in reactions as Vee's head jerked my direction. "Kenna!"

"Well, we did," I shot back. "And you know I hate suspense. If you didn't want me to blurt it out, you should have said something."

"I was trying to."

Giancarlo Rosetti held up his hands, urging the room to quiet down. "Why don't you start at the beginning," he suggested. "Sofia, would you please take notes?" He indicated a black leather notebook, a metal pen that looked similar to something Vee had used during her brief calligraphy obsession, and a bottle of ink in the middle of the table.

Sofia eagerly snatched up the book. "Sì, Giani," which she pronounced *Johnny*. She dipped the tip of the steel pen into the ink and nodded at Vee and me. "Continue, please."

"From the beginning," Fiona reminded us.

I slid a sidelong glance at Vee, who raised her brows indicating that I should finish what I started. Letting go of Duncan's hand so I could better explain, I started over. "Fine. Vee and I were shopping in the village — browsing for accent pieces for my room — we were thinking jewel tones. We bought some candles and pillows, and I picked up some new pairs of socks. When Eòran took the bags to the carriage, there was a popping sound, and a whirring — like in a movie."

"Kenna," Vee interrupted, stopping me with a small frown.

"Oh, right, most of you don't know what a movie is. It's like one of Calum the storyteller's Scottish legends — only real. Not that movies are real, because they're not. They're fiction — except the ones based on true stories. But the point is that this didn't feel real — it was like something from a made-up story — except it really happened to us. Which makes it surreal. Right?"

Vee placed a hand on my shoulder. "Maybe we should back up. The day before we got — uh — *sucked* out of Doon, we saw something strange. In the middle of the tournament, we saw cars — transportation vehicles from the modern world."

Jamie's brow furrowed as he leaned toward Veronica. "What?"

Calmly, Vee blinked at him. "I didn't understand what it meant, or if it meant anything. The hallucination came and went so quickly that I doubted my own senses. I thought maybe I'd imagined it ... except Kenna saw it too."

I shook my head up and down to corroborate her story. "We thought it was PSTD — post-stress trauma disorder or something." My fingers sought Duncan's under the table. "If we thought it meant anything serious, we would've told you. Truly."

Duncan squeezed my hand in reassurance. "I believe you, woman. We both believe you, right, brother?"

Jamie glowered at his little brother before refocusing on Vee. As soon as he did, his features softened and he took her hand in his. "Aye. O' course I believe ye. But I wish ye would've told me."

"I was going to," she murmured "but then ... we were gone."

"Can you tell us about that?" Oliver's quiet voice cut through the intimacy of the moment. "Where you were, time of day, what exactly you experienced, and anything else strange that might have happened directly before or after the event." He and Adam were also taking notes, but with mechanical pencils that they must have brought with them when they crossed the bridge.

Vee let go of Jamie's hand and steepled her fingers on top of the table in front of her. "Like Kenna said, we were shopping in the village. We ducked into the backstreet behind Dinwiddie's Leather Shop for some confidential girl talk." She cast an apologetic glance at Eòran. "When we reached the other end of the alley and were about to step back onto the street, everything went dark. I felt a sensation like I was being pulled by my guts through space. Then with a pop, I was back on the street corner. Except instead of Doon, Kenna and I were standing on a sidewalk in the middle of Alloway."

"Incredible." Gabby's breathless voice mirrored the delight in her face. By the look of her, you'd have thought we'd traveled to Oz or Narnia instead of the plain old modern world. "Then what happened?"

With a shrug, Vee continued, "We went to Dunbrae Cottage for some supplies."

"After Vee puked her guts out — in the street, right in front of a cop," I added, earning me a sharp poke in the ribs with her elbow.

Son of a Sondheim!

I started to give my friend the stink eye when she mouthed *safe room.* That's right — she wanted to give Jamie the truth in

85

pieces so he didn't lock her up like Rapunzel. Visions of Vee singing about winding and binding and minding her hair filled my brain, so it almost didn't register when Emily brushed her bangs out of her eyes and asked, "Were you feeling bad again, Your Highness?"

"We were both a bit out of it," I sputtered, noting the way Jamie's eyes narrowed at Vee as well as the way Duncan's lips pressed flat as he observed his brother's silent reaction. Knowing that we would both have some 'splaining to do in private, I added, "Getting sucked out of one world into another takes a lot out of you."

"Technically," Adam corrected, pushing up his glasses on his nose while making notes, "it's the same world. Just different dimensions."

Oliver nodded. Tapping Adam's paper, he said, "I wonder if we might borrow the Rings of Aontacht for a couple of days in order to test them in various locations around Doon."

"Not goin' to happen." "Out of the question, lads." Jamie and Duncan answered at the same time, speaking over on another.

Both scientists finally looked up, completely startled by the vehemence of the MacCraes' reactions. Oliver frowned in confusion while Adam cocked his blond head to the side like he was trying to figure out an alien species. "But there's much we could potentially learn by studying the rings and their interaction with the environment. Even if we could borrow them for —"

"Nay." Jamie cut Adam off. "The only reason the lasses are here with us now is because of those rings. They're no' to take them off. Under any circumstances."

"Aye," Duncan echoed, crossing his arms over his broad chest. The only thing more formidable than the MacCrae brothers at odds with each other was when they were in agreement.

The poor science nerds never even stood a chance. And honestly, as long as I was wearing my uncle Cam's ring I didn't feel completely helpless. If I got sucked out again, I had a means of getting back across the Brig o' Doon.

Jamie flashed the scientists a magnanimous smile. "Aside from the rings, anything you require is at your disposal."

Adam nodded as Oliver said, "Thank you. We'd like to examine the alleyway, as well as the bridge. Gather some samples, run some tests."

"Of course. I'll personally see that our brightest pages and guards are reassigned to your detail." He scribbled a couple of quick notes and gestured for Eòran, who I still thought of as Mutton Chops — but now in the most affectionate of terms. Mutton Chops shuffled back to the door, cracked it open, and passed the messages to the guard stationed on the outside.

Fiona cleared her throat delicately, drawing everyone's attention. "I'd like to examine the witch's book o' spells. Perhaps there's somethin' there that will help us make sense o' this."

For the first time all afternoon, Gabriella Rosetti appeared unsettled. "Do you really think the Witch of Doon is behind this?"

Sofia took her sister's hand. "For everyone's sake, I hope not. But we must examine every possibility. So I'll help Fiona."

Emily chimed up next. "Ana and I will handle the rest of the library."

"Sure," Analisa said drily. "Em and I are whiz bangs at research."

Gabby pursed her lips, looking anxiously from her sister to the others. She reminded me of the awkward sophomore girl desperately trying to hang with seniors. "What should I do?"

I expected one of the girls to include her, but it was Giancarlo who spoke up. "You're wonderful with people. I was thinking of conducting interviews, under the guise of writing a book about the history of the Destined. You are so good at putting others at ease, I would welcome your help."

Gabby's gaze darted to Vee, who nodded her approval. Gabby sat straighter, seeming to glow with confidence now that she had a purpose. "Yes, of course I'll help."

Duncan addressed Fergus. "For the time being, we should move Mackenna into the queen's chambers and triple the guards." Then he turned to his brother. "Anything to add?"

After a moment of thought, Jamie replied, "If there are no objections, the other ladies can take turns staying the night with them."

Around the table, every female head bobbed. Gabby clapped her hands together rapturously while Sofia and Emily furiously scribbled notes. The latter murmured, "I'll draw up a sleepover rotation."

Issuing a small huff, Vee turned to Prince Overprotective. "I like a good slumber party as much as the next girl — but don't you think you're going a bit overboard?"

"Nay." Jamie quirked his brow. "Unless ye'd rather have me as a slumber companion."

Blushing beet red, Vee dropped her face to her hand in mortification. To make matters worse, Duncan said with mock outrage, "Why does he get to sleep over? If Jamie's stayin' the night then I'm stayin' too."

"And me," Fergus interjected, wiggling his eyebrows suggestively. "Where Fiona sleeps, so do I."

Making a rude noise that was uniquely Italian, Giancarlo demanded, "Why do you *ragazzi* get to have all the fun. *Perché.* I want to sleep over too."

"Knock it off, you lot." Analisa barked. She glared at the

testosterone-bearing members of the group as she declared in her clipped London accent, "The queen's sleepovers are strictly girls only — no boys allowed."

Giancarlo Rosetti batted his inky lashes seductively. "Where is the fun in that, *carina*?" he teased, causing Analisa to chuckle in spite of herself.

"Well then — " Jamie stood and rolled his shoulders to get out the kinks. "With the queen's permission, I think we're ready to adjourn."

Before Vee could speak, I bounced to my feet with Duncan close behind. "Wait. What about Vee and me? What's our job?"

Jamie glanced from me to his royal girlfriend. Ever the gallant prince, he extended his hand and helped Vee stand up. "Your job is to be safe — after a little visit with Doc Benoir."

Taking the level headed approach, Vee cupped his stubble-covered jaw. "Jamie, I feel fine."

"Just a precaution, love."

Duncan wrapped his arms around my waist. His warm breath sent shivers down the sensitive skin of the side of my neck as he spoke. "You too, woman."

"Seriously!" I whined. "What did I ever do to you?" He raised his brows, and I immediately caved. "Fine."

"Thank you," he murmured. "And if ye wouldna mind terribly, I'd like to hear more about your adventures in Chicago."

CHAPTER 9

Veronica

The arched wooden door of Jamie's suite loomed in front of me as daunting as a miniature Mount Doom. I leaned against the stone wall at my back and pulled in a deep breath. It was time to come clean ... again. Dizziness, headaches, muscle weakness, as well as heart palpitations, had haunted me for weeks, and I'd kept it to myself. But what happened to me in Alloway went beyond the usual, and I'd faced the fact that I may not survive another attack.

Assuming I was even still in Doon come morning.

A wave of nausea rolled through my stomach, and I pushed off the wall, putting one foot in front of the other. Jamie had invited me to have dinner with him in his chambers, which normally would have my pulse racing. I hadn't been in the princes' tower since we first arrived in Doon, and I'd never stepped foot inside Jamie's room. Somehow seeing where he slept and spent his free time felt like a big deal — a glimpse into his complicated soul.

I lifted a hand to knock, but the door whooshed open before

my knuckles connected. Jamie filled the entrance, solid and strong, his honey-brown eyes crinkled at the corners. His lips followed suit and slid into a lazy grin, sweeping all other thoughts out of my mind.

"Hi," I managed to whisper, my knees going a little weak.

"Welcome to my humble abode, love." He swept his arm out in a shallow bow and opened the door wide.

I didn't know where to look first. Expecting something similar to Duncan's suite, I was completely blown away by the contrast. Where Duncan's sitting room was bright and open, Jamie's was dark and enveloping. The only sources of light were a fire crackling in the hearth, a few scattered candles, and the gold-orange sunset peeking through floor-to-ceiling burgundy drapes.

Overstuffed brown leather sofas and chairs were flanked by sturdy, rough-hewn tables that looked as if Jamie could've made them with his own hands. But what drew me in were the cherrywood shelves that covered almost every wall, overflowing with ... stuff.

I moved into the room and toward the bookcases, almost reverently. The first shelf at my eye level contained an eclectic assortment of items — an enormous conch shell, a six-inch miniature of the Eiffel Tower, a pair of battered Nikes, and a long, narrow horn with rustic-looking designs carved around the surface. I felt the magnetic awareness of Jamie coming up behind me as I reached out and ran a fingertip over the engraving. "What's this?"

"Tha's one of my new favorites." He reached around me and lifted it from the stand. I turned as he sucked in a deep breath and then put the smaller opening to his mouth and blew, causing a deep, droning sound to resonate through the room.

I giggled as he lowered the horn.

"'Tis a miniature Australian didgeridoo. The originals are over a meter long."

"Where did you get it?"

"I bought it from Oliver."

"The inventor? He just got here." I took the instrument, astonished how light it felt in my hands. "I'm surprised he would part with it."

Jamie waggled his tawny brows. "Didna ye know I'm filthy rich?"

"And humble," I teased as I placed the horn back in its stand. "Clearly, I'm fortunate to be in your presence." I threw a smirk over my shoulder and then turned back to scan the wall of shelves brimming with items from all over the world. A Grecian urn depicting frozen figures in relief sat between a model of a Harley Davidson and a hand-painted Chinese dragon. I wandered over to a tall wooden bow propped in the corner beside an animal-skin quiver full of feather-tipped arrows. I was reminded of the American Indian I'd seen fletching arrows my first day in the Doon marketplace and of my astonishment at the diversity here.

I turned in a slow circle, unable to comprehend all the artifacts and what they might represent to the one who had collected them. It was the room of a world traveler who'd never left his own backyard.

And it amazed and broke my heart in equal portions. "Jamie, this is …" I broke off, at a loss for what to say.

I slumped against the back of a chair and he stepped close, his kilt brushing my knees.

"Hey, why do ye look so sad?" He lifted my chin with a single finger and his dark eyes fastened to mine.

"It's just all this stuff …" I wasn't sure how to continue without insulting him. "You'll never get to see or do —"

He began to shake his head before I even finished. "Nay, this is no' signifying all the places I wish I could go." He swept his hand in a wide arch. "I feel like I've already been to each place or experience tha' these items represent because o' the detailed descriptions their original owners shared wi' me. When I look at them, they remind me to respect all the nations embodied in our great kingdom. And what a delicate balance it takes to lead such a meldin' of individuals."

I blinked up at him in awe. "Oh."

He cupped my elbow and guided me to my feet. I leaned into him as he brushed the hair off my shoulder, his warm caress lingering on my back.

"Would I like to sail the Pacific or climb Mount Everest or ride a motorcycle?" He quirked a rakish grin and I could see him astride a Harley, the wind tossing his hair around his face. "Aye. But—"

"Everything has a price." I quoted the lesson his mother had imparted to him and he'd shared with me. Since becoming queen, I'd lived this principle. It forced me to see both sides of every decision, and it made me a better ruler.

"Yes." His lids lowered to half-mast, his voice a warm caress. "And I have ever' thing I need right here."

Not for long.

The thought jumped into my head unbidden and the room gave a quick tilt. I took a step to the side and Jamie gripped my arms. "Vee?" His sharp gaze searched my face.

"I'm fine. Just hungry." I needed to tell him, but not yet. I wanted this dinner to be special. A memory we could both keep with us—whatever the future held.

As if in answer to my need, a knock sounded on the door. Jamie led me to a small round table in front of the fire, where he pulled out my chair and called for the person to enter. Several people filed into the room; two liveried waiters carried trays of sumptuous-smelling covered dishes, followed by Eòran, and then Blaz at his heels.

My dog bounded toward me, his long, pink tongue lolling out of his head. I braced myself as he jumped half into my lap, getting in a slobbery lick before Eòran pulled him back.

"He missed ye, yer Majesty," my guard rumbled. "Was mopin' about the kitchen. Wouldna eat a morsel."

As the staff arranged our meal and lit the candles on the table, I fought through a wave of dizziness and leaned into Blaz, hugging his bristly neck and nuzzling his face. "Did you miss me, you big baby?" He gave a soft whimper in answer and laid his heavy head on my shoulder. When he seemed satisfied that he'd regained his rightful place in my heart, he pulled back and cocked his head. His liquid eyes stared solemnly into mine and his paw tapped my knee, giving a low whine as if he knew something was off. I'd heard that dogs could sense illness in their owners, but I hadn't believed it until that moment. His intelligent gaze locked on mine, he patted my knee several times. "It's okay, boy," I whispered. "I'll be fine. Go lay down."

"M'Laird, Chef Mags instructed us to stay and serve the meal," I overheard one of the waiters say.

"Thank you. That willna be necessary. But give Mags our regards," Jamie replied.

"Yes, sir," the waiters answered in tandem before filing out of the room.

Blaz, after giving me one last lick, hopped down and headed to the hearthrug where he turned in half a dozen circles before curling up for a nap. Jamie held the door open, brows arched expectantly. I followed his gaze to Eòran whose hands were clasped behind him as he perused the items on a nearby shelf.

Jamie and I exchanged an amused look before he cleared his throat. The guard didn't turn.

Unfolding a napkin and placing it in my lap, I asked, "Was there something else, Eòran?"

He meandered over to the windows, his limp barely noticeable, and tested each latch. Unless Addie sent flying monkeys after me, I didn't see how the windows at the top of a castle tower could possibly be a safety issue.

"I just thought ye might need some ..." He wandered the perimeter of the room, then paused and poked his head into the open door of Jamie's bedroom. "Extra security." My guard turned, spread his legs wide, and crossed his arms, settling in directly in front of the doorway.

My hand flew to my mouth as I tried to hide a giggle. The sweet man wanted to protect me ... from Jamie. But when my gaze wandered to where my prince stood rigid by the door, his expression growing darker by the second, the laughter died in my throat. Clearly, he was insulted by Eòran's lack of confidence. But I was touched. The guard didn't know Jamie like I did. Didn't know that honor and integrity ruled his every action. Didn't understand that he was harder on himself than anyone else could be.

Shooting Jamie a "down boy" look, I rose and walked over to where Eòran stood. "You don't need to worry. I'm one hundred percent safe with him."

"I've seen the way he looks at ye, lass," Eòran replied under his breath, his hazel eyes latching on mine. "I'm not so old that I dinna know what that means."

I placed my hand lightly on his forearm. "Eòran, Jamie would *never* hurt me."

He started to interrupt, but I talked over him. "*Or* take advantage of me." I squeezed his arm and stepped back, offering a smile. "You need to trust us."

Lines tightened around his mouth and his shoulders slumped. "'Tis just ... yer father isna here, and I feel responsible for ye."

My heart did a funny little skip. "I ... thank you," I managed to force out over the lump in my throat.

He uncrossed his arms and leaned in as if he might hug me, but then turned on his heel and marched across the room. He paused at the door.

"Eòran, I vow to respect her above myself." Jamie's tone sounded strained, his eyes intense.

My guard gave a terse nod. "Make that far above, lad." And then he was gone.

Jamie closed the door, and blew out a loud breath before turning to me. "Shall we?"

I made my way back to the cozy, candlelit table. The savory scents of roasted meat and fresh-baked bread made my mouth water, but then my stomach clenched in rebellion. My famously insatiable appetite had been missing for weeks. Since my illness, I'd been so used to covering up how I truly felt, the lie slipped out easily. "Yes, I'm starving!"

I sat and spread the napkin across my lap again, focusing on smoothing out every last wrinkle. I couldn't even meet Jamie's eyes — how was I going to tell him the truth?

He leaned over the table and whisked the metal dome from my plate. "Coq au vin," Jamie pronounced in a perfect French accent. "Mag's specialty."

The dish looked sumptuous. Golden-brown chicken and mushrooms smothered in a burgundy wine sauce, herb-smashed potatoes, and a miniature rosemary tart on the side. Something thick and bitter coated my throat. I swallowed hard.

Jamie poured us each a glass of chilled cider and then sat

and said a blessing over the food. While I prayed for strength and for the words to say what needed to be said.

After saying amen, Jamie dug in, and I took my time slathering butter on a warm slice of bread. I'd managed to choke down a few bites of food when I noticed Jamie's plate was empty. I laughed despite myself. "Hungry?"

His eyes sparkled across the table as he shoved another hunk of bread into his mouth and said around it, "Perhaps a wee bit."

Reminded of our first "date" at Muir Lea, I teased, "We never did pass that edict, but that doesn't seem to stop you from talking with your mouth full."

A wide grin coaxed out the long dimples in his cheeks.

As I watched the perfect boy who had been chosen for me, and I for him, my heart drummed an accelerating cadence in my chest. Like the timer on a bomb counting down. My thoughts must have shown on my face, because Jamie's smile faded and his eyes drilled to mine.

I shot to my feet, not caring that my chair crashed to the floor behind me, and rushed around the table. Jamie scooted back, but before he could rise, I sat on his lap and threw my arms around his neck. Digging my fingers into his hair, I lost myself in his eyes, memorizing the exact shade of rich brown, and the splash of gold around the pupil. He blinked thick, dark lashes. "Vee?"

I refused to waste a moment of whatever time we had left.

Drinking his warm breath, I lowered my mouth to his and kissed his top lip softly. His chest expanded, and I could feel his heart rate accelerate as I moved to his bottom lip. Cupping his stubble-covered cheeks, I angled my head and pressed our mouths flush, tasting salty-sweet butter on his lips.

One hand was flat against my lower back, his other tangled

in my hair. Heat licked through me, uncurling in my belly as he kissed me with a desperation that mirrored my own. My hands ran over his neck, his arms, his muscled chest, before coming to rest against the bare skin of his neck. His skin felt impossibly warm, the vibration of his pulse thumping in rhythm with my own.

Drawing a ragged breath, he moved to the sensitive skin below my jaw. I tilted my head to give him better access and shrugged off the suddenly itchy material of my cardigan. His large fingers locked around my upper arms, pulling me closer. His mouth drifted lower on my throat, igniting my skin.

If I were to die, this is how I would go. In Jamie's arms.

Wanting his mouth back on mine, I took his face in my hands and lifted it up. He kissed me slowly, savoring my lips. Fire raced in my blood, flooding my senses. Needing to get closer, I reached down and untied the strings holding his shirt together, and spread the material wide.

With a gasp, Jamie gripped my hands and pulled away.

But I didn't want to stop. Didn't want reality to intrude on my blissful oblivion. I leaned in.

Jamie drew back with a groan. "Yer makin' it blasted difficult to keep my promise, lass."

I blinked at him, disoriented.

He lifted a hand and covered his mouth, his fingers digging into his cheeks as he searched my face. Heat rushed up my neck. What was I doing? Hastily, I began to extricate myself from him.

"Let me," he whispered and put his hands under my arms, lifting me from his lap.

As I stood fiddling with my dress, shaking and dizzy, he rushed over and picked up my chair. He carried it to his side of the table and sat it facing his. He gestured for me to sit, which

I did with great reluctance. The ticking clock in my chest sped up once again.

Jamie sat and raked the hair off his forehead. "What is goin' on with you?" He leaned forward and braced his elbows on his knees, one side of his mouth quirking. "No' that I'm complainin', mind ye, but this isna like you."

Latching my eyes on his, I took both his large hands in mine. "Promise me something."

Without a second's hesitation he replied, "Anythin'."

I stared at our laced fingers, noticing my hands appeared small in his. Delicate. I loved his hands. Broad and sun-darkened, with a map of powerful veins across the back. Straight, strong fingers, his palms peppered with calluses. They were not the hands of a sit-on-his-throne-and-bark-orders monarch, but those of a leader who ruled by example — by digging in elbows deep to clean up after a party, by training every single day so he could protect his people with his life.

Jamie stroked my fingers with his thumb. "Verranica?"

Tears rising, I blinked them away, but I couldn't look him in the face; instead, I stared at the space above his left shoulder. "If something ... happens to me ... promise me you'll choose another queen."

His silence forced me to look back at him. A furrow appeared over his left brow, and his fingers tightened almost painfully. "Dinna talk like that."

"I'm serious. We have to expect it to happen again." I pushed out a sigh and glanced at the crackling fire. "Something is trying to push me out of the kingdom. What if I can't make it back next time?"

"There willna be a next time. And if there is, you'll have the rings."

"Jamie." I forced my gaze back to his, but I couldn't form

the words that would add to his fear. Couldn't tell him that the sickness that had almost taken me from him once was back. Instead, I focused on convincing him to do the right thing if I were gone — for any reason. "We have to think like rulers. If something happens to me, you'll need a queen beside you. Someone to temper that hotheadedness of yours. And … and I think Sofia Rosetti is the perfect choice."

His brows lowered over his eyes and he sat back, dropping my hands.

I'd thought about this a lot. Sofia grew up side-by-side with Jamie, knowing she could be Doon's next queen. Perhaps it wasn't a coincidence that she'd missed her Calling. Maybe it was so she'd be open to this new purpose for her life. To take my place.

I attempted a smile, but felt my lips quiver. "Sofia is smart and compassionate and she loves Doon. And … I know …" I swallowed hard. "I know she could make a great co-ruler."

Jamie sprang out of his chair and stalked to the hearth. He ran his fingers through his tawny hair and then linked them against the back of his neck as he paced, his every stilted movement evidence of his head warring with his heart. After several tense minutes, he leaned against the mantle and stared into the fire.

As much as the thought of him being with someone else fractured my heart, I needed him to agree to this promise. Needed to know Doon would have two strong rulers, and that he wouldn't turn bitter and hard without me.

Blaz whined and shifted to lay his head on Jamie's boot. But when Jamie ignored him, he rose and slunk off into the bedroom.

After several more drawn-out moments of silence, Jamie shook his head and spat, "Nay." He strode back to the table and went down on one knee before me, his dark gaze blazing into mine, the telltale vein ticking in his throat. "Verranica, I would do anythin' you asked. I'd kill a thousand witches and their undead armies for you." He cradled my clasped hands in his, his voice a rough whisper. "I'd crawl through hell and back. But dinna ask this of me. Dinna ask me to replace you."

Tears burned my eyes and throat, love for this boy threatening to overwhelm me, but I buried my emotion, pushed it down into the deepest well of my soul so that my voice became cold and unrecognizable. "I'm not asking you to replace me in your heart, just on the throne." He shook his head and I sat straighter. "Fine. If you won't agree, then I'll write a legal decree ... binding in the event of my death."

Jamie blinked at me like he didn't know who I was, his limp hands dropping from my lap. He'd poured his heart out to me and I'd shut him down like a true ice queen.

But the suppression cost me, and I began to shake. My limbs trembled so hard, I wrapped my arms around myself and bent at the waist. Pain splintered through my chest, my vision faded in and out, and I wondered if I'd even get a chance to wrap up my affairs.

"You're no' pushing me out. Dinna let an evil scheme steal your faith. There is nowhere you can go, *nothin'* that can keep us from finding our way back to each other. *This* is the Protector's will." His voice broke in a ragged edge, but he pushed through it. "Do you hear me, Verranica? Doon is your Calling and you ... *you* are mine." His hand splayed on my back. "Vee? You're burning up." He leaned down to look into my face, and that's when I noticed my pendant had slipped out of my dress.

"What in all that's holy!?" With a hard yank, he snapped the chain off my neck.

As if a cool breeze blew a screen of smoke from my eyes, my vision began to clear. The tightening in my chest loosened and my equilibrium returned. I sat up.

Jamie dropped the pendant on the floor and smashed it with the heel of his boot as if it were a poisonous spider.

"What are you doing?"

He moved his foot, and the pendant winked back in the candlelight, whole and undamaged. I stood, the strength in my legs like an old friend I'd missed terribly. The shaking was gone, the chills faded to a comfortable warmth. And suddenly I knew — it had been the pendant all along.

"Jamie I . . . I didn't know."

"You got this from the witch's cottage, didn't you?" he practically spat.

I took a step toward him, my hands spread in a pleading gesture. "Yes, I found it there when we discovered the spell book. I recognized the necklace from Queen Lynnette's portrait. I couldn't stand the thought of something so precious to her rotting away in that evil place."

He took two steps and clasped my arms in an iron grip, his face like granite. "Tha' pendant killed Queen Lynnette."

"But . . . how?" I sputtered, trying to put the pieces together. "She gave it to the coven as an act of good faith when she promised them the throne of Doon. It's what she thought would save the people. I . . . I wore it for courage."

Jamie's dark gaze moved over my face, and the softness returned to his eyes as he yanked me to his chest and encircled me in his arms. His mouth pressed to my hair, he murmured, "Dear Lord, I almost lost you."

I hugged him fiercely and then pulled back. "But I still don't get it. How did it kill Lynnette if the witches had it? And why did it make me sick?"

Jamie palmed my cheek. "Ye feel cooler now. Are you all right? Any heart palpitations or dizziness?"

I blinked in wonder and I shook my head. "I'm fine." I hadn't realized how bad my health had deteriorated until I started to feel like myself again.

Relief sparkled in Jamie's eyes as he let me go and walked back to stare at the jewel-encrusted luckenbooth on the stone floor. "Ye didna wear it all the time, did you?"

All the times I felt most like myself over the last weeks … the céilidh dance, the day we crossed back to Doon from Alloway … I hadn't been wearing the pendant. Feeling like an utter moron, I replied, "No, but when I collapsed the first time, I'd been wearing it for a solid seven days. Why didn't it kill me then?"

"Because you're stronger than Lynnette ever was. And the curse was no' meant for you." He stroked his chin. "But perhaps because it was meant for the queen of Doon, the longer ye wore it the stronger its hold on you became. And the more it ate away at you when it touched yer flesh."

I shivered hard.

Jamie wrapped an arm around my shoulders. "From what we've been able to gather, the coven used the pendant to create a curse tha' bound Lynnette to her vow to relinquish the throne. The broach became symbolic of her soul. It was her most prized possession, and she gave it over to evil because she was afraid — weak. She lost faith tha' good would triumph over evil, and it ended her life."

"So this pendant represents Addie's claim to the throne of Doon, and I've been wearing it?" My voice spiraled higher with every word. How could I have fallen into that witch's plan again? Fury burned through my chest as I grabbed the chain off the floor. Before Jamie could stop me, I darted around the table and hurled the pendant into the fire with a shriek. "You will *never* have power over me again!"

There was an ominous hiss and then black-violet sparks flew up the chimney, purple flames licking out as if consuming the fire. A whoosh of icy air touched my face and Jamie yanked me back. The door burst open behind us.

A body slammed into both Jamie and me, tackling us to the floor so that my face was buried in the carpet. A boom shook the room, followed by the tinkling of shattering glass. And then silence.

I lifted my head to find Eòran half on top of both of us, shards of purple debris coating his hair and beard. "Yer Majesty? My Laird? Are ye all right?"

I met Jamie's eyes and then nodded, watching the purple ash as it fell from my hair. "Jamie?"

"I'm fine, love. Tha' is, I will be if this thousand-pound boulder you call a guard would get off of me," he teased.

Eòran lifted up with a groan, limping backward on his bad leg. Jamie shot to his feet and steadied Eòran with a hand on his shoulder. "Thank you, my good man."

My guard nodded, and they both turned and extended a hand to help me up. I took each of their hands and let them tug me to my feet. Jamie ran his fingers through his hair and then shook like a dog, sending sprinkles of purple everywhere.

Eòran scanned the room. Everything in a twenty-foot radius of the hearth was coated in plum-colored dust. "What the devil was that?"

I wiped the ash from my arms, and the tiny shards, like iridescent sparkles, stuck to my fingertips. I'd seen this before.

Picking up a lantern from the table, I made my way to the hearth and squatted in front of the now-dark fireplace.

Jamie crouched beside me as I sifted through the heap of ash with a brass poker.

"Be careful."

"I am. But the frozen flames and the purple ash, it's exactly what happened when Fiona and I broke the curse on Aunt

Gracie's journal, the night Addie kidnapped you." I kept digging. "But I have to be sure."

Eòran moved to stand behind us, the candelabra in his hand throwing wavering ribbons of light onto the hearth. "What are ye lookin' for?"

Just then the tip of the poker clinked against metal. Maneuvering the hook, I lifted the pendant from the rubble. "I'm looking for this." Charred and twisted almost beyond recognition, the luckenbooth hung from the blackened chain.

"We need to find Fiona." I turned to Jamie. "I think we broke the curse."

CHAPTER 10

Mackenna

If déjà vu all over again was a thing, I was having it ... again. The only other time I'd been in the royal chapel, the group had been solely focused on breaking the curse wrapped around my aunt Gracie's journal. What Vee was describing to us now, with the pendant and the shards of purple debris, made my stomach sour. The Witch of Doon definitely had a signature to her curses.

The charred remains of the luckenbooth rested on a small dais in the middle of the chapel annex off to one side of the main sanctuary. The windowless, rectangular room felt like a tomb, even with a ton of candles blazing from the altar at the far end. Three of the four walls were covered in floor to ceiling box-like panels that varied in size and reminded me more than a little bit of the mausoleum where my mom's ashes had been buried.

One of those boxes contained the witches' book of spells. Now, Queen Lynnette's pendant would go in another. When Vee and I had first arrived in Doon, and our rings had been confiscated, they had also been kept in here.

Without meaning to, I touched the silver and emerald ring on my right hand. I'd promised not to take it off until we'd solved whatever had been going on. If only the cause could be attributed to the cursed luckenbooth. But of course not. That would be too neat and tidy for real life.

"You're *sure* this isn't what sucked us out of Doon?" I asked lamely as Fergus lifted the pendant with a pair of fireplace tongs and placed it into one of the boxes near the altar.

Fiona shook her head so that her strawberry blonde curls bounced around her grave face. "Nay. Not likely."

Over her shoulder, Adam added, "Especially since it caused Vee to become ill long before the two of you were transported to the modern world. More likely, it's a different curse or something else entirely."

Next to him Oliver cleared his throat, and I noticed his eyes glowed with their own light — that of a science nerd about to get his geek on. "We'd like permission to study the pendant and the spell book. Maybe there's an electro-magnetic signature we can identify. Something that will tell us if there are other cursed objects in Doon."

With a quick glance at Jamie and Duncan to ensure they were on board, Vee replied, "Of course. Anything you want."

"Thank you." Oliver's gazed dipped longingly to the ruby ring on her hand before he remembered himself. Sheepishly he said, "I'd like to start tonight."

Jamie grasped Oliver's hand. "Thank you, man. Your dedication is greatly appreciated." Then taking Vee's arm, he guided her toward the exit with Fergus and Fiona close behind. As I started to follow, Duncan's large hand settled against the small of my back, his touch anchoring me to his side and his kingdom.

As we made our way through the corridors and Fergus and Duncan began to discuss boy things — borders surveys and whether to postpone their next training exercises — Fiona fell in step with me.

In her quiet, non-judgey way, she said, "I sense ye still have some questions about the luckenbooth. Put your mind at ease by askin'."

That's all the invitation I needed. "If the curse was meant for Queen Lynnette, why was Vee getting sick?"

"As far as I can discern, the spell was cast to kill the queen o' Doon. Thankfully, Vee is verra resilient and the spell had been partly used up on its intended victim." She shook her head ruefully. "Tis a blessing that our queen is a much stronger lass than the locket's first victim."

I snorted in response. "I still don't get why Lynnette made the deal with the witches. She should've known better."

Fiona touched my arm, and as we walked through the long north corridor, her green eyes began to shimmer. "People do all sorts of unthinkable acts when they're desperate. Regardless o' her reasons, Queen Lynnette made a terrible bargain to save her kingdom. By opening up her soul to evil, she gave the coven the means ta destroy her."

"Such a tragic fate."

"Perhaps," Fiona agreed in her musing tone that meant she was about to contradict me. "But without her sacrifice, King Angus never would've petitioned the Protector ta save our kingdom. There would've been no miracle o' deliverance ..." She trailed off, her head tipped to the side as she let the implication sink in.

"And Duncan and I would have never met."

"Nor Veronica and Jamie," she added.

"So the Protector caused Lynnette to make that bargain?"

"Nay, she did it of her own free will. But the Protector used the situation for his glory, in spite of her weakness."

"If the Protector could do that, why didn't he save Lynnette?" I challenged as we approached the corridor to our tower.

"Because her actions had consequences. All our actions do."

"So he allowed the witches to punish Lynnette for her lack of faith."

"He allowed her to reap the consequences of her choices, yes. But he also honored the intentions of Lynnette's heart. Ultimately, she wanted to protect her people, and although she wasn't around to see it, her deepest desire was granted. Doon was saved. Which I suspect had been his plan all along."

As I wound my way through the castle, I envied Fiona her faith. Life would be so much easier if I could trust there was a perfect plan behind everything, and that someday I would be able to look back and see clearly how everything played out exactly as it was meant to be.

I woke up to knocking on the bedroom door and Vee's freshly painted toes poking into my cheek. We were sleeping head to toe, just as we had when we were little, when sleeping at the foot of the bed seemed the pinnacle of ten-year-old rebelliousness.

"Your Highness, Mackenna." Emily's soft but insistent voice pierced the dark in tandem with the shaft of light from the cracked door. "Come quick. Adam's at the door. He thinks he found something."

Vee and I rolled to sitting positions with minimal collision. By the time my feet hit the floor, Emily had crossed the room to light the wall sconces. My eyes clamped shut against the golden onslaught. Blind as well as sleep-dumb, I fumbled with heavy limbs for a robe while my feet wriggled on the floor like sightless moles in search of my slippers.

I heard, rather than saw, Emily cross the room to help us.

As if by magic, soft slippers slid onto my feet. A strong hand grasped mine and hoisted me to standing. A second hand joined the first, securing a fluffy robe over my favorite fleecy pajamas that proclaimed, "Make Musicals, not War."

Forcing my eyes open, I noticed that Vee was kneeling beside Blaz and whispering in his ear. She wore Jamie's dark green robe over her sleep shorts and tank top. It was about a zillion sizes too big on her. I caught the way she slyly buried her nose into the collar and inhaled, making me wish I had something from my own prince to wear.

Before my thoughts could wander further down the path of Duncan's clothing, Emily held the door to the sitting room open for us. In the adjoining room, Adam paused mid-pace. He regarded us with feverishly bright eyes as he ran his hands through his short salt-and-pepper hair. The gray would've made any other guy look older, but it merely accentuated the scientist's baby face and long, inky lashes. From a purely objective girl perspective, he was a cute guy, even more so when his face flushed with new knowledge.

Adam gave Vee a quick deferential nod. "I'm sorry to disturb you, but Oliver and I found something." He didn't need to explain that we needed to go with him — the urgency of his discovery was imprinted on his face.

Vee led Blaz to his dog bed and told the puppy to stay. He obediently swallowed a whine as Vee, Emily, and I walked out of the queen's chambers and followed Adam down the stairs. Three night guards flanked us as we wound our way through the castle toward the chapel.

When we were a little over halfway there, Adam stopped and turned back toward us. The spacing of the wall sconces in the stone hallway caused half his face to be in shadow, reminding me of a Batman villain as he said, "Oliver went to fetch the princes. But we really need to gather everyone. Your Highness, might we send the guards to get the others?"

Thankfully, everyone had quarters in the castle. Castle MacCrae provided apartments to any who wanted to live within its walls, and consequently attracted most of the singles in the kingdom. They usually moved back to the village after marriage, with the exception of Fergus and Fiona, who'd been given a suite in the southeast tower. Eòran lived in the army barracks on the south wall above the dungeons, and the rest of our group had individual apartments along the eastern corridor.

Vee issued a command in the form of a request to the guards, who obediently scattered, leaving just the four of us to resume our trek through the castle. At the next intersection, Adam turned left. Emily and I followed, but Vee stopped. We backtracked a couple of steps as my bestie frowned at our guide. "The chapel is the other way."

Adam shrugged nervously, his expression sheepish as he explained, "I know that. I probably should have mentioned that what we found in the chapel is connected to the throne room. We need to go there first."

"But the others ..." Vee glanced back the way we came.

"No worries," he replied. "Oliver and the princes will meet us up ahead and then we'll fill the others in when we get to the chapel. You're really going to want to see this."

For a split second his self-conscious veneer cracked and I saw a flash of annoyance, but before I could puzzle it out, he resumed leading the way. I guess I couldn't find fault with his impatience, as he was obviously anxious to show us his discovery. At the next corridor, we went right and down a short hallway to the darkened throne room.

I remembered the room vividly from my first trip to Doon and more recently due to a private tour of Castle MacCrae hosted by Duncan. In addition to a single throne on a marble dais at one end, the formal receiving hall had three entrances. The general assembly entrance, the way we had come, was for the people. The ornate door to the right side of the throne led to an antechamber and the old king's quarters, which had remained vacant since his death. The heavy, wooden door off to the left of the dais connected to the keep — a fortress within a fortress, or panic room, as Vee had aptly called it. It was impenetrable when closed and barred from the opposite side, allowing the royal family to flee the throne room and be safe within an instant — though it hadn't been needed since before the Miracle. Duncan had whispered that bit of information against my neck in breathy gasps between kisses. Hands down the best tour I'd ever been on.

Deep in memories, I collided with Vee, who narrowly missed crashing into Emily. Adam stopped in front of Vee's throne, rubbing his hands together in anticipation of the information he was about to share. His gleaming eyes swept the three of us as he cleared his throat nervously. "First, in order for you to get the full effect, I'm going to need the Rings of Aontacht."

Vee's eyes widened but the look of surprise was quickly replaced with a scowl. "I'm really not comfortable with us taking our rings off."

Beside her, Emily hesitantly suggested, "Perhaps we should wait for the princes."

Adam's nervousness vanished. For the first time since I'd known him, he looked unbalanced — like someone who tortured kittens for kicks. With a humorless chuckle, he replied, "I'm afraid I must insist."

Quicker than I would have thought possible, Adam grabbed Emily. He twisted her arm behind her back as he held her in front of him like a shield. At her throat he held a wicked looking dagger that seemed to have materialized out of thin air.

"I'll take those rings now." Adam's smirk caused goose pimples across my flesh.

"No, Your Highness," Emily croaked. Her terrified eyes were so large that she resembled one of those ceramic figurines that were more creepy than precious.

"Your choice, Your Highness. The rings or Emily's life." To emphasize the point, he pressed the tip of his dagger into the soft flesh underneath Emily's jaw. She yelped as a tiny stream of blood trickled down her neck.

"Stop!" Vee pleaded. Adam paused, lifting the blade slightly as he waited to see what she would do next. With big, slow movements, she slid the ring off her finger. "There's no need to do that. We'll give you the rings. Okay?"

She turned to me. "You too, Kenna. Give Adam your ring. Calmly ... there's no need to *panic*."

I wasn't panicked. Freaked out — yes. Possibly in shock. But not panicked. As I slipped my uncle Cam's ring from my finger, I realized Vee was staring at me like I was the densest girl in the universe. Why? Because I wasn't appropriately reacting to the situation with fear? If I truly felt like our lives were in danger, I'd be plotting to barricade us in the panic room.

Oh — the *panic* room!

Vee's gaze flicked to the heavy wooden door behind me and then back to my face. I saw in her expression the moment she realized I got her unspoken message. Resisting the urge to glance over my shoulder at the door to the keep, I stepped toward Adam. When I was an arm's length away, he said, "That's far enough. Set your ring on the throne and back away."

Doing as he instructed, I stepped onto the dais and placed my ring on the red velvet seat cushion of the throne. Without taking my eyes off of Adam, I backed away from the chair and began edging toward the door that led to the keep.

"Now you, Your Highness." Adam nodded toward where my ring sat.

Slowly, Vee climbed the dais and crossed to her throne. She placed her ring toward the back of the chair — about as far away from mine as possible. Smart — Adam wouldn't be able to scoop them both up at once. Then she shuffled backward until her body brushed mine.

Concealing her action with her body, she slipped her hand into mine. Being two organisms who shared the same brain, we tensed and waited for the right moment to run. Which, to me, was ten minutes ago.

As soon as Vee stepped away from the throne, Adam giggled, an airy, high-pitched sound at odds with the person I thought I knew. His hungry eyes devoured his prize as he murmured, "Too easy." He might as well have crooned, "We wants it, we needs it."

Vee squeezed my hand, a quick burst of pressure and release meaning *be ready.* "The princes will be here any second," she said.

Now Adam laughed outright. "You stupid little impostor. No princes are coming to your rescue. And before you ask, Oliver's sound asleep in the chapel. I drugged him."

In one fluid movement, Adam wrenched Emily's arm up, forcing her to her knees, then pushed her onto the hard stone floor by placing his knee between her shoulder blades. With her cheek against the ground, facing the main entrance, all I could see was the back of her head.

Crouching next to her, Adam murmured, "Stay. If you move — at all — I'll slit your throat. Nod if you understand and agree." Emily's head bobbed once.

Satisfied, Adam straightened and climbed the marble dais.

From the opposite side of the throne, he pointed his knife at us. "Don't you two move either. I have something very special planned for you."

As Adam scooped up the first ring, Vee demanded, "Why are you doing this?"

He paused. His head tilted our direction and I saw the complete and total devotion that fueled his purpose. "Because *she* asked me to."

The instant he turned his attention to getting the second ring, Vee's hand clenched mine in a bone-crushing grip. *Now!*

I sprang toward the door to the keep, dragging Vee with me as she shouted, "Emily, run!"

Adam growled. Aware that he was mere steps behind us, I reached the door and let go of Vee's hand to fumble with the latch. The door gave way and I stumbled forward, using my momentum to curve around to the other side.

As I turned, I saw Adam lunge at Vee and grab the back of her robe. Her eyes widened as she thrashed to get away. Reaching across the doorway, I clutched the front of her tank top and tugged. With a wriggle, she shed the robe like a snake and sling-shotted into the room. Praying the discarded sleepwear didn't block the door, I shouldered it closed, just as something — make that someone — slammed into the other side. I staggered back a step from the impact, but then Vee was next to me, adding her force to mine.

The door banged shut and I barked, "Lower the sneck."

"The what?"

"The latchy thing." She clicked the metal lever into place and then wrestled with the top wooden crossbar. It slid across the door as Adam battered the other side, the impact followed by a spine-chilling howl. We hurried to bolt the remaining five crossbars into place. Once the entrance was secured, we collapsed against the door, huffing like the big bad wolf.

Vee shot me an incredulous glare. "Sneck?"

"What? That's what it's called." I remembered it distinctly because Duncan had whispered the word against the side of my neck.

High slits along one wall diffused the incoming moonlight so that the room appeared murky, barely bright enough for me to see her roll her eyes. "Since you were so studious on your recent tour, what about other ways in or out?"

"All the doors are locked. You have to have the key. This is the only one left open, because it's off the throne room." I gave her a moment for that to sink in before asking, "Do you think Emily got away?"

"I think so. I saw her running down the aisle."

Good. She could get medical help and others would learn Adam had us trapped. When Duncan and Jamie heard about this, they would pummel him into dust. Hopefully after we got some answers.

"That psycho said, 'Because, she asked me to.'" Chills cascaded up my arms, making me wish I had more than just a pajama top for warmth. "It's got to be Addie, right?"

Pacing away from the door, Vee scrubbed her face with her hand. "That would be my guess."

"But she's forbidden from crossing into Doon, isn't she?"

Vee turned around to regard me with somber eyes. "Yes, but she seems particularly awesome at finding loopholes. Like enchanting Gideon or when she sent Lucius Jobe across the bridge to do her bidding."

"Lucas Who?"

"*Lucius Jobe*. I read about him when we were researching the limbus. He was Addie's minion. She sent him across the

Brig o' Doon two Centennials ago to sabotage the kingdom from inside. What we need to figure out is if Adam was already the witch's lackey when he came to Doon or if she somehow corrupted him from inside the kingdom."

"I don't see how it matters. Either way, Adam's embraced the dark side."

Pacing away, Vee mused, "If he's like Gideon, he can be saved."

I thought about the overzealous guard who'd wasted away under the influence of an evil enchantment that caused him to do unspeakable things. "But Addie's curse corrupted Gideon from the inside out. By the time we figured out what was going on, he looked like Skeletor — cadaverous and bulge-eyed. Adam looks great for an evil henchman."

Vee gasped at me from the opposite end of the room. "That's it. Gideon wasted away because his will rebelled against Addie. He didn't want to do evil things. Adam seems to enjoy doing them. He comes alive — "

"Because he was the witch's flunky long before he came to Doon," I said, finishing her thought.

Holy Schwartz! We'd blindly embraced him. Let him into the Scooby Gang, asked for his help with the limbus. I blinked at Vee, who'd moved farther into the room. The chamber, which hadn't seemed particularly large before, now looked to be the size of a football field. The murky light touched Vee's head but allowed shadows to swallow up her body. Those shadows seemed to carry her away even more ... Or was I the one being carried?

I tried to move closer, reaching out. But I couldn't make much progress. The shadows held me back, clinging to my arms and legs like vines. It was like fighting through an invisible jungle.

Vee was also struggling. I could see her straining forward. She called my name but she sounded distant, her shout barely carrying over the whooshing in my ears. No. Not my ears — the whooshing noise came from behind me, appearing much closer and louder than my best friend.

With a final burst of effort, I lunged for Vee's hand. Our fingers touched for an instant, and then I was plunging backward into the dark. Spinning into nothingness, I lost Vee, the room, everything but the nauseating sensation of blindly swirling out of control. I was Dorothy Gale — but without a house, minus a little dog, and with no hope of encountering a good witch at the other end of my journey. I was at the mercy of evil, helpless to resist the Wicked Witch of Doon.

CHAPTER 11

Veronica

Painful prickles raced along my spine, across my shoulders, and down to my fingertips. My eyes fluttered open — pink-and-green-striped curtains, matching coverlet, an outline on the wall where my "Dance is Life" poster used to hang, a desk covered with stacks of paper shoved in the corner. My room, but not my room. Two large filing cabinets stood against the far wall, my old dresser long gone. I squeezed my eyes closed and willed myself to wake up. My chest rose and fell as I struggled to pull in enough oxygen. I clutched the scratchy synthetic fabric beneath me.

This had to be a nightmare.

"Bob! Start the coffee. I overslept!"

At the sound of my mom's screeching voice, I popped up, the room spinning around me. I pressed my palms against my closed lids. Blood roared in my ears. "Please let this be a dream. Please let this be a dream," I pleaded.

A memory rushed back — Adam's maniacal face, the throne room, the rings, Kenna and I running to the keep. Emily. Oh no, I'd given Adam the rings! I rubbed my empty finger, bereft of the weight and security the ring provided — a link to the Protector of Doon. And I'd given it away willingly, to save Emily, but as a result Doon had lost their queen. A stronger ruler would never have sacrificed their own safety for one individual. But the blood pouring down her neck … Adam would've killed her to get to the rings.

I buried my face in my hands as a horrifying thought occurred to me; what if this wasn't the dream? What if Doon had been one big, fat, movie-length dream? I'd had those before, dreams that felt so lifelike that when I woke up I could feel it and taste it for hours afterward. But surely my giant guardian Fergus hadn't been just a dream? My gifted advisor and friend Fiona? My loyal-to-a-fault sentinel Eòran? The Rosettis? Blaz? The castle with the most spectacular view on the planet? Duncan, the big brother I'd always wanted?

Jamie? My breath hitched on a sob.

Looking back, it all seemed too fantastical to be real. How could *I,* an eighteen-year-old ex-cheerleader from the Midwest, have ruled a kingdom? How could a boy that noble and beautiful exist?

A short screech shattered my musings and I looked up to find my mom framed in the doorway, her mouth opening and closing like a guppy's. "Veronica? What are you doing … I mean, where did you come from?"

"Good question," I muttered.

"What?"

"Mom, how long have I been gone?"

"Is this some kind of joke?" Her brows pinched over her nose.

"Where did I go after I left here?"

"You ran off just like your daddy." She waved her hand dismissively.

If I'd run off, then where was Kenna?

Kenna. Of course! She'd been in Doon with me, and she'd been with me in the keep. She could confirm it hadn't been a dream. Now all I needed to do was find her. I jumped off the bed. "I need your cell phone."

"Not until I get some answers, young lady!" Janet propped her hands on her hips, barring the door.

"Who're you talking to, dumplin'?"

Bob the Slob, fatter and slobbier than before, stood behind my mother, his eyes scanning me from head to toe. "Oh, hey, Veronica. When did you get back?"

I crossed my arms in front of my tank-top-clad chest. "Mom, may I *please* use your cell phone?"

"What happened to yours?"

I'd left it in my tower room on the bedside table, so I could listen to my music as I fell asleep. The answer popped so readily into my brain that it had to be the truth. Didn't it?

"I left it … um …" When it came to lying on the spot, I was a Padawan to my BFF's Jedi. As a result I blurted, "It's in my suitcase and the airline lost it."

Janet cocked a brow. "Why on God's green earth would you put your cell phone in your suitcase? Seriously, Ronnie, of all the harebrained, stupid things to do. Don't you dare think that I'll replace — "

I didn't dare think anything when it came to Janet. I stepped forward, raised my brows, and stared her in the eyes. "I need to use your cell phone immediately."

Janet blinked once, twice, three times, and then stepped back out of my way.

"Ohh … little Vee's grown a backbone." Bob's voice, deep and whiny at the same time, made me want to punch him.

"Mom, where's the phone?"

Deep brackets appeared around her mouth before she answered. "In the kitchen, by my purse."

Rushing through the hallway and into the cramped kitchen, I ignored the sick waves of déjà vu washing over me. After five long years, I knew every crack in the plaster and every creak in the floorboards. The tiny house, held together with duct tape and a prayer, was all we'd been able to afford after my dad left. It made me wonder what Janet and Bob were still doing in this dump.

I stumbled over a peeled-up corner of linoleum and grabbed Janet's smartphone off the counter. Scrolling through the contacts, I searched for the name Walter Reid. If I ended up here, then maybe Kenna ended up with her dad in Arkansas.

I'd spent half my life glued to Kenna's side — surely my mom had her family's contact information programmed into her phone. But after scrolling through the "R" section twice, I'd come up empty. I keyed in a "W," praying it would be under his first name. I scanned the short section of contacts and the blood froze in my veins.

Welling, Paul. I clicked on my dad's name with a trembling finger. It was a local number. My pulse accelerated, and my heart pounded in my ears as my finger hovered over the call icon next to his name.

"Vee, I need that back. You showing up here out of the blue is going to make me late."

Janet's voice snapped me back to reality. I *had* to find my best friend. Quickly committing my dad's number to memory, I switched to the Internet.

"I just need three minutes, Mom." I glanced up and met her eyes, the lump in my throat growing larger by the second. "Please."

Her expression softened in a rare show of vulnerability, and in that moment, she was my mom again. The one who read me bedtime stories, braided my hair with rainbow ribbons, and watched movies with me when I was sick — the woman she'd been before my dad broke her heart. "Maybe I should take the day off work."

Tears burned behind my eyes and I stepped toward her, ready to throw myself into her arms and sob like a baby.

"No way, Janet." Bob stomped into the kitchen as he tugged a sweat-stained ball cap onto his head. "If you miss another day, you'll lose that job. And they're talkin' layoffs at the quarry."

Janet whipped around and shoved a finger in Bob's chest. "You said you were looking for another job. What happened to the construction position? Or the delivery job? You're really a ..."

Tuning out their squabbling, I searched *whitepages.com*. When I found a Walter Reid on the correct street, I tapped the screen to connect the call.

As the phone rang, I moved into the living room, farther away from the noise. Three rings. *Please pick up.* Five rings. *Please let her be there.* Seven rings.

Please God ...

"This is Walter Reid, If you're getting this message —"

No idea what to say, I ended the call.

"I have to go, Ronnie. Give me my phone." Back to her old charming self, Janet stuck her hand out and glared.

Reluctantly, I gave it back to her.

"Don't think you're off the hook either. We'll be having a long discussion tonight about your future. And if it involves you staying here longer than one night, you'll be paying your part of the rent."

"Come *on*, Janet!" Bob yelled from the kitchen. Apparently they only had one car, because Janet turned and followed him out the back door. With a slam and a squeal of tires, I was alone.

Curling into a ball, I rocked back and forth on the sofa, willing the tears to come. But I felt numb — hollow and emptied out. Like my heart had been torn from my chest and I'd never feel anything again.

Then I heard Jamie's voice, deep and ragged, so clear it sounded as if he were in the room.

" ... *Dinna let an evil scheme steal your faith. There is nowhere you can go ... nothin' that can keep us from finding our way back to each other ... Do you hear me, Verranica? Doon is your Calling and you ... you* are mine."

Finally, the tears came.

CHAPTER 12

Mackenna

I shifted in the darkness thinking about how a comforter was fittingly named. The soft weight formed a cozy cocoon that enveloped me in a pleasant sleep. Every time my brain tried to tell me to get up, the comforter lulled me back to dreamland. Whatever the day would bring in the kingdom of Doon could wait while I snoozed for just a few more minutes. Something about that thought wasn't quite right ...

I blinked at the bedside alarm clock. Five fifteen in the morning — too early for man or beast. Wait ... since when did Doon have power?

I sat straight up in bed, searching the cluttered space. At the far end of the room the electric glow of a digital clock cast a greenish tinge against the wall. The faint memory of burrito stink filled my senses as I oriented myself to the familiar surroundings: microwave, fridge, desk/dressing/dining room table, single chair, and my bed. The walls were decorated with Broadway posters and the snuggly comforter depicted two silhouettes, one light, one dark ... and green. Glinda and

Elphaba — a present from my dad when I'd left Arkansas for my internship.

Holy Hammerstein! I was in Chicago, in my studio apartment.

The confusion of waking up in my old space caused me to struggle out of my comforter's siren pull and stagger to my feet. I still had on the fleecy pajamas I'd specially chosen for my slumber party with Vee and Emily. What exactly had happened?

The doorknob began to jiggle, causing hope to blossom in my chest that Duncan would be on the other side. But if that were the case, wouldn't he knock? He wouldn't just open the door and barge in. The only person I knew cocky enough to do that was Adrenaline Theatre's Artistic Director, Weston Ballard.

In my mind's eye, Wes's entitled face morphed into Adam's as the events of my last few minutes in Doon came rushing back. The science nerd I thought was a friend had stolen my ring, along with Vee's, and somehow forced us out of the kingdom.

My heart began to accelerate as the door knob turned with a soft click. I edged backwards forgetting about the bed until I landed on the mattress with a thump. Light spilled into the room from the hallway as the door opened, illuminating the intruder. Not Duncan or Wes, but a petite, female form. The bands around my chest loosed and my breath whooshed out in relief. The sound drew the girl's attention. Her head whipped in my direction and she screamed. Before I could stop myself, I started screaming back.

For several seconds we shrieked at one another in the darkness until the girl flipped on the light. Blinking like mole-men against the harsh glare, we both fell silent.

"Kenna? Is that you?" Her voice was vaguely familiar, but since I was essentially blind, I couldn't place it.

"Oh my gosh — it *is* you." The girl's form rushed over to the bed. "We were all so worried. How are you?"

"Okay ..." Or not. Up close, I could see the girl's delicate upturned nose and brilliant red curls. She reminded me of — me. Only her hair at the roots was nearly black, and suddenly I could picture her with a dark pixie cut. "Jeanie?"

"Yes." The girl nodded like I was an amnesiac grasping for lost memories. Which didn't explain why she had a key to my place or my last season's hairdo.

Extricating my hands from hers with an awkward tug, I asked, "What are you doing in my apartment?"

"You had to ... leave suddenly." Jeanie glanced away, her cheeks reddening. "So Wes made an arrangement with the landlord so I could sublet."

"Where exactly did I go?"

Her gaze returned to me, eyes narrowed like I was an escaped mental patient. "Rehab ... Don't you remember?"

That's how Weston explained my impromptu disappearance? That I was a druggie? Swallowing my outrage, I arranged my features into what I hoped made me appear contrite. "I do — that is, I wanted to know what Wes told people. How much does everyone know?"

Jeanie nodded sympathetically. "At first, Wes didn't want to share the details of your addiction, but after the *BroadwayWorld.com* article, all the gory details were public." She had the decency to wince. "Sorry."

"It's fine." I'd chosen Duncan, and Wes had gotten back at me by spreading his rehab rumor and elevating Jeanie to fill my void. It was nothing I couldn't live with. Heck, the rehab scandal might've even helped my career. Not that it would matter unless I decided not to return to Doon.

But I would return, because that's where Duncan belonged. And Vee...

Memories of being ripped from my bestie swirled in my brain like the tornado montage from *The Wizard of Oz*. Had Vee ended up back in the modern world too? And if so, where? I had the strangest impulse to look for Vee under the bed or in the closet. But my bestie had never set foot in my Chicago apartment.

Turning my attention back toward Jeanie, I asked, "Can I borrow your phone, please?"

She reached into her bag and then handed me her cell. I stood and paced to the opposite end of the room as I punched in Vee's numbers ... and promptly got an out of order message. That was a good sign, right? Dialing 411, I asked for Janet Welling in Bainbridge, Indiana ... No such listing.

Of course, Janet had gotten married again, and I had no idea what Bob the Slob's last name was. With a giggle, I entertained the thought of asking information for a listing for Janet the Slob.

"Are you okay, Kenna?"

I turned to find Jeanie frowning. Note to self: dial back the hysteria. Instead of answering her, I asked, "Can I make one more call?"

She reluctantly nodded, and I punched in my home number. After a couple rings, my father's reassuring voice sounded. "This is Walter Reid. If you're getting this message, Meredith and I are still on our *extended* honeymoon in Fiji. If this is an emergency, you can leave a message, and our house sitter will pass it along. Otherwise, I'll call you when I return. *If* I return."

Dad got married? If I had any doubt about my time in Doon, which I didn't, this was the clincher. There's no other conceivable reason why I would've missed his wedding. Mixed emotions burned in my throat, but I pushed them down as I rushed to leave a message. "Dad? It's Kenna. I need to talk to you but I don't have a number where I can be reached. And I don't remember your cell number. But I'll call you back, okay?"

I disconnected the call, realizing too late that I'd forgotten to say congratulations. Disappointment burned in my throat that I'd missed his big day, but I stuffed the feelings down.

I had other things to stress over at the moment. For starters, I had to find Vee.

Jeanie had begun to tidy up our apartment, so I did a quick Google search on her cell. With a half-formed plan in place, I intercepted her at my desk/dressing/dining room table to return the phone. Glancing around at my once-beloved memorabilia, I said, "I can't stay. I have to go back."

Jeanie nodded compassionately. "That's probably a good idea."

A sinking feeling dominated my stomach as I forced myself to continue. "Can I borrow some money? I need to catch a bus to Indianapolis and then take a taxi."

The other girl's eyes narrowed like my request was code for *I need to go see my dealer.* "How much money?"

"Sixty bucks? And I don't suppose any of my old clothes are lying around?"

Chagrined, Jeanie bit at her lip. "Sorry. I would have kept them but they were way too big..."

She trailed off with a shrug forcing me to ask, "Can you loan me an outfit and some shoes?" When she frowned at the request I added, "I swear I'll pay you back. And you can keep anything in my apartment — the posters, the signed playbills, the furniture, all of it."

"What about when you come back?" Jeanie insisted.

"I'm not coming back. Really. I promise." The words caused a slight sinking sensation in the pit of my stomach that I refused to analyze.

Jeanie walked to the dresser and pulled out a pair of faded yoga pants and a ratty T-shirt. I hurried to the bathroom to change and rinse the acidic aftertaste of fear from my mouth. When I emerged, she was waiting by the open door with an empty grocery bag and a pair of flip-flops. I stuffed my jammies into the bag and wriggled my feet into the shoes, which were a size too small.

Then she handed me three twenty-dollar bills that, judging from the look on her face, were hard to part with. I knew how much Adrenaline interns didn't make — she was probably giving me her entire emergency fund. Taking the money, I repeated, "I'll pay you back. I swear."

"Since I'm never going to see you again, you don't have to. Just do me one favor." She paused until I nodded my consent. "Get help, Kenna."

"I am," I said, thinking of Vee and her marvelous, puzzle-solving brain. "Will you do me one favor as well?"

She raised her eyebrows as I reached for one of her stray crimson curls. "Don't let Wes turn you into me. He's not worth it. Stand up for yourself and be the person you're meant to be."

With a final word of thanks, I left Jeanie to ponder who she was and turned my thoughts toward the journey ahead. If I'd woken up in my bed in Chicago, I had a hunch where Vee had turned up — if she'd turned up. As I contemplated the day-long trip to Bainbridge, Indiana, I wondered which I dreaded more: arriving to find out Vee had been sucked out of Doon too, or discovering she hadn't and that I would be left to figure this out all alone.

CHAPTER 13

Veronica

The streets of Bainbridge felt dull and lifeless in the autumn chill. People passed, avoiding each other's eyes as they hurried to their next destination. Cars zoomed by, splashing oil-darkened slush and belching exhaust. My eyes watered with the onslaught, and I yanked up my scarf to cover my nose. The breeze swirled dead leaves around my feet and up inside Janet's too-large fleece jacket. I shoved my hands into the pockets and hunched my shoulders, praying with every step for this nightmare to end, for a miracle that would take me back to my home. Back to Doon.

After Janet and Bob had left and my hysteria subsided, I'd scavenged some clothes from Mom's closet and made myself a bowl of cereal that tasted like cardboard. I'd stared at the TV as manic characters incited canned laughter in an endless cycle of ridiculousness until I couldn't take it anymore. So I'd headed out to find a job. Janet's ultimatum had been clear — pay rent or get out. And sadly, I didn't have any place to get out to.

My old dance studio had welcomed me with tiny tutued

bodies pirouetting to the sweet notes of Tchaikovsky, sweeping me back in time to all the years I'd spent teaching there. But the tranquility didn't last long; my high school happy place had become a means to an end. When I'd found the owner, she'd greeted me with a hug and informed me there were no openings at the moment. She'd offered to put in a good word for me at her sister's ice cream shop. I'd thanked her and headed back out into the cold.

Unable to accept the epic fall of going from Queen of Doon to Queen of Dairy, I'd decided to head back to Janet's. The job search could wait another day.

On my old street, my steps slowed to a shuffle as I passed the same old rusted-out car parked in front of the house with pink shutters, the yard covered in over a hundred faded lawn ornaments. I then ducked under the branches of a weeping willow that had overhung the sidewalk for as long as I could remember. Nothing had changed in Bainbridge. But much like Alice after her adventures in Wonderland, I didn't fit here anymore — I couldn't go back to yesterday because I was a different person then.

Or was I?

Perhaps I was that same insecure girl I'd always been. Waves of doubt washed over me, tugging me down until I slumped into the damp grass beside the curb.

Had my time in Doon been real? Or had my vision of Jamie in the school parking lot been a gateway to madness, each hallucination sucking me deeper into my own head? My pulse thrummed in time with my accelerating heart. Was it possible that I'd invented an imaginary world to escape my crappy life, then awoken back at home with some kind of selective memory loss?

If that were true, a straightjacket could be in my very near future. I hugged my legs and lowered my forehead to my bent knees, searching my brain for a glimpse of reality, pleas over-laying every thought.

Please, show me what's true.

My head spun, and I no longer sat on the cold curb, but walked in a sunlit rainbow of wild flowers, my hand ensconced in warm, strong fingers as Jamie's eyes shone into mine. Then the scene changed and I twirled in time to a frenetic fiddle, amidst hoots of encouragement as Doonians kicked up their heels around me.

Please, show me.

The weight of a diadem on my head, the eyes of the people pressing into me from every angle, and their deafening cheers as I announced the defeat of the limbus.

At the edge of the Brig o' Doon, my best friend by my side — I whispered a prayer, and the ring blazed on my finger, its power pushing back the darkness.

Warmth spread inside my soul and I lifted my head, the doubts melting away like snow. No matter how far I went, or how fear tried to strangle me, Doon was a part of me. Always. Maybe that was faith — knowing something as truth, even without proof.

There had to be a reason that the Protector allowed a sinister force to thrust me back to my old life — something I needed to do or learn in the modern world. I walked faster. A purpose that would help me become a better leader, or help me defeat the witch once and for all. I began to run. Just like when Kenna and I found the rings at Aunt Gracie's cottage. This was no coincidence.

Blind hope spurred me toward something I couldn't see. Doon was my destiny, and no matter what Addie was up to, nothing and *no one* would keep me from it. I ran harder, push-ing my legs to their physical limit.

Our rundown house came into view and my miracle sat on the crumbling front stairs, the glow of her crimson hair unmistakable.

"Kenna!"

At my yell, she jumped up and bolted across the lawn to meet me. We flew into each other's arms, the collision almost knocking us off our feet.

"Vee, oh my gosh, I was so scared you might not be here! That I'd guessed wrong. I had no idea where to look for you if you weren't in Bainbridge."

"How did you know to check here?" I leaned back to take in her precious face, but held tight to her arms. "Where did you come from?"

"Chicago. But can I tell you all this inside? I'm freezing."

I looped my arm through hers, unwilling to let her go, and led her into the house.

After shutting the front door and locking it behind us, I felt comfortable enough to release my hold on her. I walked over and clicked on a lamp.

Kenna stopped and surveyed the cramped living room. "It looks exactly the same. Down to the blue floral sofa and glass-top tables."

I shook my head. "I know. It's like after everything we've been through, everything that's changed in our lives, it shouldn't be the same."

As I shrugged off my coat, she walked over and lifted the ratty rainbow afghan my great-gram had crocheted for me. "This thing's seen better days."

I could just picture Bob the Slob cuddled up with it, wearing nothing but his tighty-whities. "You *may* not want to touch that."

She dropped it like a hot tamale. "Why do you think your mom hasn't done any updating?"

"I don't know. I think they sold Janet's car too." I shrugged. "Are you hungry?"

"Starving! All they had at the bus station were hot dogs and microwaved pizza. Seriously, how did we ever eat that st — " Kenna's eyes flew wide and she cut herself off. "What in the wide world of Sondheim are you wearing?"

Glancing down to see black lace and cleavage, I yanked the sweater up as far as the material allowed. I'd had to borrow clothes from Janet, including a bra and clean underwear. "I couldn't exactly look for a job in my tank and sleep shorts."

"Really? Animal-print leggings and white platform boots." She wiggled her brows and shot me a smirk. "What kind of job were you looking for exactly?"

Admittedly, I hadn't paid much attention to what I'd put on, but this was pretty bad. Then my eyes landed on Kenna's stretched-out yoga pants, paint-splattered T-shirt, and too-small floral flip-flops — her blackened heels hanging a good inch over the backs. My giggle morphed into a full-blown belly laugh. "We're a long way from custom gowns and handmade slippers."

"No kidding." Kenna shook her head as she entered the kitchen and opened cabinets, taking out bread and two paper plates. "You try traveling over two hundred miles dressed like a hobo. An old lady tried to give me a dollar at the bus station. And I was tempted to take it!"

She chuckled, but the thought of her trekking across the Midwest all alone in the freezing weather with no coat and only flip-flops on her feet sobered me. "I'm sorry, Ken. I'm so glad you made it here safe and sound. Let's get something to eat and then you can fill me in."

After gathering a simple meal of PB&J sandwiches and chips, we sat on my bed cross-legged, just like we did when we were kids. Kenna updated me quickly on how she'd borrowed money from the girl who had taken over her old life and used it to catch a bus to Indianapolis, and then a taxi to Bainbridge. I was impressed.

"These, I've missed." Kenna popped a chip into her mouth and closed her eyes in ecstasy. "Do you think we could open a Lay's factory in Doon?"

"Ha, ha." I took a swig of milk. "Speaking of Doon—"

"Where were you when I got here?"

"I was looking for a way to earn enough money to pay Janet rent *and* get back to Scotland. Do you think your dad could float us the money? I tried to call him this morning but there was no answer."

"That's because he's on his honeymoon in Fiji."

"What? Your dad got married?"

Kenna glanced down at her paper plate and swirled a blob of grape jelly with her finger. "Missing stuff like that is one of the costs of my choice to live in Doon." She glanced up, tears glinting in her eyes. "Vee, I have to get back to Duncan. We have to find a way!"

I put down my plate and scooted close, until our crossed knees touched. "We will, I promise. We just have to think. How can we get money fast?"

She licked the jelly off her finger and dabbed at her eyes before grinning at my leopard-print leggings and skin-tight sweater.

"Don't even go there."

She giggled. Then her eyes lit up. "What about the MacCrae's solicitors? They have access to Jamie and Duncan's fortune— technically, it's your fortune too. Do you think they'd wire us the money?"

"We could try ..." I tapped my chin. "What's the firm called?"

"I don't know. How many solicitation firms could there possibly be in London?"

I buried my head in my hands, the hope that had surged inside me crushed in seconds. We had to get back to Scotland. But even if we both worked two jobs, it would take us a month to save up the money. Not to mention that neither one of us had passports.

Kenna reached over and snapped the super resilient material of my pants. "We could always sell off some of your mom's very valuable wardrobe. Speaking of which …" I looked up as she dug into the waistband of her yoga pants and pulled out a wad of crumpled bills. "I've got eight bucks. Think that will be enough to get both of us some clothes that don't suck at Thrifty Threads?"

"That's actually a good idea … and today's BOGO Thursday!" In middle school, we'd loved upcycling at Thrifty Threads, scouring for clothes we could improve and make our own with a few creative alterations. I jumped off the bed, grabbed both our plates, and threw them into the wastebasket. "Let's go. I don't want to be here when Janet and the Slob get home."

Our plans to get back to Doon would have to wait until after we'd found sensible footwear.

The glare of the florescent bulbs inside the thrift store only served to highlight the shabby assortment of clothes jammed into the racks. Upcycling didn't seem as fun as it used to. I turned to a shelf of shoes and selected a pair of purple Chucks in size nine and a half. "Kenna! These might work."

She rushed over and cradled the battered tennies like a newborn. "These babies take me straight back to my Goth days!"

The ten-block walk from Janet's house to downtown Bainbridge required drastic measures for my BFF, and since Janet and I wore a size seven shoe, that left Bob's closet as her only option. Even after she'd lined her feet with two pairs of clean socks before slipping on the size eleven loafers, she claimed she'd never get the stench out of her skin.

"Think I could put these on now? I'll just tell the cashier."

"Go for it." I shrugged as I turned back to the rack and found a pair of cute lace-up boots in my size.

"That is *so* not fair." Kenna slipped off Bob's shoes and kicked them under a rack of dresses. "As much as I love me some Chucks, next to you it looks like I'm wearing clown shoes."

"*Veronica Welling*, is that you?"

The hairs rose on the back of my neck. That Barbie Doll-on-helium voice could only belong to one person in the universe. My feet rooted to the floor, I glanced over my shoulder. Stephanie Heartford, captain of the cheer squad, boyfriend-stealing bane of my high school existence, stalked toward us.

Kenna moved to my side, our shoulders touching as we closed ranks in our classic defense mechanism.

"And Mackenna Reid! If this isn't just a sweet little reunion." Stephanie clasped her perfectly manicured hands in front of her Burberry clad chest. "What are y'all doing here? I just stopped by to drop off last season's wardrobe. I certainly didn't expect to see two of my old classmates."

"We're dropping clothes off—"

"—to make Halloween costumes."

Kenna and I spoke over one another, making no sense whatsoever. I poked her with my elbow, signaling that I'd do the talking.

Stephanie's baby blues widened and she scanned us from head to toe, her bubblegum pink lips twisting in a smirk. "I had no idea the fashions in Europe were so ... *retro.*" Read: disgusting.

"Yeah, well ..."

"Ronnie, you did move to Ireland, right?" She gave her head a toss, sending blonde curls tumbling behind her shoulder. "Your mom said you met someone."

"Scotland," I corrected, and started to tell her not to call me Ronnie, but she didn't even pause.

"Oh! Did it not work out? I'm *so* sorry." She shifted her designer bag in front of her, displaying a gold-embroidered coach and four emblem, and I was hit with a memory of Jamie picking me up in front of the castle in his carriage before the céilidh and presenting me with wild flowers he'd gathered himself. My throat closed.

Sensing blood in the water, Steph's grin widened. "Eric and I are getting married." She wiggled the fingers of her left hand, showing off a square-cut diamond engagement ring that must have cost more than Janet's house. "He's the new marketing VP at Daddy's company. Daddy says he's never seen someone with such a natural gift for business."

My ex-boyfriend had only graduated because I'd tutored him in three subjects. I had a feeling his new position had more to do with Mr. Heartford making his little girl happy than Eric's sudden aptitude for marketing. But I didn't say any of that, instead I blurted, "Well ... um ... congratulations." Flustered, I glanced down at the scuffed toes of Janet's hideous boots. Part of me wanted to brag right back in Stephanie's Clinique-spackled face. But what could I say? *Good for you, Steph. I'm a queen. I rule an enchanted kingdom and have a divine Calling with the most amazing boy on the planet.* But I couldn't say any of that. I felt like a kid again — like that high school girl who had no idea who she was.

Kenna tugged on my elbow. "We need to get going. See you around, Stephanie."

"Wait. How long are you guys in town? We're hosting a fund-raiser for the high school. After the flood, they're in desperate need of a new gymnasium. I just can't stand the thought of those poor children not having a sports facility for basketball games! And where would the girls practice cheer?"

I almost smiled. That was Steph, saving the world one cheerleader at a time.

"We won't be here long." Mackenna shuffled backward. "A few days at most."

"Well, that's perfect! The fundraiser is a formal dinner this Saturday at the country club." Her eyes narrowed as she cupped her hand around her mouth and false whispered, "They have a formalwear section here. I think they still have my old prom dress. Now that I do zumba, it's too big for me."

Dropping her hand, her gaze darted to Kenna. "They might even have a few plus-sized gowns."

"Hey, now." Kenna stepped up and got in Stephanie's face. "Just because I'm not a size double zero, that doesn't make me fat —"

I grabbed Kenna's arm and yanked her away from Stephanie, who'd gone sallow beneath her spray tan.

"I — I better go." Stephanie hightailed it out of the shoe section and then called over her shoulder. "Hope to see you Saturday, Ronnie!"

"Why'd you stop me?" Kenna demanded. "I could've snapped her like a toothpick."

"Yeah, and it would take me weeks to earn enough money to bail you out of jail." I steered her toward the women's clothing section. "Have you forgotten you have no ID?"

Kenna groused as we searched the racks, selecting jeans,

sweaters, and matching yellow down-filled coats — not ideal, but the sizes were right, and they were the only jackets we could find that didn't reek of cigarette smoke. After changing in the dressing room, we plunked down seven bucks and eighty-nine cents and stuffed Kenna's borrowed clothes in a trash can by the door.

Warm and comfortable, but resembling Tweedle-Dee and Tweedle-Dum in our poufy neon coats, we headed back to Janet's. We walked in silence, my brain churning furiously to form a plan. But short of begging a loan from Steph and Eric — I'd rather swim the Atlantic with sharks on my heels — there was no way around it; we'd both have to get jobs.

But whether we had to work for months flipping burgers or wait for Mr. Reid to return from his extended honeymoon, I would find a way to get us back to the Brig o' Doon. And then I'd camp on its ancient stones until the portal opened.

I would find a way back to my kingdom and my prince, even if it took the next hundred years.

CHAPTER 14

Mackenna

When we were little girls, Vee always wanted to escape into her favorite stories. Even as a child, I'd known on some level that her parents were at the root of her fairy tale obsession. In a land far, far away, she could believe that something magical waited on the horizon of her life, and that some fated day in the future, someone special would arrive to set her free from the trolls who raised her. But that day wasn't today.

We walked through the warped front door to discover Janet sitting on the couch drinking boxed wine from a plastic cup at four in the afternoon. Pausing mid-sentence, Vee blinked at the unexpected sight of her half-sloshed parent. "What are you doing home?"

"None of your business." Janet glowered at Vee. "Did'ja get a job yet?"

Quick as lightning, Vee shifted the plastic bag with Janet's outfit and Bob's shoes behind her back. "I'm looking, but there are not a whole lot of options in Bainbridge, Mom."

"Well, Bob and I talked about it, and if you don't have a job by the weekend, you're out."

Hopefully, we'd have another option by then, like my dad returning early from paradise — because I couldn't imagine imposing more than one night on Janet and Bob's "hospitality." Hoping to ease the tension in the room, I chirped from over Vee's shoulder, "Hi, Mrs. Welling."

Janet grunted at me and took another slug of wine.

My bestie jiggled the bag and gestured with her head toward the hall. Quietly slipping the bag off her fingertips, I headed toward Vee's old room while she blocked me from Janet's view. "Kenna's going to sleep over, okay?"

With another grunt, Janet said, "You two're on your own for dinner. And that don't mean raiding the pantry. Bob paid for those groceries and he doesn't stand for freeloadin'."

"That's fine. We already ate." With a resigned sigh, Vee turned away from her waste of a parental unit.

As she shut the door behind us, I plopped on her bed. Her striped coverlet, the one she'd proudly bought with her first dance studio check, had seen better days. Like a white trash version of *Goldilocks*, cigarette burns and grease stains pockmarked the faded fabric as if some chain-smoking fiend had been eating nachos in her bed. Vee noticed what had drawn my focus and said, "Bob's brother stayed here, for a while."

As I sprang to my feet, she added, "It's okay. I washed the bedding this morning. With bleach."

I collapsed once again onto the sagging bed as Vee quietly opened her door and checked the hall. With a silent gesture, she slipped out of the room to return the borrowed clothing. Her house looked more rundown than I remembered. And not just the house, Bainbridge in general. Granted, it had been a few years since I'd spent any considerable time in my hometown, but compared to other places I'd lived, Doon and Chicago, the place I'd grown up in seemed devoid of color and vitality.

When Vee returned, she cast me an apologetic smile. "The calendar says it's Bob's bowling night, and my mom's asleep, so we should be fine."

I suspected "asleep" was code for "passed out cold." Growing up, Janet had often behaved inappropriately — acting like she was our BFF, doing us up fancy before we had any business wearing makeup, and padding our bras — but in all that time, she'd never been outwardly rude. "Janet's more ... intense than I remember."

"She got fired again." Vee sat next to me and the ancient mattress dipped so that our shoulders softly collided. "Bob's gonna have a fit."

"Why should you care?"

"Because I do, and so should you." She scooched up toward the headboard and I counterbalanced by scooting to face her with my legs crisscross applesauce. "We've got to stay somewhere until your dad gets back. Or would you prefer to take your chances sleeping at the bus station?"

"No." Although the bus trip had not been overly traumatic, I'd had more than my share of creeper dudes trying to befriend me. "What if we asked Mrs. Russo if we could stay?"

When we were little, Vee, her ex-boyfriend, and I had spent many nights watching *The Goonies* in the Russo's bonus room. Eric's mom always had a soft spot for Vee, so after our encounter with Cheerzilla at the thrift store, I couldn't help wondering how she felt about her new daughter-in-law-to-be.

"Are you really suggesting that we expose ourselves to more of Stephanie's ridicule?"

I looked up to see my best friend giving me the look I had dubbed the Evil Highney: arched eyebrow, flat mouth, lifted chin. "That's the look you should have given Steph at the thrift store!"

Her features immediately softened. "What look?"

"You know, that condescending look you give someone who isn't obeying you. The one that makes you look like a villain in a Disney film." She continued to stare at me blankly so I did my best to imitate the expression, but could only hold it for a second or two before I cracked. "The Evil Highney."

"You have a name for it?" she asked incredulously.

"We all do ... behind your back, Your Highness."

Vee looked seriously injured so I scooted up the bed and put my hands on her knees. "It's a good look. Effective. I wish you'd used it on Stephanie—that would've shut her up."

With a rueful shake of her head, Vee confessed, "I couldn't think of a single thing to say that wouldn't make me sound like a lunatic. I felt like I was in high school all over again."

"I wish you had one of your gowns from Doon. Then you could go to that charity ball, and put her in her place—"

With a regal wave of her hand, she cut me off. "None of that matters. What's important is getting back home."

The word "home" slithered across my skin. Where was that, exactly? Not Bainbridge or the apartment in Chicago—and although my heart missed Duncan fiercely, I found myself in no rush to return to Doon with its constant threat of evil seeking to devour that world. Why couldn't it just be a normal place without all the life and death intrigue?

Rather than vocalize my thoughts, I asked, "What are we going to do?"

Vee shrugged, seemingly at a loss. "Get jobs. Wait for your dad. Try to track down the MacCrae solicitor."

"I suppose robbing a bank is out?" Rather than dignify me with an answer, she rolled her eyes.

"Fine," I replied. "But we should at least go through the couch cushions and see if we can scrounge up enough money to buy a lottery ticket."

For some reason, *this* — out of everything we'd had to deal with in the past twenty-four hours — caused Vee to snap. "Why? Are you feeling lucky? 'Cause I'm not."

She clutched a pillow to her stomach. "If I was lucky, I wouldn't have run into Steph on one of the most humiliating days of my life. If I was lucky, I would've figured out that Adam was Team Addie. If I was *lucky*, I'd still be in Doon with Jamie!"

Yes, the situation sucked, but I knew deep in my soul that we'd eventually be okay. "Hey, it was just a joke." *Sort of.*

"And for the record," she said, "I don't really believe in luck."

I wrapped my arms around my bent knees. "Do you think Jamie and Duncan know what happened with Adam?"

"Depends on how much time has passed ... there and here." After another pause, she said, "They'll come for us."

In a voice pitched so low that I could barely make out my own words, I replied, "What if they don't ... or can't?"

She took my hands, waiting until I lifted my gaze to hers. "Then we'll go to the bridge and find a way across. We'll figure it out *together*."

"Okay."

I could already see the gears in her head churning with the lists of potential obstacles needing to be faced and conquered in order to achieve our goal.

As we settled in for bed, I couldn't help but envy Sleeping Beauty in the tiniest of ways. She didn't have to wake up in somebody else's bed. Her happily-ever-after didn't depend on fighting the evil Maleficent or hacking her way through a barrier of thorns. All she had to do was sleep and awaken to true love's kiss. I didn't know which was more unrealistic: getting saved by the handsome prince or waking up after years of sedation fresh and lovely as a rose blossom. But I guess even the slumbering princess would eventually have to reconcile her past and her present. When you wake up altogether different, there must always be a reckoning.

The night was filled with garbled fairy tales — half fantasy, half nightmare. Nothing unfolded as it had in the stories. I was in the middle of it all, somehow at fault for the deviations. And no matter how much I assured the characters — in song, of course — that things would work out in the end, they didn't believe me.

I awoke, startled out of my dreams, and feeling like Sleeping Booty. Drool oozed from the corner of my mouth, my eyes were crusted up, and my hair — I couldn't even go there without copious amounts of caffeine.

Blinking into the weak light of morning, I heard the garbled chime of the doorbell, realizing that's what had jerked me from my fitful sleep. I could also hear water running and vaguely remembered Vee saying something about a shower before I dozed off again.

The dying doorbell sounded again. From Vee's room, I could clearly hear Janet as she opened the door. "What do you want?"

"Pardon me, madam. I'm o' the hope that Verranica is here."

"And Mackenna."

The deep Scottish brogues had me on my feet, sprinting down the short hall, and pushing past Janet before I fully comprehended what was going on. The minute I saw Duncan, I hurled myself at him. His arms crushed me in an iron grip as I buried my face into his chest.

Duncan's lips brushed the top of my head, punctuating his words. "Shhh, woman."

Belatedly, I registered that his body shuddered between each shaky kiss. I pulled back slightly to look in his gorgeous, tortured face. His velvety-chocolate eyes shimmered with equal parts horror and relief. Readjusting his grip, he clutched my body with one hand while the other touched my cheek. For a second his hand rested against my skin as if to reassure its owner that I was indeed real, then his trembling fingers swept at the wetness under my eye.

That was the moment I realized that I was weeping — and not just a couple of relieved tears, but full-on ugly crying. Salty tracks and snot marked the spot over his heart where my face had been pressed against his shirt.

Beside us, Jamie fidgeted. "Excuse me, but is Verranica here?"

"Who're you?" Janet demanded.

"I'm James MacCrae," he stated with the practiced air of someone who'd been well rehearsed. "And this is my brother, Duncan."

Janet grasped the collar of her ratty nightgown closed as if the expensively-dressed guys with the cultured accents were home invaders intent on robbing and pillaging. She lifted her chin toward a man dressed in black standing at attention next to a small but impressive looking limousine. "Who's that?"

Without bothering to turn around, he grunted. "Stevens. Please, may I see Verranica?"

Janet turned her attention toward the stunning oldest MacCrae brother. Even in a fitted T-shirt and hoodie, he exuded power. "How do you know Ronnie exactly?"

Knowing how much Vee hated that nickname, I flinched inwardly while Jamie took a beat to connect that he and Janet were speaking about the same girl.

"I'm her betro—" Recognizing the odd word choice, he halted. I interjected "boyfriend" at the same time Duncan said "fiancé."

Janet's eyes narrowed suspiciously. "Did you knock her up? Is that why you're here?"

Brows puzzled, Jamie glanced at me impatiently. I was *not* about to translate that for him. He was already a bundle of barely contained anxiety. If he knew what Vee's mom was implying, he'd lose his composure for sure. To Janet I said, "No. She's not." And then to Jamie, I explained, "Vee's in the shower."

Jamie made a move to go inside and then realized that he'd not officially been invited. Using more restraint that I would've thought him capable of, he asked Janet, "Might I wait for her in your parlor?" As he spoke, he looked as if he was in pain, causing images of Edward and Bella in Biology class to flash through my head. Too bad Jamie wasn't a sparkly vampire—that would shut Janet up.

Still clutching her collar while taking a wary step back, she replied sullenly, "Suit yourself."

I expected Jamie to barrel into the shabby house, but he surprised me again by turning to the uniformed driver standing next to the car. "We might be a short while, Stevens."

"As you wish, Your Lordship."

At the word "lordship," Janet's eyebrows lifted toward her Clairol-tinted hair. Modesty forgotten, she let the edges of her collar fall open as she dropped into a wobbly approximation of a curtsy. "Please come in, Your Lordship."

Jamie entered first, with Janet scurrying close behind. When I made a move to follow, Duncan placed a restraining hand on my arm. When the door shut between them and us, he spun me around. The intensity of his dark eyes caused a ripple of goose bumps to shoot from my fingertips all the way to my toes, making me aware that I was only wearing sleep pants and a cotton top.

I shifted self-consciously as Duncan closed the distance between us. His solid chest pressed into mine, trapping me against the closed door. "Wait," I hissed. Not into PDA, I glanced over his shoulder. Stevens had tactfully retreated into the driver's seat and was reading a book.

An instantaneous flash of heat ignited my skin as my gaze returned to that of the boy who'd traveled halfway around the globe for me — again. Between one heartbeat and the next my arms reached for his neck as he braced me against the door. His forehead dropped to mine and for a moment we shared the same breath.

"I'm never going to let go of you," Duncan whispered.

"Okay." I could feel the hysteria building in my chest again.

Then Duncan's lips were on mine and there was no more thought of anything but his kisses. His arms bracing the door on either side of my chest kept him from crushing me, but my heart and soul were already flattened by the devastating weight of loving him.

The door's peephole dug into the back of my head, but I barely felt it. Nothing could hurt me now. Not even the heavens, which anointed our reunion with a fine, misty drizzle. We were together at last. A little fall of rain could hardly touch us under the circumstances.

Several minutes later, we came up for air, foreheads pressed together, panting in unison. I returned to myself in degrees, first aware of my own body and then my surroundings. The rain had increased in force. The back of Duncan's pale blue button-down shirt and jeans were soaked. Wedged against the door, sheltered by a tiny overhang and my giant Scottish boyfriend, I remained relatively dry.

As I regained my wits, Duncan's eyes fluttered shut. His trembling hand caressed my cheek as he murmured something over and over. So low that I had to strain to hear, he whispered, "I found ye. I found ye. I found ye."

"Yes," I replied, breaking his reverie.

He opened his agonized eyes. "Can ye forgive me, Mackenna?"

"For what? Coming to my rescue?"

"Nay," His voice hitched. "For failing you."

"Failing me? How?"

"I didna protect you ... from Adam ... from disappearing."

"You know about Adam?"

"Aye. He's now in the dungeons of Castle MacCrae under constant guard. He'll no' harm ye again."

I started to ask for more details, then realized I didn't want to think about that yet. I wanted to be in this moment. "How did you find me?"

"The lass from Chicago, Jeanie. She looked up your route on her wee phone." He smiled his bone-melting, lopsided grin. "Are you ready to go back to Doon?"

Was I? Rather than answer directly, I stated, "Vee and I don't have money, or any ID."

"Vee's rich, as are Jamie and I. We've money enough for all."

"We still need identification. Birth certificates, social security cards, drivers licenses, and passports. All that takes time."

"No' if you have the kind of money that we do. It buys private jets and pilots who pay no mind to papers. Plus, I've got ID." I remembered the fake ID that Duncan had used on his last trip into the modern world. He was right, as usual — with his credentials and an unlimited bank account, we could go back to Scotland right away. But the news of Adam's capture eliminated any urgency I'd felt about returning.

Regardless of how I felt, I knew Vee would be anxious to get back. Anticipation of her reaction caused me to push lightly at Duncan's chest. "Let's go round up Vee and Jamie then."

I stepped into the living room just in time to see Jamie perched on the end of the couch next to the dubious afghan. Janet handed him a chipped coffee mug on a small plastic plate doubling as a saucer. "Your tea, Your Lordship."

Looking as uncomfortable as his hostess, Jamie accepted the drink. He sipped awkwardly as the sound of the running shower underscored the tension in the otherwise silent room. Between sips, Jamie glanced down the hall like he was one swallow away from ripping the bathroom door from the hinges.

Taking pity on him, I said, "Vee should be finished any moment."

"I hope so," lamented Janet, sounding more like Jack's beleaguered mother from *Into the Woods* than her usual self. "I can barely afford to pay the water bill as it is, let alone with two extra girls in the house."

Was she really trying to hit up her daughter's boyfriend for money?

Feeling increasingly uncomfortable, I mumbled something about checking on Vee and bolted down the hall. If I didn't hurry her along, Janet would con Jamie into taking her back to Doon with us. And I was not about to let that troll manipulate her way into my best friend's happily-ever-after.

CHAPTER 15

Veronica

Enveloped in a cocoon of steam and hot water, my tears mixed with the shower spray. Jamie's sweet brogue had echoed through my dreams all night. *"Verranica ... I will find you. I will find you ..."* I'd woken up sobbing.

When had I become so dependent? I leaned my forehead against the slick tiles. I'd pretty much been on my own since the age of twelve. After dad split, and then Kenna moved, I'd learned to take care of myself. Now I felt weak ... like a part of my soul was missing without Jamie. Without his strength and his humor ... without that look he gave me that said I was his whole world.

Ridiculous.

I'm a queen. Thousands of people depended on me. I needed to stop bawling like a love sick baby and find a way to get back to my kingdom.

A pounding on the door made me jump. I stuck my head outside the curtain and swiped at my leaky eyes. "Yes?"

"Get out here," Kenna called. "I've got a surrprriise for you."

I suppressed a groan, but turned off the water and grabbed a towel, drying off anyway. Kenna's *surrprriises* always straddled the line between joy and pain. Like the time she wanted to cheer me up after my first heartbreak, and coerced a cute older boy into dressing like Santa Claus and jumping out of a box on my front porch. He serenaded me with a creative Christmas rap and then sprinted back to his car and took off with a squeal of tires. The residual humiliation had lasted for weeks. My BFF always meant well, but as I pulled on my old robe I'd found stuffed in the back of the linen closet, I wondered what she'd planned this time — a Rogers and Hammerstein serenade with her old drama pals? Or maybe some fresh-baked chocolate chip cookies burnt to a crisp?

I combed my wet hair off my face. Neither one of us could cook worth a darn. Good thing we had Mags. I set the comb down and gripped the sink. Did the old chef miss us? Did the people wonder where I'd gone? Did they even know, or had Jamie made up an excuse to protect them from the truth — that their queen had disappeared and may never return? I stared at my reflection. My throat was already so raw that when I swallowed it felt like I'd eaten glass. I refused to give into tears again.

A knock jerked me out of my morose thoughts.

"Just a sec!" I called, praying a full marching band wasn't about to see me in my fuzzy pink robe.

I pulled open the door and my world stopped spinning. My prince, beautiful and larger than life, filled the doorway. A tiny smile played around his mouth, his eyes speaking a hundred silent words.

I couldn't move. Couldn't speak. Afraid to even blink, in case the vision evaporated.

His lips tilted, pulling out a dimple in one stubble-covered cheek. "I've seen a lot o' *interesting* fashions in the modern world, but this is by far the most encitin'."

His deep honeyed voice snapped me out of my stupor, the provocative nature of his words proof that Jamie stood before me in truth. In my dreams, he was perfect. But seeing him in a heather-gray hoodie and jeans, he was more than perfect—he was real.

My knees shook, and my heart rose into my throat, but I forced myself to lean a hip against the bathroom counter. Crossing my arms in front of my chest, I arched a brow. "What took you so long?"

He stepped closer and leaned against the doorframe, mirroring my casual posture. He was almost a foot taller than me, but in this tiny house, he appeared Thor-like. "There were complications, of a sort." His dark eyes sparkled like a sky blanketed with stars, but they didn't release me for a moment. "This being my first time out o' Doon, many modern inventions captured my attention." He shrugged a broad shoulder. "Automobiles, ice cream, television, chili dogs ... ye couldna blame me for wantin' to try them all. I figured ye wouldna mind waiting."

"Is that so?" I took a step closer, so only a foot separated us.

His lids lowered a fraction, his gaze devouring me. "Aye."

A gravitational pull tugged us toward one another, and we both stepped forward. I wound my arms around his neck, threading my fingers into the silken hair resting against his neck and rose on my toes. "Then perhaps I should remind you what you were missing."

"Verranica ..." The deep timbre of my name on his lips reverberated through me as he lowered his mouth to mine.

So much for Ms. Independent. When his arms encircled me, electricity shot through me from my tingling scalp to my curling toes like magic, and I never wanted to let him go.

"Hey." A voice grumbled behind us. "I need to use it."

All the magic came to a grinding halt. I clenched my teeth as I glanced past Jamie's shoulder to see Bob the Slob, or *Blob* as Kenna had aptly named him, wearing nothing but his tighty-whities and a frown.

Bob's eyes focused, and he stumbled back a step. "Who the heck are *you*?"

Jamie released me, but as he turned, his hand slid down my arm and he linked his fingers through mine. "Sir, I'm — " His words cut off and his entire body tensed as he stepped in front of me. "Yer attire is highly inappropriate, sir. There is a lady present."

As expected, Bob threw his head back and laughed. "A lady? That's funny. Vee's *far* from a lady! Where'd you dig this guy up? Benny Hill?" Bob chuckled as he scratched his head.

Jamie met my gaze, his face like granite, his eyes blazing. "I'll be right back, love." He released my hand and stalked forward, shutting the bathroom door behind him.

I heard a startled, "Hey! Who'd you ..."

Unable to resist, I cracked open the door and peeked through. Jamie, growling in Bob's face, backed him down the hallway. "... owe her respect. And dinna show yourself until you are properly clothed."

I bit my lip against a giggle.

"This is *my* house, and I'll dress any way I want." Bob jammed a finger into Jamie's shoulder. "That girl is trash, just like her mother. She should be respecting *me*!"

I tensed just before Jamie's fist connected with the Slob's jaw with a loud crack, followed by a crash as Bob's significant weight hit the floor. Jamie turned and met my wide-eyed gaze. He shrugged as if in apology, but there was no need. In fact, I had to suppress the urge to cheer. I flew out the door and threw myself into his arms. "You're my hero, you know that?"

"And you are my heroine." I felt his lips against the top of my head. "Now, can ye get dressed so we can go? I dinna think I'll be welcome here much longer."

In confirmation to his words, Janet came running down the hall. "What on earth happened?"

Jamie set me on my feet and stepped to one side as I pointed. "Bob had a little accident."

"Sugar Dumplin'!" She shrieked when she spotted him crumpled on the floor moaning.

"Shall I stand guard while ye change?" Jamie asked.

"No, I'll be fine. I think Bob got the message." I held his gaze, my mind switching gears like a racecar driver. "But I have a million questions about Adam and the rings and Doon — "

"Vee ..." He rubbed my shoulder. "We need to get back to the airport. Change and then we can talk. I'll be waitin' outside."

"'Kay. Just give me a few minutes. I need to say good-bye to my mom."

Jamie searched my face, and seeming satisfied with what he found there, kissed my mouth and headed outside. I threw on my thrift-store outfit, and then wove my wet hair into a loose braid. With no other clothes to pack, I stared at my old room and then shut the door. There was nothing left of me here.

Janet waited in the living room, curled on the sofa, black mascara streaking her face. "So you're leaving with *His Lordship*?"

I glanced out the window above her head and my jaw almost dropped at the gleaming Mercedes limo parked outside. It looked like something the president of the United States would ride in, all bulletproof and beautiful. The windows were dark, but I had to assume Kenna and Duncan were waiting inside. Then something Janet said struck a chord. "His Lordship?"

Janet waved a hand toward the window. "You know tall, blond, and gorgeous out there?"

I smiled. I'd used the same three words to describe him myself not so long ago. Now he was so much more. But the similarity in our thought process made me pause, when all I wanted to do was dash out the door.

Perching on the edge of the sofa, I took Janet's hand. "Mom, what happened to your car?"

She sniffled and rubbed her nose. "When Bob's brother, Randy, stayed with us for a while ... When I came home from work one day, my car was gone, and so was Randy. The worst part is, I don't know if Randy took it or if Bob sold it to pay his gambling debts."

"I'm sorry." The Slob was worse than I thought.

Janet turned, her red-rimmed eyes meeting mine. "Do you love that boy, Ronnie? Clearly, he loves you, but do you want to go with him? 'Cause if not, you and me, we could start over somewhere together."

My eyes began to burn. A part of me wanted to take her with us, but I knew that wasn't how it worked. "I do love Jamie, more than I ever thought possible. And I want to go back with him. I'm sorry, but where we're going, there's no way you can come." Her mouth crumbled. "But Mom, you don't have to stay here. You can do better than Blob ... I mean — "

Her giggle cut me off. "That's actually kinda perfect." Then her laughter dissolved into sobs. "I don't ... know how ... to be alone."

I took her other hand and squeezed her fingers tight. "Yes, you do! You took care of me when ... when Dad took off. You're stronger than you know."

She wiped under her eyes. "You've changed. You're not my little Ronnie anymore."

I hadn't been for a long time, but I didn't need to say that. "Tell me you'll try, Mom. Try to make it on your own. Then, down the road, you can be with someone because you want to — not because you're afraid of the alternative."

"I will." She sniffled and wiped her nose. "I'll try."

"Good." I gave her an encouraging nod and decided right then, I'd send her some money before returning to Doon. The MacCrae coffers could handle it. I just prayed she'd keep it to herself and really use it to make a fresh start. I released her hands and stood. "I need to go."

Janet rose and wrapped me in a tight hug.

"Mom, do you have any idea where Dad is?"

She stiffened in my arms.

"I'd like to try and speak with him. Maybe see him before I go back to Do — I mean Scotland."

"Last I heard he was shacking up with some bimbo in Indianapolis. He's not going to want to see you."

I pulled away. Despite all the time that had passed, she still hated him for abandoning us. For the first time I saw how that hatred kept her frozen in time, never able to move on with her life. "How could you possibly know that?"

"When are you going to get it through your head that he doesn't care about us anymore?"

It was an argument we'd had over and over. I'd insist Dad needed us and might be too ashamed to reach out, while Mom would argue he didn't give a fig.

"Stay away from him, Veronica. For your own good."

"And you don't think he'd want to see his only daughter before she leaves the country, maybe forever?"

Her face hardened. "No. I don't. All that selfish jerk cares about is his freedom."

This coming from the woman who'd treated me more like a roommate than a daughter. I couldn't hear any more. "I have to go."

"Vee, wait." She touched my upper arm. "I'm … I'm sorry. About your daddy. About me. Everything."

She hadn't really been a parent to me for years, but she was still my mom. I turned into her arms and we held each other for a long time. Until we heard a groan. "Janet …"

I disentangled myself from her arms and looked into her watery eyes. "Remember what I said. You can make it on your own."

She nodded, the muscles in her throat contracting. My own chest tight with emotion, I turned and walked out, shutting the door on my past.

CHAPTER 16

Mackenna

Whizzing along the Indiana highway, I was experiencing a *My Fair Lady* moment: homeless, bus station girl taken under the patronage of a Scottish prince, who buys her sparkly flip-flops that fit. It was *loverly* riding in the back of a modern limo with no impending Doonian disasters to spoil the moment.

Stevens lowered the tinted window that separated us from him. "Your pilot called, sir. There's a hurricane shutting down the eastern seaboard. It's doubtful you'll be able to fly out before Sunday."

Vee, who was seated backwards next to Jamie, angled her body to better see the driver. "So we're stuck here for the weekend?"

"Yes, miss."

A sensation much like relief blossomed in my chest. I wouldn't be quitting the modern world just yet. But the news that brought me respite had the opposite effect on Vee. Her brows lowered as her eyes sparked with concern.

With a gentle touch to her cheek, Jamie murmured, "It'll be all right, love." Then to Stevens he replied, "We'll need accommodations at the finest inn in Indianapolis."

"Very well, sir. I'll arrange for it."

The driver raised the partition between us. I had to hand it to Stevens, he hadn't batted an eyelash when Jamie said the word *inn*. Knowing the MacCraes, the man was being well paid for his discretion.

Vee swiveled around to regard both MacCrae brothers. "What about Adam?"

Gruffly, Jamie answered, "Adam is under guard in the dungeon."

"Aye." Duncan gently squeezed my hand. "He'll no' be causin' any more mischief in Doon."

Still unsettled, Vee chewed anxiously at her lip. "We think he's working for Addie."

"Fiona discerned the same thing," Jamie stated. "She found the spell responsible for pushing ye out of Doon in the witches' book and translated the first bit."

Duncan nodded. "That's how we knew where to look."

"Aye. Fiona sensed that ye'd been transported to America. With Adam in Doon, Adelaide was able to cast some sort of sending spell that carried the both of you back to your former places in the modern world. Fiona thinks the Rings of Aontacht protected you from the witch's first two attempts. That's why Adam took the rings."

Squeezing my hand tighter, Duncan supplied, "We wouldna have known if Emily hadn't gotten away."

Vee heaved a sigh of relief. "So, she's okay."

"Aye," Jamie confirmed. "Doc Benoir says she'll be just fine."

As the limo gently swayed down the highway, we lapsed into silence. No matter how many times I kept trying to wrap my brain around Adam's treachery, I still felt baffled. Searching Duncan's face, I demanded, "Why would Adam help a witch?"

"Likely he's convinced that Adelaide's in love with him — just like what happened with Lucius Jobe. Once Adam pledged his body and soul to her, she could make him do whatever she wished."

Vee had also mentioned Lucius Jobe — that he'd entered into Doon out of misguided love to Adelaide, but that was as much of the story as I knew. "Remind me what Lucius did?"

Jamie answered me, but his eyes kept straying to my best friend as he spoke. "At one point in the late seventeen hundreds, the Rings of Aontacht were lost in the modern world. Addie got her hands on the emerald ring and coerced Lucius Jobe to use it to enter Doon on her behalf, since she couldna enter herself. Lucius arrived in Doon with the claim that his dreams led him to the ring and the bridge."

The story finally clicked. "Oh yeah, that's why everyone in Doon was so suspicious of us when we first arrived."

Duncan squeezed my hand and continued where his brother had left off. "Once inside the kingdom, Lucius poisoned livestock, killed a couple of farmers, and was finally caught tryin' to breach the border that surrounds the witches' cottage. He claimed idle curiosity had caused him to trespass, but the king didna believe him."

Vee leaned forward, her gaze darting from one brother to the other. "What do you think Lucius was trying to do?"

"Nobody knows for certain." Jamie shook his head. "They were too terrified to think to question him. Lucius was sentenced to death, but before he could be hanged, he took his own life."

Twisting the tip of her braid around her finger, Vee mused, "It makes sense that Lucius and Adam were after the same thing. Were you able to get any information out of him?"

Duncan exchanged a look with Jamie. "I wish it were that simple. After Emily escaped ... When we finally cornered Adam, he'd cut out his tongue."

"Cut out his tongue?" Vee's wide blue eyes locked on mine as my stomach churned and I tried to un-see the image of Adam with a gushing mouth, bloody knife in one hand, tongue — wriggling like a lizard tail — in the other.

"Aye." Duncan nodded. "That way he'll no' be made to talk. Fergus's men are working on getting information ... by other means."

With a frown, Vee asked, "You're sure Doon is safe?"

"Aye." Jamie looked back and forth between his girlfriend and me. "Just to be sure, Fiona is translating the rest of the spell in the hope of learning what Addie and Adam planned to do next. She's also trying to figure out how they communicated with one another." Jamie paused and met Vee's worried gaze.

"Regardless, my queen," Duncan interjected, "we dinna have a choice. We canna fly in a hurricane."

Vee bit at her lip, a tipoff she was not convinced. "So what do we do now?"

Jamie exchanged another glance with Duncan. He hesitated as if suddenly unsure of himself. "I'd love to see a wee bit o' the modern world."

Mouth quirked in amusement, Vee shot me a quick glance as she bit back a smile. "Indiana isn't all that exciting."

As if the state itself took offense to her words, the Indianapolis skyline appeared outside of Duncan's window. Jamie's eyes went wide as he gawked in awe. "It is to me. Surely we can find a way to pass the time."

Vee reached back to twist her hair around her fist. "I dunno."

Such *fol-de-rol,* as Cinderella's fairy godmother would say. Even if I hadn't been witness to the exchange at the thrift store,

I would still be able to tell from her behavior that she wanted *something*. Something that was very possible now that Jamie had appeared. Time to wave my magic wand. "Vee wants to go to a charity fund-raiser in Bainbridge tomorrow night. It's formal."

"Kenna!" From her position across from me, she kicked my ankle.

"Ow! Tell me I'm wrong, that some part of you doesn't want to get all fancy and go to that event on the arm of a freakin' hot prince."

The freakin' hot prince in question made a uniquely Scottish sound of offense. "Och! I'm sittin' right here."

Rather than look his way, I kept staring Vee down until she broke. "I don't know," she mumbled. "Okay, maybe I've fantasized about attending, but we've got other things to worry about."

"Actually we don't. We can't leave until Sunday, Jamie said so. So I vote we should make the most of this unexpected weekend in the Midwest. Who's with me?" I grabbed Duncan's hand and lifted it with mine high into the air. A second later, Jamie's arm shot up.

Outnumbered, Vee halfheartedly raised her hand. "Fine."

"I suppose we should shop for tomorrow night, then." Jamie rubbed his hands together. "Gowns for ye lasses. Proper attire for m' brother and me."

"Oh, Duncan and I aren't going with you," I hastily replied. Getting dolled up and facing down Steph was my bestie's revenge fantasy, not mine.

Vee favored me with the Evil Highney. "You're not?"

"Well — I mean — we kinda —" Doing some cracking of my own, I pleaded silently with Duncan for help.

"Nay," he chuckled, amused by my sudden loss of bravado. "We're going to have a romp about Chicago."

To quell Vee's look of betrayal, I amended, "But I'll still need something fabulous to wear. So I'm in on the shopping."

Eyes glued to the passing urban scenery, Jamie asked, "Do you have a local shop in mind?"

"We've got something better than a shop." Vee grinned impishly at me, and as I read the lustful look in her eyes, we both said, "We've got the mall."

CHAPTER 17

Veronica

Jamie sauntered toward me carrying a double-stuffed cookie and a supersized blueberry slushy, the boyish grin on his face doing funny things to my heart. For the first time since I'd known him, he was immersed in the joy of the moment. He took an enormous bite of the dark chocolate and icing-stuffed concoction, and his eyes rolled back in his head.

"Mmm ..." He paused in front of me before taking another bite. "We need to get the recipe for this and take it back to Mags." At least that's what I thought he said around his food-stuffed mouth.

"Ya think?" I stood on my toes and kissed a glob of frosting off of his dimpled chin. "We'll add it to the list, alongside corn dogs, jalapeño poppers, cherry Coke, cinnamon-sugar pretzel bites ..."

I watched as he finished the cookie in two bites and then licked his fingers.

"Seriously?" I'd been laughing so much since Jamie showed up at my bathroom door in Bainbridge that my cheeks hurt, but I couldn't stop the giggle from escaping. "Get a napkin, pig-boy."

He lifted his chin, stared down his nose, and adopted a formal British accent. "'Tis an ill cook that cannot lick his own fingers."

"Is that Shakespeare?"

"Aye."

Slapping his arm, I ranted, "I can't *believe* out of all the Shakespeare you have stored in that brilliant brain of yours, that's the line you choose to quote to me."

I turned to stalk away, but he grabbed my arm and pulled me back against him, his warm breath stirring the hairs by my ear. "The course of true love never did run smooth."

"You can say that again," I mumbled as I took his hand, and tugged him away from the Tollhouse Café. "I'm thinking you should slow down on the junk food for a while."

Jamie narrowed his eyes. "Lass, I'm a Scotsman. We eat sheep's brains and haggis for breakfast. I think I can handle a wee bit o' *junk food*, as ye call it." Jamie rubbed his flat stomach while taking another long draw of slushy.

"You have no idea what's in junk food. It has all kinds of chemicals and preservatives your body isn't used to."

But Jamie'd already moved on. Like a child at Disney World, his attention ping-ponged from one thing to the other with no transitions. I listened as he contemplated the pros and cons of installing skylights in the castle roof. But a part of me was distracted by the miracle of the moment. If he'd been born here, in my time, this would be a typical date for us — strolling through the mall, checking out the shops, grabbing a bite to eat — or several bites in Jamie's case. Just like average American teenagers.

Being on his arm, everyone who saw us knowing we were

together, made me feel like a kite on a string. But then I glimpsed a mannequin dressed in a formal gown and tiara, and I crashed to earth in a sudden downdraft. We weren't average teens. A kingdom of people relied on us to lead them, and awaited our return, and I was what? Feeling giddy to show off my gorgeous boyfriend, as I shopped and he devoured funnel cakes?

I squeezed Jamie's hand and pulled him to a stop in front of a shoe store window. "Do you think we should try to fly the opposite direction of the storm? Like head to the west and then turn back toward Scotland?"

Jamie's sable gaze searched my face. "Stevens checked into all the possible flight scenarios. What you're suggestin' would only save us a few hours. But besides tha', the air patterns are too unstable." He took a draw from his drink, the slurping noise indicating he'd finished all thirty ounces of sugary goodness. Maybe Scotsmen really did have stomachs of steel. "And I believe there is a gala Mackenna said you would like to attend."

"I don't have to go to that."

He tossed his empty cup in a nearby wastebasket, and then turned back to me and arched a brow in question. "What of these *disgusting*"—he made air quotes, which always cracked me up—"clothes yer wearin'. Dinna ye need to do a bit of shoppin'?"

If there was one way to distract me, it was shopping.

Two hours and an insane amount of money later, we left my favorite store laden with bags full of sweaters, jackets, skirts, jeans, matching accessories, and even new underwear. I'd never shopped without a budget. In fact, I'd never purchased anything from a store that hadn't been from the clearance rack. And it had been a blast, even with the sales girls — and one guy — fawning all over Jamie. He'd been polite and charming, but his attention had never wavered from me.

I wrapped my arm around his waist as we walked, giving him a quick hug. "Thank you for that."

"Yer welcome, love. But 'tis your money as well."

Jamie'd gotten into the shopping spirit too, purchasing chinos soft as butter, fitted T's, and a charcoal-gray Henley that hugged his broad shoulders to perfection.

"I still havena found an item to add to my collection. Somethin' thoroughly American."

He'd been searching for a souvenir he could take back to Doon and add to his shelf, but so far the perfect item had eluded us.

"I think I have an idea."

I led him in the opposite direction, walking fast past the food court and into a hunting supply store that took up an entire city block. I'd been there once before as a little girl, but I pushed back the memories of picking out fishing equipment with my dad, determined to focus on Jamie.

It was like entering a different world. Jamie lit up like a flash bulb, various expressions of wonder chasing across his face as he took in each department. A two-story waterfall splashed into a clear tank full of live fish. Hunting platforms of all shapes and sizes were braced in realistic looking trees. There was a wall of colorful duck decoys and whistles, and an entire section of camouflage outposts and binoculars for bird watching. I knew he'd feel at home here. Even in an enchanted kingdom, boys loved their toys.

"Is that what I think it is?" Jamie rushed off toward a lifelike stuffed moose. Compared to the various animal heads at the hunting lodge back in Doon, this thing was a monster.

"I'd read about the size of these creatures, but ..." His voice trailed off as he stopped, his head tilting back to look up into the moose's glass eye. At just over six feet tall, Jamie's head was even with the beast's shoulder, it's antlers at least as wide as he was tall.

"Saints! What is that?" And he took off again.

By the time I'd caught up with him, a clerk was handing him a massive crossbow.

"You've chosen wisely." The clerk turned his cap backward and pointed out the features of the weapon. "This baby is top of the line. Fires bolts at three hundred sixty-five feet per second with just the touch of the trigger."

"Och no?" Jamie rested the bow on his shoulder and squinted down the sight.

To his credit, the clerk didn't break stride at Jamie's odd speech. "What do you hunt?"

"Deer, wild boar, the occasional bear." Jamie slanted a glance at me and winked.

"Well this thing has plenty of power for that type of game. We also have an extensive rifle section."

Catching his eye, I shook my head. Doon wasn't ready for guns, and I hoped it never would be.

I could almost read Jamie's thoughts as he inspected the bow — being weaponless made him feel out of control, vulnerable. "I'll take one o' these along with the arrows, a carrying case, and any accessories ye might recommend."

"Yes, sir. But ... er ... don't you wanna know how much it costs first?"

"It's no matter." Jamie handed the crossbow over. "Now where would ye keep your best swords?"

The guy blinked.

I snorted a laugh and linked my arm through Jamie's, squeezing his forearm. "He's such a jokester!"

Jamie chuckled, playing along. "Aye, I meant blades."

"Oh! Yes, sir, we have a wide selection of hunting knives. Right this way."

After Jamie had purchased his crossbow, several wicked

looking knives and holsters, along with a set of throwing daggers for his brother, we headed back into the mall.

"Want to go back to the hotel and check the weather?" I suggested. "Maybe the hurricane changed course and we can fly out tonight."

Jamie took the heavy shopping bag out of my hand. "I'm anxious to return to Doon as well, but Sam Champion said the storm is gainin' strength."

I chuckled at the way he said the meteorologist's name as if he knew him personally. Jamie had been glued to the enormous flat screen in our penthouse suite all morning, flipping between the Weather Channel and ESPN. According to Duncan, Jamie'd started watching the World Series on the plane and in the limo. Jamie claimed it calmed him. But an image of him lounging on a sofa, a Big Gulp and a pile of hot wings at his side, a game controller in his hand, only reinforced my instincts to get him home as soon as possible. Couch-potato Jamie was not a pretty picture.

"We can go right? Since you found your memento?"

He repositioned the crossbow bag on his shoulder and then put his arm around me as we walked. "Nay, these are practical tools. I have somethin' else in mind."

We made a beeline for the sporting goods store where Jamie began selecting bats, gloves, baseballs, hats, and matching jerseys. "I canna wait to teach Lachlan and the Crew this amazin' game. 'Tis deceptively complex, each play requirin' a myriad of strategies. But I imagine I'll be rather good at it."

Inspired to get in on the action, I held up an extra-extra-large Giants jersey and taunted, "Yeah, well, I get Fergus."

His eyes met mine and narrowed. "Is tha' a challenge?"

"You bet your adorable dimples, it is. My team will crush yours. Especially with Analisa as my base stealer."

With a mock scowl, he said, "Fine. But Duncan and Gabby are mine. That girl can run like the wind."

The trash talking escalated as we debated what we needed to purchase and what could be re-created in Doon. By the time we finished equipping two entire baseball teams, our bill in the thousands, the clerk volunteered to personally deliver our purchases to the hotel. We gratefully agreed and then headed back out to search for Kenna and Duncan.

I stopped at a mirrored column, pulled my braid over my right shoulder, and tugged on my new Royals hat. I had no idea if they were a good team, I just liked the color ... and the name.

"That looks quite fetchin' on ye." Jamie met my eyes in the reflection his eyes glinting as he teased, "I may even prefer it to your crown."

I knew exactly what he meant. He'd picked out a fitted Yankees hat for himself. Something about the black cap pulled low over his eyes, his sandy blond hair curling under the edge and against the tan skin of his neck made me want to fan myself. But I settled for entwining my arm with his and laying my head on his shoulder.

He slowed, lifting his nose like a bloodhound. "What is tha' heavenly fragrance?"

I took a deep breath and drew in the scrumptious scents of fried dough and cinnamon.

"Churros." Jamie read the sign on a nearby kiosk. "I have a mind to try those."

Amazed, I shook my head. "Haven't you eaten enough?"

"That I have. And yet I will eat them whilst I still may."

Was that more Shakespeare or the wisdom of a boy king? Either way, as he took my hand and led me to the end of the churro line, his words resonated. I had to have faith that when we crossed the bridge, Doon would be there waiting and safe.

Our forever. But for this minute window of time, I would enjoy the nows. "I'll take an order of those too."

"Tha's my girl." He quirked a grin that drew out the long dimples in both his cheeks. "I'll make a proper Scotswoman out of ye yet."

CHAPTER 18

Mackenna

The comforting thing about malls is that they're basically the same from one end of the country to the other: same stores, same food, same roving groups of families, same loiterers, the same kids and hipsters. A city of strangers — some come to work, some to play. Sure, a variance existed here or there just to keep things interesting, a unique attraction or a shop with local flair, but all in all there was a sameness. The mall was a slice of home.

And that uniformity, while soothing, was the reason I got bored so quickly. Though Vee could go from store to store, comparing items and sale prices, I was good for two or three stores tops. After that, I tended to sprawl in a chair near the changing rooms and serenade the people trying things on while my bestie shopped for the both of us.

I wasn't sure what to expect with Duncan. Yes, the mall was a new experience for him, but what kind of mall guy was he? His brother was easy to figure; all googly eyed with wonder, he would go into each and every store to check out the wares, even the ones that Vee probably preferred he didn't.

But Duncan ... He'd been surprisingly without opinion since we changed our plans. Even now, he was waiting for me to respond as to what I wanted to do. Instead, I said, "I'm on to you, buster."

His brow creased in genuine confusion. "What do you mean?"

"The way you keep deferring to Jamie. I know it's his first real trip here, but it's kind of yours too. So cut the chivalry act and tell me what *you* want to do."

He frowned at me, looking vaguely uncomfortable with my demand. "Seriously," I added. "We're not moving from this spot until you answer me. There must be a few things that you'd like to do."

After a moment he said, "Aye. There might be a couple of things."

"What's the first one?"

"I rather fancied the look of those tartan trousers in the shop we passed," he replied in all sincerity.

My lips started to twitch and I resisted the urge to smirk. Of all the things in the modern world to experience ... "Tartan trousers?"

"Aye."

Gershwin love him, if the boy wanted plaid pants, then I vowed to be okay with it. "Show me."

We backtracked to a dimly lit store, with pounding music that had been a staple in my Goth phase. He pointed to a mannequin just inside the entry next to the life-sized *Supernatural* cutouts. "Those're the ones."

I helped him find a pair in roughly his size. While Duncan went to try them on, visions of *Brigadoon*, dancing men in plaid pants leaping around Gene Kelly and Cyd Cherise, occupied my head. Repeating the mantra *I will not laugh, I will not laugh, I will not laugh,* as I waited. I did my best to vanquish the mental image of twirling Scotsmen.

When Duncan stepped out of the dressing room, however, it was no laughing matter. The pants fit perfectly—low on the hips, snug but not skinny-jean tight in the legs. A chain, connected to the side belt loop, disappeared into the back pocket. To finish off the outfit, he wore a black Ramones T-shirt he must have grabbed on his way in to change.

His bare feet added an air of genuineness to the ensemble, like he wasn't dressing up to go out but wore those types of clothes around the house on a daily basis ... while strumming on his guitar in search of one great song. *Glory!*

A gaggle of girls passing by came to an abrupt halt in the entryway, openly staring and giggling. When Duncan noticed them, a couple of the more daring ones offered him a coy wave. He acknowledged them with a respectful "Good day, lassies" and then instantly dismissed their blatant adoration as he turned to me. The politeness in his face transformed into a dazzling smile as his brows lifted questioningly. "Aye or nay?"

Feeling like one of his admirers, I blinked trying to regain my equilibrium. "Aye. Definitely, aye."

With a nod, he padded back to the dressing room. The gaggle watched his retreating plaid-clad backside, their collective sigh intermingling with mine.

Feeling an immense burst of pride and more than a bit of comradery, I said, "That's my boyfriend."

Wearing a dreamy expression, one of the more vocal girls asked, "Is he from England?"

I shook my head. "Nope, Scottish."

"We LOVE Scotland!" they cried in unison.

"You should go someday," I said, rather enjoying the way their worshipful attention had transferred to me as the other half of the hot plaid pants guy and someone who'd made the pilgrimage to the faraway land of kilts. "It's really beautiful."

They nodded at me and then refocused on each other, chattering about senior year and an epic graduation trip. In their enthusiasm, I was forgotten, and they moved on. Which was just as well, because Duncan stepped out of the dressing room a moment later looking as heart-stoppingly gorgeous in his jeans, blue button-down shirt, and black Chucks. I watched him pay the clerk — who kept toying with her blue hair while she helped him.

He approached me with an easy, crooked grin, and no clue how devastating he was to the opposite sex. "Finished."

I laced my fingers through his free hand and drew his adorable knuckles to my lips for a kiss. "What next?"

"Can we go to the bookshop? I'm of a mind to get the rest of the dragon series that I started when I came for ye in Chicago."

A half hour later, Duncan had four thick books and a mug of Earl Gray tea. I took a leisurely sip of my cappuccino, content to sit in the little mall café and do nothing. I wasn't much of a literature girl myself — it never made sense to waste oodles of time reading when you could accomplish the movie version in two hours. But I could watch my boyfriend read all afternoon.

When he lost himself in a book, his face developed that far-off, meditative look that dreamers get. It reminded me of how I felt the first time I heard certain Sondheim songs — like I needed to dwell in that moment until the words imprinted on my soul.

"Whatcha thinkin' of, woman?" I returned from my musings to discover Duncan's inquisitive gaze contemplating me as if I were a facet of his story come to life. I distinctly remembered the first time I saw that particular expression — he'd been Finn to me then, my beloved summer playmate. Never mind that the passage of time in Doon made it impossible for us to have been the same age at the same time. Or that the closed portal on the bridge would've prohibited him from crossing into my world and vice versa. That was the mystery of the Calling. Our spirits had been speaking to one another for most of our lives.

I could picture the August afternoon when I'd scrambled away from my aunt's cottage to meet him at the bridge. He was sitting off to one side in the grass, his dark head haloed by the sun as he bent over a book. I was eight and returning to America the following morning.

In that moment, Finn had looked so peaceful — so perfect — that I froze halfway across the bridge and tried to memorize him so when I returned home, I'd carry a little piece of him with me.

Sensing my nearness, he'd looked up at me then with the same mixture of fascination and contentment. In the space between one heartbeat and the next, he drew me in to share in his perfection. Smiling at the man Finn had become, I asked, "Do you remember that summer when I was eight? What you said to me right before I left?"

"Aye. You asked me if I would still be there when ye returned the following summer."

"And you said, 'Yes' or rather 'Aye,'" I amended with a chuckle.

His intimate gaze caused our surroundings to disappear so that I existed both in the moment and in our shared memory at the same time. Duncan reached across the table, taking my hand in his. "And you asked, 'What if your ma doesna let you come back?'"

"You said I need never fear because you would always come

for me. That it was your solemn pledge and promise. And you always came — when I stopped traveling to Scotland, when I abandoned you ... even when I was ripped away. Here you are."

"'Tis my solemn pledge and promise."

The pad of his thumb brushed lightly across the back of my hand, sending little shockwaves of sensation up my arm to reverberate in my chest. I loved him so much that speaking the words seemed woefully insufficient.

As I struggled to put my epic feelings into mere words, he spoke again. "From the first moment I laid my eyes on ye, my life was twined with yours. When you're gone, I exist but cease to live. I canna take a deep breath or taste food, or sleep soundly or hear the sweetness of music. I'm a husk."

"Apart, we're single notes," I said, echoing his sentiments. "But together, we're more. We're — a symphony."

"Aye."

A melody was not enough. Melodies were transient. You could pick them out of the air, hum them for a bit, and then let them go. You could alter a melody to someone's specific interpretation, the same way you could try to change for the sake of love as I'd seen so many girls do. But a symphony ... a symphony was like unconditional love. The parts wouldn't change to suit the whims of the conductor. A symphony was written. Just as Duncan and I had been since childhood.

"There you are!" Vee approached from the direction of the food court with Jamie in tow. Doing a poor job of appearing stoic, the oldest MacCrae's free hand pressed against his stomach like he was trying to staunch a bullet wound, his face a sickly shade of green.

Duncan closed his book and stood. "What did ye do to my brother?"

"What did I do? He did it to himself." Vee released Jamie,

who slumped into the chair his brother had just vacated. "I warned him about eating a second helping of churros."

"They were delicious," Jamie groaned. He attempted to straighten up, thought better of it, and doubled back over with his face in his hands. "Oufph."

Duncan made a sound of reproach. "Jamie, what would the lads say if they could see ye caterwauling o'er a wee belly ache?"

"They'd know to eat churros in moderation," he replied in a muffled voice.

Vee circled behind the poor Scotsman to rub his back. "Maybe we should get him some medicine."

"We had a governess who used to give us castor oil and treacle," Duncan stated, nudging Jamie's leg with his knee. "How's that sound, laddie?"

Jamie groaned again but managed to straighten up in his chair. "Try it and ye'll live to regret it, little brother." He reached behind to capture Vee's arm and gently pull her to his side. "Verranica, go find yerself a bonnie dress for tomorrow night. I'll just take a wee nap while I wait for ye here."

Torn between the need to soothe her boyfriend and the allure of dress shopping, she hesitated. "If you're sure you're going to be okay?"

"Aye. 'Tis only a slight digestive concern." He slouched back in his seat, extending his legs and crossing them at the ankles. "It'll pass in no time."

"Okay." She bent and kissed his forehead before addressing Duncan. "If I take Kenna with me, do you think you can take care of him?"

"Aye." Duncan's eyes darted to his abandoned book, revealing the real reason he'd so readily agreed to babysit. He'd keep Jamie company if it meant he could get back to his dragon tales.

I stood as Duncan crossed to me and cupped my cheek with

his rough hand. "Have fun, woman. And dinna worry about the time." He gave me a peck on the lips before Vee slipped her hand in mine and pulled me away.

"I need to stop at a makeup counter too," she said. Her eyes were already glowing with the prospect of a whole new look. The girl did love a good makeover. We both did.

After a dozen steps or so, she stopped dead in her tracks. "Kenna. I am not going anywhere with you if you keep that up."

"Keep what up?"

"Humming 'Popular'. It makes me feel like some social experiment."

I hadn't even realized I was humming, but I had definitely been getting my inner Galinda on in my head. I shrugged without feeling the slightest bit of remorse. "You know how the idea of a *makeover* sets me off. *La laaaa, la laaaa. You'll be pop —*"

"Kenna!"

"Sorry."

But I really wasn't. This was my perfect moment: Duncan dreamily lost in a book, Jamie belly ache notwithstanding, being his charming, charismatic self, and me and Vee, underscored by the perfect Broadway show as we did our thing. The moment was so epic that even Indianapolis seemed like a Midwest equivalent of the Emerald City ... and on this one short day, before returning to Doon, we would have a lifetime of fun.

CHAPTER 19

Veronica

The next day I had a *now* hangover. The fun of being in the moment had caught up to me with a vengeance. I sat curled on the leather sofa in our penthouse suite, cradling a cup of peppermint tea. Churros and double chocolate milkshakes, then cheeseburgers and fries for dinner followed by a *Lord of the Rings* movie marathon with popcorn, soda, and king-sized Reese's Cups had been a blast. The best part: watching emotions play across Jamie's face during the movies, and seeing him flinch and ghost the movements of the sword fights with his hands.

I'd finally had to confiscate the remote, after he'd hit the pause button five times during the first movie to explain why a particular attack sequence would never work. It wasn't that he didn't understand the concept of fiction, the warrior in him just had a hard time suspending reality.

But today, after just a few hours of sleep, my head ached and I felt as energetic as a slug.

"We're headed to the Windy City," Kenna announced as she

and Duncan paused by the door, both of them dressed in a punk chic mashup of leather and plaid. Was that a chain dangling from Duncan's hip? I moved to my knees on the couch to get a better look.

"Make sure to ride the Navy Pier Ferris wheel," I called. "I hear it's especially fun on blustery days." Kenna shot me a glare that could melt a polar ice cap, and I burst out laughing. The last time I'd made Kenna ride a Ferris wheel, it had been an autumn day much like this one, and she'd puked her guts out in six different languages. Heights were not her thing — at least not heights combined with swaying metal death traps.

"What's so funny?" A sleep-mussed Jamie walked out of the room he shared with his brother. His eyes still heavy, he lifted the edge of his pale blue T-shirt and rubbed his washboard stomach.

My heart did a twirl in my chest. I jumped up and flew into his arms.

He wrapped an arm around my waist and held me to his side, then kissed my temple. "Good morn', love."

"Well, I guess tha's our signal," Duncan remarked.

"Have fun, you crazy kids." Kenna grabbed her purse. "And give that Gucci-toting hag, Stephanie, my regards!"

The door clicked shut, and I nuzzled the warm spot where Jamie's neck met his shoulder. Then I leaned back and gazed into his eyes. "Did you sleep well?"

"Nay. Stayin' away from you for the last few hours was one of the hardest things I've ever had to do." He tucked my hair behind my ear and then ran his fingers down my jawline. I shivered. "My dreams were haunted by visions o' you disapperin' again."

He trailed kisses across my forehead and down to my cheekbone. I stood on my toes and tilted my head, biting my lip as his mouth fastened to the pulse throbbing in my neck.

And then there was a knock on the door.

"Saints," Jamie growled. "Who is that at this blasted hour?"

"It's after ten o'clock." I disentangled my limbs from his. "I ordered strawberry pancakes!"

The thought of syrup and butter oozing over a fluffy stack of cakes had me jogging to the door. Incredibly, I was hungry again. Hair of the dog and all that.

We had our breakfast in a bay alcove with windows overlooking the city. But we didn't pay much attention to the view. With no pending disaster hovering over us, no petitioners awaiting an audience, or royal advisors vying for my attention, we were free to focus on one another without distractions. So we talked about everything from our childhoods to the present, swapping stories until I'd laughed so hard my stomach hurt.

Jamie told me about the time he and Giancarlo Rosetti stole Sean MacNally's horse and left it to wander in the bogs.

"No wonder he hates you!"

Not long ago, Sean had led a resistance against the crown that resulted in him kidnapping Kenna and me and forcing us to enter the witch's evil limbus — which had been our plan anyway. Admittedly, he was a sandwich short of a picnic, because he'd also had Jamie restrained and then rammed his fist into his gut. Not the smartest thing to do to his future king. And as a result of his transgressions, Sean was a current resident of Castle MacCrae's slimiest dungeon efficiency, complete with chamber pot and flea-infested mattress. Which, all things considered, was better than the traditional punishment for treason. Jamie and I'd had quite a row about that one.

Jamie chuckled, pulling me back to his story. "Nay, Sean hated me long before that. But he deserved more than a misplaced horse after what he did to Gabriella."

I untucked my foot from under me and leaned forward at the mention of my eager lady-in-waiting. "What did he do? Sean's several years older than Gabby, right?"

"Aye, by four years. But in Doon, children twelve years and older are instructed in the same classroom, and Gabby made the mistake of correctin' Sean during a math lesson." Jamie shook his head. "In retaliation, he dumped a reeking bucket of manure on her head and told her if she rubbed it in hard enough it would melt away the wee freckles on her face. Her da had to submerge her repeatedly in an enormous vat of tomato sauce to get the stench out o' her hair and skin. There was no pizza in Doon for a week!"

After our laughter died down, Jamie stared into his coffee thoughtfully. "Sean was always a lone wolf. Or he used to be …"

"What do you mean?"

Jamie glanced out the window. "When Duncan and I learned to hunt, our father told us to steer clear o' the wolf pack. Tha' without them the natural order o' things in Doon would deteriorate. He also warned tha', although physically smaller than bears, the wolves' strength resided in their numbers, making them the top predators in the kingdom."

He shifted his gaze to me, but his thoughts were nowhere near metropolitan Indiana. "One day, we were huntin' wi' Da and came across a wolf eatin' a wee rabbit. It was the largest wolf I'd ever seen. Thick silver fur quivering, it lifted its head and barred massive teeth drippin' wi' blood. It growled so low, the sound echoed in the soles of my feet. But before I could turn and run, Da took it out wi' a single arrow."

"I thought he told you not to hunt the wolves?"

His eyes focused on my face, and a corner of his mouth quirked. "Tha's exactly what I asked. My father said it was a lone wolf, one tha' had separated from the pack. He told us lone wolves are desperate and weak, regardless of their appearance o' strength."

"I never thought of it like that before."

"Nor had I." Jamie took a slow sip of his coffee, then lowered his cup and cocked a brow. "Sean only became powerful wi' a pack around him. Divest him o' the men who had his back and he became nothin' but a burbling grouse."

As Jamie added two more pancakes to his plate, I mulled over his story. Something about it resonated, but before I could work it out, he began to ask me questions about my childhood. Now that he knew so much about my world, he seemed curious about everything. Like my favorite movies, when I'd learned to ride a bicycle, and who'd taken me to my first dance — which happened to be my ex-boyfriend and childhood friend, Eric.

I took a sip of my fourth cup of coffee. "You'll meet Eric tonight at the fundraiser. He and Stephanie are engaged." I lifted my fingers and made air quotes.

"Stephanie used to be your friend, eh?" Jamie set down his fork. "Now she's betrothed to your ex-boyfriend?"

I nodded, and watched the wheels spinning behind his eyes. "Was he unfaithful to ye?"

"I ... well ..." I tucked my other leg underneath me. "Do you remember when you appeared to me the first time? I was sitting in my car crying and you held out your handkerchief?" That handkerchief had somehow stayed in my world when he'd disappeared, and then disintegrated in my hands. But at that point I'd thought he was nothing more than a hot Scottish figment of my imagination.

He nodded. "Aye. I longed to hold ye in my arms. Comfort you. But couldna reach ye."

Going a little gooshy, I sighed as I reached across the table and linked our fingers, running my thumb across the prominent veins on the back of his hand. "That was the day I found out Eric was cheating on me with Steph."

Jamie tensed, thunderclouds gathering on his face. "And ye say he's goin' to be at the ball this evening?"

"It's not a ball, it's a party. And I forbid you to punch anyone tonight. Do you hear me?" I gave his hand a hard squeeze and then let go. "I couldn't care less about Eric and Steph. And you definitely don't want to experience the modern justice system."

He gave a noncommittal shrug, but when I arched my brows, he promised to keep his fists to himself.

Glancing at the clock, I pushed back my chair, the bacon and pancakes tangling in my gut. I could put it off no longer. "I need to ... I need to make a call."

Jamie's sharp gaze latched onto my face. I swallowed hard. I couldn't tell him what I was about to do. I couldn't talk about it. I just had to do it. If I didn't, I might never work the nerve up again.

"Of course." He wiped his mouth with a cloth napkin and stood, ever the gentleman.

I twisted my hair up behind my head and tied it into a knot, pulling the strands so tight my eyes watered.

"Is everythin' okay?"

"It's fine." I took a deep breath and rose to my feet. "Just something I've been putting off."

He nodded. "I'll be right here."

On trembling legs, I made my way into the bedroom and shut the door. It took me three tries to dial the number correctly even though I'd had it memorized for days. Would he know my voice? It began to ring. Would he want to see me right away? I paced in front of the window. Was he here in Indianapolis? *Five rings.* I hadn't thought of the possibility that he wouldn't answer. *Seven rings.* If I left a message, what could I say?

"Yeah?"

The voice was groggy with sleep, but I knew it instantly. "Dad?"

Silence.

"It's Veronica."

"Huh?"

"Veronica, Dad." My voice dwindled to a whisper. "Your … your daughter."

More silence.

I clenched my eyes closed, trying to stop the hot tears from streaking down my cheeks as I pushed on. "Dad, I'm in town for a few days and I was … I was hoping we could get together."

"That's not a good idea."

"I'm leaving the country and I don't know when I'll be back — *if* I'll be back." I hated the pleading tone that had entered my voice.

He sighed. "I'm not anyone's father anymore."

"But, Dad — "

"I hope you have a happy life." Did his voice catch? Or was I projecting my own emotions? "Good-bye, Vee-Vee."

The line went dead.

"Dad!"

I pulled the phone away from my ear and stared at it as if his face would appear there. As if staring at it hard enough might rewind the past. Make him love me again.

My chest constricted, my throat aching with the effort to hold back sobs. He didn't want me. It hadn't been just Mom who drove him away. It had been me too.

Suddenly, I couldn't breathe. The loss burned like a flesh wound exposed to the open air. I had to get away, find a way to close it again. I swiped my eyes dry, threw my sweater on over my pajamas, and slipped on my shoes.

Dashing out of the bedroom, I ran for the front door. But before I could open it, Jamie was there. He stood blocking my path. My escape.

"Move!" I pushed against his shoulders.

"Nay. You're not disappearin' on me again." He widened his stance. "I canna let ye run away."

"I want to be alone." Like the strike of a match, my grief morphed into anger. I stood on my toes and got in his face. "Get. Out. Of. My. Way!"

He put his hands on both my shoulders, his dark gaze searching mine. "What is it, love? Let me help you."

His comforting words reopened the flood gates and the sobs broke loose.

Jamie's expression crumpled and he pulled me to his chest, wrapping me up in his arms. "You're scarin' me. Tell me what's hurt ye." I could feel his warm lips press to the top of my head.

"I ... I ... called ... my ... my dad."

The hand Jamie'd been running down my hair stilled on my back. "What did he say?"

"He doesn't want ... want to ... see me. Ever ... ever again."

His entire body stiffened, and then he squeezed me against his chest — like if he held on tight enough he could absorb my hurt. But a part of me recoiled from him. That rejected little girl that lived inside of me screamed that no man could be trusted. That Jamie could eventually leave me too.

I leaned back, swiped the tears off my cheeks, and looked into his eyes. "I have to go. I need to be alone." I pulled out of his arms and held up my hand to show him that I wore one of the rings. "I'll be safe."

"But ye canna—"

"No, Jamie." I snapped. "This is *my* world. I'll be fine on my own."

Hurt flashed across his features before he nodded and moved to the side, a muscle flexing in his jaw.

Without looking back, I slipped out the door with nothing more in mind than outrunning my grief.

CHAPTER 20

Mackenna

Duncan caressed her smooth curves, the look of absolute rapture on his face making me a bit regretful that I'd agreed to his crazy suggestion. "She'll do," he stated in that Scottish brogue that was half growl, half purr, and one hundred percent boy lust. "You're a wee, bonnie lass. Aren't ye?"

Refusing to go all jealous over a hunk of metal, I interjected, "Do you even know how to drive?"

"How hard could it be?" he asked with a crooked grin. On the short walk from the hotel to the car lot, Duncan had explained it'd been a desire of his since the first time I stuffed him into a horseless carriage to drive one. Since he was too young to rent, ID or not, Stevens had directed him to a lot that sold vintage sports cars.

"This is a stick shift."

"Aye." He had no idea what I meant but he was too far gone to care. With another gentle stroke across her hood, he announced, "I mean to have her."

Duncan had immediately singled out a candy-apple red

Corvette convertible for his intended. Although used, the car was in cherry condition according to the sales guy.

With a resigned chuckle I gave in. "Okay, Braveheart. Don't say I didn't warn you."

"This one," Duncan cooed, his eyes never leaving the bright, shiny paint job.

The sales guy nodded. He wasn't bothered that the boy in front of him was unequipped to handle such a complex piece of machinery. All he cared about was the driver's license and the platinum card in the boy's outstretched hand.

I, on the other hand, had all kinds of misgivings. "What are we going to do with *it* when we head back to Scotland?"

"I don't know. Give 'er to Vee's mum?"

"Janet? No way." Janet and Blob would never get such an expensive gift, even over my dead body.

Duncan just shrugged. "Dinna worry. When the time comes, I'm sure we'll find the right home for her."

The Corvette wasn't a horse! But I guess, in a weird way, she was the modern version of his beloved Mabel. Whatever delusions I'd had of Duncan bonding with her quickly vanished as the boy tried to drive his new pet off the lot. With a complete lack of finesse, he jerked the car to life; she lunged forward and then immediately stalled.

"Try easing up on the clutch a little more slowly," I suggested. The salesman had covered the basics: clutch, brake, gas, and shift positions — but driving a manual was a skill, not something that could be mastered without extensive practice.

I remembered, not-so-fondly, the driving lessons with my dad in his old, manual transmission Fiat. After the first driving lesson, I predicted I'd get whiplash before I would get the hang of the pedals. But my poor father had stuck by me, and by me, and by me as I learned to drive the thing. It'd taken more than three months.

Duncan started the car again, this time reacting too slowly. With the clutch engaged, the car revved without moving, and when he eased off, it shot forward, grinding as it demanded to shift into higher gears.

"Shift into second!" I commanded. Gears crunched as I added, "Don't forget the clutch."

The car slowed and then bolted forward again as Duncan figured out second gear. But when he tried for third, again at my urging, it stalled in the middle of the road.

Looking dazed, Duncan threw up his hands in frustration. "This modern contraption is broken. I think the shopkeeper hornswoggled me."

Tempted to do the "I told you so" dance, I reigned myself in. Duncan's manhood had been injured enough by the trip down the street. In the rearview mirror, I could see a growing knot of sales people at the end of the block watching the spectacle that was my boyfriend learning to drive.

I flashed Duncan a sympathetic grimace. "Before you take the car back, mind if I give her a try?"

Duncan favored me with a gallant nod of his head. "Be my guest." As I climbed out of the car to trade places with him, I noticed money being exchanged by the group of onlookers. I pitied the fools that had bet on him to make it to the corner.

Melting into the driver's seat, I instantly changed my mind about Duncan's new pet. Ensconced in sweet-smelling leather, with the steering wheel in my left hand and the stick shift in my right, I experienced a similar rush to the one I got at curtain call. Yet another modern world pleasure I would soon leave behind.

No longer in a mocking mood, I turned to my boyfriend and instructed him on how to adjust his seat for maximum comfort. Seat belts fastened, I pressed in the clutch and turned on the ignition. The resulting purr seemed to come from the core of my being, the effect of car and driver becoming one.

"Now relax and enjoy the ride," I said with a wink.

Smoothly shifting into first gear and easing off the brake, I pressed the accelerator while letting up on the clutch. As the Corvette sprang to life, modern horse-power coursed through me like a drug. By the time I shifted into sixth gear on the highway, Duncan regarded me with something akin to awe.

"Ye've got a gift, woman. I'm man enough to admit when I've been bested."

"You don't mind?"

"Nay." He reclined his seat slightly, stretching out as best he could in the restricted space. "Watching you drive my bonnie lass might even be better than drivin' her m'self."

The boy was amazing. How easily he laid his ego at my feet. As I followed the signs for I–65 north, I wondered what other revelations about him our day in Chicago would bring.

When the stages of Chicago went dark for the night, the city's theater folk could be found at the Green Room Lounge, eating deep dish pizza and singing karaoke. On any given night you might get or give an impromptu performance from a Hollywood celebrity or a Broadway A-lister: and if you were lucky, sing a duet with them. Seated in a green leather booth, for the first time that I could remember, I felt at home.

Duncan toyed with the edge of his playbill as we waited for food. His face displayed a thoughtful frown of concentration. But I had no idea if the reaction was positive or negative.

I'd deliberately not spoken about the show on the way to the restaurant so that he'd have time to process. I wanted him to love *Wicked* as much as I did, but I recognized that his perspective was vastly different from mine. "So?"

The pucker between his brows eased as his dark gaze met mine. "'Twas lovely. I liked how the story portrayed an unexpected perspective. And the music — "

"I know, right?"

"Aye …" He picked up a breadstick, broke it in the middle, and offered me half. "Although I canna help but think 'tis a dangerous precedent to romanticize evil. Witches, demons, sorcerers, and the like as noble, misunderstood creatures is great fiction. When someone chooses to serve evil, they sacrifice the part of themselves with the capacity to embrace goodness."

Taking a bite, he chewed thoughtfully before continuing. "There's an essay I read once in the castle library. It was gathered during the Centennial in the late eighteen hundreds. The author, Edmund Burke, stated, 'When bad men combine, the good must associate; else they will fall, one by one, an unpitied sacrifice in a contemptible struggle.'"

"That sounds a lot like something one of our presidents — famous leaders — said. 'The only thing necessary for the triumph of evil is for good men to do nothing.'"

I happened to remember the quote because of a paper I'd been forced to write senior year. While other kids illustrated the Kennedy quote with examples of Hitler and Rwanda, I'd used Horton's decision to protect the Whos despite the scorn of the entire jungle. As part of my presentation I'd sung "Alone in the Universe" with fellow thespian Dani Diaz and earned a solid B for my efforts.

"That's an apt statement. Makes me think o' Sean MacNally's lot," Duncan replied, refocusing my thoughts from an elephant's noble quest to save a world on a clover to a world hidden from modern civilization. "Too many lads fell under his sway. Now that he's imprisoned though, most o' the others have disavowed him."

I'd been wondering about the sentiments of Sean's followers now that he was locked up. Not that I had any concerns about them breaking Sean out of the dungeon. I knew from firsthand experience how impossible that was — even for cheerleader ninjas. Still, a wave of relief surged over me at Duncan's words. I gave his hand an appreciative squeeze as our tattooed server placed a deep dish masterpiece between us.

Duncan's eyes widened as he took it in. "Where's the cheese?"

"On the inside. Along with the meat," I explained as I maneuvered a three-inch thick slice onto each of our plates.

I watched expectantly as Duncan took his first gooey bite. He made a throaty noise of ecstasy somewhere between "mmm" and "ahh" as he slowly chewed and swallowed. When his tongue darted out to capture a little bead of tomato sauce at the corner of his lips, my own mouth began to water.

I attacked my own piece with gusto in lieu of accosting the boy across from me. "Good, huh?"

"Aye. Do you think we could bring a recipe back for Mario?" he asked before using his knife to balance another chunk on his upside-down fork and shoving it in his mouth.

"I'm not sure you could convert him to Chicago style." I chuckled at the thought of an anecdote Gabriella Rosetti had recently told us about the first time her brother Matteo featured haggis pizza. He got banned from the kitchen permanently, or at least until the local demand for his creation got him reinstated and the specialty pie permanently on the menu. "He's kind of a purist when it comes to pizza. You might have better luck with Mags."

I savored another forkful as music swelled, signaling the

commencement of the after-hours entertainment. Joey, the owner and emcee, always kicked off the night with a group sing-along of "There's No Business Like Show Business" from *Annie Get Your Gun*. As the final word "show" faded, Joey took the mike.

"Beloveds," he crooned. "We have a very special treat for you tonight. Not only a Green Room Lounge favorite, but a true star." I held my breath along with the rest of the room waiting to know which shining example of musical theater perfection was about to grace the stage. There were so many performers I had hoped to see live: Idina, Raul, Kristin, Kelli, Jeremy, Audra, Brian, Sutton, Darren, JRB, NPH — the list could go on and on.

Joey paused dramatically, beaming at his captivated audience. "Please welcome back to our humble stage, the dazzling and unforgettable Mackenna Reid."

What?

In complete shock, I turned to Duncan, who was wildly applauding along with the rest of the patrons. With a grin that rivaled that of the club host, he tipped his head toward the stage. "What are ye waitin' for? Go on, woman."

Still reeling, I got to my feet and wound my way to the stage where Joey, who smelled of lilac and pomade, pulled me into a hug. "Welcome home, honey," he murmured into my ear. "The first set is yours."

As he let go, my brain started frantically indexing my repertoire. He'd given me the set, which was 8 – 10 songs — so what would I sing? I hadn't thought to prepare anything. Thanks be to Kandor and Ebb, the patron saints of all things Chicago, I'd been preparing for a moment like this my whole life.

I made a quick mental list of songs that I would sing for the last time. I'd never be able to take sheet music for them all back to Doon ... and even if I did, who would appreciate them like this crowd? Which caused me to wonder what exactly I would do with my own theater when I crossed the bridge?

I couldn't think about that now. So instead, I sang. Gloriously.

When my set was finished, I wound my way through the adoring crowd back to my even more adoring boyfriend. As I slid into the booth next to him, he kissed my cheek. "I'm so verra fortunate that you chose me."

He meant over *all* of this … As I struggled to respond, I noticed a girl sitting alone at a corner table. It took a moment longer to recognize the brunette as Jeanie. Having given up her single white female homage to me, her hair was once again its natural color and in a cute pixie cut. Her makeup and clothes were back to her own unique style as well.

Turning to Duncan, I asked, "Can I borrow a couple hundred dollars?"

Duncan's eyes narrowed. "Nay. But ye can *have* anything you need. This money's not mine or yours. It's ours." He peeled off a hundred dollar bill for himself and gave me the rest.

"Thank you," I said as I accepted it.

"Can ye no' tell me what you need the money for?"

I hadn't meant to be cryptic. Caught up in so many emotions, I wasn't thinking clearly. I nodded toward the girl. "It's for Jeanie. When I showed up in the modern world, she loaned me money."

I'd taken a few steps when Duncan said, "Wait." As I turned around, he handed me the spare set of Corvette keys. "Jeanie rendered a service to you when you were in great need. I, too, am in her debt. Besides, my bonnie lass will need someone to take care of her after we go home. I'll have Stevens arrange the papers and transport the car to the girl."

Adding Duncan's generosity to the list of the day's revelations, I walked over to Jeanie's table. At my approach, she looked up nervously. With her short black hair and dramatic eye makeup, she looked like herself again. "You were truly great, Kenna."

"Thanks." I slid into the chair opposite her. "How are you?"

"I'm good," she hedged. "I took your advice. Broke up with Weston. He's threatening to have me blackballed from Equity, but he's all talk. I didn't expect to see you here. I thought you were gone for good."

"My boyfriend and I got delayed because of the hurricane. But I'm glad I ran into you." I held out the money and keys. "Thank you again for helping me get to Bainbridge. You saved my life."

A bit flustered, she took the wad of cash and hastily thumbed through it. "Kenna, this is seven hundred dollars!"

"I know. And keys to our Corvette. We're headed back to Scotland, so we won't need it. We'll have Duncan's valet bring you the car and title next week." Realizing what transferring ownership would require, I added, "And he'll have a check for the taxes on the car and the first year's insurance."

I still held the extra set of keys, and when I tried to give them to her, she waved them away. "Kenna. I wasn't really nice to you when you showed up at the apartment."

"And yet you still helped. You should give yourself more credit. And don't worry about Wes. You're talented enough to make it on your own."

I watched as the effect of my words softened her features. "You really think so?"

"Yes." I placed the key in her palm and closed her hand around it. "In fact, I'd really like you to sing a duet with me in the next set."

Jeanie's eyes pooled with tears. "Okay. If you're sure."

"Totally." As I stood to leave, Jeanie captured my hand in hers. "You should stay here. It's where you belong."

How wonderful it would be to stay … continue building my career, sing at the Green Room Lounge afterhours. If I asked, Duncan would stay for me. That had been his intention once upon a time, so I knew he'd agree. But how was him giving up his world for me any better than me giving up my world for him? Either way, one of us would be displaced. And if we stayed, the other part of his heart and mine, Jamie and Vee, would be cut off. Doon may never feel like home, but it's where my true family was. And for the sake of my family, I would go back and do my best to build a life and a theater that I could be proud of.

CHAPTER 21

Veronica

There were lots of lies I used to tell myself, and sometimes other people. Little stories to lessen the pain or explain why my dad couldn't make it to another Father-Daughter dance or ballet recital.

He worked deep undercover for the CIA, and wanted desperately to return home but couldn't risk exposing our identities to the terrorists he tracked. Or he died in battle, a war hero. Or he nursed sick children in Uganda and, though it pained him to be so far away, there were just so many lives he needed to save.

I used to sit in my room after a bad day and imagine he would come in and wrap me in his arms, shower me with unconditional love, and tell me he would protect me at any cost. Lies had kept me from falling apart.

After two hours of jogging in aimless circles, I couldn't escape the truth — that my father was a selfish drug-addict who couldn't be bothered with the child he'd given life to.

I swiped my keycard and let myself into the penthouse. With

no more fabrications to protect me, I felt exposed, yet oddly liberated. There were no more excuses, just the harsh truth, and for the first time I could see things clearly. It had been *my* strength that had sustained me, even through the lies — and maybe because of them, I hadn't turned bitter. Like Janet.

Maybe this was part of what I needed to learn here — that, unlike my mom, I *could* stand on my own.

I slipped off my sweater and spied Jamie on the terrace. He leaned against the railing, his hair blowing against his cheeks, the strands glinting in the sun.

I crossed the room and joined him outside. "Hey."

He glanced over his shoulder with a tight smile.

My heart squeezed. I'd hurt him. I moved closer and stood so our shoulders were touching. "Can I get a do-over?"

He glanced down at me and arched a brow, a gesture that meant he didn't understand something I'd said.

"Sorry, I mean ..." I ran my hands over the smooth metal of the railing while I gathered my thoughts. "What I mean is, I'd like to start over and react differently than I did earlier. I'm sorry I pushed you away."

"Thank ye for that, lass." His brows crouched over his nose. "But you were hurt. That man — " He straightened and raked the hair off his forehead, his anger and his need to comfort me fighting a battle across his face. He finally leaned back against the balustrade and slanted a glance in my direction. "Can I ask ye somethin'?"

The way he looked at me, as if my answer could change the course of the future, made me swallow before whispering, "Yes."

"When I asked you to get engaged, ye hesitated. Can you tell me why?"

Clearly, he'd been doing some thinking of his own. "Do you mean handfasted?"

"Aye. In Doon, they're one in the same."

"But I read that it meant after we're handfasted, we would be engaged for a year and a day."

"Our engagement can last for any length of time we like." The planes of his face hardened. "You're still hesitatin'. I dinna understand why."

I blinked several times and then turned away. He was right. Even though I loved him with every cell of my body, heart, and soul, the idea of marriage turned me into a goopy mess of emotions that were not all sunshine and light.

I stared at the people below us, going about their business like colorful ants, and wondered if any of them had been rejected by their fathers. If any of them had a mother who only cared about what they could do for her. If any of them questioned the meaning of love.

My reluctance to become handfasted to Jamie was complicated, but I knew I owed him some kind of explanation. So I took a deep breath and plunged in.

"Before my dad left, my parents fought all the time. About everything from what brand of ketchup to buy, to serious stuff like my dad's job hopping. But I remember a time when I was little, they held hands and kissed … they were peaceful and happy … in love." I paused and glanced at Jamie's profile, all hard angles and noble lines. He was like an unattainable wish I would have made as a child. Not because he was beautiful, but because he was everything I'd ever dreamed of — valiant and passionate and brilliant. And underneath the facade, sweet and kindhearted, and sometimes silly.

And I was terrified of losing him.

He turned and searched my face. "Tha's what I've been tryin' to puzzle out. What do your parents' failures have to do with us?"

"We're so happy together now, but it scares me a little." Pressure built behind my eyes, but I had no tears left. "I worry that once we're officially bound to one another, the mystery will be gone. That, like my parents, we'll start bickering and getting on each other's nerves. That we won't be *in love* anymore. And ... and then you'll move on without me."

His lips pressed together and a furrow appeared over his left brow. "Ye act as if what we have is fragile. Tha' if one of us tugs too hard one way or the other we might sit down and decide it isna worth the effort."

"I—"

"Nay, let me finish. You've got to stop putting barriers up against me." He took my shoulders in a firm grip, his eyes drilling into mine. "I am not yer father, Verranica. I willna give up on ye. I love tha' you challenge me, tha' ye push me to be better. We have a divine Calling, yes. But even if we dinna, I would choose you. Over and over I will choose you until you get it through your thick-as-granite skull that I will *always* choose you."

A smile bloomed from somewhere deep inside me, my heart inflating until it felt too large to fit inside my chest. I took a step toward him. "I choose you too."

He pulled me into his arms. "I'm verra sorry about your da. I wish I could meet him just once and explain everything he's missin' by not knowing you."

I nodded against his chest, my throat too constricted to speak.

After several long moments, he leaned back and lifted my chin. "Better now?"

"Yes, much."

"Good." Jamie flashed his brash grin. "Now, go get dressed so ye can show me off at this party."

I shook my head and shoved his shoulder. "Arrogant pig."

He tugged me against his chest and lowered his head. His lips brushed mine and then he pulled back, still so close I felt the vibration against my mouth as he whispered, "Aye, but I'm *your* arrogant pig."

The black fabric flowed over my skin like water, hugging my curves as if the dress had been made for me. Synthetic material had its advantages. I adjusted the strap and turned to look over one shoulder at my reflection, admiring the back of the gown, which dipped all the way to my waist. At the store, in the dressing room, Kenna's exact words had been, "That dress is going to blow Jamie MacCrae's mind."

I pointed my toe to admire my new strappy black and silver four-inch heels. She was right. He would either love it or throw a blanket around my shoulders and refuse to let me leave the hotel room. Either way, I couldn't wait to see his reaction. Quietly, I opened the bedroom door. Jamie sat on the edge of the couch with his elbows resting on his knees, watching baseball.

I cleared my throat and struck a pose with my hand on my hip.

No reaction.

"James Thomas." It's what his mother used to call him, I was told, and it got his attention every time.

"Oh sorry, I was just ..." He grabbed the remote and clicked off the TV. "The Yankees are behind by one, in the eighth innin'. We can watch it in the lim — " His gaze landed on me and he froze like an effigy, one arm stretched out as he set the remote on the table. " — o."

I pivoted so he could see the plunging back.

He didn't speak, but I could hear him coming up behind me. When I felt his warm breath against my bare skin, I glanced at him over my shoulder. His eyes were fastened to my exposed back, his jaw unhinged. I turned around. "So, do you like it?"

He swallowed, and when he spoke the rough edge to his voice sent delicious chills down my spine. "Did my heart love till now? Forswear it, sight! For I ne'er saw true beauty till this night."

"Now *that's* more like it." There were definite advantages to dating a Shakespearean scholar.

He reached out, but then lowered his arm and shoved both his hands into his tuxedo pants pockets. "I dinna rightly know if I should touch ye. But I've a mind to keep ye here all to meself." His fierce gaze made my breath catch.

"Don't tempt me." My eyes swept over him, every line of his muscled body highlighted by the precise cut of his suit. Warmth rushed through my veins and pooled in my gut. I took a step closer to him and flattened my palm against his chest, and the heat of his skin reached me through the crisp, white material of his shirt. He watched me, not moving a muscle, not breathing. Our gazes locked, and time stood still. We had the penthouse all to ourselves for the rest of the night.

I gripped the silken lapel of his jacket and took another step closer, tilting my chin to look up into his face. But the dangerous glint in his eyes — the barely leashed control — reminded me of a warning he'd once given me about dangling bait in front of a hungry shark.

Releasing my hold on him, I took several steps back. I would never want to tempt either of us to do something we'd later regret.

Proving we were on the same wavelength, he quirked a wicked grin. "Smart move, love. I'm feelin' decidedly un-prince like this night."

I grabbed my wrap and crystal-studded bag and headed for the door. "Let's get out of here while we still can."

The country club had your typical old-money feel. Expensive but slightly outdated décor. The air permeated by decades of Coco Chanel mixed with the enduring scent of cigar smoke. Just inside the entry hall, I was greeted by my old cheer squad member, Amber, who sat at a table handing out nametags and place cards. With her dyed blond curls and carroty spray-tan, she was clearly still a one hundred percent pure, grade-A Stephanie clone.

"Oh, hi, Ronnie! Steph said you might be coming." I bit my lip at the nickname. Besides Janet, Stephanie and her clones were the only ones who ever called me that. But for one night, I could endure it.

Amber searched the seating chart and then found my place card. "Well, this says, 'Ronnie Welling and guest,' and I can see that you're alone. Steph thought that might be the case. So I'll just —"

"Verranica, the gentleman takin' the coats is from Edinburgh."

Amber blinked, and then her gaze widened like an anime character with stars for eyes.

I took Jamie's arm. "Amber, this is my fiancé."

Jamie stared at me, one corner of his mouth lifting. It was the first time I'd admitted to our commitment to one another. But after today, I knew it was time to claim this great love I'd been given. It didn't mean I couldn't stand on my own. I'd already proven that I could.

Jamie turned to Amber and extended his hand. "James Thomas Kellan MacCrae, the fourth. But ye can call me Jamie."

She shook Jamie's hand and then handed us our nametags and table number, continuing to ogle him like she'd never seen the male species before.

"Well, tha' was peculiar."

I led him into the dining room. "Get used to it."

We paused at the entryway, the party already in full swing. Round tables rimmed the dance floor where couples mingled and chatted. A DJ on the far end of the room played a soft instrumental. I spotted one of my old teachers with his wife and waved. He returned the gesture enthusiastically. The crowd appeared to be a mix of older and younger couples.

We stepped farther into the room and I gasped — plastered all over the walls were enormous posters of Bainbridge High athletes in action. We wandered toward our assigned table, and hanging directly behind it was a six-foot-wide Stephanie in full cheer regalia, her limbs stretched into a herkie.

A giggle bubbled up in my throat as my gaze moved to the next life-sized poster: Eric shooting a basketball, its edges trimmed close like a Fathead wall decal. Was this a shrine or a fund-raiser? The next banner showed Amber and Steph in cheer formation. I turned in a circle and realized every poster featured our graduating class, but none of them included me. The closest I came to being represented was a group photo where you could see part of my hair and arm on the cropped edge. But I didn't feel the least disappointed.

"Veronica? I can't believe you *actually* made it." The words, spoken in the tone of a dog's squeak toy, made me turn.

"I wouldn't've missed it, Steph." I smiled, determined to be gracious even if it killed me.

Stephanie's gaze raked over my gown, and when she apparently couldn't find fault, her lips slid into a snide smirk. "Nice dress. It's quite an improvement over the leopard-print pants and hooker boots."

In my peripheral vision, I saw Jamie arch an inquiring brow, which unfortunately drew the eyes of the snake.

"And who might *you* be, darlin'?" Steph flipped her blonde curls behind her bare shoulders and slinked toward my boyfriend.

My stomach clenched as she got into Jamie's space and ran her nails down the sleeve of his coat. But Jamie wasn't falling for it. He glared at her hand until she pulled it back to her chest and then fiddled with the low neckline of her dress. "I'm Stephanie Heartford, your hostess with the mostest." She tittered, and I felt embarrassed for her. Did she really just say that? I met Jamie's gaze over Stephanie's head. Amusement played over his expression, and I let the tension flow out of my shoulders. He crossed his arms in front of his chest. "I am James MacCrae, Verranica's fiancé."

Stephanie whipped around so fast her hair smacked Jamie's chest. She stared at my left hand, and then I realized our mistake. A catlike smirk twisted her mouth. "Where's your ring?"

"I — " I wore the Ring of Aontacht on my right hand, and it's unique design would pass for an unconventional engagement ring ... if Steph hadn't already noticed my naked left finger.

"What'd you do? Rent him from Hot British Escorts 'R' Us?" She tilted her head back and let loose a cackle that would've put the Witch of Doon to shame. "Oh, Ronnie, I'm sooo glad you came."

She marched off, making a beeline for a group of cheer-bots.

I sunk into a nearby chair and watched as ten sets of eyes stared in our direction. The girls I used to cheer with snickered behind their hands, and then split up to spread the latest gossip. *So* high school.

Jamie pulled out the seat beside me and sat so our knees touched. "Dinna let that daft cow get to ye." He leaned forward and took my hand. "Yer crown is no' what makes you a queen. And you are betrothed to me, even without a ring." He lifted my left hand and kissed the back of my fingers, his steady gaze glued to my face.

"What did I ever do to deserve you?"

He stood and pulled me to my feet, then leaned down to whisper in my ear. "You must be a verra good girl."

Surprised I didn't turn into a puddle right there, I let him lead me to the dance floor as the strains of one of my favorite Lady Antebellum songs began. He spun me in a circle and then placed his broad hand on my lower back and took the other one firmly in his. As always, we fell into perfect rhythm with one another, our movements flowing together until we were like one person. Heads turned to watch us as we deftly waltzed past. And by the end of the song, there was a smattering of applause, and I saw we were the only ones on the floor.

"Well now, wasn't *that* entertaining!" Stephanie's amplified voice cut through the crowd.

She stood on the stage gripping the DJ's microphone with a manic air as she fought to pull the attention back to herself. "I bet you wish you'd had a dance partner like him at senior prom, Ronnie." She smirked and shook her head. "Oh, that's right, you weren't there."

My spine went ridged and Jamie tightened his arm around my waist. Prom had been one of Eric and my "off" weeks — we'd had quite a few. In hindsight, I was pretty sure I knew why.

Barreling on, Stephanie announced dinner, gave instructions for the auction, and promised more dancing to follow. "Then we'll show 'em how it's done. Won't we, babe?"

I followed her gaze across the crowd to Eric's flushed face.

He was either appropriately embarrassed by his fiancé's behavior or he'd been to the bar one too many times. He caught my eye and flashed the trademark Russo grin. I was surprised to feel nothing. Not even anger. He was part of a past that no longer defined me.

"Jamie, I think I've seen enough. Let's make a donation and then get out of here."

"Are ye sure? Leavin' this soon would appear as a retreat to your enemy."

Knowing he was right, I sighed. "Okay, one more hour."

Dinner turned out to be surprisingly fun. We were seated with Phyllis and her boyfriend, who were home for the weekend from Purdue, and an older couple I didn't know. Phyllis had been one of my few allies on the cheer squad, given we were in some AP courses together. We spent the evening trading stories about college life and my adventures with Scottish cuisine. The older couple had just returned from a European cruise—although they'd never been to Alloway. Then the discussion turned to baseball and Jamie kept up with the guys at the table as if he'd watched the American game his entire life.

After dessert, the DJ started a fast set, and I immediately recognized the opening of a Justin Timberlake song.

"Oh! Remember this one, Vee?" Phyllis threw down her napkin, and grabbed my hand, pulling me out of my chair. I glanced over my shoulder at Jamie, who shot me a wink. He knew I couldn't resist a chance to dance—or, thanks to the playlist on my phone, a JT song.

Phyllis and I kicked off our shoes, lifted our arms, and shimmied onto the middle of the floor. After a few failed attempts at synchronization, we found our place in our old hip-hop cheer-dance routine. A few other girls joined in, and by the end of the song the whole squad had picked up the routine and danced along. Even Stephanie, who seemed determined to turn every move into something vulgar. But I was having too much fun to care.

After several more songs, I made my way back to our table with my updo falling down around my shoulders and a sheen of sweat coating my skin.

"Hey." Jamie rose to greet me. "Did ye have fun?"

Drawn to him by forces beyond my control, I stepped close and weaved my fingers into the back of his hair. His warm knuckles traced down my spine, sending tingles all over my body, and then he wrapped his arm around me, pulling me close. He lowered his head and kissed me until the room began to spin, and I had to grip his shoulders to keep from floating away.

When he pulled back, he flashed a wolfish leer. "Tha' should put an end to any doubts you're truly mine."

"Aren't you incredibly thoughtful?"

"'Tis a sacrifice, but I try."

After asking Jamie to make a shamefully large donation, I headed to the restroom. We could've paid for twelve entire school buildings, but I didn't want to make it too easy for Stephanie. Especially knowing she'd take all the credit.

While in the bathroom stall, a group of girls came in, chattering over one another like a flock of magpies. I reached to undo the latch, but stopped when I heard my name.

"Did you see Veronica's date? Aye yai yai! That boy is smokin'!"

"He reminds me of that one British actor, Alex —"

"But hotter!"

The next voice I recognized as Amber's. "Yeah, but Steph said she's lying about them being engaged."

"Ring or not, the way he watches her ..."

"Like a starving man at a buffet."

"And he can't stop touching her ..."

"The way they danced!"

"It's as if they've been dancing together forever."

There was a pause and someone sighed.

"I think they're really in love."

I smiled to myself as they all agreed, even Amber. Not wanting to answer the million questions they would throw at me, I waited until everyone left before coming out. I washed up and was reapplying my lipstick when the door swung open and Eric sauntered in.

I spun around. "This is the lady's room."

He leaned a hip against the counter beside me; his tie was loose around his neck, his blue eyes unfocused. "I know that. I came in to talk to you."

I hadn't spoken a word to him all night. We'd grown up down the street from one another, but he'd killed our friendship when he chose to cheat on me. "Get out."

"Just give me a second, Vee." He stood and moved into my space, and his breath practically made me secondhand drunk.

I stepped back, but he followed. "I think about you a lot ..."

"Eric, just stop. I have a strong suspicion you won't even remember this tomorrow."

He moved closer, and I leaned away, the bare skin of my back stinging as it hit the cold marble counter top.

"I heard you aren't really engaged to that pretty-boy Scotsman. But I bet I can make you happy."

"That pretty-boy Scotsman is going to beat you into next week if you don't back up. Right. Now." I gritted my teeth and tried to sidestep, but he blocked me. He was so close I could smell his Axe body spray — the same scent he'd worn since he hit puberty.

"Come with me, Vee. Now. My car's out back." He rubbed my arm, and his skin felt clammy against mine. "We could leave this town and never look back."

I'd once longed for this moment, dreamt of us escaping Bainbridge together. His arm moved around me, and he rubbed my back, his hand traveling up to the nape of my neck. I shivered in revulsion.

"See, you want me too." He lowered his head, whispering in my ear. "You can't deny it."

The door swung open behind him and Phyllis stopped dead in her tracks. She took one look at us and breathed, "I'll get Jamie." And fled back out the door.

"Eric, seriously, you need to go." I gave his chest a warning push, but he didn't move. "I don't want to see you get hurt."

But it was as if I hadn't spoken. "I saw you watching me while you were dancing. It was just like old times. Like we'd never broken up." He tightened his grip on the back of my neck and leaned his head toward mine, puckering his lips.

Acting on instinct, I closed my fist, reared back, and punched him in the eye. The sickening smack of flesh on flesh sounded just as Jamie and Phyllis rushed in. Eric released me and stumbled back, clutching his face. "What'd you do that for?"

Jamie stalked forward, his eyes churning with a mix of intense emotion. I could almost feel the fury radiating from him. Then the emotionless mask descended over his expression, and I knew Eric was in trouble. "Jamie, I've got this."

I grabbed Eric's sleeve and towed him out the door. Still clutching his eye, he followed like a beaten puppy as we entered the dining room. Spying Stephanie with a gathering of clones, I dragged him over and gave him a push so he stumbled into the middle of the group.

Stephanie demanded, "What the —"

But I interrupted her. "You might want to keep your boy on a tighter leash. He just followed me into the ladies and tried to kiss me." Then I lifted my chin and unleashed the Evil Highney. "And don't *ever* call me Ronnie again. My name is Veronica."

Leaving her sputtering behind me, I pivoted on my heel and strode across the room to where Jamie stood in the doorway. "Let's dance."

"Yes, my queen." He tipped his head in a bow, eyes glowing with admiration.

Taking his hand, I led him onto the floor. Then I linked my arms around his neck, and he followed my lead, settling his hands on my waist. We swayed to the music like we were average American teenagers at prom. But for the first time, I didn't care that I'd missed my senior prom. And I had no interest in being average.

"I thought ye said no fightin'."

"I didn't say anything about me." I lowered one of my arms and shook my stinging knuckles. "Ow, that hurt!"

"Try no' to be a lone wolf next time." He took my hand and lifted my bruised fingers to his lips. "You know I've got yer back, love."

Then he wrapped me in his arms and I laid my head on his chest, listening to the steady beat of his heart. And that's when it hit me — trying to handle everything on my own wasn't smart.

After being hurt by Eric, Janet, and my dad, I'd learned it was safer to stand alone. And thanks to them, I knew that I could. It was why I'd kept secrets from the people I should've trusted the most — about the cursed journal, the luckenbooth pendant, my illness — the list could go on and on. So many times I'd shouldered the responsibility instead of sharing the weight. All because I believed that relying on others made me weak.

But there was a world of difference between the unhealthy dependence I'd witnessed between Janet and Bob, and a group of trusted friends working together to bring each other up. Pack leaders surrounded themselves with strong individuals, and relied on each of their talents — *that* was a position of strength.

As queen, I held the power to do it all on my own. But ... I lifted my head and met Jamie's radiant gaze — with the amazing people surrounding me, why would I ever choose to stand alone again?

I smiled into my future king's eyes. "The modern world has been ... educational, but I'm ready to go home. Back to Doon."

CHAPTER 22

Mackenna

Stepping into Doon from modern-day Scotland reminded me of a recurring dream I used to have. I was playing Éponine in the Broadway revival of *Les Misérables* and crushing it. After my death scene, I stepped into the alley behind the theater to get some air. Suddenly I was no longer in New York. In that slow-motion way that dreams often go bad, ragged revolutionaries were racing past me in the cobbled street, shouting to one another in French. I turned just as the army rounded the corner and fired. Pain seared through me, and I crumpled to the ground — with no boy to comfort me and no fall of rain to wash me clean of the past. Then I woke up.

I always hated that dream.

With a brilliant flash of light, day turned to night as the modern world reformed into medieval stillness. Our little group walked to the end of the bridge as we struggled to acclimate to our new surroundings. The temperature, which had been in the fifties, dropped at least twenty degrees. The air stung my nose and throat as I breathed it in and then exhaled in a visible cloud. Duncan pulled me into the sphere of his warmth as Jamie held up a hand in warning. Quietly, he said, "There are supposed to be men waiting here."

Vee shivered, blinking to adjust to the darkness. "Is that snow on the ground?"

"Aye," Jamie answered, kicking at a frozen patch of white with the tip of his brand-new Nike. The uneven ground, so recently scorched by the limbus, glistened with little clumps of snow. The lack of undergrowth caused the charred trees to stand out in stark, shadowy relief, creating the overall effect of a haunted wood. I had the impression that if I stepped off the bridge, I, too, would be leached of color.

Jamie set the half dozen bags he'd been carrying down just off to the side of the bridge. He removed his prized ball cap and placed it on Vee's head. Next he slipped off his jacket and draped it over her shoulders. "Stay with Mackenna and m' brother whilst I go have a look about."

With a severe nod, Duncan stepped away from me. Quietly shedding his own bags next to Jamie's, he accepted the crossbow his brother thrust at him. For an instant, the princes' eyes locked, and the fierce unspoken message they exchanged caused the hairs on the back of my neck to rise. Something was wrong. Both boys were on alert, bodies tensed and ready — but ready for what, exactly?

Rather than using the flashlight tucked in his belt, Jamie pulled out his recently purchased hunting knife and crept toward the skeletal tree line. Earlier, I'd poked fun at Surfer Dude's rampant shopping spree at the hunting store, teasing that he'd gone commando — which made Vee blush. But now I took it all back. In a dangerous situation, I preferred the MacCraes armed to the teeth.

As Jamie disappeared into the night, Vee slipped her arm

through mine. We huddled behind Duncan, our senses straining for some indication of what was happening. After a few seconds, we heard a high-pitched whistle.

My heart began to race as I looked to Vee, whose wide eyes mirrored my own. As if sensing our fear, Duncan whispered over his shoulder, "Tha's Jamie." Another whistle answered in the night, causing Duncan to whip back around and ready his weapon.

"Who goes there?" Jamie's voice echoed through the woods.

"'Tis Fergus."

Like a two-headed girl with one brain from a sideshow attraction, Vee and I sighed in unison — until Duncan held up a hand cautioning us to remain quiet.

"What's the password?" Jamie shouted.

"Horatio," Fergus answered.

Duncan's shoulders sagged in visible relief as he said, "It's okay."

Vee frowned, and I quietly explained, "It's something they do on their training exercises. 'Horatio' means friend while 'Laertes' means traitor or foe."

"From *Hamlet*," she replied.

"I guess." In truth, I'd never thought about why they'd used those specific passwords. I'd been too busy teasing Duncan about playing war games. However, standing at the mouth of the Brig o' Doon in the middle of the night, I vowed to never joke about the MacCraes' games ever again. Coming from Indiana by way of Arkansas, I had no concept of what it took to fight for your life or defend a nation against an enemy, but some terrible foreboding whispered that may not always be true.

A moment later, Jamie emerged from the blackness. "Fergus's camp is o'er yonder, just a wee bit." Taking Vee's hand, he led her toward the spooky forest as Duncan and I followed.

No one spoke as we wound our way through the devastation. We emerged from the woods into a clearing — the same one where Sean MacNally and his men had held the princes while Vee and I faced the zombie fungus.

Fergus stood in front of a tidy campsite, the shelter shaped more like a teepee than a festival tent. Only the curl of smoke rising through the hole in the top announced its presence.

When we approached, the big Scotsman hugged each of us. Leaving Jamie for last, he said, "Took your time, didn't ye?"

"Sorry, lad." Jamie stepped back. "Where're my men?"

"I sent them away."

"Why?" Duncan asked.

"I wanted to speak to the four of you in confidence. Fiona's discovered something."

Vee stepped forward, her voice strained. "What is it?"

"I'll let Fiona tell ye herself." He lifted the flap of his tent, revealing a small fire in the center. Vee ducked inside with me close behind. Fiona flung herself at the both of us and we squeezed one another for nearly a minute. When we finally let go, I noticed the tent was indeed more like a teepee than anything else. The air was warm from the fire and smoke free. Thick woolen plaids littered the ground, creating a soft place to sit or sleep. It was actually kind of homey.

As Fiona turned toward the light, I forgot about the tent. She looked terrible. Bruise-like circles accentuated her sunken eyes. Her strawberry-blonde hair needed a good brushing. The firelight made her appear haggard and angular, nothing like the sassy and curvy girl we'd left.

"Fiona, what's the matter?" I took her hand as her grave eyes darted between me and her queen.

"I was wrong about the nature o' the spell that forced ye out o' Doon. Sorely wrong. I thought it was a sending spell, something Adelaide worked through Adam to remove ye from Doon."

"It wasn't?" Vee stepped closer.

"Nay. When I'd translated the last of it, I realized my mistake." Her grave, green eyes begged us for forgiveness for the error. "It wasn't a sending spell. 'Twas a *retrieving* spell."

"What's the difference?" Duncan asked.

"A retrieving spell is used by a witch to claim something that once belonged to them."

"The locket that Queen Lynnette gave Addie?" I prompted. "The one Vee took?"

Fiona shook her head. "I'd considered that, but it doesna explain why you were also a target. I think she did it to reclaim her magic."

"What are you talking about?" Jamie demanded.

Unruffled by the two princes frowning down at her, she continued. "In a retrieving spell, the body is physically separated from the essence being retrieved. The essence is pulled one way while the body is forced in the other."

I thought back to the castle keep and the terrible ripping sensation that accompanied my spiral into blackness. Feeling nauseous all over again, I mumbled, "That's exactly what it felt like."

Vee nodded and placed a hand over her mouth like she was about to hurl. She swayed, and Jamie lunged for her arm to keep her from staggering too close to the fire.

"Let's sit," Jamie suggested, mostly, I suspected, for Vee's benefit. He settled her on his lap while I sunk next to her with Duncan at my side.

When we were situated around the fire, Fiona continued to explain. "When Vee confronted Adelaide in Alloway and Kenna confronted the limbus, they both defeated essential portions of the witch's power. But energy doesn't just vanish ... I think she purposely let Vee and Kenna win so she could make them her vessels — deposit some of her magic in each of them. If I'm right, she buried it deep enough that neither would even know they had it."

"Why would she do that? It doesn't make any sense." I resented being anyone's vessel, especially the unwitting dupe of a nasty old witch.

Fiona suddenly looked pained, the kind of expression I imagined someone would get when they had to break very bad news to another person. "It does if she wanted to shed all her magic."

Vee chewed at her lip. "Why would she ... No."

"Aye," Fiona affirmed. "So she could cross inta Doon."

Turning pale as the Ghost of Christmas Past, Vee whispered, "So Addie's trying to get back into Doon?"

With a heavy glance at Fergus, she said, "I'm afraid 'tis far worse, my queen. Adelaide could have only worked this spell if she was already in Doon."

Horror contorted Vee's features. "How?"

Jamie, doing his best to mask his own shock while comforting his fiancé, supplied, "Without her power, she might've crossed the Brig o' Doon with the Destined."

"Aye." Fergus, who'd mostly remained silent as he sat behind his tiny wife, looked over our heads at Duncan and Jamie. "Tha's precisely what Fiona thinks ... that she used up the last bit of her magic ta conceal her true appearance."

Duncan's arm tightened around me, trying to protect me from the awful truth. "She could've crossed the Brig o' Doon as anyone."

But the Destined had crossed into Doon months ago, before our getting kicked out of Doon, even before the limbus. "I'm confused. If Addie had no magic when she crossed over, then she shouldn't have been able to cast the zombie fungus curse. Right?"

"Actually, she didn't need her magic for that." At my blank look, Fiona elaborated. "The power was already in the Pictish Stone, the curse written upon it — it was ancient magic. Adelaide must've set it up before she fled, before the Miracle, in anticipation of one day returning. All she would have to do when she crossed over was touch the stone with a bead of her blood."

Vee began to twist the ends of her hair, a physical manifestation of her brain going into overdrive. "So I get how she triggered the limbus. And stashing her power in Kenna and me, while hard to believe, isn't out of the realm of possibility. But how in the world did she manage to cast a retrieving spell?"

"I dinna know for certain, but I suspect that when Adelaide seduced Adam and he surrendered his will ta her, she would've regained a little power. But the retrieving spell is complex — it has to be done precisely. In order to cast it, she would have need of her spell book."

"Which I stupidly found for her!" Vee pounded the ground with the palm of her hand.

Capturing her hand, Jamie lifted it to his lips. "Ye couldna know, love."

"Vee's right," I said. "Because of us, Addie's in Doon with her magic, and hiding in plain sight."

Suddenly, I felt exhausted. I sagged against Duncan, whose fingers began to knead the side of my neck. "How many people know about this?" he asked.

"Just Fiona and me," Fergus answered. "We thought it best, until we had a chance to consult with you."

Vee caught Fergus's gaze. "Where do the people think you are?"

"At the hunting lodge, having a bit of a honeymoon get-away." Fergus took a stick and began to stoke the fire.

"Then who's in charge?" Jamie's normally smooth voice sounded strained.

"The queen's advisors." Fergus threw the stick into the flames.

Vee sprang to her feet. "They have no idea how much danger we're in. We need to get back to the castle."

"I've got a wagon over yonder." Fergus nodded in the direction I guessed was the road. "I couldna bring more horses for fear of arousing suspicion."

"Good thinking, man." Jamie stood and took Vee's hand.

Vee's face appeared as hard as stone in the firelight, her transformation from modern teen into medieval queen happening in the space of our terrible conversation. "Before we head back, I think we need to agree to keep Fiona's discovery between the six of us. Addie could be any one of the Destined and she could have others besides Adam under her influence. Since we can't be sure, we have no idea whom we can trust."

Jamie nodded. "Trust no one."

"But the six of us." Duncan completed his brother's thought, and they exchanged a weighted look.

"Agreed." Fiona stood and bowed her head to her queen.

Fergus and I echoed our agreement, but my mind already raced with the possibilities. Over twenty Destined had entered the kingdom during that last crazy Centennial. The night we *thought* we'd defeated the witch. Who knew how many were working for the other side or what they'd been up to right under our noses?

We stepped out of the tent into the pre-dawn morning, hesitating slightly at the sight of snow flurries being flung about by the arctic wind. How foolish we'd been — crossing the Brig

225

o' Doon loaded with modern-day souvenirs and presents like tourists coming home from Disneyland. The whole time Addie had been using us to execute her plot of revenge.

And to think I'd almost made it easier for her still … if I'd stayed in Chicago, kept Duncan with me.

No more. I would not serve the Witch of Doon — not even unintentionally. I was actively and deliberately choosing sides. Mackenna Reid was from this moment on Team Doon!

CHAPTER 23

Veronica

The next afternoon, I paced in front of a roaring fire, my full skirts whooshing with every step. As much as I wanted to wear one of my comfortable maxidresses, layers had become a must. The air inside the castle was too drafty for anything but wool.

An eerie howl echoed through the room as another icy gale pummeled the castle. Without central heat and modern insulation, the two-foot-thick stone walls were little protection against the falling temperatures. I shivered, drew my ermine-lined cape tighter around me, and stopped in front of the diamond panes of my office windows. From here, the fields looked like the sparkling backdrop of a Christmas card. But I knew better.

This was no short-lived summer blizzard set off by a girl's naive attempts at heroism, but the bitter, ground-freezing cold of mid-winter. According to Jamie, the kingdom's climate was temperate all year round. They may experience a bit of snow around the holidays, but nothing like this. If I'd held any lingering doubt that Addie had found a way into Doon and regained her magic, I need look no further for confirmation than out my window.

As my advisors had repeatedly pointed out that morning, Doon's enchantment was linked to the weather — a physical manifestation of its state of peace or unrest. My advisory cabinet, which Fiona and I privately referred to as "the three Wise Men," were ancient and, in most cases, astute, but this time they lacked a key bit of information. And for now, I was inclined to let them draw their own conclusions.

A knock on the door announced the arrival of Fiona, who came in bearing sustenance. My dear friend set the tea service on the low table in front of the fire and then curtsied. "I brought ye some o' yer favorite cakes."

"Oh, you're a lifesaver! I haven't eaten all day." I strode over to the table and popped an entire miniature cinnamon muffin in my mouth.

Normally, as my chief consultant, Fiona would've been part of my earlier meeting, but lying was not one of her gifts. I'd seen her try, and her face flamed, her hands shook, and sweat popped out on her forehead. Considering the Wise Men were already on alert, we couldn't risk her revealing our secrets.

Fiona handed me a cup of steaming tea, and we both turned as Fergus barreled through the door. "Och! Is it truly necessary that *everyone* be searched and disarmed before seein' ye?"

"Fergus!" Fiona hissed. "Show respect."

"Er ... sorry, Yer Majesty." My giant friend bowed, his almost translucent skin flaming from his neck to his forehead.

"No worries, Fergus. But you know I can't show preferential treatment to anyone. Especially now."

"Aye, but need that git Eòran be so blasted thorough in his body search?" Fergus jammed the tail of his shirt back into his waistband, took ahold of his wide belt, and did a wiggle to readjust his kilt.

I bit my lip against a laugh as Fiona glared at her husband and pointed to a seat by the fire.

His clothes finally in proper order, Fergus sank into the indicated chair and reached for a scone. "So how'd ye fare?"

"Aye, how did it go?" Jamie came in, followed by Kenna and Duncan.

"Lock the door," I replied.

Duncan did as I asked. "That bad, eh?"

After we all settled around the coffee table, I perched on the edge of the sofa and related my morning meeting. "The Wise Men are beginning to speculate on the reasons for the weather change. Their current theory is it's linked to whatever force pushed Kenna and me out of Doon." I glanced at Fiona. "Which is partially true."

She nodded, and I explained the rest. "I suggested to them that the force has been contained now that Adam is in custody, but I don't think they're buying it. They believe that if I don't make a statement soon, the people will begin to draw their own conclusions, and their ideas could be far worse than the truth. We'd then be dealing with mass hysteria."

"I doubt they could conceive of anythin' worse than the witch masquerading as one of them." Jamie shifted forward onto the edge of the sofa beside me and took my hand in his.

"Does that mean we should tell everyone?" Kenna asked. "Hope the truth will bring the witch out of hiding?"

Duncan, who was balanced on the arm of Kenna's chair, said, "Then we lose the element of surprise."

Fergus popped three cakes into his mouth and swallowed them in one gulp. "As far as we know, Addie doesna know we're aware she's here."

"Do you think when she pushed us out of Doon she was trying to break the enchantment itself?" Kenna asked.

The fire crackled into the silence as we all contemplated that possibility.

"Nay." Jamie shook his head. "In order to break the covenant protecting us, a Doonian would ha' to leave willingly."

I turned to him. "So if I took someone to the border and tried to force them back to the normal world, what would happen?"

"In theory, nothing." The curl of Jamie's lips told me his words were more than speculation. "The portals are the only way in or out."

"Spill." My gaze shifted to Duncan, who chuckled. "What did you guys do?"

"'Twas an accident." Duncan smiled at his brother. "At least I think it was."

"Aye." Jamie smirked. "We were huntin' in the northeastern corner and one of us shot a huge buck. The animal wasna mortally wounded and ran off."

Duncan picked up the story. "We both claimed to ha' fired the shot, and instead of goin' after the deer to see whose arrow had pierced its skin we decided to fight about it."

Jamie practically laughed the next words. "In the course of the brawl, I shoved Duncan and he fell back. We didna even realize we were at the border until he bounced back at me with a force that flattened me to the ground."

When their laughter died down, Kenna voiced the question I'd been thinking. "What did it feel like, Duncan?"

"Like I'd fallen against a mattress made of springy clouds. It gave a little at first, then spit me back out."

Jamie sobered a bit. "Scared us so badly, we sat there and stared at it for a good spell. Until we got the brilliant idea to throw rocks at it."

Duncan leaned forward with a grin. "And one flew back and smashed Jamie in the mouth!"

Jamie touched his upper lip where he had the tiniest ghost of a scar, one that I'd never thought to ask him about. "Aye, then it wasna so fun anymore."

Kissing the tip of my index finger, I pressed it to the little imperfection above his lip. "Your mouth seems to have recovered." Standing, I moved to face the group with my back to the fire. "Any theories on which of the Destined is really Addie?" I turned to Fiona. "She could be male or female, correct?"

"Aye." Fiona nodded. "She could even be a child."

There had been a mother and daughter from Austria who'd crossed the bridge together during the most recent Centennial. "But that would blow the theory that she'd enthralled Adam through some form of infatuation."

"There are all sorts o' love," Duncan interjected. "Didna Adam mention losin' a wife and daughter in a car accident?"

A chill raced down my spine and my knees went weak at the thought of the adorable little girl with the enormous hazel eyes and blonde pigtails. If evil could hide in that pure, beautiful package, it would shake my faith to the core.

"Too obvious, I think." Jamie caught and held my gaze, and I knew he was right.

"What about Emily?" My assistant had been a godsend, taking care of all the details that, as a new queen, I couldn't possibly handle on my own. But as I'd told Fergus, I couldn't afford to give anyone preferential treatment.

Fergus shook his great head. "Nay. She had a Calling with Drew Forrester."

I exchanged a glance with Kenna, noting the green tinge of her skin. Drew had been the first victim of the zombie fungus, and my BFF had killed him in order to save me. "He was a soul-less monster, Ken."

"Tha's right. He died the day he fell into the limbus." Duncan lifted her hand and tucked it under his arm, encasing her fingers in his other hand.

"Oliver and Adam have been quite chummy since crossin' the bridge," Fergus suggested.

"True." I thought back. The scientists had bonded almost immediately, spending much of their free time together.

"I'll bring Oliver in for questionin'," Jamie volunteered.

"No," I protested. "Remember, we need to act as normal as possible, so as not to give away our advantage. Invite him for an ale or something." I tapped my chin. "You could ask him to build that electric generator for the castle that we were talking about on the flight back to Scotland."

Jamie's lips tilted and his eyes burned into mine at the reminder of our time spent on the private jet. "Of course, my queen." Discussing modern technology had been a very small portion of our in-flight entertainment.

I broke eye contact and grabbed a notepad and quill off the table while clearing my throat. "Um … okay then. Let's divide the Destined among us and do a little subtle digging. Write down anything suspicious, anything at all that seems off."

After deciding who would talk to whom, everyone began to gather their things and make their way toward the door. But I stayed seated, double checking my list. I tapped the feather against my chin, knowing I'd forgotten something essential. It came to me in a flash, and I shot to my feet. "Wait."

The group quieted and turned to face me. "I suggest we each seek the guidance of the Protector in helping us to discover the witch's true identity."

Everyone agreed, and when they'd filed out, I shut the door

and returned to my desk in order to finish up the paperwork that had piled up during my absence. Even with the witch out there, I needed to deal with these issues in order to keep up the appearance of normalcy. And, I needed a way to calm my racing mind. Fiona had divided my correspondence into two piles: "Urgent" and "Not as urgent." Halfway through the five-alarm pile, I came across a letter from Gregory Forrester—the man who'd lost his arm trying to pull his brother Drew out of the limbus.

Your Royal Highness, Queen Veronica,

I wish to request an audience at your earliest convenience. Finally having mustered up the emotional and mental strength to go through my brother's things, I came across something that could be of interest to you. Due to its delicate nature, I do not wish to discuss the details in writing. Please send for me anytime, day or night, and I will respond with the upmost expediency.

Your loyal subject,

Gregory Forrester

My relationship with Gregory had gotten off to a rocky start. The first time we met, the flesh was melting off of his arm and he accused me of causing the curse that killed his brother. But after Kenna and I defeated the limbus, I'd paid Gregory a visit. Explaining what his brother had become, and what had ultimately happened to him, proved one of the hardest conversations of my life.

Gregory had surprised me by thanking me for destroying the abomination that had taken control of his brother's body. He'd even dropped to a knee and pledged to me right there in his living room. Humbling, to say the least.

An icy finger of air found its way down the nape of my neck as the wind rattled the windows behind me, the bare branches of a nearby tree tapping and scratching the glass like wintery nails. Resisting the urge to look over my shoulder, I pulled my cape tighter and read the letter once more for clues as to why Fiona would've placed it in the urgent pile.

Deciding to set it aside to ask her later, I stood and walked over to the bookcase. Something had been niggling at the back of my mind since I'd realized retrieving the spell book from the witch's cottage had played right into Addie's hands. I pulled down a book on Scottish symbols and flipped to the luckenbooth. I traced the sketch of the intertwined hearts topped by a crown in the upper left corner of the page. In Celtic mythology, some symbols were incorruptible, while others held a greater capacity for conducting malevolence. I had a hard time believing something so beautiful could carry a curse. I'd always believed Lynette's pendant was a gift given out of love.

Scanning the page, I found one legend that claimed the luckenbooth had originally been designed as a token of love and devotion, and had been given by Mary Queen of Scots to Lord Darnley. Another story maintained that it was an engagement brooch given to her by the Dauphin of France, who later became her husband.

Interesting, but unhelpful. I skimmed down the page. *See also Double Witch's Heart on page 419.*

I turned to the corresponding page, and my gut clenched; the drawing of entwined hearts was almost identical to the luckenbooth. I began to read, walking back to my desk. A red glow drew my attention, causing me to stop and stare at the ring on my right hand. And that's when the world exploded.

The windows shattered, blasting glass shards across the room. Arctic wind tore at my hair and clothes. With a terrible groan, a dark shape blocked out the sun, falling toward me. I dropped to the ground, my cape blowing over my head. Blindly, I scrabbled away from a great wrenching sound that vibrated in my chest, as if the very fabric of the earth were being torn apart. An avalanche of cracks and crunches, like hundreds of bones snapping, resounded behind me, prompting me to crawl faster.

When I reached the far side of my office, I collapsed behind a chair, just as a massive crash shook the room. Afraid to move, I gripped the leather arm of my merger shield, praying we weren't under attack.

Eòran yelled my name and banged on the door, but my muscles refused to cooperate with my brain as I awaited the next strike. When it didn't come, and the screaming outside the room became frantic, I forced myself to move. Peering over the arm of the chair, I discovered an enormous tree inside my office. The trunk, wider than my shoulders, had split my desk completely in half. Dull light filtered through a gnarl of jumbled, dirt-covered roots that protruded from the empty window casing. The oak had been completely uprooted.

Still crouching, I moved forward slowly, stepping over snapped limbs and clumps of leaves. My desk chair had been flattened into kindling. And in a flash of clarity I saw myself there beneath it, broken and bleeding, my lifeless eyes staring back at me. Two more seconds, and I would've been sitting in that chair.

The door vibrated as guards tried to knock it down. Barely able to stand on my trembling legs, I picked my way around the tangle of branches to the door and unlocked it.

Eòran came stumbling into the room, followed by a stream of royal guards. "My queen!" He paused mid-stride, taking in the uprooted tree. He hesitated for only a moment before turning to where I leaned against the wall for support, and steered me out into the hall. As he issued orders that sounded like gibberish to my ears, he lifted me into his arms.

An hour later, I lay propped in my bed with covers tucked up to my chin, running my fingers through Blaz's bristly fur, but I couldn't stop shaking. Kenna handed me a mug of something stronger than tea. "Here, Mags said to drink all of this."

I brought it to my lips and inhaled the warm, spicy fragrance before taking a sip. The liquid burned a pleasant path to my stomach. After everything we'd been through, I couldn't say why *this* had put me in my bed. Maybe the vision I'd seen of myself, as if I were hovering above my body while the life leached out of it, had pushed me over the edge.

Kenna stoked the fire. "Is your head okay? That cut looked pretty nasty."

"It's fine." I touched the bandage on my forehead. That I'd only received this wound and a few small scratches was a miracle in itself.

A door slammed in the outer room and I jumped, prompting Blaz to catapult off the bed with a sharp bark.

"Verranica!" Heavy footfalls preceded Jamie's arrival. He ran into my room, his eyes wild until they landed on my face, and then he stopped, drinking me in. His chest heaved as if he'd sprinted up the hundred and twenty-some stairs to my tower.

"I'm fine." I set my cup on the nightstand and pushed up, sitting straighter.

The muscles of his throat contracted, and he strode forward, gathering me in his arms. "Holy Saints in heaven, I saw the tree …" His voice broke off and he squeezed me tighter.

For a moment, I nestled into the crook of his neck and pressed my nose against his skin. His unique scent of crisp pine and rain-washed air chased away the last of my chills, warming me like nothing else could.

"I'll just give you two some alone time." Over Jamie's shoulder, I watched Kenna walk toward the door.

"Wait, Ken, don't go yet."

Jamie released me and sat, his weight dipping the mattress. I shifted to counterbalance and motioned Kenna back. When she hesitated, I patted the coverlet on my opposite side.

Sandwiched between the two people I loved most in the world, I felt safe enough to say, "Earlier, after our meeting, I'm one-hundred percent sure I did not bolt my office door." From their blank looks, I realized I needed to clarify. "When the tree … fell, Eòran couldn't get to me because the door was locked tight. And …" I hesitated. "My ring lit up, warning me just before it happened."

Silence.

Jamie raked the hair off his forehead, the planes of his cheekbones taking on a deep reddish hue. Worried about his blood pressure, I grabbed the cup off my nightstand and thrust it at him. "Here, drink this."

Kenna took my hand. "Do you think Addie did this? Smashed the tree through your window?"

Jamie set down the empty cup. "I'm sorry to do this, Verranica, but I'm doublin' your guard and you canna leave your suite. You'll need someone trustworthy watchin' your back every moment. Even in the loo. I'll ha' Fiona and Kenna take shifts."

Kenna nodded, her eyes like large silver dollars in her pale face.

Warm at last, I pushed the covers down to my waist. "Let's not overreact. We don't know for sure the tree wasn't just a freak accident."

"I dinna believe in coincidence." Jamie's jaw hardened and

he turned to my BFF. "Mackenna, you have the gift of sight. I'd like for ye to inspect Vee's office, the door, and the tree inside and out. Look for any traces of magic."

Kenna blinked and glanced between us. "Just because I could see the limbus doesn't mean I can see magic — or curses, or whatever. I could be a one-hit wonder."

Jamie shook his head. "Perhaps you have not seen, because ye weren't lookin'. It's likely Addie used some sort of spell to cloak her magic. She may be evil incarnate, but she is no' daft. Ye'll ha' to look closely."

"I'm not sure I'll be able to see anything." Kenna stood, her shoulders set with resolve. "But I'll try."

"I'm coming with you." I threw the covers aside and started to scramble off the bed, but paused when the room began to spin.

"Vee, you need to rest." My friend lifted her palm to me, her voice soft but firm. "Let me do this one thing for you. Let me help *you* for once."

Remembering what I'd learned about trusting my pack, I watched her walk away, but said a quick prayer for her safety and asked the Protector to sharpen her vision. I hated the worry I felt every time one of my loved ones left a room, like it could be the last time I saw them alive.

Jamie held out the blankets, and I crawled back under. When he'd tucked me in, he situated himself on the bed beside me, stretching out his long legs as he put his arm around my shoulders. With Blaz's warm body nestled in on my other side, I snuggled in. But instead of feeling cozy, I felt restless, my mind refusing to relax.

Winter blasted the windows of my tower, rattling the glass in their frames, a constant reminder of the evil that lurked just out of sight. I fingered the Ring of Aontacht, turning it and rubbing each symbol with the pad of my thumb. Its energy flowed up my arm and filled my soul with reassurance. We were not powerless in this fight.

"I'll agree to the extra guards and someone to watch my back, but I'm not hiding in this room."

Jamie stiffened. "This is the safest place in the castle. The most defensible."

"Think about it — Addie tried to murder me with an ancient curse locked in a pendant. And when that didn't work, she pushed me out of Doon multiple times. Then when I came back, she hurtled a tree at me." Jamie's profile hardened as he stared out the window. "Her attempts are getting less artful and more desperate."

He pulled his arm from around my shoulders and shifted to face me, his eyes dark with concern, his mouth pressed in a firm line. His first instinct was to protect me, his Calling and his queen, so I appealed to the strategic side of his brain.

"You told me yourself, an early retreat would be a victory for my enemy."

"Aye, but tha' was — "

I shushed him with a finger on his lips. "What better way to draw her out than for me to flaunt myself throughout the kingdom? The more desperate she gets, the more vulnerable she becomes."

A muscle ticked in Jamie's jaw. "I dinna like it."

I took his hand in mine. "I don't like any of this, but the sooner we can bring this thing to a head, the sooner it can end." And I could bring back the baseball-cap-wearing, churro-eating boy whose carefree grin could power a small city.

Meeting Jamie's solemn gaze, I lifted my chin with determination. "Besides, Addie should've learned by now. I'm not that easy to kill."

CHAPTER 24

Mackenna

If I lived to be three hundred years old — and now that I was back in Doon, it was not outside the realm of possibility — I would still never understand the appeal of sports musicals. Whoever conceived that *Rocky*, an underdog story about a boxer, would be better with song and dance numbers had undisputedly taken one too many punches to the head. The boxical had debuted on Broadway the summer I'd lived in Chicago and, aside from a pretty song about rain, had failed to inspire . . . confirming my belief that show tunes and sports did not mix well.

Yet, as I stared down my straw-stuffed bag of animal hide while in the village's first girls-only gym, I couldn't help but hum "The Eye of the Tiger." As I faced an entire hour dedicated to jabbing and kicking my way through Analisa's class, I decided I'd much rather be performing *Rocky* than reenacting it.

Fortunately for me, the instructor was late. And while some of the Destined girls were using the time to get their *Crouching Tiger, Hidden Dragon* on, I was more interested in observing than demonstrating my Kung Fu Panda skills, if I'd had any to begin with … which I didn't.

Smack!

I staggered back several steps, flailing my arms like a scarecrow.

Vee steadied herself before frowning at me. "You're supposed to be holding the bag for me."

"Sorry," I muttered, stepping back up and bracing my arms against the leather. "I was surveilling the crowd. That's a word, right?"

"Not so loud," she hissed, ignoring my question. She steadied her posture and took a slow, deep breath. Exhaling in a roar, she landed a single punch that made my teeth rattle.

"Geez. Remind me not to get on your bad side. Did someone pee in your Cheerios?" I leaned into the bag as she set her feet, lowered her chin, and jabbed again.

"Just picturing a certain—" She stopped and glanced around before whispering, "*Wicked* person's face."

But which person? Of the two dozen or so Destined who had either crossed the bridge or trekked through the mountains at the last Centennial, I only knew a handful well. Did the witch have other minions doing her bidding while she walked around pretending to be one of us?

I'd lain awake the night before thinking about the Destined, and no matter how I scrutinized them, my mind always came back to Ana, the criminal who'd claimed to have been Called to Doon for service. Something about her set me on edge, but I'd been hesitant to voice my suspicions because of her friendship with my boyfriend. If I was going to accuse her of being the witch, I needed more than a gut feeling. I needed solid proof.

Speaking of the devil, Analisa burst through the storefront door. Clad from head to toe in black Lycra and spandex, her modern attire indicated that she'd specifically packed work-out clothes for her trip across the bridge. That in itself seemed highly suspect to me. And with her two-tone hair gathered in a sleek ponytail, she reminded me of a Japanese assassin.

"Sorry I'm late, girls. I took a long run in the castle gardens and lost track of time. We'll get started in just a moment." Other than a red nose, she didn't look like she'd been out in the elements — no perspiration dotting her face, no panting for breath. Either she was one of those fitness freaks who never got winded or she'd been up to no good.

I watched her stretch her long, graceful limbs, looking for signs of decay underneath the facade. What if I'd been too quick to dismiss that burning in my gut as jealousy when it'd been something else entirely? I opened my mouth to voice my suspicions to Vee just as Ana called out, "Let's get started, shall we?"

After ten more minutes of holding the bag while Vee did combination drills, I was wobbly. When it came time to switch, I motioned for Fiona to take over and stumbled to the door in search of air.

As I stepped outside, I could feel eyes staring at my back. With a sudden pivot, I caught the impression of Ana's smirking face as she turned back to the class. How could I prove she was a card-carrying member of the Evil League of Evil before she pulled out her freeze ray and stopped the world?

"Do ye think Analisa's the Witch of Doon?" Sofia's voice at my shoulder startled me. I shifted my attention to see Jamie's petite ex-girlfriend watching my reaction through shrewd ebony eyes. With the howling wind, I hadn't heard her follow me out.

Quickly checking my reaction, I glanced at Eòran to make sure he hadn't overheard. Fortunately, Mutton Chops seemed riveted by the queen getting her ninja skills on. I tugged on Sofia's arm to guide her away from the gym window and asked, "Why would you say that?"

"Because I'm observant." The bitter wind tugged dark spirals out of her braid, so that the whip-like tendrils lashed at her cheeks. She'd thought to grab a couple of plaid wraps, which she'd draped around her small body to keep out the cold, and proved her attention-paying skills by handing me one. As the woolen warmth settled around me, I nodded for her to continue.

"The weather never changed like this when Lucius Jobe crossed inta Doon."

"How can you be sure?" Vee'd scoured every book in the library that had anything to do with the Witch of Doon or her known minion, Lucius. If there'd been any record of weather, Vee'd have mentioned it. What did Sofia Rosetti have access to that the queen didn't?

Looking fairly pleased with herself, she offered me a sly smile. "I reviewed all the interviews that my brother and sister conducted and cross referenced them with the queen's research notes." Before I could inquire how she got Vee's notes, she supplied, "Fiona got them for me. She wasna simply being kind when she said I had much to contribute."

To have this girl echo my suspicions about Analisa seem a bit convenient. Either Sofia had more information than she was sharing or she was fishing for confirmation ... or worse, she was working for the big bad. "So the freaky change in weather makes you think the witch is actually in Doon? Even though she never breached the border before."

"Aye." She shoved a tangle of curls back from her face and tucked it behind her ear. "And if ye ask me what proof I have, I've none. Just the same as ye'll find no mention of weather in any of the Lucius Jobe reports. But I feel the truth, deep inside o' me. The witch is here. I know it as surely as I know my name is Sofia Maria Rosetti."

I didn't want to offend her, but she also had been sure she'd had a Calling with a boy on the outside world, and he'd failed to materialize when the portal on the bridge opened. As carefully as I could, I said, "Didn't your instincts also lead you to believe that you had a Calling?"

Pain flashed across her face. For a moment I could read all the hope, longing, pain, and confusion that she'd experienced with her supposed Calling. "I wasna wrong about that," she answered fiercely. "I can't explain why he didna cross the bridge at the Centennial except to say that the Protector's ways are no' my own. We will meet at the appointed time—I have faith it will be so."

Analisa's class shifted from heavy bags to sparring as partners. I watched as Fiona claimed Vee before Gabby could swoop in. The younger Rosetti sister, while usually harmless, didn't know her own strength.

"Another thing." Sofia gestured toward Ana on the other side of the glass. "She was lying about where she was."

"How could you know that?"

She huddled closer to me, but we both kept our focus on what was happening in the gym. "Because I have a keen sense of right and wrong. I kin usually tell when someone is lying. She came from the opposite direction of Castle MacCrae, most likely from the road that leads inta the forest. That excuse about losing track of time in the gardens wasna true."

I angled my body to look squarely at Sofia. "So you're a human lie detector?"

"Nay." Sofia shook her head. "Nothing so grand. I canna discern the supernatural realms, or see shades of evil magic. I dinna have prophetic dreams like some — but my intuition is hardly ever wrong. Fiona's mum once told me where facts are the knowledge o' the mind, intuition is the knowledge o' the soul. I've learned ta trust my instincts, even when I lack the evidence ta prove them."

I guess on some level that made sense. Acting was about going with your gut, but I'd never thought about instincts being equally weighted with facts. "And your instincts are telling you that Addie is in Doon?"

She met my challenge with unwavering eye contact. "Aye."

"How do I know you're not one of the witch's minions?"

"I canna prove it, other than to say listen to your own instincts. My destiny — perhaps even my Calling — is intertwined with what's happening. I am supposed to stand with you." She pressed a clutched fist to her chest, her wide eyes meeting mine unwaveringly. "I know it in the core of my being; it's soul knowledge."

Fiona trusted her, as demonstrated by their sharing information about Vee's notes and their collaboration on the spell book. As I dug deep down, I felt I might be able to trust her as well. "We know the witch crossed into Doon with the Destined, but we're not sure who she's pretending to be. Your instincts are telling you it's Analisa?"

Sofia's confidence didn't waiver as she said, "I canna say for certain. All I can claim is that Analisa lied about where she'd been. From that I can conclude tha' she also lied about what she was up to. It's suspicious, but not a certainty that she's the witch. I've been trying to narrow down the Destined."

"That's what we've been trying to do." Her brow lifted in question, so I supplied, "Fergus and Fiona, the princes, Vee and me. Just the six of us."

Placing her hand on my arm, Sofia replied, "Now seven.

Not only is it my kingdom, my family and friends, who're in peril — it's my destiny to stand with you." Then more shyly she asked, "Will ye come with me ta speak ta Veronica when class is over?"

"Sure."

As I contemplated the best way to get Sofia into our inner circle, a castle page hurried up to Eòran with a written message. Mutton Chops scanned the note and then dismissed the page without the slightest change in expression. After a moment, he crossed to the gym door, cracked it open, and calmly asked to speak to the queen.

Draping a plaid around her sweaty body, Vee slipped from the gym into the frigid outdoors with Fiona in tow. Mutton Chops handed her the note. The wind whipped her ponytail into a frenzy as she read the contents. Unlike her guard, her face revealed plenty — and none of it good.

After a long pause, she looked at us, her eyes filled with shock. "Gregory Forrester is dead."

Fiona let out a soft gasp. "What happened?"

"He fell onto the saw that cuts logs in half." She shook her head as if trying to contradict the contents of the letter. "Is that a common mill accident?"

"Nay, Yer Highness." Eòran answered. His hairy face was still passive but I thought I detected worry in his beady eyes.

Biting her lip, proving that she had more on her mind than she was vocalizing, Vee said, "Please excuse us, Sofia."

"Wait." I placed my hand on the girl's arm to keep her from leaving. "Sofia knows the witch is in Doon."

"Kenna!" Vee's brow furrowed as she cast a quick glance at Eòran.

For the first time since the day I met him, Mutton Chop's careful composure cracked. But just as quickly as he'd lost it, he reined himself in, his face once again a stoic mask. "'Tis all right, yer majesty. I've had my suspicions."

Vee searched his face for several seconds. Then, apparently satisfied with what she found, she turned back to me and Sofia. "How?"

Fiona, who'd been hanging back to watch for eavesdroppers, stepped forward. "Sofia's gifted wi' a strong intuition."

"Dinna worry, Your Highness," Sofia whispered, trailing off as a group of men, both Doonians and Destined, walked past. "I havna spoken my suspicions to a living soul, except to Kenna. I only shared my theory because I believe that I might be of service to ye."

Vee's sharp gaze moved from Sofia's earnest face, to mine, and then to Fiona before settling back on the girl in question. "Okay. Please stay, Sofie. Jamie and I were supposed to go to the mill later today to meet with Gregory." She paused and glanced up at the sky, blinking away tears. "I can't believe he's really gone."

Before I could reach out to comfort her, Eòran stepped into our circle and scowled, his badger-like face puckering with deep, craggy lines. "Tha's not on your agenda for this afternoon. In fact, Prince Jamie said the two of ye were in want of some alone time and had me dismiss the guards."

Grimacing apologetically, Vee answered, "I know — and I'm sorry. Gregory had something urgent to discuss, so he asked us to meet him at the mill in secret."

"Your Highness," he scolded. "I canna protect ye if I am no' privy ta your plans."

"You're right." Vee nodded. "I'll keep you in the loop from now on. Who else knows about Gregory's accident?"

"I expect the whole village will know shortly." Eòran cleared his throat. "But I'm afeared, Your Highness, this wasna an accident."

Vee shivered hard and pulled her wrap tighter. "I was thinking the same thing. We need to be very careful. Gregory knew something, something about his brother that he wasn't comfortable putting in writing. Now we may never know what that was."

Her voice caught, and I moved over to take her hand. "We need to call a meeting as soon as possible. Tell the princes what we've learned. Compare notes."

"But no' at the castle." Eòran crossed his arms in front of his chest. "Secret passages and spy holes make it near impossible to guarantee privacy."

"My mum's cottage in the village is empty," Fiona suggested. "She's staying in the castle wi' me and Fergus for the time being. Safer that way."

But was the castle safer? Gregory didn't think so, and neither did Eòran. Not to mention the tree that nearly squashed my bestie like a bug. As long as the witch lurked through the streets of Doon, safety was an illusion.

"We should wear peasant disguises," I said as my brain started whirling with costuming possibilities. "Like Cinderella when she goes back into the woods in act two."

"That's perfect," Vee said, her voice strong again now that we had a course of action. She met each one of our gazes. "Tonight. Under the cover of darkness. Mrs. Fairshaw's cottage. Make sure you aren't followed."

CHAPTER 25

Veronica

The deep-hooded cloak concealed my face and blocked the worst of the icy wind as I made my way through the deserted streets of the village. A steady fall of snow sifted the light of the oil lanterns, creating deep shadows around every corner. I'd left Blaz behind and given Eòran the task of guarding my suite, both of them much too telling. Tonight I wasn't a queen surrounded by a bevy of guards, but a girl delivering a basket of cakes to an ill relative. If my borrowed cloak were red, instead of dingy brown, I'd fit neatly into a fairy tale.

As I neared the center of town, all the shops were closed and dark, everyone huddled inside by their toasty hearths. I envisioned myself curled up by the fire in Jamie's strong arms, the heat of his body keeping me warm. The thought alone spiked my internal temperature by several degrees.

But instead of cuddling with my fiancé on this frigid night, we'd rode to the village in a cart laden with barrels full of grain. After stowing the cart in the stables behind the Rosetti Tavern, we'd split up and continued on foot.

A loud screech gave me a start as a crow landed on a nearby awning, its jet-black eyes tracking me as I passed. Visions of the demonic zombie crow Kenna and I had encountered in the limbus pushed my feet faster. With a great flap of wings, a second crow landed on a nearby lamppost, a third cawing as it swooped over my head. I pulled my cloak tighter and resisted the powerful urge to glance behind me where Jamie trailed at a distance.

Practically running, I rushed off the main road and headed down a side street, the rapid fall of snow blinding me. A piercing wind moaned, followed by a shuffle and drag that had my heart catapulting into my throat. I stumbled on an uneven stone, righted myself, and sprinted forward. What if it hadn't been the limbus that created zombie creatures, but Addie? She'd been here all along ... there could be more.

Something grabbed me, a low voice rumbling through the stillness. "Whoa, there."

I spun with my fist raised, then exhaled a frustrated breath. "Jamie! You scared the daylights out of me!"

White teeth flashed, the rest of his face shadowed by his hood. "Sorry, love. You're goin' the wrong way. Fairshaw Cottage is the next street down." He took my arm and steered me back the way I'd just come.

Working to regulate my breathing, I panted, "I thought we were arriving separately?"

"No need. The streets are empty." He tucked me closer and pushed his cloak back a bit so I could see the still sun-darkened planes of his face. "Why were ye frightened?"

He didn't know the gory details of my run-in with the crow from hell, and I didn't feel like sharing. "I don't like crows."

Jamie's deep laughter rolled through the night. "Mayhaps they donna like you either."

"You have no idea."

The tiny stone cottage sat dark, surrounded by a frozen garden suspended in mid-autumn bloom — almost as if it had been trapped in time. As we walked up the path, a shiver shook through me, and Jamie pulled me closer to his side, mistaking my apprehension for cold.

Noticing the pristine snow beneath our feet, my steps slowed. I hated how my voice quivered when I asked, "I thought the others were arriving before us?"

Jamie stopped under the shelter of a tree and turned me to face him, his brows hunched over his eyes. "What's going on wi' you? Yesterday you were practically ready to throw yerself at Addie to draw her out. Now you're as jumpy as a feral cat. I've never seen ye this way." He reached inside the shelter of my hood and cupped my jaw, his tone softening. "Is it Gregory's death tha's got ye so shaken?"

"That's part of it. But there's something else ..." I searched his dark gaze as light snow fell between us and a perfect star-shaped flake landed on his nose before melting into his skin. Tears flooded my eyes, the beauty of the night clouded by what I now knew — something big was coming. "I had another vi — "

"Are the two of ye gonna stand there and make lovey faces all night?"

We turned to find Fergus in the open doorway.

"We're all waitin' on ye." He ducked back inside, bending to fit through the doorframe.

At my surprised look, Jamie explained, "I instructed them to enter through the back door, so if anyone recognizes us they'll think we're seekin' a bit of privacy. You were about to tell me somethin' ..."

"I think it's best if I tell you inside." We walked toward the house, and I linked our gloved fingers, his powerful heat seeping through two layers of leather. "I'd rather say it once."

After we were all settled around the large farmhouse table in the dining room, our only light a single candelabra, Jamie turned to Duncan. "Are the premises secure?"

Duncan gave a single nod. "We searched the house and grounds. It's all clear."

I sat straighter in my chair. "All right, then let's begin with our interviews of the Destined." Fiona pulled out paper and quill to take notes, and I turned to my left. "Mackenna, what did you discover?"

My BFF turned toward the newest addition to our core team. "Sofia thinks that Analisa is lying about where she was this morning."

Sofia's dark curls bounced as she nodded. "Aye."

Duncan leaned forward, his eyes skipping around the table. "I know Ana better than anyone here. She wouldna hurt a fly."

That assessment took it a bit too far. My upper thigh still ached where she'd demonstrated a proper defensive kick that afternoon. But I also knew Duncan's statement would only add fuel to Kenna's distrust. I would've felt the same if Jamie were buddy-buddy with the beautiful British girl.

As I'd feared, Kenna leaned toward Duncan with narrowed eyes. Before she could open her mouth, I stated in a firm voice, "So noted. Fergus? What did you find out?"

Following a quick turn around the table where each of us recounted our conversations with our assigned Destined, I determined we were no closer to discovering the witch's identity than we'd been the day before. The debate could last all night, but what I'd learned couldn't wait.

"There's something else." Every gaze in the room locked on me. Afraid that if I looked at Jamie I'd burst into tears, I turned to Kenna and searched her eyes for strength. She gave me an encouraging smile and took my hand under the table. I cleared my throat and began again. "I've had a vision."

Fiona sucked in a breath. "When?"

"This evening after dinner, I touched my crown — the one that used to be Jamie's mother's — to remove it from my hair, and I fell into a waking dream." Jamie's large fingers encased my other hand, his unique energy flowing through my veins. I lifted my chin and met each set of eyes around the table as I spoke. "No longer in my tower, I was outside, gazing up at a huge statue of a woman ... a queen. The monument was made of two different materials; one half shined like metal and the other half appeared softer, like clay. The ground shook, and the softer part of the statue crumbled. I lifted my arms as a large chunk fell toward me, and when I opened my eyes I was looking out over a desolate landscape from a great height." I shook my head and raised my eyes to the ceiling, fighting the tears burning the backs of my eyes. My friend and my prince squeezed my hands tighter, and I continued. "I was inside the statue and watched as pieces of Doon's cornfields, forests, the village ... all of it began to break off and fly away, disintegrating into nothingness."

"That doesna mean — "

I cut Fiona off. "There's more. I looked into the distance and saw all of Doon's people running for their lives. They split like waves, one half heading toward the mountains while the other half was led across the Brig o' Doon by someone ..." I glanced at Jamie and then Duncan. "A soldier wearing the MacCrae tartan draped across his chest led a mass of people out of Doon. I couldn't see his face. But even as half of myself was crumbling away, I knew what I saw was right — that in order to save us all, these people would have to leave the kingdom."

I paused and let that sink in before I said, "Then I saw a

battle. Fighting, blood, and death everywhere. I blinked, and I was back on the ground staring up at the statue—it had changed. It was now completely made of steel, whole and strong, and it wore a gleaming golden crown. I couldn't tell if the statue was male or female—it was as if it were both. I spun around and Doon was whole again.

"As I came back into consciousness, I heard a voice." I took a deep breath and closed my eyes, focusing on reciting the exact words. "It said, 'You will be pressed on every side, but not crushed; perplexed, but not in despair; persecuted, but not abandoned; struck down, but not destroyed. Trust. Use the armor I've given you. And a kingdom will rise up that will stand forever.'"

Silence hung in the air. The apocalypse barreling toward us could not be stopped by pulling the rubber mask off the witch and sending her away in a paddy wagon. A full-out war was coming. The unknown sacrifices that would be required of us already felt like a paralyzing weight.

"Then we must go on the offense." Jamie's voice resounded in the quiet.

"Nay, not yet." Duncan shook his dark head. "We canna reveal our hand."

"Ye heard what is coming." Jamie leaned forward. "I will no' sit idly by, waitin' for the witch to strike first!"

Duncan stiffened, his voice raising. "What would ye suggest? Imprisoning *all* the Destined until someone escapes by magic?"

Jamie slapped his hands on the table, his eyes narrowing at his brother. "Something like that, yes."

"We canna! It goes against every precept of Doon's culture. Free will to choose—"

"They will have no will at all if we donna protect them from the evil within their midst."

"Are you truly suggesting we arrest the Destined to force Addie's hand? Those people are innocent until proven guilty."

"Extreme situations require extreme action. We need to force her out of hiding. Show her we aren't defenseless pigs waitin' for the slaughter!" Jamie's entire body tensed, ready to spring.

I shot to my feet to break up the fight, but the floor moved, and I flopped back into my chair. "What the —"

" — Saints was that?" Jamie finished my question as the room shook and rivulets of dust rained down on us. Wide-eyed, we sat for several beats as the shaking grew stronger. A vase on the sideboard toppled over with a crash.

"Earthquake," Mackenna gasped. "We need to duck and cover."

A picture slid off the wall, clattering to the floor.

"Doon doesna have such things," Duncan replied, reaching for her.

"It could now th —" The candelabra toppled, cutting her off. Several of the candles winked out. Fergus and Sofia grabbed the ones that didn't and extinguished them.

In the pitch black, Jamie stood, and pulled me up by our linked hands. "I think it's comin' from outside."

Chairs screeched across the wood floor as everyone else lurched to their feet. Holding on to one another for balance, we staggered to the front of the house. I'd never been in an earth-quake, but that's what this felt like — like the ground would split open and swallow us whole. The rumble grew louder as we reached the front door. I skipped over an oil lamp rolling across the floor, lost my hold on Jamie's hand, and stumbled outside into the snowy yard.

And stopped to stare in awe.

Hundreds of cattle thundered past on the narrow street, their eyes wild like they were being chased by a ravenous T-rex.

My heart banged in time with their clattering hooves, but the sight loosened something inside my chest, and I almost smiled. This was no natural — or even supernatural — disaster. Just a bunch of terrified cows.

I turned to see all my friends lined up across the lawn, varying levels of bewilderment on each of their faces. A giggle bubbled up inside me, and I squeezed Kenna's arm, her gray eyes clear with amusement. In fact, I could see each one of my friend's expressions in perfect clarity, lit with dancing light. Goosebumps chased across my skin as I searched for the source of the odd glow. I spun around to discover the cottage roof ablaze, crackling with *purple* fire.

I opened my mouth to scream a warning, but the air was sucked from my lungs, and everything slowed to the frame-by-frame motion of a dream ... then *BOOM!*

A flash of light blinded me as a blast of boiling heat slammed me off my feet and into the air.

CHAPTER 26

Mackenna

Violet explosions blossomed beneath my eyelids as I struggled to free myself of whatever was binding me. It felt like a straitjacket, but blazing hot and pliable. Whatever it was, it had an iron grip. I thrashed about, trying to yell but making no sound. *If I could just raise my knee for some leverage ...* I bent my left leg and a lightning bolt of pain shot through me, turning the blooms under my lids white. As the wave of agony receded, I realized that I must be dreaming. If I could just go back to sleep, the world would right itself again.

"Mackenna. Open your eyes, lass." From miles away, Duncan's voice infiltrated my sleepy haze. "I've got you."

Another muffled voice — Vee's — said, "Don't let her go to sleep."

Why would my boyfriend and my bestie be so cruel as to rouse me in the middle of the night? It wasn't time to get up. Couldn't they see that? I was about to jump over the moon. I opened my mouth and tried to tell them so, but the only thing that came out was a muffled, "Moooo."

Something between a pat and a slap stung my right cheek and then my left. Then my right again, followed by the left, then right — I tried to bat the irritating sensation away but my hands were captured. Still far off, Duncan's muffled voice commanded, "Open your eyes, woman."

My lids battled opened in a series of blinks. Duncan's dirty face loomed over me. He'd been so far away a moment ago. I wanted to ask how he'd gotten to me so quickly, but the instant I opened my mouth, warm air — sooty, with the faint flavor of toasted marshmallows — filled my nose. I gagged.

Duncan pressed a handkerchief to my face. His lips were moving, but with all the other sensations assaulting my senses, I couldn't make out his words. I inhaled cautiously into the cloth. The scent of lavender flowed through me. As my body settled, I stared at Duncan. His lips — such lovely, kissable lips — moved again. I could barely make out their question. "Can ye sit up?"

I nodded once and slowly inhaled as he lifted me up. He crouched next to me, gently probing my face and neck with gentle fingertips and a tight smile that didn't quite reach his eyes. "How do ye feel?"

"WHY ARE YOU WHISPERING?" I asked.

His mouth moved again and I thought he said, "I'm not."

"SPEAK LOUDER!"

He lifted a hand toward my cheek and snapped his fingers. At least, I assumed that was what he was doing. The motion was right, but produced no sound. I never knew he couldn't snap. Vee and I had once had a teacher, in third grade, who couldn't snap. The entire class had been thoroughly entertained watching her try.

"WHAT ARE YOU DOING?"

With a frown Duncan snapped in quick succession. "Can ye no' hear that?"

"NO." If I hadn't been carefully watching him, I never would have figured out what he asked. The boy seriously needed to speak up.

A flash of light flared over his shoulder and drew my attention toward a bigger picture. Fire had nearly gutted Fiona's mom's cottage. I could feel the heat of it on my exposed skin. Lifting my arm, I marveled at the tattered fabric that had once been a sleeve. Continuing my examination, I noted that my skirt and shawl were also in shreds.

Duncan's peasant costume was equally ragged, trousers shredded nearly to the knees, half of his tunic ripped open, and a long, thick shard of wood stuck out of his shoulder. When I pointed, Duncan shrugged off his impaled bicep as if it were a minor annoyance, like a mosquito. With his good arm, he reached across his body and yanked the wood. Blood spurted from the wound when it slid free.

As I watched the shard and the blood, the sounds of the night came whooshing in. I could hear the crackle of the fire, the frantic cries of my friends, and an awful ringing sound. Ripping off a ruined portion of my skirt, I pressed the fabric against his shoulder to staunch the blood flow. "You need to keep pressure on it."

"'TIS JUS' A FLESH WOUND," he shouted.

"Why are you yelling at me?"

"Got your hearing back, did ye?" He waited for me to nod before continuing with an impish grin. "It's just a wee nick. I've had worse than this during my war games. Tear off another length o' skirt and I'll bind it up."

I did as he requested. While Duncan bound his wounds, I turned to look for my friends. Fergus, Fiona, and Sofia were getting to their feet. Other than Sofie cradling her arm, they seemed relatively okay. Vee and Jamie were already standing, the former picking debris out of the latter's hair.

Once his shoulder binding was secure, Duncan stood and hoisted me to my feet. Other than the ringing in my head and a busted-up left knee, I appeared to be in good shape. Leaning on my big, strong boyfriend for support, we limped our way over to where the others were gathered, and I stupidly asked, "What happened?"

"Ye started mooing at the top of your lungs," Fergus answered.

His wife backhanded his arm and supplied, "My mum's cottage exploded."

I stared at her as I digested that information, trying to fit it into my patchy last few minutes. "Are you okay?"

"Aye," Fiona answered. "Rattled is all. I landed atop Fergus, which was like fallin' into a cloud. But I busted his lip with my head."

The giant chuckled, swiping at the trickle of blood still oozing from his mouth. "I always knew my wee wife was hardheaded. It's one of her best qualities."

I looked beyond Fergus to Sofia, who was gingerly holding her right arm in her left. "Bruised is all," she replied to my unspoken question. "Nothing that canna be fixed with a little ice."

Next to her Vee and Jamie had swapped roles like a pair of grooming monkeys. "We're fine," Vee said in an octave higher than usual. "It could have been a lot worse."

Agreed. My knee was already starting to feel better but my recollection of falling on it was fuzzy. "Did something fall on me?"

"That would've been me." Duncan supplied matter-of-factly. "I tackled ye to the ground."

"What do you mean tackled me?"

"Just as it sounds, woman. I threw ye to the ground and covered your body with my own." He grimaced, in what I thought was remembrance but soon recognized as pain.

Circling behind him, I got a good look at his back. The shirt and coat he'd been wearing were riddled with large charred holes. The exposed skin was blistered and embedded with dozens of wooden splinters. Unable to stop myself, a small gasp escaped from my lips as my eyes filled with tears. "We need to get you to Doc Benoir."

"It can wait," Duncan grunted. "We've got more pressing matters to tend to."

"Aye," Jamie said, levelling his gaze on his younger brother. "Now will you concede that we need ta take action?"

Rather than argue, Duncan's intense gaze shifted to Vee. "I defer to my queen."

With a nod, Vee addressed the group. "I'm not waiting around for Adelaide to make another move that might get me or someone else killed. We have to go on the offensive." A tiny rivulet of blood trickled from her previous temple injury down the side of her face. She wiped it away so that it streaked her cheekbone like war paint.

While taking the offensive made for a good sound bite, it was hardly actionable. "What do you suggest? We take the Destined aside one at a time and ask them if they're the Wicked Witch of Doon?"

Vee arched her eyebrow at me. "You got a better idea?"

Was she serious — and had she really just shot me the Evil Highney? "Any idea has got to be better than that."

"Why don't you say what you really think?"

Despite her sarcasm, I couldn't stop the words from spewing out. "Fine. I think you're way out of your depth. You've got the crown and the castle but you've got no clue how to defeat the witch."

"I'm doing the best that I can!" she huffed.

"And it nearly got us killed!"

"Stop! Just stop it!" Sofia's voice, entirely too big for the tiny person it was coming from, penetrated my red haze. I took a breath and saw five sets of eyes staring at Vee and me in shock. I could count on one hand the number of real fights we'd had in our thirteen years of friendship. They were always the result of major stress, and we always felt horrible afterward.

After taking a deep, slow breath, I nodded for Sofia to continue. "You're both right," she said. "We do need to go on the offensive, and Kenna's on to something."

"What? Asking each of the Destined if they're the witch? I wasn't serious."

Sofia's ebony curls bobbed up and down. "Sort of. What if we hold a fealty ceremony?"

Like I was supposed to know what that was. "A what?"

Duncan's chest pressed against my back as his hands wrapped around my shoulders. "It's where all the citizens pledge their loyalty to the Protector and the crown as we did for Jamie at his coronation.

"Aye," Sofia continued. "After Lucius Jobe divided the land, the king held a fealty ceremony to unite the people."

But Vee dismissed the idea with a shake of her head. "Adelaide would never pledge herself to me or the Protector."

Sofia gestured with her good arm. "That's the point. She'll be forced inta revealing herself. Your vision implies we are a kingdom divided. Why not unite us and ferret out the witch at the same time?"

Understanding sparked in Vee's turquoise eyes. "Whichever Destined refuses to pledge is the witch."

"That could actually work." Fiona glanced to her husband. "What say you, Fergus?"

He scratched his baby-smooth chin. "We'd have to be prepared. Have triple guards at every exit."

With a hasty glance over her shoulder at the crackling fire, Vee asked, "How soon do you think we can do this?"

Jamie looked to Duncan, seeking his silent agreement. "Two days. All we need do is issue a decree. We can have pages go to every door in the kingdom."

"After the fealty ceremony, it's customary to hold a feast," Fergus said, rubbing his large hand over his rumbling stomach. How he could think about food after nearly being incinerated was beyond me.

Fiona chuckled. "Mags won't be happy about the short notice, but she'll accommodate the request."

The anticipation of doing something was making us all a bit giddy after the latest brush with death. Gleefully, Vee looked from one face to another. "Two days, then. Let's take out Addie before she can strike again."

CHAPTER 27

Veronica

As the Wise Men filed out of my temporary office within Jamie's suite, I moved over to the windows and began a few deep breathing exercises. Already meetinged-out, I had all of three minutes to pull myself together before my next one began. I took several cleansing breaths and positioned my arms and legs in a warrior pose.

My morning had begun at dawn with Giancarlo, his sister Gabriela, and Fergus. I'd given them the job of going out among the people before the official fealty announcement arrived. Charismatic and liked by everyone, the three of them were perfect good-will ambassadors to the crown, talking up the idea of uniting the kingdom and healing the fissures of doubt caused by Sean MacNally and his gang of dissenters.

Slow exhale.

Three grueling hours with the Wise Men had followed. I'd steered my advisors into believing the fealty ceremony had been their brilliant idea, and then we'd hammered out all the nuances of the royal decree. The wording of the announcement was a delicate matter, but my cabinet didn't know about the secret weapons I'd already dispatched just after sunrise.

I focused on elongating my muscles, filled my lungs again, and brought my hands together, arching into a half moon. The laces of my bodice strained against the movement, and I longed to change out of my full skirts into sweats and a T-shirt, but a visual representation of my power had never been more important.

Straightening, I pushed out a breath, readjusted my crown, and rolled my shoulders as a knock sounded on the door. "Come in!" I called, walking back to the seating area in front of the fire. The door opened, and a lanky bundle of fur raced into the room. "Blaz!"

He jumped up, his oversized paws now reaching above my waist. Never having had a pet before, I was astounded at how fast he grew. "I missed you, buddy." I bent and let him lick my cheek.

Eòran moved into the room and stoked the fire. "The laird asked me to send him up to ye once his training was finished for the day."

Jamie knew I would need a bit of comfort. I quirked a grin as I sat and nuzzled my puppy's silky ears. It had been Jamie's idea that I use his suite as my new office. Access to my own rooms was being limited to a chosen few, and his tower was just as easily defensible. But meeting in this room had other advantages — like his scent permeating the air, and the strength I gained from all the carefully chosen objects around me, including the Yankee's baseball cap that sat on the shelf within my line of sight.

I thanked Eòran as he left the room, and another guard announced the arrival of the next person on my agenda. My personal assistant, Emily, bustled into the room, a leather-bound notebook and quill in her hand.

The girl dipped into an awkward curtsy. "Your Majesty."

"Emily." I indicated the seat across from me. "Please sit down."

Before the girl's bottom had even touched the cushion, she began to talk. "Your Majesty, as you requested, I've ensured the sick and elderly have extra provisions, including firewood." She sucked in a breath, made a check on her paper, and continued on. "For the weekly feast we'll be serving duck à l'orange, roasted parsnips, creamed corn, fresh bread and butter, of course, and a dessert of apple and pecan tarts with fresh cream. Your dress will be — "

"Emily." I leaned forward and touched her hand, and she glanced up at me with startled blue eyes. "That all sounds perfect, but I first need to ask how you're doing?"

She blinked, and I noticed a faint purple bruise along her left cheekbone where Adam had hit her. Something like lava bubbled up within me, and I had to work to unclench my jaw and soften my tone. "After what happened with Adam, and now the accident with Gregory ... are you okay?"

"Ye ... yes, ma'am." She nodded, her light-brown bangs falling to cover her forehead as she focused on the notes in front of her. "I'm sorry to say that I never got to know Gregory very well. It's kind of like the grief you feel when you see a tragedy on TV — it's terribly sad, but doesn't affect your everyday life, so you move on." Her head whipped up. "That probably sounded horribly insensitive! I'm sorry — "

"It's fine. I understand." And I did. Death was a part of life, and she didn't know that Gregory had likely been murdered by a force of evil that sought to destroy our kingdom and everyone in it. I shivered hard and pulled my hand from hers. Folding my fingers in my lap, I met her startled gaze. "I also wanted to thank you for keeping Adam's betrayal a secret. We'd hoped we had contained the issue with his imprisonment, but …" I was unsure how much to say. But, as had become more and more common lately, she finished my thought.

"But you're concerned he's not the only one."

I searched her face before answering, her bow-like mouth set in plump, slightly blotchy cheeks, her solemn gaze meeting mine. Did she know something she wasn't sharing? "We're considering several possibilities. Including factions of Sean MacNally's gang causing dissention within the kingdom. Which leads me to our next topic."

I paused and took a sip of lukewarm tea before continuing. "This week's feast will follow a special ceremony. A royal decree is being issued throughout the kingdom as we speak." Suddenly very thirsty, I downed the rest of my tea. Emily waited with quill poised above parchment. "Announcing a fealty ceremony."

My assistant began to scribble and then paused and looked up, her head cocking to one side. "Didn't everyone already give you fealty during your coronation?"

"Actually, no. If you remember, there was a group fealty declaration, but not an individual one. The ceremony was truncated, partly due to the limbus and partly because we planned to have a kingdom-wide fealty once Jamie and I wed."

I poured more tea for myself, the pot trembling in my shaky fingers. Would we ever be married now? I wanted to wake up every morning and see his face, have him rule by my side as our Calling intended. All my silly reservations had disappeared during our time in the modern world. Perhaps the witch had done me a favor of sorts. I understood now that there were no guarantees of tomorrow. And I wanted to spend every moment I could with Jamie. But saving our kingdom came before my romantic dreams.

"Emily, would you like some tea?" I steadied the pot with my other hand.

"No ... thank you, Majesty." Her gaze flicked from the teapot to my face. "So you wish to unite the kingdom? That is ... verra wise." Something rich and pure shone from her eyes; respect, and maybe even love. And I almost told her the real reason for the fealty ceremony, but swallowed the words and commented, "You're picking up the accent here."

"Oh?" Her cheeks stained pink. "I ... I ... di ... didn't realize."

"I find myself doing the same thing at times." Sensing her embarrassment, I changed the subject. "Any thoughts on what I should wear to the ceremony?"

Emily lifted her quill and focused on her notepad. "I believe we can make a few alterations to your gown for the weekly feast ..." Her hand sped across the paper in arching strokes. "To make it more majestic, maybe even a bit somber."

After another moment, she flipped the paper around to show me a drawing of a sweeping ball gown, fit for ... well, for a queen. "What do you think about burgundy with a black overlay and onyx crystal-beaded trim?"

I met her gaze, and despite all the heaviness in my world, grinned like a girl who'd just found the perfect prom dress. "It's gorgeous."

A knock sounded just before Eòran poked his head into the room. "Yer Highness, yer next appointment has arrived."

Emily sprung to her feet and rushed to the door, calling over her shoulder, "So much time and so little to do."

Before I could ask her if she'd quoted Willy Wonka on purpose, Oliver marched through the door.

"Thanks, mate." He nodded at Eòran, who tailed him into the room. "I can take it from here."

Blaz, who'd been sniffing around the hearth, trotted to my side and stood at attention, tail down, ears up. Maybe some of Jamie's guard-dog training had sunk in after all.

Oliver dipped his head in an abbreviated bow and then flopped into the chair across from me without being invited. Eòran's face went dark, and he took a huge step forward as if to yank the Australian out of his seat and make him show proper respect. But I caught his gaze and stopped him with a shake of my head. My guard retreated, but stood by the open door, his arms crossed in front of his chest.

"Oliver, would you like some tea?"

"Why are you cutting me out?"

Startled by his hostile tone, I set the teapot down with a clang.

"Where's Adam?" Oliver leaned forward, his tanned fingers gripping the arms of the chair. "And don't tell me he's still ill, because I checked with the bloke at the clinic, and he isn't there."

A low growl sounded from Blaz's throat and I put a hand on his bristly head to calm him. I eyed a stormy-faced Eòran, hoping he would understand I wished to handle this myself.

Oliver went on, "Last time I saw him, he was as fit as a Mallee bull!"

"Adam tried to kill me." I dropped the bomb and watched Oliver's face for signs that what I'd said wasn't a surprise. He froze, his expression a comical mask of outrage and shock, and then he melted back into his chair like a popped balloon. No darting eyes, fidgeting hands, enlarged pupils, or flaring nostrils. He was either an Oscar-worthy actor, or he had no clue that his friend had tried to harm me.

Then again, I'd been fooled by Addie's disguises before.

"To be honest, we've *cut you out*"— I made an air quote with my right hand —"because we aren't sure where your loyalties lie."

He released the bridge of his nose and slanted a glance in my direction. "What's that supposed to mean?"

"Exactly what it sounds like, *mate*." Jamie strode into the room, and stopped by my side. He and Duncan had spent the morning inventorying weapons and meeting with the metal forgers. As he bent to kiss my cheek, I noticed that the burn on his jaw had scabbed over neatly. "Sorry I'm late, love. How's the arm?"

I touched my bicep where a flaming piece of wood had caught my dress on fire the night before. "Still sore, but Fiona's healing ointment has worked wonders."

Oliver sat upright, his eyes alert. "What happened?"

"Just an accident." I waved it off, unwilling to share that we'd been in Fairshaw Cottage just before it exploded into a million match-like pieces. Thank the Protector that stampede had lured us outside. I'd lain awake half the night thinking through every angle of what had happened, and I woke up knowing that cattle charge had not happened by chance. I was coming around to Jamie's belief that there were no coincidences — at least, not in Doon. I'd been saved too many times to believe otherwise.

"I finished the generator you asked me to build." Oliver's statement pulled me out of my musings. He sat ridged in his chair, a flush appearing on the slope of his cheekbones. "I used scrap bits of metal to construct a wind turbine and then set it up on the southeast battlements. With the gust we're having, it should be charged in a few hours." He scrubbed a hand over his dark hair and fixed steady eyes on Jamie and then myself. "I've done everything you asked me to do without fail and without question. My loyalty lies with Doon."

"What drew ye here, Oliver?" Jamie asked, still standing beside my chair. "How were ye Called to us?"

The Australian shifted in his seat and turned to stare into the fire, his throat contracting as he swallowed. A Calling, no matter the purpose, was intensely personal. Like myself, most believed themselves to be going a little insane before accepting that Doon could be real. Oliver's hesitation to speak about what Called him here convinced me of his innocence more than anything else.

Without turning back to us, he began to speak. "I had a good life in Melbourne, by most standards. I'd patented several inventions and then sold them to the highest bidder. International corporations had begun seeking me out to create their latest technology. I had more money than I'd ever dreamed of, but ..." His brow furrowed. "But it felt empty. I had mates and women ... lots of them." He shrugged and glanced at me with a small smile. "But no end goal. Until the dreams started. It was as if I'd been to paradise while I slept and brutally yanked back to real life when I woke. It wasn't just that Doon was beautiful. The feeling of belonging and purpose ... it was like being Called home even though I'd lived in Melbourne all my life." He met my gaze, his eyes liquefying, and I knew he told the truth.

"Thank you, Oliver. I think you've answered our question. I'm sorry to have to tell you this, but we believe Adam was sent here by the Witch of Doon."

Jamie squeezed my shoulder in warning.

"You mean Adam didn't have a Calling to come to Doon?" Oliver questioned.

"We are no' sure of that," Jamie answered. "But do ye remember him actin' suspicious? Did he say or do anythin' that could give us insight into his motivations?"

Oliver thought for a moment and then shook his head. "No, I'm sorry."

I glanced up at Jamie and he nodded.

"That will be all for now, Oliver. Thank you." I stood and shook his hand.

Next, Jamie took his hand and held it. By the pained look on Oliver's face, it was not a gentle hold. "Donna say a word of this to anyone. If ye want our trust, ye'll ha' to prove ye're worthy of it."

Oliver nodded. "You can count on me, mate."

Jamie released his hand. "Good."

After the inventor left and we were alone, Jamie said, "I dinna believe him."

"I do." I moved to the sofa where a pile of paperwork waited for my attention. "His Calling story rings true to me."

"Ye're too trusting." He crossed his arms in front of his chest, feet spread wide.

Too tired to argue, I picked up the petition on the top of the pile. "You're probably right."

Jamie's eyebrows arched into his hair. "Tha's it?"

"That's it." I shrugged and turned back to my paperwork.

"I need to change out of these dusty clothes and then I'll return to help ye with those petitions."

He strode into the bedroom and my thoughts kept circling back to the two conversations I'd just had. I knew I was missing something, but my tired brain couldn't seem to latch onto it.

I'd read the first paragraph of the document in my hand three times and was nearing my fourth when the door swung open and my BFF burst into the room dressed in head to toe black. "Come on, Highney. Field trip time."

I slumped back into the cushions. "I wish. But I've got a ton of paperwork. Maybe after dinner?"

"This is important." A heavy sack landed with a thump beside me. "And requires a costume change."

Untying the drawstring bag, I found a pair of thick leggings, a wool tunic, a cloak, and fur-lined boots — all in black. "Why do I feel like we're about to play out a scene from *Pretty Little Liars*?"

"Ha, ha." She stopped in front of me, gripping her hips. "Gather your royal fiancé and let's be off."

I sighed in resignation. I wasn't getting anything done here anyway. "Fine. Where are we going?"

Kenna's gaze darkened and her voice dipped an octave as she replied, "Into the woods..."

CHAPTER 28

Mackenna

We rode in relative silence through the wintery woodlands to Gregory and Drew Forresters' mill. The wind tugged at the hood of my fur-lined cloak, boxing my ears until my eyes watered. Duncan pulled me closer to him, but it did little good against the storm. At a farm just outside of the village, we'd switched our carriage for a sled and two sturdy work horses that plodded along unaffected by weather.

"Maybe we should turn back." Although Vee shouted, I had to strain to catch each word before the wind snatched it away.

Jamie and Duncan shook their heads in unison. Bending his head toward my ear, Duncan said, "Can ye not see how the storm's picked up since we set off on this course? The witch wants us ta turn back."

I assumed Jamie, who was talking to Vee, was saying something similar. When his lips stopped moving, she nodded and pointed over my shoulder. Sitting backward in the sled had its disadvantages, like not being able to get that first glimpse of our destination.

Abandoning the battle to keep my hood up, I twisted in my seat to see the mill in the distance. *Blessed Leonard Bernstein*, we'd arrived! As soon as the horses came to a stop, the MacCrae brothers catapulted over the sides of the sled.

I watched as Duncan and his brother efficiently hitched the horses to a post. Then Duncan jogged back to help me out of the sled. Other than a slight stiffness in his gait, there were no outward signs of the burns across his back. Still, I was attuned enough to catch how he occasionally stifled a wince when he moved the wrong way.

Not wanting to cause him any further pain, I readied myself to jump down. Before I could leap, Duncan dug both hands into the slope of my hips and hoisted me out as effortlessly as if I were a doll, which I certainly was not. He set me on the snowy ground but kept his hold of my hips. Leaning his face to mine he said, "Jamie and I want to have a wee word with the mill foreman. His cottage is just over yon bridge. You and Veronica go inta the office and get warm. We'll join ye shortly."

Anxious to get inside, I looped my arm through Vee's and propelled us toward the little office. As we staggered forward, stray bits of hair escaped, our matching ponytails lashing our faces. Like *Side Show*'s conjoined sisters, we pushed our way inside as a single being. Vee, the Violet to my Daisy, shrank against me as she blinked into the dark, enclosed space. "Brrr. It's cold in here," she lamented, her words accompanied by white bursts of breath.

My teeth chattered in agreement. "Where are all the workers?"

"Jamie said they won't come back. They believe the mill is cursed."

"Smart guys." I pulled my cloak tighter about my shoulders, scanning the walls of the Forresters' office. "Is there a thermostat in this place?"

"We have to make a fire," she replied.

"And you know how to do that?"

"Yup. Jamie taught me." She pointed to a pile of sticks in the corner. "Grab some kindling, please, while I get the tinderbox."

I grabbed an armful of branches and turned back to Vee, who was staring thoughtfully at the fireplace. "What is it?"

"There's something in the ashes. Hand me a stick, please." Her focus didn't leave the charred remains in the fireplace.

I placed a long twig in her outstretched hand, watching as she knelt to stir the cinders. "Any idea what it was?"

"Paper," she mused. "Maybe letters. Looks like parchment. But it's hard to tell. Maybe Fiona will be able to see something." Vee set down the stick and began to scoop the ashes into a copper bucket next to the hearth.

When she was finished, I set the stack of kindling next to her. Since I couldn't make a fire without matches or a lighter, I decided to put the bucket by the door, so we wouldn't forget it. The ashes weren't heavy — nevertheless, handling them made me feel vaguely uneasy — kind of the way I felt if I was forced to handle raw meat.

Holding my breath, I crossed to the door in long strides. I set the bucket near the entrance and the discomfort lifted. With Vee thoroughly occupied across the room, I decided to try an experiment. I touched the handle of the bucket, and the unpleasant sensations returned. As soon as I lifted my hand, they were gone. Staring at the ashes, I noticed tiny bits of purple, shimmering like glitter. Strange that Vee hadn't mentioned them.

When I asked her as much, she looked at me as if I'd grown an extra head. With the fire crackling in the hearth, she stood and crossed to me. "What are you talking about, Ken?"

"There," I said, pointing into the bucket of ashes. "See those tiny purple sparks?"

Vee shook her head. "Nope."

It was like the zombie fungus all over again. I was seeing things that no one else could. Then it hit me. "The purple in the ashes — it's magic. The witch must've burned the papers."

Vee's eyes widened as she filled in more gaps. "They must be related to whatever Gregory wanted to tell me."

"You said he didn't want to talk in the castle, right?"

She nodded. "He said it wasn't safe."

"Out of all the places you guys could have met, he asked you to come all the way to the mill," I said thinking aloud. "What if there's more here? Some kind of hidden clue?"

Vee chuckled. "I think you've seen one too many episodes of *Scooby Doo*, Ken. Life is never that convenient."

"Still," I said with a shrug. "We're here and we've got nothing better to do, do we?"

"Okay," she sighed. "We might as well search the office. You take the desk and I'll examine the bookcase."

I walked over to the desk and began to carefully sift through the contents of each drawer, taking extra care to discover any secret compartments. There were ledgers and invoices, ink and quills, and even an odd button or two, but no hidden spaces and nothing resembling a clue.

Just as I finished with the last drawer, Duncan and Jamie returned. Stamping off snow, they gravitated toward the fireplace, and Vee and I gravitated toward them. In tandem, Jamie wrapped his arm around Vee as Duncan pulled me against his side. For some minutes we stood in silence, enjoying the peace, warmth, and relative safety of the moment. At last Vee asked, "Did you find out anything?"

Jamie continued to stare at the fire, his voice low. "Aye. The foreman said that Gregory had been acting peculiar all morn'. Then when the rest of the lads were preparing a wagon with a shipment of lumber, Gregory started up the saw. A moment later, he was dead ..."

After Jamie paused again, Duncan continued. "He also said that the lad seemed to just lay down on the rollers. Before any o' the others could get to him, he was sawn in half."

I could feel his tremor of revulsion as it moved through him. I knew Duncan well enough to guess that he was wondering if he could have saved poor Gregory by being at the mill. But there was nothing that anyone could have done.

To ease his needless guilt, I laid my head on his shoulder, saying, "Vee noticed paper fragments in the fireplace. Whatever burned there bore the markings of Addie's magic — I saw little purple sparks in the ashes. We put everything in a bucket to take back to the castle."

Duncan placed a soft kiss on the top of my head. "Did ye find anything else?"

"Nope. Vee and I searched the desk and the bookshelf, but there's not much else here."

Duncan turned in a slow circle, his face pinched in confusion, "What happened to the bunkhouse?"

Vee blinked from one brother to the other. "The what?"

"The bunkhouse," Jamie explained. "It's a small barracks. The Forresters sometimes slept here when they were particularly busy. That's odd. The entrance used to be right where that bookshelf is."

Duncan and Jamie crossed to the shelves. On the count of three they hoisted and moved it to the side, revealing a dark space. Before Jamie could even ask for a little illumination, Duncan had lit a candle from the hearth. He handed it to his brother and then lit another for himself.

Both princes disappeared into the gloom as Vee and I hovered at the opening. The room was rectangular, narrow with a wooden bunk on each side and just enough room in the middle to walk. In the flickering light, words were visible on the walls. The same sentence written over and over — hundreds of times in the cramped space.

She asked me to.

Pointing to the words with a shiver, Vee asked, "Is that blood?"

"Aye," Duncan answered while turning in a circle. "And there are two sets of handwriting, Drew's and Gregory's most likely."

"So Addie got to both of them." Vee's grave face looked sunken in the candlelight.

Jamie hastily blew out his candle and exited the bunkhouse to take his queen's arm. "I think we've seen enough. Let's go home."

Following in his brother's wake, Duncan slipped his arm through mine. He paused long enough to grab the bucket of magic ashes, and then escorted me from the mill. As soon as we shut the door behind us, the weather picked up like a ferocious beast. Before we could get to the sled, the wind captured the bucket in Duncan's hand. His arm wrenched behind him, aggravating his recent back injury. With a yelp of pain, he let the ashes go.

The bucket tumbled to the ground and the wind caught the ashes, sucking them up into a purple cyclone. We stared in shock as the tempest lifted the debris into the sky. Within seconds, all evidence of what had burned in the Forrester's fireplace was gone.

As Jamie helped Vee into the sled and untethered the horses, I stopped Duncan in his tracks. "I can't help but wonder if we should be drawing Addie out. She got to Adam and Gregory — maybe even Drew. What happens when we provoke her? We have to assume she's even more powerful than when we faced her in Alloway. Doesn't this seem like a reckless idea?"

"Aye." He grimaced, his dark features even more pronounced against his pain-paled skin. "But what other choice do we have? We canna just sit around and wait for her to kill again."

He cupped the sides of my face, tipping my head up while he looked down at me. "We'll have six dozen men on alert, and I canna believe she'll show her true self in front of everyone. The witch not only wants the kingdom, she wants the souls in it. She'll need to proceed carefully."

I wanted — desperately — to believe him. That our crazy plan would work. "But what if she doesn't? What if she goes full-on big-bad in front of everyone?"

Duncan's warm fingers lingered against my cheeks. His eyes drank me in like a condemned man saying his final good-byes. "I pray that it never comes to that." Which wasn't an answer.

CHAPTER 29

Veronica

My grandfather once told me that our character is defined in the moments when we think we can't go on: when we're terrified to give a presentation, or stand up to the person we're most afraid of, or lay dying of cancer in a hospital bed. In those moments we choose weakness or courage. When my grandpa passed on, he looked death in the face and welcomed it, because even though he couldn't see what waited for him on the other side, he had faith — a belief that had sprouted from thousands of choices, tiny seeds that had grown into an unshakable oak tree.

In the antechamber off the throne room, I took my last few minutes alone to examine my reflection. The fiery jewels of my new tiara glinted against the dark hair piled on top of my head, the up-do creating an illusion of height. I adjusted the folds of my regal, floor-length mantle, and the tiny gemstones and gold thread swirling over the snowy fabric sparkled in the light. I lifted my chin, set my jaw, and gazed into my determined eyes. And a queen stared back.

But on the inside I trembled like a sapling in the wind. I faced an opponent that was not only a psychotic killer with the aspirations of Hitler and the powers of Voldemort, she was invisible. When I stepped into the throne room, I might as well be wearing a red and white bull's-eye. Addie could be anywhere — watching me from the audience and guffawing at my feeble attempts to draw her out, or lurking in the shadows ready to zap me dead on the spot.

Squeezing my eyes closed, my heart beat a tattoo that stole my breath. Why had I been chosen for this role? Why would Doon's Protector choose a young, broken girl from the Midwest with no magic, and no special skills outside of executing a perfect pirouette, to lead a kingdom into war? I balled my hands into fists and flung my head back, ranting at the twenty-foot ceiling, "How am I supposed to do this?"

"With our help."

I glanced in the mirror to find my best friend and my fiancé entering the room. I whirled around, too grateful to have them with me to be embarrassed that they'd witnessed my moment of weakness.

Jamie moved to my side. "You're no' alone, Verranica."

Kenna's eyes latched onto mine. "We're all in this together."

"My ma always said there is power in unity." Jamie's voice was soft, but firm. "Individually, we may be no match for the witch, but woven together we're unbreakable."

"Like a four-stranded cord," Duncan said as he entered the room.

Or a wolf pack, I thought with a secret smile.

"Make tha' seven." We all turned to see Fergus and Fiona slip through the door before Duncan closed it.

Kenna, utilizing her brilliant observations skills, commented, "I may not be a math girl, but I think you just skipped a number."

"Donna ever forget the Protector." Fiona took my hand and then Kenna's and lifted our rings into the light, their stones shining pure and strong. "There is untapped power in each o' you that you only need call on at the appropriate time."

Kenna and I exchanged a long look. Together, we could do this. We had to.

"Speakin' o' the time." Fergus tilted his head toward the doorway. "Everyone is assembled."

"All of the Destined?" I asked.

My enormous friend bowed. "Aye, Yer Majesty, they're all here."

Jamie stepped forward. "Are the guards stationed around the perimeter?"

"And interspersed among the crowd?" Duncan added.

"Aye, my lairds," Fergus responded with a nod.

Kenna bumped my shoulder and muttered, "Why do I feel like we're the last people on the *Titanic*? Clearly, I get to be the Unsinkable Molly Brown." She flipped her red hair over her shoulder with a flourish and batted her eyes at me. "You can be Kate Winslet. Sorry about your luck, Jamie."

I rolled my eyes and bit my lip against a grin. Her grim humor had a way of forcing me outside of myself — lacing even the darkest circumstances with hope. I grabbed her hand and pulled her close.

Fiona took Fergus's hand and gathered us all into a tight circle where she said a quick, ardent prayer. As she asked for the witch to be revealed and for each of us to have the strength and wisdom to stop Addie's evil plans, something bloomed inside of me, fortifying my spine and pushing out my fear.

I'd been Called here for a purpose — a destiny that was inexplicably linked with not only my best friend and my prince, but a malevolent force that had stalked Doon for centuries. I didn't understand why I'd been made queen at this moment in time. But the choice of how I would face the challenge was mine — and I chose to stand as an unwavering oak.

Lifting my head, I leveled my gaze on each one of my loved ones' faces in turn. "Addie may have thought she gained the advantage by entering Doon, but she's on *our* turf now." There were several impassioned 'Ayes' before I continued. "We're about to bring that witch's reign of terror to its final end. No more epilogues, sequels, or comebacks. This is it." I lifted my chin, my next words ringing out, "We do this for Doon."

Jamie's eyes blazed into mine, his voice deep and strong. "For Doon."

Our fingers still linked, Kenna raised my and Duncan's hands above our heads. "For Doon!"

Then everyone lifted their arms into the air and declared in unison, "For Doon!"

Following a few more encouraging words, we broke our huddle and my friends began to file out of the room. I was to wait until Reverend Guthrie spoke his piece about the fealty being a covenant with the Protector before making my grand entrance. I'd turned to look over my notes for the ceremony when warm fingers wrapped my upper arm. Despite the gravity of the moment, I smiled — I would know his touch a thousand feet beneath the ocean.

"I've a gift for ye."

I set down my paper and looked up into Jamie's eyes, so often hard and guarded, shining bright with love, and perhaps a hint of anguish. After being queen, I understood why he'd learned to hide his feelings from the world. But I could read his beautiful face like a favorite book, and it made me giddy knowing I was the only one.

"You do?"

He released my arm to withdraw something from his pocket, and I noticed his appearance for the first time that evening. He wore his dress kilt, a formal black jacket draped with the MacCrae tartan, a jeweled sword at his hip—and he'd cut his hair. The short layers were swept up and off of his forehead, the sides and back trimmed close. I stepped into him and ran my hand down the nape of his broad neck, missing the way the strands used to curl around my fingers. The style accentuated his sharp cheekbones and strong nose, making him appear older, and somehow more ... Jamie. "Why did you cut your hair?"

A muscle flexed in his jaw, a furrow appearing above his left brow. "For battle."

My gut tightened, and I felt the blood drain from my face. I knew it was coming, the vision had been crystal clear, but I still hoped it could be avoided somehow. That we could take the witch by surprise and end this before it spiraled out of control.

"Hey." He cupped my cheek, his hand dwarfing my face. "Donna lose courage, love. I've been preparin' for this all of my life. But I donna want to talk about that right now." His thumb brushed over my cheek, setting my skin on fire despite all the other emotions fighting for my attention. Intensity tightening his lips, he released my face and then placed something in my hand.

I glanced down to find a bunch of ribbons, each strand saturated in the vibrant colors of a rainbow.

"They're for our handfastin'," he explained.

My heart did a twirl in my chest as I remembered that multicolored cords were used to bind the couple's hands together in a symbol of commitment.

He tipped up my chin, his dark eyes penetrating my soul. "Verranica, I vow to ye that no matter what happens, we will be handfasted within a fortnight. Nothing will keep me from makin' you mine in truth."

The reasons for the Completing had never been clearer to me than in the days since I'd returned to Doon. Jamie's calm-in-the-storm-strength, flawless logic, and natural leadership were the perfect complement to my blind determination, idealism, and sometimes reckless enthusiasm. I *needed* him by my side for the good of the kingdom, and my heart.

I glanced at him under my lashes. "How soon after the handfasting can we marry?"

He broke into a full-blown, dimpled grin. "As soon as ye like."

I arched a brow. "The next day?"

He gathered me in his arms, and lowered his head until his mouth hovered a hairsbreadth from mine. I drank in his sweet breath as the low timbre of his voice vibrated inside me. "The same day."

Our lips met, and the rest of the world faded away, everything but Jamie's touch — the liquid fire of his mouth moving on mine, the electric caress of his fingers on my neck, my face. He cupped my cheeks, his mouth sliding across mine with bone-melting deliberation. Stars danced behind my eyelids as he nipped my bottom lip and then caught me when my knees buckled beneath me.

A knock sounded and we broke apart. The air charged and heavy between us, we each panted for breath. Jamie's gaze pierced mine, his eyes communicating all he couldn't say — whatever happened after we stepped from this room, he was mine and I was his. Forever.

I swiped a hand across my tingling lips and straightened my shoulders. "Let's do this."

He nodded once and presented his bent elbow to me. After

ensuring the ribbons were tucked safely in the pocket of my skirt, I placed my hand on his forearm. "Blaz?"

"He's with Lachlan and his family."

I looked up into Jamie's dark eyes one last time, the flecks of gold shining like a beacon. "Thank you."

He winked, making me smile as Fergus opened the door. "'Tis time."

After traversing a short hallway, we entered the packed throne room. The crowd felt unnaturally hushed as the horns split the silence, announcing my arrival.

"Presenting your Called monarch, the brave and honorable, her Majesty Queen Veronica!"

Jamie squeezed my hand and I separated my arm from his, walking forward on numb feet. As I reached the center of the dais, a cheer went up, followed by applause, every Doonian rising to their feet. The show of unmitigated support fortified the steely resolve growing inside of me, and I beamed. These were my people, my family, my home, and I would stop at nothing to protect them.

CHAPTER 30

Mackenna

Some of my most and least favorite musicals had to do with royalty — always in a totally fictional, myths-and-legends kind of way. Maybe if I'd grown up in the UK with real monarchs, it would be easier to wrap my mind around royals as more than the stuff of fairy tales. But my American childhood had conditioned me for fantasy, not politics.

I stood in the front of the throne room watching as the MacCrae princes, first Jamie and then Duncan, knelt in front of my bestie on the sacred stone Doonians called the *Liath Fàil* and pledged their lives. In that moment there were no relationships outside a queen and her loyal subjects. In my mind Vee and I were two parts of a whole, equal and complimentary pieces. But in Doon that was no longer true. Vee was the leader of the country, followed by the royal family. Even when I married Duncan, I would be, at best, fourth in the pecking order.

Could I pledge my allegiance as her subservient and faithful subject in total sincerity? She was practically my sister — I couldn't envision a day when she would not take my thoughts and feelings into account, but if it ever were to happen, could I obediently follow? Could I sacrifice my own will to hers? That's what was on the line.

As I puzzled out what the vow meant for me personally, Vee's advisors, the Wise Men, made their oaths. After them came Fergus and the queen's royal guard. It had been Duncan's brilliant idea to have the advisors and soldiers pledge before the other citizens. He hoped it would make them less susceptible to the witch's influence. After making their vows, the queen's guard lined the far aisles on both sides of the throne room — another tactical decision. These men would control the flow of subjects as the rest of the Doonians made their vows and filed back into place.

To my right, Fiona squeezed my wrist. "Our turn," she whispered and turned toward the center aisle, her gentle grip encouraging me to do the same. Behind me, Analisa, Emily, Sofia, and Gabriella followed. As Vee's inner circle, we would make our vows next.

Still feeling mildly conflicted, I silently watched Fiona climb the two steps to the altar and gracefully drop to one knee. As she pledged her fealty, I worried about our plan. What were the odds that we could identify and apprehend Addie without casualties?

After kissing the brilliant red stone of the ring on Vee's finger, Fiona rose, and then it was my turn. Suddenly, my legs went wobbly as I rushed up the two steps to the altar to speak the oath that would forever change the dynamic between me and my other half. For a moment I just stared, searching beneath the crown and mantle for the girl who'd shared all my deepest secrets since kindergarten. Reverend Guthrie cleared his throat. "Kneel, please."

I immediately dropped to one knee on the rough sandstone

slab in the center of the dais. The momentum of my movement caused me to sway off balance. Before I could go sprawling on my butt, Vee's hand grabbed mine. As she steadied me, I glimpsed a flash of metallic color at her wrist. I didn't need more than a glance to know it was half of a silver heart encrusted with fake jewels that read *ST ... NDS*. The matching other half of the charm bracelet, *BE ... FRIE* was somewhere on the dresser back in my turret room. It had been our Christmas gifts to one another back in first grade, bought with our own money. That she would wear it for this occasion brought tears to my eyes. As my best friend, I trusted her with my whole life. I could and would trust her as my queen.

"Ready?" she asked softly.

I nodded and then spoke the words that Duncan had helped me rehearse. "I, Mackenna Louise Reid, promise on my faith that I will, now and always, remain loyal to my queen. Will never cause her harm, and will, in all things, observe my homage to the kingdom o' Doon. I pledge my devoted counsel in all situations and vow to protect the queen with my life, against all persons and in all circumstances, in loyalty and without deceit."

The little charm tinkled as I reached for her hand and kissed the Ring of Aontacht. She helped me rise and then crushed me in one of her bear hugs. For only me to hear, she said, "I couldn't do this without you. I love you."

I left the dais feeling vaguely lightheaded when Analisa's voice shattered the reverence of the room. "Sorry, Veronica. I just can't."

I whirled around to see Analisa towering over Vee directly in the center of the altar. "I've been tryin' to justify kneeling down to you, but it goes against my grain. It's not in my nature to follow blindly."

My heart lodged in my throat, cutting off my air. I glanced toward Duncan, who had his hand out, preventing the guard from moving in. "Ana," he cautioned. "Think carefully. Not pledging fealty to the queen is an act of treason. You could be imprisoned."

"That's tyranny, innit? Forcing me to pledge obedience. I won't do it." Analisa whirled to face the crowd. "I've been Called to Doon, same as many of you. Maybe it's time for modern government — a democracy. Maybe that's why we were Called here, to change the way things work."

With a pained expression, Duncan dropped his hand. He shared a look with Jamie, who ordered, "Arrest her."

The guards rushed toward the dais as the crowd erupted in chaos. Seeing that she was trapped, Ana grabbed Vee's arm. "You don't have to do this, Vee. We can agree to disagree and live peaceably."

As the initial wave of soldiers reached Analisa, Giancarlo Rosetti jumped to his feet, pleading with Vee to let Ana go. The guards tackled Analisa, who still had a grip on Vee. Suddenly Giancarlo and the rest of the Rosetti boys were flinging themselves into the middle of the guard. With a growl, Fergus joined the scuffle. From the outside, it looked like a single organism of arms and legs and teeth.

Somewhere in the middle of the chaos were Doon's queen and Analisa. And any minute now Ana could go full-on big-bad. "Hurry!" I yelled.

I could see Jamie and Duncan on the opposite side of the fighting mass, ineffectively trying to reach Vee. Suddenly the fighting shifted, and Vee was thrust away from the rabble. Unable to get to her across the bodies, I could only watch as she flailed backward and crashed into the unforgiving stone floor. Her crown toppled from her head and clattered down the steps, sliding to a stop in the middle of the aisle.

After the sudden burst of commotion, the room became still. All eyes turned to the queen, and she picked herself up from the floor. Her elaborate hairdo now hung in haphazard wisps around her head as she raised herself to her full height.

With an unwavering gaze, she addressed her guard. "Fergus, take half your men and please escort Analisa and the Rosettis to the dungeon. Make sure you isolate them. I'll send word when the fealty ceremony is over."

Mario Rosetti stepped into the aisle flanked by his wife. "Your Majesty, Giani did not mean any harm. He was defending his *amore* — his love, and his *fratelli* were defending him. *Per piacere*, be lenient with my *ragazzi*."

Queen Veronica listened imperiously. "Right now they are only charged with disrupting the ceremony, which must be finished. I will be willing to discuss leniency after. Fergus, take them to the dungeon."

As half the royal guard escorted Analisa and the Rosetti boys out of the throne room, something niggled inside my brain. If Analisa was the witch, why hadn't she revealed herself ... or zapped the guard with her magic? Surely there wasn't an advantage to continuing to keep secret who and what she was.

Vee walked back to the center of the dais and smoothed out her gown. In a calm, authoritative voice she said, "Let's continue with the ceremony. My crown, please."

I moved toward the aisle to retrieve Vee's crown, but Emily beat me. Holding the circlet in her hands, she offered me a sweet smile. "I've got this."

The girl climbed the steps and crossed to face Vee on the sacred stone. "Did ye know, Veronica, that you're standing on the true Liath Fàil, the Stone of Scone? The one sent to Westminster Abbey in 1296 was a fake. The real coronation stone has been hidden in Doon this whole time. This stone is able to turn peasants into rulers. And unlike a glass slipper or a sword encased in rock, its power is real."

Emily's words were pleasant, but as she spoke, Vee's face turned pale, her eyes growing wide and alarmed. The remaining guards, along with Eòran, Jamie, and Duncan, were still toward the back of the room as Emily turned to face the crowd. While holding Vee's crown, her free hand slipped into the bodice of her dress to reveal Queen Lynnette's charred luckenbooth pendant. Then, with a smile that chilled my blood, she grasped the crown with both hands and held it up over her head.

"My fellow Doonians, I am Adelaide Blackmore Cadell, rightful queen o' Doon — come to claim my throne." Emily placed the diadem on her head. "Wee Veronica is right. The fealty ceremony must continue. Only now, you will pledge your undying allegiance to me."

CHAPTER 31

Veronica

The soft curves of Emily's face began to morph before my eyes. In a flash of nightmarish déjà vu, I watched as her hair lightened to a golden blonde and grew like Play-Doh out of her skull and down her back. My assistant's rounded cheeks sharpened, and the skin of her face pulled tight over high cheekbones, her nose thinning and elongating. She arched her back and the extra weight Emily carried disappeared like an illusion, to reveal the tall, athletic frame of a twenty-something woman.

Not a woman, a witch.

With a quick flick of her wrist, the drab gray dress Emily had worn transformed into a blood-red silk gown, the exact shade of the jewels in my crown — the one *she* now wore. The very crown she'd designed for me.

No. Not for me, for her. I'd counted Emily among my friends. I clenched my hands into fists as the betrayal washed over me.

Addie ran her hands down the smooth material hugging her hips. "Ah, much better."

Her brilliant violet eyes focused on me, and the unnatural light there dropped my stomach to the floor. Her lips tilted as she touched the damaged luckenbooth hanging around her neck. "This little bauble no longer holds any power, thanks to you, my dear." Her voice slithered around me like a python squeezing my chest. I sucked in a deep breath as she went on. "But I'm nothing if not sentimental, and this piece represents a promise. A promise Queen Lynnette made to my family long ago. Do you know what that was?"

Unwilling to give her the smallest concession, I lifted my chin and replied, "No."

"Liar! You know your throne is rightfully mine!" She took a step toward me, her hand reaching out as a ball of light formed in her palm. "But we canna have two queens, now can we?"

"Stand down, witch!" Jamie leapt onto the stage, followed by Duncan, Eòran, and several of the royal guard. Jamie, sword raised, pressed forward cautiously. "Surrender and I will no' run ye through."

Addie froze, the magic in her palm retreating as the guards circled her, their swords raised. "Why, Prince Jamie," she cooed, her words taking on an almost physical quality. "I thought we had an understanding."

My gaze darted to her hand, her fingers twisting in a circular motion as she worked to enthrall him. To steal his will. I searched Jamie's face, his expression hadn't changed, but he couldn't get close enough to Addie to do any damage.

Jamie's eyes darted to Duncan, who gave a slight nod before he leapt forward, but it was as if he'd hit a wall, and stumbled back.

My turn. There was authority in the royal monarch of Doon, a link to the covenant that gave the chosen ruler's words a weight that a subject of Doon could not resist. With no idea whether or not Addie still qualified under that heading, I stepped forward on shaky legs and raised my voice so the entire throne room could hear. "Adelaide Blackmore Cadell, by the authority of the crown, you are under arrest for high treason—"

Addie turned, her eyes narrowed, but before she could lift her hands in my direction, Duncan tried again, his dirk aimed at her throat. A shriek split the air, and both Addie's arms flew out. Violet light flashed from her hands, blasting everyone around her off their feet. I staggered back, but didn't fall. Not so for Jamie, Duncan, and the entire royal guard, who flew through the air, landing hard.

"Enough!" Addie screamed as she swiped the blood from her neck and stared at the red streaks on her hand. She leveled murderous eyes on Duncan's sprawled form. "You, young prince, will die for this!"

She raised her palm, and black fire arched toward him.

I heard Kenna shriek as the magic hit Duncan. He writhed, his limbs convulsing, but after a few seconds, he fought through it and staggered to his feet. Sword in hand, eyes blazing, Duncan advanced.

I searched for Jamie and found him dazedly rising from where he'd landed on the other side of the stage.

Addie's brow furrowed. She took a powerful breath, and then threw out both her hands, delivering double streams of fire. "I said, *die!*"

"NO!" I screamed.

The magic slammed into Duncan and he stumbled back, his face contorting in agony. Out of the corner of my eye, I saw a blur of red and aqua as Kenna raced past. Jamie rushed in from the other direction, both of them headed into the line of fire. Without further thought, I ran, ducked my head, and tackled

Addie to the ground. The black flames flashed harmlessly over the crowd before going out.

Stunned, Addie lay still. As I heard feet pounding toward us, the words *stop her* repeated in my head. I rolled to the side and grabbed Duncan's abandoned knife. Addie, coming out of her daze, sat up and shot flames in my direction just as I slammed the blade into her other hand, pinning it to the stage. Her screech of pain seemed to channel into the magic she flung at me. I braced for the blow. But nothing happened.

A white glow had sprung up from my ring like a shield, glowing all around me, just like the limbus when Kenna and I had ventured inside. Glancing up at the crowd that had gathered around us, I registered the shock and awe on each of their faces. I met Jamie's fierce stare, and he stepped forward, but I shook my head, willing him to stay put. He paused, tension coiled in every muscle. Carefully, I rose to my feet.

Addie closed her fist, cutting off the spell. "So you're somehow protecting yourself and your inner circle. But what happens when I do this?" Her eyes narrowed just before she pulled the knife out of her hand and flung it with perfect precision into the chest of one of my royal guardsmen. The man toppled over, eyes wide.

"Ah ... so they can be killed." Addie stood, healing the wound in her hand with one zap.

Jamie and several others sprang forward, but the witch was ready. With a broad sweep of her arm, a charcoal cloud enveloped them, petrifying every one of those who'd sworn fealty to me like statues in Medusa's garden. "I may no' be able to hurt your minions, but I can stop them."

"They're *not* my minions!" I raised my ring and focused all my energy into some kind of unfreezing spell. When nothing happened, Addie threw back her head and cackled. A rumble cut her laughter short.

Chaos erupted from the crowd, followed by shouts as the Doonians rallied.

"Let's get her, mates!" Oliver's voice was unmistakable.

"Aye!"

"She canna stop us all!"

Addie lifted her wrist in an inpatient flick, and sent a wave of smoke rolling through the rest of the Doonians, solidifying them as well.

With a snap of her fingers, Adam and Sean MacNally pushed through the frozen bodies, their enthrallment clear in the vacant look in both their eyes. They each grabbed one of my arms, pinning them to my sides. I jerked against their iron grips, but they only tightened their hold.

Addie glided forward, her vivid gaze burning into me like a laser beam. "I may not be able to hurt you, *wee queen*, but I will have my way yet. Wait and see."

I wanted to spit in her smug face, scream insults that would scorch her ears for centuries. But I was terrified she would plunge a knife into someone else's heart. I needed to keep her talking. "You know killing me won't work. The throne would only pass down to Jamie, and if you kill him, to Duncan, and so on until you've killed every last Doonian. Then who would you rule?"

Her contemplative gaze swept me from head to toe. "I had hoped, since ye are not Doon-born, that I could kill ye, and then your pretty prince would be so heartbroken he would be putty in my hands. I see my mistake now. The Covenant is linked to the ruler. The Protection of Doon resides inside o' you." She drew a circle with her finger in front of my chest, purple light hanging in the air like the aftermath of a sparkler. "But I can destroy you in a thousand little ways, and in the end I *will* take your precious kingdom."

I swallowed hard, and forced myself to stare into her evil gaze. "The Protector gave me a vision." Straining toward her, I growled, "You. Will. Lose."

"Ah, your precious Protector." Addie stretched the word out. "Means nothing to me."

Turning her back, she began to pace. "For the next portion of our entertainment, you will be my silent captive. If you interrupt me in any way ..." She gave a sharp nod as another one of her mindless slaves came forward. The bald head and disfigurement of his face were unmistakable. Gideon. As I noted the alertness of his expression, I realized he wasn't enchanted, but serving the witch of his own free will. My heart gave a squeeze. He'd fooled us all.

A grin split Gideon's face, and he pulled a young teen up the stairs of the platform. A bob of bronze waves framed wide-brown eyes—Greta, one of the kids in the Crew.

As Gideon yanked Greta past where Jamie stood, my prince remained immobile, but his eyes followed. The fear I read there sparked a fire in me, and I rammed the heel of my boot down hard on Sean's foot. He released me, but Adam held tight. I spun and thrust a fist into Adam's stomach. Sean caught my arm and drew me back.

"Get off of me!" Wild, I struggled against them, kicking and twisting. "She's just a child!"

The smack hit my cheek with the force of a sledge hammer, knocking my head sideways as pain exploded in my left eye. Squinting through tears, Addie's smug face wavered before me.

"As I was saying." She arched one dark brow, her scarlet lips curling up. "You will watch in silence, or Gideon will snap the girl's wee, freckled neck."

CHAPTER 32

Mackenna

Scene Freeze. How I hated this game!

I concentrated on staying rigid as Gideon dragged Greta past me. I had no doubt that Addie would have her killed if I tried anything. Besides, no one was in any immediate danger, except from boredom as Addie strutted around Vee and her frozen subjects like a malevolent peacock.

If this were a play, now would be the time for an expository speech from the antagonist explaining how they came to this point. Addie was not about to disappoint. The only way she could be more cliché is if she wore a pointy black hat and carried a broom.

In a low tone, meant not to be overheard by the Doonians, Addie began her victory gloat. "Ah, Veronica. You canna have any inkling how revolting the past months have been — constricted as unshapely, sad Emily ... without my magic, kowtowing to you. 'Yes, Your Highness. Right away, Your Highness.' Mustering up tears for that simpleton Drew Forrester. Having to deal with his overly inquisitive brother. Seducing Adam and

Sean into believin' they were my one and only love." She chuckled. "So odious ... but so worth the trouble."

"And using you and your insipid friend as vessels to regain my magic — such poetic justice. You two did everything I wanted — carried my magic inta Doon, retrieved my spell book, and liberated the rest of my power buried deep within the Pictish stone. I jus' want you ta know, I couldna be here without you."

She glanced at Gideon, whose hands were wrapped around the young girl's neck. "Remember, Your Highness, one word and she dies. The same goes for you, Mackenna."

I held my breath and forced myself not to react as Addie turned to me. "I know your stage tricks, dearie. Fool me twice ... well, I'm too smart for that. Do we have an understanding?"

Greta yipped as Gideon tightened his grip in warning and Addie's brows lifted to emphasize her point. I slowly nodded, and she responded with a wide smile. "Lovely. Let's continue with the fealty ceremony, shall we?"

She reached for Queen Lynnette's locket, lifting it over her head. "Unfortunately, I've had ta part with the ring I'd planned to use on the occasion, but the locket should do nicely." She wound the chain around her finger in an improvised ring.

"Citizens of Doon, my dear subjects." She addressed the crowd like Evita speaking to her adoring masses. "I've waited a long time to take my place among ye as your rightful queen. If ye pledge to me, ye will find me a most benevolent ruler, as ye shall now see."

She waved her long fingers so that a hazy purple tendril of magic began to slither through the crowd. "Eòran, step forward."

Not of his own will, Vee's most dedicated guard lurched forward with jerky, resistant steps. When he came to a frozen stop in front of Addie, she reached out and stroked his bushy face with long purple nails. "Dear Eòran. You are a most loyal protector. I've need of men like you. Will you swear to serve me as your one true queen and ruler of Doon?"

Eòran's face began to contort, turning scarlet beneath his gray mutton chops. Clearly he had a lot to say on the subject despite being frozen.

Bemused, Addie watched him for a moment and then with a snap of her fingers said, "You may speak freely."

" ... if ye were the last person on earth!"

Addie's mouth dipped into a disappointed moue. "So I take it that's a no?"

"I will never serve you, witch."

"I understand." She regarded the scruffy guard with a pained expression. "Now that ye've had your say, what say we put that tongue o' yours ta better use?"

Eòran's eyes bulged from his head as she waved her fingers in front of his face. His stubby hands clutched at his throat as he opened his mouth and made noises that were somewhere between a hiss and a groan. Inside his mouth, where his tongue should have been, was only a slug-like stump.

Slowly, Adam's closed mouth spread into a wide, vindicated smile. Releasing Vee's arm, he dropped to one knee and pressed his lips to Addie's hand. He kissed the pendant multiple times before smiling up at her. "Thank you, my queen! Thank you!"

I exchanged a glance with Vee. Still held by Sean, and with the threat of Greta's life hanging in the balance, she remained silent — but I could read the horror on her face as clear as day. As Adam pledged his fealty, I swept the crowd noting how many eyes of the frozen Doonians projected palpable reactions of shock and awe.

What did Addie have to gain by mutilating Eòran? As if she was reading my thoughts, Addie straightened her shoulders and spoke to the crowd. "Many of you are infirm. You're in need of restoration. I can heal you, just as I've done to Adam. If you follow me, I will make you better than whole. I will make you strong and sound. All ye need to do is pledge to me. There is nothing to fear ... Step forward and be transformed."

At first nothing happened. Then an elderly man began to hobble forward on spindly bowlegs with the use of a walking stick. He deliberately avoided looking at Vee as he passed. I watched breathlessly as he knelt in front of the witch and pledged his oath. As he kissed the pendant, Addie flicked a shower of purple sparks over his head.

The man gasped, "My legs!" and then rose without use of his stick. Instead of an infirmed eighty-year-old, he had the hardy appearance of a man who'd worked out every day of his long life. He turned in an athletic circle and then bowed low over Addie's outstretched hand. "Thank you, my queen."

As he descended the dais to stand off to one side of his new queen, a couple ventured forward cradling a small child. They stopped hesitantly in front of the witch, the woman's eyes darting uncertainly to Vee. She mouthed the words, "I'm sorry." Then to Addie, she begged, "Heal my child!"

They held out their sleeping daughter, who appeared to be four or five. Addie stroked the child's damp hair, her face a deceptive mask of compassion. "Your wee bairn is sickly."

"Aye, Your Highness," answered the mother.

"Canna ye save her?" pleaded the father.

"Aye." Addie continued to stroke the child's head, leaving trails of purple sparks until the sleeping child's eyes blinked open. As soon as their daughter awoke, the couple dropped to their knees and pledged their lives, including their daughter's, to the witch. After kissing her pendant, they rose and took their place among the witch's new minions.

The couple was replaced by two more Doonians in search of physical healing — a man with an eye patch and an old woman with a permanent hunch.

People were actually buying her miracle healer act!

I met Vee's startled gaze. Due to our almost psychic connection, I could tell she wanted to warn them as desperately as I did. But we dared not speak for Greta's sake. So I continued to watch in mute horror as the witch restored the next pledge's sight. And then the hunchback's posture.

Healings performed, Addie addressed the crowd again. "As ye can see, I am a monarch of great power and great compassion. It is my intention ta lead Doon into an unprecedented age o' prosperity. All who join me will share in the wealth and blessings that only I can provide. Your false queen would lead you inta war. One ye canna win. I offer an alternative without bloodshed, without strife. All ye need do is swear fealty to me."

"'Tis true." Sean MacNally's voice rang through the hollow space. "My queen is a remarkable woman and a natural-born Doonian. The throne was stolen from her long ago. I urge my lads to follow in my example and pledge to Doon's one true queen."

In the wake of Sean's words, several men stepped forward, some alone and others with wives and families in tow. I guessed they were all Sean's cohorts who'd opposed Vee's rule since she first became their queen. I noted that Duncan and Jamie were straining to move without success. It was as if the witch's spell could measure intention and was only freeing those who truly wanted to drink her wicked Kool-Aid.

Nearly thirty Doonians made vows to Addie — bowing to her, kissing Lynnette's pendant. Each person descended the dais slightly changed. They seemed stronger, with a vague zeal that I couldn't help but feel was a result of them willingly sacrificing their free will. I had no doubt that if and when the time came, Addie would make them puppets, not caring what happened to them as long as they did her bidding.

When the line of her would-be subjects died down, Addie scanned the remaining group. "Are there any more good folk who want ta come forward? Come now."

When the witch had claimed the crown, Sofia and Gabby had retreated back to our row. They now stared sullenly at the floor. Behind them I noted Roddy McPhee and his wife doing the same. Lachlan and Blaz were nowhere to be seen. Come to think of it, other than Greta, all of the kids that made up Jamie's Crew seemed to be absent. Addie, however, didn't seem to notice that an entire generation seemed to have vanished.

When no other citizens responded to her appeal, she nodded at the remnant. "Please dinna make the mistake of backing the wrong queen. Veronica canna save ye. However, to prove I am a fair and benevolent ruler, I will give you 'til the morrow to change your mind. Think on this … Each day I will demand a life from each family, either in service or in death. Swear fealty to me or watch them die."

Addie turned to her underlings, who were gathered in front of the dais. "Take the rest of the Doonians to the dungeons. Make sure that families stay together. They have much to discuss before daybreak."

About a dozen men broke from Addie's mass of new followers to escort the rest of the people to the dungeon. Just as had happened with Eòran, those enthralled walked with jerky, halting steps toward the back of the hall.

Once the room was clear of all the unclaimed, Addie's benevolent mask melted away. Unfortunately, her followers didn't seem to notice her true, rotten self.

"For those of you who've pledged to the false queen, you may save those you love from the executioner's gallows by recanting your oath and swearing fealty to me. Shall we begin?"

CHAPTER 33

Veronica

Horror didn't begin to describe what I felt as I watched several of my royal guards, men who I'd talked to and joked with, who'd watched over me morning and night, kneel before Addie and denounce their vow to me. But as a part of me died inside, the senseless choice they were making hurt me most — the choice that would separate them from the Covenant that had protected them for centuries.

After a dozen of my guardsmen had pledged, Addie spun to face me, her violet eyes dancing with delight. "Your turn, queenie." She strutted forward, stopping less than a foot away to tower over me. "As you can see, ye canna stop me from gainin' your people's fealty. Hand over the throne and no one else has to die."

A part of me wanted to give in, to stop the killing and torture. Shutting out Addie's impatient face, I squeezed my eyes closed and searched for guidance. If surrendering the throne saved lives, wasn't it worth it? Something inside of me stilled. Queen Lynnette had believed the same thing.

She'd made the choice for them. If I did the same, I'd be turning every Doonian over to a malevolent ruler and robbing them of the chance to choose light over dark, good over evil. This wasn't about me, or even those I loved most. My decision changed the fate of an entire *kingdom*. The Protector's vision had been clear — we would win, but we had to fight.

I opened my eyes, lifted my chin, and stared into the gaze of evil incarnate before uttering one word: "No."

Rage hardened every muscle in Addie's face, stripping away her beauty. "You imbecile! You have no power! Who are *you* to say no to *me*?"

Monster-Addie whipped up a clawed hand, and I flinched, ready for the blow, but she spun away on her heel. When she turned back, a placid calm had replaced her anger, restoring her attractive facade.

"Fine. I will execute the ones you love," she commented as if discussing the weather. "And their corpses will be strung up in the courtyard as a reminder for those who refuse me." She leered then, wide and full of such malicious joy that it froze the blood in my veins.

She tapped a crimson nail against her lips. "Hmm … let's see. Should we start with the least important and work our way up?" She paused in front of Eòran, shook her head, and then walked to where Fiona stood petrified, her hand reaching toward the dais. "This one has special gifts." Addie ran the tip of her fingernail down my friend's cheek hard enough to draw blood.

I lurched, causing Sean to tighten his grip, but dared not cry out for fear my reaction might encourage her to act.

Addie moved on, but there was no sense of relief as she paused before Kenna. "Or perhaps the fiery sidekick?"

"Stuff it, witch!" Kenna jerked against the guard who held

her arms. Addie chuckled and shook her head. Her dismissal of my best friend almost made me smile, because I knew someday she would learn what I already knew — Mackenna Reid was a force of nature.

Addie ambled around the stage, hands clasped behind her back. When she passed the place where Gideon had been holding Greta, I noticed they were missing. But before I had time to contemplate their whereabouts, Addie stopped directly in front of Jamie and Duncan, who stood frozen side-by-side. She gripped her waist and tilted her hip, striking a pose.

"Hmm … the heir or the spare? An age-old question, really. Does one gravitate toward the mercurial, brooding brother, or the cheery, loyal one? Both so incredibly appealing." She reached out and stroked each of their cheeks. Jamie blinked and stared past Addie's shoulder, his eyes never leaving mine. I swallowed, hard.

"You seem to be quite fond of your friend's boy toy," Addie's voice slithered through the silence. "But I've always believed in startin' from a position o' strength."

She turned back to me and clasped her hands in front of her chest, her face lighting like a rich kid on Christmas morning. "The crown prince it is!"

"No," I whispered, tears pooling in my eyes. I couldn't do this. I couldn't sacrifice Jamie.

"You can stop it, ye know." Addie tipped her head to the side, her face transforming in an imitation of compassion. "Just hand me the throne, swear your fealty to me, and everyone in this room lives."

"I won't." I shook my head, unsure if I was denying her or my traitorous heart.

"All right, then. To prove my great benevolence, I'll grant you the same reprieve as the rest o' Doon. Ye shall have a nice overnight stay in the dungeon to think it over. And, if ye promise to behave, I will give ye a moment to say your good-byes."

I bobbed my head in agreement, and then Addie turned back to Jamie. "I trust you will convince her to do the right thing." She swept her palm through the air, releasing him from her spell.

Jamie strained against the guards as they escorted him to the middle of the stage. Addie nodded. "Ye may release him. They aren't goin' anywhere."

Sean let me go and I ran to meet Jamie, but when I tried to throw my arms around him, he held my shoulders, keeping me at arm's length. His velvet gaze caressed my face, his words soft, but strong. "Ye have to let me go. Your Calling is greater — "

"No." I hated the desperation in my voice, but I couldn't stop it. "I can't. I won't!" Forgetting my earlier resolve, I lowered my voice, my next words only for him. "Together, nothing can stop us. If I give her what she wants, we live to fight another day."

Jamie pulled me closer. Our faces inches apart, I met his eyes and the tears there almost broke me. "Verranica, one of us *will* live to fight another day, and that must be you." He pressed his lips against my forehead. "The Protector will be with you."

Grief and fear welled, choking off my protests. He'd already given up.

"Wrong answer, James." Addie stepped between us and got in Jamie's face. "Let's see your mighty Protector stop me from hanging you until your beautiful eyes bulge out of your skull."

Jamie moved back, drawing her away from me as he spoke. "Adelaide, I have no need to defend myself, or our Protector. If he who I serve is willin' to deliver me from your hand, let him do so. But if not, know this." Jamie crossed his arms and spread his feet, his eyes blazing. "I will *never* serve you, or bow down to you."

"Seize him!" Jamie didn't fight when guards swarmed and yanked him to his knees. Addie's face flamed as red as her dress. "You dare to mock me, when you are in chains at my feet?" She flicked her wrist, her words becoming reality as heavy shackles appeared on Jamie's wrists and ankles. "We shall see how brash you are swinging at the end of a rope!"

Jamie lifted his head, his tone edged with steel. "'Tis no' arrogance. 'Tis faith. If ye knew the difference, your need for vengeance would no' consume you."

"Be silent!" Magic flew from Addie's palm.

I stared in amazement at Jamie's frozen form, defiant even in repose. I'd been wrong; he hadn't given up. He just knew where to place his trust, and it was time I did the same.

Addie whipped around. "What will it be, queenie? Your prince's head or the throne?"

The witch thought she'd forced me into a corner. Given me an impossible choice. But I would not choose between Jamie and Doon.

Balling my fists at my sides, I stared her down. "I was Called here by the Protector to serve this kingdom. The throne is not mine to give."

Addie's eyes widened and then narrowed. "What rubbish! You stole the crown from your *soulmate* in order to save his miserable life. Which, given the circumstances, I find hilariously ironic."

"You would, since you have no concept of love," I spat.

Her gaze focused behind me, and Sean yanked my arms behind my back. "Perhaps a night o' solitary confinement will dampen some of that nauseating self-righteousness."

Addie flung up her arm. "Guards! Take them to the dungeons."

There was a scuffle as Kenna fought. "I am not going back to that disgusting place!"

"On second thought, take them to the lower dungeon." A slow smile slid across Addie's lips. "And throw the wee queen in the hole."

CHAPTER 34

Mackenna

The regular dungeon, the one I'd become intimately acquainted with — twice — was homey compared with the dank cell in the lower dungeon. The tiny rectangular cubicle had no lights and no furniture, unless you counted the mound of moldy hay in one corner … which I definitely didn't. Below ground level, the walls oozed liquid that putrefied along much of the floor. The claustrophobic space made it impossible to pace, perhaps all the better since the ground was mostly slick and nasty. And the stomach-revolting smell … I couldn't even go there.

Fiona and I huddled together, peering through the bars at the single flickering torch next to the heavy door at the close end of the corridor. The only way in or out of the lower dungeon was through that door. The other direction was a dead end leading into sheer blackness and what Addie had called "the hole." If I thought my accommodations were icky, I couldn't even fathom what Vee was facing in that pit in the ground.

"How long do you think we've been in here?"

Blood had dried in a long welt on the side of Fiona's face. "Impossible to reckon. Hours."

"Do you think it's close to morning?"

"I canna tell. Askin' me will no' change that." She shoved a limp strawberry-blonde curl behind her ear. "Sorry. I dinna mean to snap. I'm afearin' for my husband, and the others."

"I'm sure they're okay." For now.

Commotion reverberated down the hall from the lighted end of the corridor. A moment later, a mass of shadows filled the dungeon entrance. My mind started to go down a bleak path — one where we were about to be herded into the courtyard to witness the execution of the crown prince of Doon. Fiona squeezed my hand as the shadows began to move in our direction.

"Fiona!"

The projected whisper caused my companion to visibly perk. "'Tis Fergus. He's here." She pressed her face into the rectangle of bars. "Here, Fergus!"

The big man, followed by torch-wielding shadows, raced down the passageway to his bride. "We'll get you out. Stand back." As he spoke, he inserted a key into the lock and popped the mechanism. A moment later the door swung inward.

Fergus stood in the entrance as Fiona launched herself into his arms. "Fergus, I was so scared for ye."

"Shhhh, wife. I'm sound and I'm here now."

Behind Fergus's hulking form, I recognized the other shadows as Analisa, Giancarlo, and the Rosetti twins. All of them had blossoming bruises and cuts decorating their faces. "What happened to you guys?"

Ana lifted her chin. "Emily's cronies got the jump on us. Locked us up on the floor above."

Giancarlo draped an arm over Ana's shoulder. "Lucky for us, Ana doesna go anyplace without her tools."

Patting the end of a leather folio tucked into the bodice of her gown, Ana grinned. "What kind of thief would I be if I didn't come prepared?" She handed a key to one of the Rosetti twins. "Get the rest of our lads out."

As the twins scampered off, I stared at the girl I'd been ready to burn at the stake just hours before. "I'm sorry, Ana. I thought you were — "

"I know what you thought, Mackenna. I may personally not cotton to the idea of pledging my life to the monarchy, but I am the crown's friend and ally. Especially when our kingdom is under siege. So let's skip the awkward apologies and get about taking our home back. Now, where's Veronica?"

"She's in the hole at the far end of the hall."

I turned toward the darkened end of the corridor just as Duncan stepped into view. Before my brain could command my feet to move, I was sprinting into his arms. He crushed me against him with my face buried in his neck. His unique, familiar scent of leather and sunshine banished away the darkness. I opened my mouth to speak, and the words I'd intended came out as a strangled sob.

Duncan smoothed his hand down my matted hair. "It's all right, woman. I've got ye."

Over his shoulder I heard Giancarlo swear. "None of the keys fit this door, *amore*."

"I can pick it," Analisa replied without a hint of self-doubt. "Step back, you lot, and let me work."

Still wrapped around my prince, I let Duncan move us slightly off to the side. Gently, he pulled away until we were face-to-face. His grave eyes drank me in as if he were about to go off to war. With a trembling hand he caressed my check with his rough knuckles.

"Did I ever tell ye about the time that Jamie convinced me

I could fly?" I shook my head and he continued in a somber voice. "When I was a wee lad, my brother and I used ta climb trees. Jamie always climbed faster and higher. So one time, I got it inta my wee head that I would out-climb him.

"Like a monkey, I shimmied my way to the top of a bonnie tree and called for Jamie to join me. When my brother was about halfway up, he stopped. Suddenly, he ordered me to come down. But I wasna in a mood to follow so I refused. A moment later I felt a pinch like the prick of a needle on my leg, followed by another one. You see, Jamie had noticed that I was crouched over a wasp's nest. Well, I started to panic until Jamie called out to me. 'Duncan,' said he, 'I wasna going to tell ye this until you were older, but you're special. You can fly. If you let go of the branch ye willna fall but float like a cloud.'"

I couldn't help but wonder about his point. Was he trying to occupy my mind while Ana worked on picking the lock? Impatient to get to my best friend, I bounced on the balls of my feet and prompted, "What happened?"

"Well, it never occurred to me that Jamie wouldna tell me the truth. So when the next wasp stung my hand, I let go of the branch and stepped off."

"And did you float to safety?"

"Heavens no. I dropped like a stone." Despite the tone of his story, Duncan had a strange smile on his face. "Jamie, who'd anticipated this, lunged from his perch in an attempt ta catch me on my way down. But I was fallin' too fast. I knocked m' brother from the branch and we both crashed ta the ground. Jamie broke his arm, and I suffered a cracked collarbone."

Duncan caressed my face again. "But if he hadn't acted, I would've died. Those wasps would've swarmed and I wouldna have lived to tell the tale."

Something in my chest deflated as his story solidified in my brain. "You're going after Jamie, aren't you?"

"Aye." His dark eyes pleaded with me to understand. "My brother would walk through the fires o' hell for me."

Duncan's sweet demeanor turned fierce and uncompromising, like the ruthless warrior I knew lurked deep in his soul. "As would I for him. I will save him. But if I should pay the ultimate price, I need ta know that ye will be all right."

What was he asking me? To escape to Chicago and go about my life like none of this ever happened? Peering into his unwavering eyes confirmed that was exactly what he was asking of me. "No. Just, no!"

"Be reasonable, Mackenna — "

Whatever else he'd been about to say was cut off by Analisa. "Got it."

The door swung open, but Duncan didn't move. He continued to silently plead with me to bless his suicide mission. Well, Hawaii would freeze over before I'd do that. Pulling out of his grasp, I forced my way past him. "Let's go rescue Vee."

CHAPTER 35

Veronica

No ... get away!"

Icy needles sunk into my skin, jerking me out of one nightmare and into another. I kicked out blindly and my foot connected with something squirmy as rocks and mud shifted beneath me. Freezing liquid pooled around my feet, and I scrambled back, trying to regain my tenuous purchase on the steep slope.

When they'd thrown me in, I'd landed in a waist-high pool of reeking muck, which I'd fallen back into more times than I could count. During one unfortunate foray into the slimy mire, I'd grabbed onto something that felt suspiciously like a human skull. But I couldn't be sure in the impenetrable darkness.

Digging my heels in, I found a relatively dry spot and hugged my knees, trying to calm the shaking. I'd lost all sense of time, unable to gauge if minutes or hours had passed, but despite the bone-numbing cold, I wasn't in a hurry to get out — because that would mean they were taking me to watch Jamie die.

I laid my forehead against my knees, but the damp, muddy

fabric against my skin was no comfort. I clenched my teeth against a wave of hopelessness and lifted my face. "Please, if you're out there, save us. Don't make me choose." I prayed the words over and over until my fervent pleas dwindled into repetitive chants, vacillating between begging for Jamie's life and asking for the strength to deny the witch. Rationally, I knew one thing precipitated the other, but my heart wouldn't hear logic.

An indeterminate time later, a screech sounded from above. I raised a hand against the harsh light piercing my eyes. This was it.

"Vee, are you down there?"

My heart lurched at the familiar voice and I blinked into the blinding glow. "Kenna?"

"We're lowering a ladder."

Afraid to trust my deprived senses, my voice broke as I asked, "Is that really you?"

There was a scraping sound and then a splash.

"Who do you think it is, silly? Idina Menzel?"

Tears sprung to my eyes. It was really her. As my vision adjusted, I noticed the light wasn't just coming from above. White rays glowed from my hand, the power of our rings connecting.

Trying not to look too hard at my surroundings, I rose and made my way around the edge of the cesspool toward the ladder. My sodden gown and cloak weighing me down, I had to stop on the third rung to catch my breath.

"Hurry, Vee," Kenna encouraged.

"What time is it?"

"Nearly sunrise."

The witch had given me until sunrise to change my mind.

Fear fueling me on, I raced the rest of the way up. Eòran lifted me out and set me on my feet. Before I could get my bearings, I was surrounded by soldiers and ushered through a door hidden in the recesses of the wall. We climbed a rough stone staircase and emerged in the cramped passages of the catacombs.

Several guards fanned out around us, Analisa and Giancarlo standing watch beside them. Fergus stepped forward, bowing his great head. "Yer Majesty. Please forgive me for failin' ye."

Kenna rubbed the frozen flesh of my arms.

"Fergus, there's nothing to forgive." I met Duncan's gaze as he stepped into view. "What about the rest of the people?"

"The Rosettis and your remainin' loyal guard are freeing them now." Duncan shifted from foot to foot, his fists balling and unballing reflexively.

"And Jamie?"

His eyes darkened with grief and then shuttered—so like his brother. "We havena been able to reach him."

Ignoring the squeeze of my ribcage, I ordered, "Fergus, take three of my best guards and find Jamie. If I were Addie, I'd have him in the Keep. Try there first."

Fergus gave a nod and then stooped to kiss Fiona's forehead, whispering, "I'll be back before ye miss me."

"Ye better be." She lifted her hand to caress his cheek.

His expression solidifying with determination, he turned away, rattled off the names of three guards, and they headed for the right passage.

"Fergus!" I stumbled forward, my voice breaking. "Do whatever it takes to save him."

He glanced back, his light eyes glowing in the wash of my ring. "Aye, Yer Majesty." He gave a quick bow, and then ran out of sight.

Fiona hovered at my side. "They'll be back." But I couldn't tell if her words were meant to comfort me or herself.

"Kenna." Duncan strode forward. "Stay with Vee and the rest o' the guard. I'm goin' with them."

Kenna's cheeks reddened to volcanic levels, but before she could blow, I grabbed Duncan's arm. "No, you can't. I have something more for you to do."

He spun on me, demanding, "What could be more important than savin' my brother?"

"For you and me, nothing. But I must think like a queen now." I lifted my chin and fought back the emotion clogging my throat. "I have to put Doon first."

He stared me down, his jaw flexing as he wrestled with the same internal battle I had to fight myself. I waited, needing his logic to win out over his heart before I continued.

Footsteps sounded through the corridor, moving fast in our direction. Eòran drew his sword and motioned the guards to fall in. Whispered voices and a low-pitched whine echoed toward us. I pushed past Eòran just as Blaz emerged from the left passage, followed by Lachlan, Greta, and a gang of kids. Ordering my men to stand down, I rushed forward.

A dozen faces came into view, and I realized they were all part of Jamie's Crew. "Lachlan, why aren't you escaping with the Rosettis?"

Blaz jumped up, sniffing my soiled clothing, but I pushed him down. The kids had torches and ancient-looking weapons — a mallet, some rusty swords, a hatchet. "What are you guys doing?"

Lachlan slid his sword into his belt. "We're goin' to rescue Jamie."

"Yeah." Greta stepped up next to him, dried blood scabbed on her throat where Gideon had held her at knife point. The other kids chimed in their agreement.

"He'd do the same fer us!"

"Jamie'd never leave us!"

"We can take that witch out!"

I couldn't speak; my heart had leapt into my mouth. Kenna stepped up beside me, her eyes silvered with tears as she took my hand.

Duncan flanked my other side. "You all are verra brave, but my brother would want ye to get to safety."

I couldn't've asked for a better opening. Keeping Kenna's fingers in mine, I turned to face Duncan. "That's right. He would want all of the people to get to safety. That's why I need for you to lead them out."

He stilled, his brows furrowing. "Lead them out *where*?"

"Out of the kingdom. Across the Brig o' Doon."

CHAPTER 36

Mackenna

My heart, which had leapt at Vee's words, now plummeted as Duncan scowled at the ring in the palm of her outstretched hand. "Nay. Mackenna can lead them. I'll no' leave without my brother."

"We should all go." The suggestion flew from my mouth before I'd had a chance to finish forming it. Immediately, Vee's face pinched in refusal as Duncan stared stoically at the catacomb wall. "I mean, wouldn't that be the wisest thing to do? Fergus can follow with Jamie."

My bestie leveled her gaze on me, and in that moment I barely recognized her. "I'm the queen. The ruler of Doon. The Covenant resides inside of me. I *won't* abandon my kingdom to Adelaide."

Duncan stepped in front of me, facing off with his queen. "Nor will I."

"Please." I reached out to touch his shoulder, but he shrugged me off.

"Mackenna, this is none o' your concern. Ye will do as your queen bids you."

Before he could say more, Vee interjected. "So will you, Prince MacCrae. The vision was clear. As your queen, I'm ordering you to escort the people out of Doon."

Duncan leaned forward to stare down my best friend. In all the time I'd known him, I'd only seen him as furious one other time — when the kingdom was on the verge of annihilation and his brother ordered him to babysit me. His jaw flexed as he stepped back. "As ye command, Your Majesty."

Then he whirled in my direction, pointedly ignoring me as he brushed past to growl orders at his soldiers. "Intercept the Rosettis and have them lead everyone out through the dungeon entrance." Then to others he instructed, "Get to town — round up every horse and cart ye can find. I'll take what I can from the royal stables. We rendezvous at the western paddock beyond the village. Dinna allow the people to scatter. We travel light and fast."

As the soldiers scattered to obey orders, Duncan's tortured gaze briefly connected with mine and then jerked away, leaving me to feel as if my entire world had slipped from my grasp. Focusing on the vicinity of my right ear, Duncan said, "Say your good-byes. We leave immediately."

I searched his unyielding face, wondering if he could discern my relief that Vee's command prevented him from his suicide mission. But saving him meant deserting the one person who'd stood by me my entire life. For Duncan's sake, I was about to abandon my bestie.

The girl who shared my brain took my hand in hers. "It's okay, Ken. I'm ordering you to go ... You swore an oath to me."

I knew I couldn't refuse and yet I could not bear to solidify the distance between Duncan and myself by agreeing. Twisted every way, what answer could I give except to beg in vain, "Please come with us?"

Rather than acknowledge my plea, Vee squared her shoulders in resolve. "I'm counting on you and Duncan to see my people safely across the bridge."

Fiona materialized at her side. "I'll stay with Her Majesty."

"No, Fiona." Vee leveled her gaze on our friend. "Fergus would want you to be safe. And I need you to look after the Crew. As a personal favor."

If she disagreed with the command, she did not let it show. "As ye wish, my queen. But if I may, I would petition Her Majesty to bring my Fergus safely back to me."

"I will," she promised grimly. Nothing short of death, which was a very real possibility, would cause her to break it. "Now be off. You too, Eòran."

Mutton Chops made a guttural sound as he whipped his head back and forth. Appreciation welled in Vee's eyes at her guard's blatant disobedience. He would never abandon her. As she turned to embrace him, she whispered something in his ear. Although I could not hear what was said, the way the old badger's eyes flickered in my direction made me suspicious that she was giving him a special assignment.

When she straightened, she said, "I'm counting on you, Eòran. Now you need to go. The Protector's grace go with you."

As Fiona and Eòran began to usher the Crew toward the passage that would lead to the dungeon and the exit beyond, Lachlan handed Vee a torch and one of the swords he'd tucked into his belt. "The Protector's grace remain with you, Your Majesty."

Vee placed the torch in a nearby wall sconce and the sword next to it before dropping to one knee. "You are one of my best knights. I'm counting on you to get the Crew and Blaz to safety." She kissed the dog's head and then gave him a little push. "He's yours now."

Lachlan shook his head, his dark curls bouncing in the flickering light. "Nay, Your Majesty. I'll keep him safe for ye until next time we meet. You can count on me."

"I know I can." Unshed tears, for the boy's brave words or the loss of her beloved pup or perhaps both, shimmered in her eyes.

With a few orders from Duncan, Fiona, Eòran, and the rag-tag pack of children warriors began to double back toward the dungeons.

Once they were out of earshot, Duncan said to Vee, "I will do as commanded, but I won't leave you alone."

Vee glared at him. "One guard."

A man I recognized from Duncan's "war games" stepped forward. "I will stay with the queen — protect her with my life, m'laird."

Duncan nodded in satisfaction, before addressing the remaining two soldiers, Analisa, Giancarlo, and myself. "We'll make for the Brother Cave for weapons. From there the stables and on to the rendezvous point. Your Majesty should accompany us to the cave of Robert the Bruce."

Vee took the torch and sword from the wall. To the soldier who'd volunteered to stay she said, "Go find Fergus. Let him know I'm waiting in the cave of Robert the Bruce."

Without a moment to delay, we set off for the cave where the historic leader of the Scottish rebellion discovered the strength to persevere in his battle to liberate his beloved homeland. From there, Analisa could pick the lock of the iron door leading to the cavern that the princes used as their personal gym. The Brother Cave was not only full of weapons, it was also the shortest, most clandestine route to the stables.

Darkness dwelled beyond the door that barred our escape, indicating that it was still night. As if to reassure herself, Vee muttered, "It's not morning yet." She sagged against a rock ledge, shivering in her soggy gown. Unable to acknowledge the finality of our parting, I wrapped my arm around her trembling back, trying my best to impart warmth and strength.

All too quickly I heard Ana's congratulatory exclamation as the door squeaked open. Without a word to my bestie, I jumped up and jogged into the Brother Cave. As the others gathered weapons, I ransacked trunks until I found a stash of clothes. With my back to the others, I ripped the bodice of my gown open and let the cursed thing pool around my feet. Quickly pulling a coarse tunic over my head, I kicked off my slippers and slid my feet into Duncan's ginormous spare boots.

Vee stood in the doorway, longingly watching our chaotic preparations. Crossing to her, I handed off the other pile of oversized yet dry clothes. "Here. I'm done facing the end of the world in a pretty dress. So are you."

"Thanks." She hesitated. Knowing her as well as myself, I could see her wrestling with her emotions, not only our imminent parting but her barely in-check fear of rescuing her beloved and facing Adelaide Blackmore Cadell, the terrible Witch of Doon. Holding the clothes between us like a shield, she offered me a wistful smile. "See you soon, okay?"

"Whatever." Grabbing the clothes and dropping them off to one side, I wrapped my arms around her. The minute we made contact, moisture began to seep from my eyes. With a hiccup-y sob that signified the beginning of an ugly cry, I held her as tightly as I dared. And to my utter relief, she squeezed me back.

All too soon, I felt Duncan's unyielding grip on my arm. "We need to make haste, Mackenna."

Before letting go, Vee whispered, "I love you," and I murmured it back.

Then Duncan, my own heart, pulled me out of the cave and

away from the other half of my soul. Stumbling alongside him in too-big boots, I scanned the night for some indication of the hour. Despite the inky, star-spangled sky, tendrils of pink and blue unfurled on the horizon. As I contemplated the ominous implication, a nearby rooster let loose an earsplitting crow as he heralded in the morning.

CHAPTER 37

Veronica

What had I done?

I paced in front of the empty frame that had hidden Robert the Bruce's axe for centuries and was now an empty shell. Much like Doon was about to be.

I'd followed the Protector's vision and sent the Doonians out of the kingdom. But when Fergus returned with Jamie, what would we do then? How would we fight back with so few of us left? And without my ring to shield me from the witch's magic?

Jamie would know what to do. But I couldn't shake the feeling that we were losing time. All I could picture was the counter on a bomb, the digital display ticking off the numbers until the explosion.

Reaching the end of the passage, I spun on my heel for another lap, grateful for the soft, clean fabric of the oversized tunic and leggings. A vision of Kenna's grief-stricken eyes as Duncan had pulled her away almost brought me to my knees. Would they make it to safety? Would I ever see my best friend again?

I gripped the handle of the ancient weapon and squeezed until the rough metal dug into my skin, refocusing my thoughts. I rounded a curve, and soft, golden light seeped in through the Brother Cave entrance, reminding me that Jamie was out of time. "Come on, Fergus," I muttered. "Hurry."

As the words left my mouth, the ground bucked beneath me and I tripped forward. My sword clattered to the stone floor, and I smacked hard against the wall. "What the —?" I gripped the damp stone as another tremor shook the earth. This was no bovine stampede.

The trembling stilled, and I sprinted to the entrance of the cave, gripping the bars, but the quake had collapsed part of the entrance. I shook the gate with all my strength. It wouldn't budge. Another rumble vibrated rocks the size of my fist loose from the ceiling. I had to get out before the entire castle landed on me! Running in a stumble, I scooped up my sword, grabbed a burning torch from its bracket, and headed into the narrow passage that would — hopefully — lead me back to the stairs.

The world shivered, and I slammed into the close tunnel walls like a Ping-Pong ball. A rock smacked into my shoulder, sending me tripping into an intersecting corridor. But which way? Coughing on dust, I turned in a circle and tried to recall the way we'd come. A faint chalk mark on the far wall caught the light. Jamie's old trail! I rushed toward it, thanking the Protector for my big, strong boyfriend's fear of getting lost.

I reached the next intersection just as a hard shudder brought me to my knees, pebbles cascading down all around me. Tucking into a tight ball, I covered my head and waited for the tremor to stop. When I opened my eyes, the passage Jamie had marked was blocked with an avalanche of stone.

No!

With no other choice, I regained my feet and barreled in

the other direction. I ran as fast as I could through the shaking earth. Were those footsteps behind me or just falling debris? Tunnel after tunnel, I ran, the sound of my labored breath echoing in my ears. A hard shake and I fell sideways as part of the ceiling collapsed, the displaced air almost snuffing out my torch.

I cupped the tiny flame and blew it back into life, but a pattern of sound — footfalls, not rocks — had me moving again. The witch must have sent Gideon down here to find me once she discovered I'd escaped the hole. Even though the old guard knew the catacombs better than anyone, I couldn't let him find me. *Could not* let him drag me back to Addie to make the impossible choice.

The earth stilled and the footsteps grew louder. I thought I heard my name, but I couldn't be sure over the thudding of my heart. I pushed myself to move faster.

"Vee!" Fingers grazed my shoulder.

I dropped the torch and spun around, swinging my sword in a wide arc. Metal hit metal and the impact knocked the weapon out of my hands.

A light-haired giant pulled me into his arms.

"Fergus!" I collapsed against him, my knees going weak with relief.

After returning his hug, I peered around my friend's wide shoulders to find the anxious faces of several guardsmen.

But no smirking prince. "Jamie?"

Stepping out of Fergus's embrace, I met his eyes. The earth rumbled beneath us.

He glanced up, and the moisture collecting on his blond lashes splashed onto his cheeks.

"Where's Jamie?" I whispered.

Slowly, my friend shook his head. "He did no' make it, lass."

"What do you mean?" Blood rushed into my ears, dulling my senses.

"When the witch found ye missin', she flew inta a rage and forced Jamie to the gallows." He swallowed hard. "I'm so sorry, but we couldna get to him in time. I ... I saw him from the castle window. I saw him ... drop." A great wrenching sound escaped his throat. "I'm so verra sorry."

"I ..." I blinked up at Fergus as the world fell away, leaving a gaping void beneath me.

Jamie could *not* be gone. It wasn't possible. My brave knight. The boy who made me laugh one moment and kissed me until I couldn't breathe the next. *That* boy was invincible.

My friend's crumpled face wavered through the tears pooling in my eyes, and I had the overpowering urge to comfort him. "I'm s-sure ..." My voice broke and I took a step back, lifted my chin and tried again. "I'm sure you did your best — " A sob choked off my words but I swallowed it ruthlessly. "Thank you ... for ... for trying to ... to save him."

Fergus moaned, and I gave his arm a pat. The ground swayed, and I stumbled as if my bones were made of rubber and somehow ended up on the floor. The nothingness closing in around me, I fought to focus on the guardsmen who were looking to me for direction. But only one thought looped through my brain — there had to be some mistake, Jamie MacCrae was my Calling and I was *his*.

Then, a light pushed against the numbing blackness. Swiping at my cheeks, I reached into my pocket and clutched the ribbons he'd given me. "We're getting married."

"I'm sorry?" Fergus knelt beside me.

"We're getting married," I repeated louder as I pulled the ribbons out. The rich colors blurred through the prism of my tears. "We're getting married within a fortnight."

I looked up into Fergus's face with expectation and lifted the evidence for him to see. The proof that Jamie couldn't possibly be ... gone.

Fergus' moist blue eyes met mine, and his lips pressed tight as he shook his head. "Nay, lass."

How could he know? He didn't understand. I shot to my feet and shoved the rainbow-hued strands into his face. "He promised me. Jamie promised me that *nothing* would stop us!"

"Vee." Fergus's enormous fingers closed around my hands, and he tugged them to his heart, his watery gaze shining with conviction. "Jamie'd do anythin' to keep that promise ... if he could. He loved ye more than life."

The bottom dropped out of my soul, and I pulled my hands back, stroking Jamie's last gift to me. He'd *loved* me more than his own life. Past tense. His words in the throne room echoed in my head ... *Verranica, one of us will live to fight another day, and that must be you.*

He'd known how this would end.

CHAPTER 38

Mackenna

The ground rumbled again, shaking so mightily that the wooden wheels of our wagon collapsed. As we bounced to a halt, the road before us split open like something from a big-budget action movie. "Is Doon trying to stop us?" I asked, doing my best to project over the noise of the earthquake.

"Nay," Fiona yelled in response. "'Tis likely one of the witch's spells preventing us from leaving."

Duncan dismounted from the driver's seat in one graceful leap just as the quake stopped. If the massive catastrophe rattled him, he covered it up well. Signaling the other drivers to halt, he barked, "The bridge is through yonder trees. We go from here on foot. Make haste. There's no time to lose."

Duncan helped Fiona down from the wagon before assisting me. From the way he touched me and the impassive expression in his eyes, I could have been any random villager. I hoped it was a momentary hiccup brought on by the direness of the situation. I couldn't believe that he'd bear a grudge against me because of what Vee commanded. But I was too tired and disoriented to sort through things with the ground pitching and tearing beneath us.

Without making eye contact, he barked, "Get the Crew out of the wagon!" Then he turned to the next cart driven by Mario Rosetti. Sofia, Gabriella, and Mrs. Rosetti rode with him while the Rosetti boys flanked them on horseback. "We need to get everyone across that field to the Brig o' Doon. Spread the word." Giancarlo, who had been entrusted with Duncan's horse, Mabel, galloped toward the rear to tell the others.

As Sofia and Gabriella scrambled to the ground alongside their brothers, I turned to the kids in the back of our wagon. Half of them were already out. Lachlan scooted to the edge and handed me Blaz's leash.

Vee's dog whined as I took him in my arms. His long legs dangling, I struggled to hold onto him as the poor thing trembled like a baby. Lachlan jumped from the wagon as another vibration shook the world. The boy fell onto his butt, looking vaguely appalled at the ground revolting beneath him. Blaz squirmed in my arms, desperate to get to Lachlan, who was still trying to get to his feet. Grabbing the boy's hand, I hoisted him up and handed him the dog's leash. But another quake caused us to stumble apart mid-handoff. Blaz tumbled with a yelp and then took off running toward the castle.

"I'll get him," Lachlan yelled as he ran after the pup.

"Wait!" I demanded.

I started to go after him when Mario stopped me. "Nay, *signorina*. You must open the portal on the bridge. *Addesso!* Now!" He pointed toward the field. Little fissures crisscrossed the space that stood between us and the Brig o' Doon.

I looked between the field and Lachlan's retreating form,

unsure what to do until Sofia Rosetti filled my vision. "Go to the bridge. I'll get Lachlan." She turned to her father. "Get Kenna to the bridge, Papà."

Sofia took off after the boy as Mario began to tow me across the uneven ground. Behind us I could hear Duncan urging the people to run for the bridge. As more and more Doonians stepped into the field, nature reacted in total rebellion.

The emerald ring on my finger blazed green and the earth fell away, turning crevasses into canyons. I concentrated on my feet and maneuvering over the terrain in giant boots.

As the shaking calmed, I looked back over my shoulder, trying to locate Duncan. From the back of the mass of people I noticed Lachlan, flanked by Sofia and Gabby and towing Blaz. To their right, the red glow of Vee's ring surrounded Duncan as he mounted Mabel.

Horse and rider galloped across the field like something from a Sleepy Hollow tale. At the rate they were traveling, they would make it to the portal before me. I turned my attention toward the bridge, intending to force myself to go faster, when the soil crumbled beneath me. Time stopped as my body dropped into a newly formed ravine.

Belatedly, I realized that Mario still gripped my hand. He fell to the grass trying to keep his grip while I dangled over the crack in the earth. From below, the acrid smell of sulfur stung my eyes and nose. I blinked up at Mario ... and Eòran. Mutton Chops leaned into the crevasse, helping Mario pull me up.

As I scrambled for solid ground, Eòran hoisted me to my feet. Before I could catch my breath, Duncan and Mabel approached, slowing as Eòran hefted me in the air. Duncan grabbed my arm, and with Mutton Chop's help, I swung onto the horse's back.

Once I was firmly behind Duncan and clutching on for dear

life, he resumed his charge. Behind us, the ground continued to crack. Doonians screamed as they or their loved ones tumbled into the abyss. Some of us would not survive. Even as the truth of that hit me, the light of my ring and the one Duncan wore on the tip of his pinky began to unite, merging from red and green to brilliant white.

As we cleared the final copse of trees and the Brig o' Doon came into full view, the riverbank gave way. Mabel reared back as she scrambled for solid footing. By the time I cried out, Duncan had regained control of his steed. With a clicking noise, he rerouted Mabel into the field, arcing in a wide circle. After a moment's pause he grunted, "Hold fast, Mackenna."

Before I could question why, we were galloping straight for the fissure. With a mighty bellow from her rider, Mabel leapt the newly formed ravine and skidded to a halt at the mouth of the Brig o' Doon.

I was still panting for breath as Duncan twisted in his seat, lifted me off the horse, and dismounted all in one fluid motion. With a frown of regret, he raised his hand to swat his beloved horse's rump. Worried that he was about to send the poor beast to fend for herself, I stepped between them, capturing his hand before he could strike.

"Let's take Mabel with us."

Duncan blinked at me like I was speaking pig Latin. "Can we do that?"

"We can try." When he nodded in agreement, I took the horse's reins and handed them to him. Taking his free hand, the one wearing Vee's ring, in my own, I said, "Let's get the portal open."

From our side in Doon the arch ended in a ruin halfway across. But as we stepped onto the cobbled stones, the light of our rings poured across the bridge, making it whole. The

Robert Burns memorial and the rooftops of modern-day Alloway appeared in the background.

Without warning, Duncan smacked Mabel's rump, causing her to bolt across the bridge and safely into the present. At my startled noise, he favored me with one of his heart-stopping, lopsided grins. "Dinna worry. She'll no' stray far. She's safe. We made it."

The relief that lit Duncan's face was short lived as another mighty tremor shook the ground. "Hurry, Doonians," he urged.

I glanced in the direction of the field to see the people of Doon making their way across. With Eòran's gestures, those closest to the bridge were spanning the chasm with a large fallen tree. Once it was firmly in place, Mutton Chops scurried across and others began to follow. Mid-field, I spotted Sofia with Lachlan and Blaz. They were flanked by the other Rosettis and Analisa helping the injured to pick their way toward us.

Eòran stepped onto the bridge and then stopped to urge others across. As the first of my adopted countrymen crossed the bridge, a distant rumbling began. Like an invisible tidal wave, the trees of the forest began to collapse. Closer, the patch of earth that had been wasted by the limbus fell into giant sink holes. I watched helplessly as Mr. Dinwiddie, the boot maker, and another merchant who'd been crossing the ravine stumbled from the log and tumbled into the chasm below.

Duncan's free hand captured my face. "Focus, woman!"

The dark intensity in Duncan's gaze riveted me to him as he said, "Give me your ring."

"What! Why?"

Without the slightest trace of emotion he replied, "Once we get the people across, I'll hold the bridge for you to follow." He didn't need to explain that he had no intention of coming with me; I could read it clearly in his flat eyes. To lessen the blow, he murmured, "I willna leave my brother to die."

Clenching my finger over my ring lest he try and wrench it from my finger, I stared at him, letting my outrage fuel my resolve. "And I won't let you go on a suicide mission."

"'Tis no' your decision to make."

The light coming from the rings on our intertwined hands had begun to spurt like a flashlight running out of power as the latest tremor intensified. The quake, which had to be at least an eleven on the Richter scale, continued to menace the ancient bridge. Behind my prince, a chunk of the wall crumbled away as Fiona and another group of Doonians stumbled past.

I clung to Duncan as the bridge pitched and stones dropped from the structure into the rushing river below. Glancing down I could see the Brig o' Doon splitting in half beneath our feet. If we fell into the icy river below, where would we end up? Alloway or Doon?

"Hold fast!" Duncan barked at me. Worried for my friends, I glanced back to Doon as the latest wave of destruction reached the field. Tossed by an unseen force, bodies flew through the air. In that moment I realized it was indeed a tidal wave — not of water, but of purple magic.

Unable to look away, I yelled out to Sofia and the rest of the Rosettis to hurry. Just as Lachlan stepped onto the bridge, something slammed into me. Like Jack and Jill, Duncan and I tumbled down the far side of the sloped bridge and onto the grassy riverbank of Alloway. As the world stopped spinning, I realized that Eòran had been the something that knocked us forward.

With a curse at the badger-like guard, Duncan hauled me to my feet. My ring no longer emitted any light — white, green, or otherwise. And the bridge — the bridge was missing. Not collapsed in ruin or lying in cobbled chunks across the riverbank … the Brig o' Doon had disappeared.

Lachlan, Blaz, Sofia, the other Rosettis, Analisa, and all the rest of the Doonians were gone.

epilogue

Jamie

Air rushed into my lungs and I jolted forward.

What in all that's holy?

Snow-laden trees bowed like sentinels around a frozen fountain, their heavy branches almost touching the ice-glazed lions in its center. I'd splashed in that pool as a boy.

Either the hereafter looked exactly like Doon, or, miraculously, I still lived.

I squeezed my aching temples and memories rushed back — Addie screeching about Veronica paying for her escape, a hood being lowered over my head, the earth quaking, and as I uttered my last prayer, hands gripping my arms and pulling me back. *"It is not yet your time."*

And then I'd awoken here in the castle garden.

My chest constricted. A miracle, indeed.

But what of my people? And *Veronica?*

The air cracked as a wave of violet shook the trees, preceding an ungodly shriek. "MacCrae!"

That would be Addie discovering she hadn't killed me as

planned. I leapt to my feet at a dead run — past the shrub maze, down the steps, and into the forest.

When Vee escaped, she would've gathered the people and led them away from the castle. But which direction? I paused in the lee of the dungeon entrance, the sharp wind like needles against my exposed skin.

Knowing her logical mind, my queen would seek shelter and weapons. *The hunting lodge.* I headed east into the woods. With only a dusting of snow beneath the canopy of branches, there were no tracks, but there would be other signs that hundreds had passed this way.

I slowed, searching for broken twigs, trampled grass, missing bark. And found nothing. Had they gone to the catacombs?

A piercing howl echoed through the forest, and I heard distant footfalls, followed by shouts.

"I saw somethin'!"

"There!"

"Through the trees!"

As much as I longed to turn and fight, without weapons it would do me little good. I dashed left, leapt over a fallen log and up the hill. Few people knew this forest better than I. Except perhaps Gideon. I forced my legs faster.

A hot wind brushed my face, swirling around me, warming my icy skin. I stalled and pivoted toward it, soaking in the exquisite heat and breathing in the magic.

Saints!

Shaking off the enticement, I sprinted in the opposite direction.

I had to find them — I had to find *her.*

Veronica had been right; together we were stronger. But in the witch's clutches, we became each other's weakness. Capture was not an option.

No longer hearing my pursuers, I jumped, caught the branch of a large oak, swung up, and climbed as high as I dared. Since the winter had come unnaturally early, there were plenty of leaves to conceal me. I settled into the intersection of two branches and leaned against the trunk to wait. The last time I'd climbed a tree, my idiotic brother'd woken a wasp's nest and we'd both fallen — nay, *leapt* to the ground. I flexed my left arm as my throat tightened. I'd come close to losing him that day. Lifting my face to the sky, I prayed he'd found safety. And that Veronica was with him.

I could trust Duncan with anything, even the one who defined my world. I reached into my pocket and fingered the single azure ribbon I'd kept from the set I'd given her. Providence had gifted us a second chance.

"I will find you, my heart. And I *will* keep my promise."

The adventure continues
fall 2016 in the fourth and final
book of the Doon series,

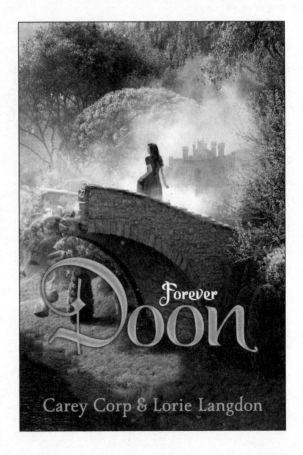

acknowledgments

Co-writing a series continues to be a challenging and rewarding labor of love. Thankfully, so many of you have crossed the bridge with us to DOON.

Thank you to:

The Protector, who orders our hearts, minds, and steps. Without Him, there would be no Doon.

Jacque Alberta, for seeing Doon in the weather, and for living and breathing this series right along with us.

The **Blink** and **Zondervan** team, for giving us the tools and support to bring the Dooniverse to the world.

Agent extraordinaire **Nicole Resciniti**, for being the first person to convert to Doonism.

Melissa Landers, our critique partner and friend, for providing benchmarking and much needed counterbalance. Can't wait to write that Doon-Alienated crossover. ;)

The **Booktubers** and **Bloggers**, especially Sasha Alsberg, Ben Alderson, Tiernan Bertrand-Essington, and Daniela Diaz for loving this series and helping countless readers to cross the bridge. We're so proud to call you friends!

The **Doon Street Team**, Amber, Amanda C., Jules, Ang, Tracy, Stephanie, Sara, Amanda S., Charity, Debz, Jessica, Rachel, Kathryn, Winona N., and Cameron, a heartfelt thank you for sharing your love of Doon with the online world and celebrating our small victories!

Mike Heath, for continuing to outdo himself one Doon cover at a time.

Artist J.C. Anguiano for his inspired Doon creations. Your illustrations are amazing!

All the **Doonians** who pour out their love of this series in art, edits, fan accounts, and encouragement on social media. You make the Dooniverse come alive!!!

Lorie would like to thank:

Tom for listening to me babble about logic issues and plot holes and the occasional prince in a kilt; Ben for sharing my love of musical inspiration; Alex for the best, most encouraging hugs on the planet; my parents, Bruce and Dinah Luneke, for your unwavering belief; Toby and Jerry Moeggenberg for your love and support; and the friends of my heart — Kelly Moe, Tricia Lacey, Laurie Pezzot, Lisa Litz, Jen Egbert — I don't spend near as much time with you as I would like, but know that you have each shaped who I am today, and I appreciate you more than you know!

Carey would like to thank:

Athena and Harrison, who support my dreams and tolerate my schedule and burnt dinners; my mom for stalking readers at her local bookstore until they buy my books; Jonathan Hunter for cheering me onward and upward; the amazing folks at Crossroads Church for nourishing my spirit; Skerryvore — whose music provided so much of the emotional landscape for my chapters; my dear friends for their overwhelming enthusiasm — especially Kelly Harris, Nancy Hemingway, Mary Jo Vanden Berg, Erica Bardeau, Tricia Giltner, the Jones Family (Roger, Judy, Madison & Megan); and my hometown peeps from Vacaville, CA!

Doon

Carey Corp & Lorie Langdon

Veronica doesn't think she's going crazy. But why can't anyone else see the mysterious blond boy who keeps popping up wherever she goes?

When her best friend, Mackenna, invites her to spend the summer in Scotland, Veronica jumps at the opportunity to leave her complicated life behind for a few months. But the Scottish countryside holds other plans. Not only has the imaginary kilted boy followed her to Alloway, she and Mackenna uncover a strange set of rings and a very unnerving letter from Mackenna's great aunt—and when the girls test the instructions Aunt Gracie left behind, they are transported to a land that defies explanation.

Doon seems like a real-life fairy tale, complete with one prince who has eyes for Mackenna and another who looks suspiciously like the boy from Veronica's daydreams. But Doon has a dark underbelly as well. The two girls could have everything they've longed for...or they could find themselves in a world that has become a nightmare.

A Doon Novel

Forever Doon

Carey Corp & Lorie Langdon

With the witch of Doon on the throne, Jamie believed dead, and Duncan and Mackenna trapped in Alloway, Veronica has no choice but to put her grief aside and prepare her remaining followers for the impending battle against the false queen and her forces. But while on a covert mission to steal a powerful elixir from the castle, Veronica discovers her true love may actually be alive, and fighting a battle of his own.

With the Brig o' Doon destroyed and the portal fragmented, Doon's forces are not only divided, but also isolated in different dimensions. With the help of a storyteller as ancient as the witch herself, Kenna and Duncan learn they must rebuild the bridge to have any chance of crossing back into Doon with their ragtag army. But when Mackenna insists on fighting as well, Duncan soon realizes the only way he can ensure her safety is to turn her into a cold-hearted killer.

For Vee, Jamie, Kenna, and Duncan, saving their kingdom while keeping their lives intact will take a miracle.

Available in stores and online!

BLINK